NEW YORK REVIEW BOOKS
CLASSICS

KILOMETER 101

MAXIM OSIPOV (b. 1963) is a Russian writer and cardiologist. In the early 1990s, he was a research fellow at the University of California, San Francisco, before returning to Moscow, where he continued to practice medicine and also founded a publishing house that specialized in medical, musical, and theological texts. In 2005, while working at a local hospital in Tarusa, a small town ninety miles from Moscow, Osipov established a charitable foundation to ensure the hospital's survival. Since 2007, he has published short stories, novellas, essays, and plays, and has won a number of literary prizes for his fiction. He has published six collections of prose, and his plays have been staged all across Russia. Osipov's writings have been translated into more than a dozen languages. He lived in Tarusa until February 2022, when he moved to Germany.

BORIS DRALYUK is the editor in chief of the *Los Angeles Review of Books*. He is the author of *My Hollywood and Other Poems* (2022), co-editor of *The Penguin Book of Russian Poetry* (2015), editor of *1917: Stories and Poems from the Russian Revolution* (2016), and translator or co-translator of volumes by Isaac Babel, Andrey Kurkov, Leo Tolstoy, Mikhail Zoshchenko, and others, including Lev Ozerov's *Portraits Without Frames* and Maxim Osipov's *Rock, Paper, Scissors, and Other Stories* (both NYRB Classics).

ALEX FLEMING is a literary translator from Russian and Swedish. Her translations include works by Maxim Osipov,

Katrine Marçal, and Sara Osman, and have appeared in *Asymptote Journal*, *Litro Magazine*, *Literary Hub*, and *Image Journal*, among others. She is also the editor of *Swedish Book Review*, a journal of new Swedish writing. She is based in London.

NICOLAS PASTERNAK SLATER is a retired hematologist turned translator. Since 1998 he has published translations from Mikhail Lermontov, Leo Tolstoy, Ivan Turgenev, Anton Chekhov, Teffi, and others, as well as Fyodor Dostoevsky's *Crime and Punishment* and two works by his uncle Boris Pasternak: *Doctor Zhivago* and *Family Correspondence 1921–1960*. He also works in collaboration with his wife, Maya Slater; their joint publications include Dostoevsky's *A Bad Business and Other Stories* and Turgenev's *Fathers and Children* (NYRB Classics).

KILOMETER 101

MAXIM OSIPOV

Edited by
BORIS DRALYUK

Translated from the Russian by
BORIS DRALYUK,
ALEX FLEMING, *and*
NICOLAS PASTERNAK SLATER

NEW YORK REVIEW BOOKS

New York

THIS IS A NEW YORK REVIEW BOOK
PUBLISHED BY THE NEW YORK REVIEW OF BOOKS
435 Hudson Street, New York, NY 10014
www.nyrb.com

The following stories have appeared elsewhere: "Sventa" in *Paris Review* (Spring
2021); "Little Lord Fauntleroy" in *Subtropics* (Spring/Summer 2021); an extract
from "Pieces on a Plane" in *Granta* (Spring 2022); "The Children of Dzhankoy" in
Hazlitt (February 2022)

Library of Congress Cataloging-in-Publication Data
Names: Osipov, Maksim, author. | Dralyuk, Boris, translator. | Fleming, Alex
    (Translator), translator. | Slater, Nicolas Pasternak, translator.
Title: Kilometer 101 / by Maxim Osipov; translated by Boris Dralyuk, Alex
    Fleming, and Nicolas Pasternak Slater.
Other titles: 101-ĭ kilometr. English
Description: New York: New York Review Books, [2022] | Series: New York
    review books classics
Identifiers: LCCN 2022000781 (print) | LCCN 2022000782 (ebook) | ISBN
    9781681376868 (paperback) | ISBN 9781681376875 (ebook)
Subjects: LCGFT: Essays. | Short stories. | Novellas.
Classification: LCC PG3492.87.S553 A1613 2022 (print) | LCC PG3492.87.S553
    (ebook) | DDC 891.78/5—dc23/eng/20220114
LC record available at https://lccn.loc.gov/2022000781
LC ebook record available at https://lccn.loc.gov/2022000782

ISBN 978-1-68137-686-8
Available as an electronic book; ISBN 978-1-68137-687-5

Printed in the United States of America on acid-free paper.
10 9 8 7 6 5 4 3 2 1

CONTENTS

SVENTA

In Lieu of a Foreword

To the memory of my parents

VNUKOVO is the smallest, most intimate of Moscow's airports, and when your flight arrives—especially if it arrives at eleven on a Saturday night—you don't expect to see much of a crowd. Stamps in the passport, baggage claim—quick and easy:

"Where are you coming from?"

"Vilnius."

"What's in the bag?"

Nothing special: books, cheese. No food embargo violated—entry granted. But then, at the exit, you're in for a surprise: a phalanx of men. This is the sort of throng that might greet a plane from Tbilisi, but these people don't look Georgian. And no solicitations either— no "Taxi, cheap taxi; taxi into town, very cheap." It's eerily quiet. You begin to squeeze your way through the crowd, and there's no end in sight. The men don't step aside, but neither do they block you deliberately; they just stand there. It's as if these muscular, beardless, middle-aged guys in dark jackets and coats simply don't see you. If the wheels of your suitcase happen to roll over their feet, they won't snap at you, won't even say a word. You feel you could pinch or poke them and they still wouldn't move. They're like a dark, incomprehensible force out of some bad dream: Who are they? Where are they going? On some kind of pilgrimage? Maybe the hajj? You'll get to the bottom of this: Where's security? Police?

Once you fight your way through to the glass door, you find that it's locked—and beyond it, on the street, there's another crowd. But this one is more diverse, made up of both men and women.

1

A policeman is stationed by the door. He's holding a vessel of some kind—of course: an oil lamp. Well, it took you a while. It's Holy Saturday: the crowds are waiting for the Holy Fire to land.[1]

"Special aircraft. From Tel Aviv."

"*Rak zeh haser lanu*"—that's all we need . . . The only Hebrew you know.

After an hour or two, the "special aircraft" will land, the television cameras will capture the authorities lighting the beardless men's oil lamps, and these lamps will travel all over Moscow, the suburbs, and the neighboring districts. At that point everyone else will be allowed to pass through the glass door. The story's been all over the papers, TV: people have flocked to Vnukovo from far and wide—"We've been coming for six years," "We have faith in our people, in our country."

Stay calm. No reason to panic. The policeman gestures with his hand:

"The third exit's operational."

You have to push your way through again, suitcase in tow. Welcome back from Lithuania.

"What feelings does this place evoke in you?" the literary correspondent of the Zarasai paper asks in English, at your book launch with Tomas, your Lithuanian translator and publisher. She's the only person in attendance who doesn't speak Russian.

"For me, Zarasai is not so much a place as it is a time in my life. I won't find better words than 'paradise lost.'"

The young woman is wary: Does the gentleman miss the USSR? "No, no. I only miss that time when my parents were alive."

"So is this your first visit to independent Lithuania?"

To independent Lithuania, yes: the first. It's good not to feel like an occupier. Took a quick jaunt through Vilnius, liked everything, but couldn't wait to get back here. You have a look around: a new library by the lake (the whole town is on the shore); the café from the early 1970s, with the interior columns—now shuttered (it used to serve two-course lunches); the Catholic church. The Soviet statue of the girl with the rifle (Marytė Melnikaitė) is gone without a trace, as if it were never there. And as is usual in such towns, the natural landscape is more attractive than anything man has constructed.

"Why haven't you visited us before?"

No good answer. All you can do is shrug. Almost forty years earlier, your father sent you a letter from here: "It's so quiet, so peaceful—in the house, outside. There's almost no one around these days, which is probably why they're so polite to me, even at the post office. From time to time you forget you're a seedy Muscovite with an overburdened conscience. You begin to see the world differently—it sinks in, penetrates."

And here is your own diary entry from fifteen years ago: "I want to go back to Zarasai, where I spent so much time—every summer, many years in a row. And instead I fly here, fly there—to places one has to visit, places it would be a shame not to see—but never to Zarasai. That means I'm not living my own life."

It's windy here, clean. The soil is sandy, and the locals like to keep things tidy. It's...desolate.

"Peaceful?" the young correspondent suggests, with a smile.

Yes, that's better. You say goodbye:

"Come back in the summer. Bring everyone."

That would be nice. But the people with whom you used to come to Zarasai aren't around anymore. One now lives in San Francisco, another in Amsterdam. You fell out with a third. Several others, including your parents and sister, have died. And so you set out for the peninsula alone. It's about two kilometers away, on the south side of the lake. You remember the road—no need for GPS or any other guides.

"A house stood here..."[2]—two stories, made of stone. Not a sign of it. Demolished. After the owners died (that much you knew), the children were divvying up the inheritance and sold the house. But the buyers didn't like the style, so they tore it down, along with all the extensions and outbuildings. Razed everything to the ground. They wanted to build something of their own, but apparently ran out of money. The neighbors give you the story. They remember your family, a little.

Strange. It was a strong, solid house—with a huge balcony, big enough for the dining table. Your family would eat out there some evenings. You had a neighbor over, a fellow Muscovite, the spitting image of Sergey Rachmaninoff. Over tea, he told you he was the Communist Party organizer at his institute. "What an honor…" Mom said, wryly. Mom was usually quiet, especially in comparison with Dad, but every once in a while she'd come out with something like this, some inopportune aside. She was only ever here in July and August, while Dad might come any time of year. In the summers he lived upstairs, and in the winters down here, approximately where you're standing right this minute. "And now a bird goes flying through / the empty space that was a window…"[3]

Poems are well and good, but the disappearance of the house really does set you back on your heels: stone, it turns out, is also short-lived. Disheartening—although, of course, there are worse things in this world. And besides, you're neither Nabokov nor Proust. Go down to the water through the pines, across the cushiony moss. The tall old pines, the slender saplings by the lake, the thickets of reeds—still there, just where you left them.

A memory: August of '78—you're about to turn fifteen. You and your classmate Kharitosha, a friend for life, have set sail in a dinghy. The vessel's name is *Dolphin*—made in East Germany, patched up every which way (back then people used to fix things, not toss them away), two sliding centerboards on the sides to prevent drift and give directional stability. A maritime adventure on Lake Zarasas. You man the jib, Kharitosha the mainsail and the tiller. Working to windward—lean out! "So long, dear mother! Farewell, my sweet! / I'm off to join the Baltic Fleet!" But one of your sliding centerboards has broken off, and you just can't get the dinghy out of the bay. The waves keep pushing you back to the shore. You take turns trying, half-heartedly, to paddle out. Dad is watching from the jetty. He's already had to wade into the cold water and push you out of the reeds several times. Avast! Kharitosha has an idea: "We should get some epoxy. Glue the goddamn board..."

"Epoxy, eh?" Standing waist-deep in water, Dad launches into a lengthy speech. *Jackasses* is the warmest word he can find for you two.

From then on, *epoxy* was the family shorthand for useless ideas. As for the dinghy, you see it later, on film, when you begin to sort through the archive. The early '60s: the *Dolphin* has a motor and no mast; Dad's at the stern; mom is water-skiing on the Oka. After dad died, you grew busier, more impetuous. Now it's time to take on another set of responsibilities: framing photos, maintaining the archive.

After you learn that the house is gone, the disappearance of the little bathhouse doesn't come as a shock—it was wooden, dilapidated. Everyone always bathed on Saturdays, and on Fridays they'd bring water up from the lake, gather wood for the fire. "We did good work," you once said to Juozas, the bathhouse's tall, skinny owner. You were ten. Juozas's huge, strong hands were black with dirt, and you very badly wanted him to like you. "Yes, we sure showed those bastards," he replied dreamily. Juozas smoked unfiltered cigarettes. The smell of burnt matches and so on. If you wanted to, you could also reminisce about all sorts of bathhouse escapades—but again, this is a travelogue, not Fellini's *Amarcord*.

And so, no more house, no more bathhouse, and even the jetty has been replaced with something tastelessly sturdy. Don't get stuck here, on the peninsula. Go get Tomas and drive to Sventa, but first— the forest.

The woman at the library gives you directions: take the highway to Degučiai, turn off toward Dusetos, then, after the second bus stop, look for the marker. "At this site, on August 26, 1941, eight thousand Jews were murdered by German fascists." The mention of *Jews* on the obelisk had always seemed impossibly brave to you; in the days of your youth, the word was used strictly in special cases—only when the authorities couldn't very well call them Soviet citizens, as they did on the monument at Babi Yar. To the left and right, a ravine, overgrown with grass; two hundred thousand Lithuanian Jews are buried in such ravines.

De-Sovietization has not left the monument untouched: the Russian inscription was removed. Was it right to do that? Not for you to decide. In this case, you would have kept it. Now there are two inscriptions, one in Yiddish and the other in Lithuanian. The Yiddish reads: "Here lie eight thousand Jews from Zarasai and the surrounding region, who perished cruelly at the hands of Nazi murderers and their collaborators on August 26, 1941. Blessed be the memory of the innocent victims." The Lithuanian version adds a clarification: "their *local* collaborators."

Some of the locals also saved Jews. Some began by shooting them but wound up saving them, and some even took the opposite route—hard to believe, but it's true.

The place is spick-and-span: a fence, a neatly trimmed little hedge, a Star of David on the obelisk, candles, Israeli flags, and little stones on the pedestal. Someone has brought a little handmade cross. This isn't how it used to be.

"The lot of Lithuanians," says Tomas, "is to be patient, to mourn."

Everyone around here knows the old joke: for his last wife, a man should pick a Lithuanian woman, so that he'll have someone to look after his grave. No, these aren't Mandelstam's "women kin to the damp earth,"[4] whose calling is to accompany the dead; on the contrary—they take the simplest, most practical approach to life's most difficult challenges.

On the way to the hotel you remember a short, gloomy old man, about sixty—one of the "locals"—with a face darkened by drink. He was a mechanic or electrician, rode around on a motorcycle with a sidecar, and had done some time in prison. "Polacks? Kill 'em all. Russians? Kill 'em all. Yids..."—eyes raised to Dad's face—"every other one."

He'd never get away with that now, but back then you had to put up with it, grudgingly: after all, you were the occupiers. Everyone called you *žydai*—which sounds so painful to a Russian-speaking Jew, but it is the only Lithuanian word for "Jews." This old man also saw himself as a victim, in every possible way. And well into the mid-1950s, Radio Free Europe gave him and his "Forest Brothers" hope: hang in there, fellas—another world war is just around the corner.

Your family used to drive down to Sventa for the whole day—with blankets, books, and food, with a volleyball, with tin cups for picking blueberries and baskets for picking mushrooms. There were holes in the car's floorboard. You could watch the asphalt beneath you. The transmission was, needless to say, manual. How you and Dad laughed at Mom when she returned from her first trip to the States, back in the late '80s, and reported that new cars had no clutch pedals. You told her she was wrong, and she agreed: You knew better about these things. And how you wish you could share this simple pleasure with your dad, this piece of automotive perfection you're now driving, though it's only a rental. No need to ask for directions this time. You have your GPS. It suggests Lake Svente—"Sventes ezers"—just what you need. These Baltic languages and their superfluous *s*'s. Your name is Maksimas now: it's right there on the book cover.

A border crossing? Is Sventa really in Latvia? Yes, sure—after all, you did use to drive to Daugavpils whenever you needed anything from an actual city. There they had a prison, and Lenin by the train station, wearing his cap with earflaps even in the blazing heat. LitSSR, LatSSR—borders weren't such serious business back then. And here's the familiar gravelly road, where you learned to drive. And here's the forest, shabby and sickly. Everything is familiar: the road and the forest.

Apparently there aren't that many tourists these days, and one can drive right up to the water. Sventa was never crowded—one of the reasons you loved it—but it used to be a state reserve: no campfires, no cars. Everything else is exactly as you remember it: that sand, that

little punt with its tarred, shiny bottom, and that old rotted jetty—
how you missed the jetty. You walk out on it and find yourself ankle-
deep in water. Then you dry your feet and look around.

"Why are you blowing your horn, young man? / Lie in this coffin—it's warm, young man." Wasn't it there, hiding behind those
trees, that you blasted your trumpet for all to hear? Scriabin's *Poem
of Ecstasy*, Wagner's *Twilight of the Gods*—you thought your roaring
was music. "No rhythm, but, on the other hand, no tune." Your pianist friend, the one who's now in Amsterdam, persuaded you to drop
the trumpet and pick up the flute—a quiet, sensitive instrument—but
you never got a feel for it. Your sense of joy is still somehow linked
to the sound of a trumpet.

On the mysteries of happiness . . . Your father ended his last letter
with this thought: "We're together. Sometimes we talk, sometimes
we don't. And I no longer ask myself whether life worked out. I catch
myself thinking: Maybe this is happiness?" You try to tell Tomas
about your parents, but how can you communicate the mystery at
the core of any individual? It's harder than translating poetry.

"Trouble can find us any day. It can find anyone, of course, but
especially us. Our goal should be to minimize our fear of trouble"—
your father always remembered how, in 1952 and '53 (the Doctors'
Plot and so on), he couldn't find even the simplest, most menial job,
how he'd almost hoped for the mass deportation to the Far East: as
long as all the Jews were together, among their own kind. His letters
were meant to instruct, to tell you something important, while your
mother's were a means of prolonging her silence. "I spent the whole
day as if I were on a train. I'd just wake up then fall back asleep. Didn't
do a thing. And now I'm just babbling, because you can't leave a letter blank."

You stand by the water a little longer, have a smoke, think a few
things you can't share, eat a mandarin. It's a bit dead around here. So
quiet. Quiet as a graveyard.

And only after returning to the hotel and studying an actual map
do you realize your mistake. Sventes, Šventas, Šventoji—Holy Lake
and Holy River—such names are found on either side of the Latvia–

Lithuania border. Lake Šventas—what your family always called Sventa—is where you had wanted to go. How did you get so lost, so turned around? Blame it on the háček: Šventas ežeras is south of Zarasai, toward Turmantas, not up north in Latvia.

Later, Tomas says:

"But Maxim, you recognized everything: the road, the lake."

"True. I did."

On the way to Vilnius, you compare impressions. For Tomas, the highlights of the trip were the massive trucks rumbling along the cobblestones in front of the church, the wind, and the hail. But you didn't notice any of that. Memory is an odd faculty: sometimes you'll sit there and listen to an entire concert, but later the only thing you'll remember is that the conductor wore red socks.

Storks and hills, and lots of water. The sky reminds you of the Netherlands, but the landscape is more expressive, because of the hills. Would you like to live here? It's the provinces, yes, but not provincial—not excessively so. Just a country in Eastern Europe. In many ways, worthy of envy. Everything here will get better and better, gradually. That is, if no one interferes.

One of your friends—a woman of advanced years—likes to preface her reminiscences with the words: "When I was a pillar of society…" Maybe she really had been, way back when. And you also find people in Lithuania who like to remember the good old days, when the grand duchy extended to the Black Sea (mainly thanks to successful marriages), but here no one draws practical conclusions from the premise of former greatness.

"You just don't know the whole truth." You've heard that said countless times by anti-European Russians in Paris, in Rome. That's all they talk about: people don't like us here, don't like us there. My friends, you know where they like us least of all? In Moscow, at home.

"Our goal should be to minimize our fear…" You weren't even twenty when you received that letter. Now you're past fifty. You say to Tomas:

"It's really quite amazing. Everything has returned. My concerns today are exactly the same as they were some thirty years ago: First, not to sink into the mud, to sully my conscience; second, not to land in jail; and third, not to miss the moment when one ought to leave, forever. And I harbor the same illusory hope I harbored then: that we'll wake up one day and find ourselves in the clear, with all this darkness behind us."

The present circumstances, however, force you to stay up at night, keep your eyes peeled, always look behind you. A witty friend will later tell you: Prince Andrey Kurbsky had similar feelings. He too ended up in Lithuania.

"Meet me at the scrapyard," texts Bóris—your friend Borechka—a great violinist who recently moved here from London. He struggles courageously with Lithuanian suffixes—*žmogus, žmonija, žmogiūkštis, žmogiškumas* (man, mankind, etc.)—although they say one can get by here with English or Russian. Háčeks, by the way, were invented by Jan Hus.

Borechka wants you to like the city. He shows you around, apologizing for anything unattractive—for instance, the scrapyard. Life here isn't lavish, but it isn't too shabby, and, most importantly, there are fewer of the prohibitions, restrictions, barriers, and other torments that have plagued Moscow in recent years. Vilnius is nice: clean, but not spotless. The neighborhood where you're staying is like a mix between Serpukhov and Paris, and the Old Town is unique.

"Every place has its problems," says the owner of a literary café, with a smile.

He's an experienced fellow. He's lived in Israel and America, almost settled in Jordan—he knows what he's talking about. But does he expect, for example, the Special Forces (who knows what they're called here?) to raid his café and take it away from him? Would he be thankful if they didn't toss him in prison, too—where Amnesty International wouldn't even think of getting involved? He's genuinely surprised: no, he expects nothing of the sort. It's a good thing the

Soviet Union collapsed! You had also dreamed of that moment, long before you got to Lithuania—back when you were reading *The Pickwick Papers* as an eight-year-old boy. You knew there was a city named London, had seen it in books and on maps, but to see it in life—forget it, son.

"The author is obviously unfamiliar with Viktor Shklovsky's theory of prose," one of the listeners says, quietly, but clearly. He's a huge Lithuanian who works at the Vilnius University Observatory. Hard not to be high-minded if you work at an observatory.

The reading, the questions—all in Russian. Who, one wonders, needed this translated book? The answer is clear: the author. "So who's going to buy the booze for the launch?" You heard this somewhere else, but for a similar reason.

Užupis is a district of independent artists, with its own jokey constitution and government (in which Tomas occupies a significant position). Here you read your story "Objects in Mirror":

"Houston . . ." Ada says thoughtfully. "Andryusha, did you know we got an apartment in Vilnius?"

Vilnius, they reason, can't save them from everything. But with an Israeli passport . . . Oh, they have Israeli passports too?[5]

And the listeners smile. At the end a Muscovite, about your age, with a doctorate in physics, comes up to you. It turns out that the apartment you're staying in belongs to him. He won't wave his Israeli passport under your nose, but he has one. That means the story rhymes with reality: the answer is a round number, not some nonsensical fraction.

"Come back often—or just move here. Believe me, you'll find a lot to like."

A friendly chat, a glass of wine—and not only one. "You just don't know the whole truth . . ." You haven't heard those words from anyone here. On your last day in Vilnius, you begin to run into your new friends in the street. Vilnius can distract and entertain you to precisely the right degree. In one of your stories, a mother asks her son: "How could I ever be sad that you're happy?" Perhaps only one's parents can truly take joy in one's happiness. Enough of that. Be a good passenger: find your seat, keep your chair in the upright position, and fasten your seat belt.

Dreams fall away, one after another—some because they come true, but most because they prove pointless. Your father wanted you to become a professor—what good is that now? Or say you find a beautiful cemetery on the other side of the river, make arrangements with the woman in charge, but then—it's all for naught. Turns out there's a quiet, cozy cemetery right here in Tarusa, on your own shore.

There is indeed a lot to like over there—that's true. But there's a lot to like here too—as long as you find a gap in this solid wall of dark, muscular men blocking the exit. But you've already said everything you had to say about these guys. Remember those you love. Remember the priest who has presided at all your family's funerals: nobility and simplicity—the best qualities to be found in the Russian people. Think about that, look at the water, and remember Lithuania.

You get home long after midnight. Now you'll log on, pull up Skype, call your family, and read from the first chapter of John, verses one through seventeen—in Old Church Slavonic, English, German, and Russian. That's the kind of Easter you'll have this year.

April 2017
Translated by Boris Dralyuk

LUXEMBURG

Stories

LITTLE LORD FAUNTLEROY

"Eric? what sort of a name is that, Eric?" demands some unknown nurse. Not out of curiosity. She disapproves.

He stops by the nurses' room. She's not embarrassed, she looks him straight in the eye, malevolently. But that's his name—why apologize for it? That's how it is. They'll get used to it, learn to live with it, his name and all the rest of him.

This is where he comes to see patients every Saturday—patients in the intensive care unit, or anyone else who's sent his way. He's the only cardiologist they have.

It's not the city, but then again, of course, it isn't the country. Something in between, neither one thing nor the other—a suburb, that's the word. The summer visitors in their dachas across the track see it in their dreams—the same thing every night, more or less: a place for disasters to happen, an amorphous nightmare. Best not to go there, even on business—and the railroad crossing has been blocked off with concrete bollards from time immemorial. Walk across, or bike across. "Get yourself a donkey," said the smart-asses.

So, coming out of Moscow, the summer dachas run along the left side of the railroad; along the right side there's chaos. High-rise tenements, factories, gray concrete office blocks. Industry has wilted here in recent years, and so much the better, they say, as far as air and water quality goes. Though people carry on living in those blocks, and even reproducing, if rather half-heartedly. The less you think about what goes on beyond those concrete bollards, the better—that way you could even stop dreaming about it.

The dachas here are good ones, in the classic style; up to just over an acre of land, with pines, and sand, and no dirt, and lots of sky. The only disadvantage is, there aren't any distant views. The trains aren't a problem, people are used to them, but the lack of vistas, and the lack of an expanse of water, even just a river—those are a pity. The lots are big, very big, and the houses all look pretty much the same: they can accommodate two families, one on each floor. That feels like an anachronism these days—what about privacy? But these houses were built in the late 1920s, for political prisoners released from czarist labor camps. No point dreaming about separate living back then. There wasn't even a Russian word for privacy.

There were enough labor camp returnees at the time for eighty-odd plots of land. Of course, the dachas have changed hands many times since then. One day he found an old certificate at the back of a storeroom: it stated that in 1881, female citizen so-and-so (a distant relation of his) had taken part in the assassination of Czar Alexander II. The certificate bore the name of a treatment center, and it was signed, stamped, and dated 1926. He never showed that certificate to anyone. Let sleeping dogs lie.

So there he was—in a dacha no worse than many others, and better even than some. Lots of pine needles, which would be good for the child. And how had he ended up on that side of the tracks? A weary smile—why ask? I'm a doctor, aren't I? They'd rushed a neighbor of his to the hospital with palpitations, she had atrial fibrillation—know what that is? It all worked out fine, they gave the little lady an electric shock and put her right. To people really close to him, he explains: I have this inner need.

It's an odd way to carry on, no denying it. Borya, once his fellow student, now a neurosurgeon, gives a broad grin. Amazing teeth.

"Love for the common man, is it? Albert Schweitzer? Or just bored with your family?" There had always been something not right about Eric. He'd have done better to finish his thesis.

No, no, he only works here Saturdays, what's his family got to do with it? One-on-one with the patient, like when he was young. But Borya won't let it drop—that's his right, he's brought Eric a supply of medicine from his own department. Borya is stocky, muscular, and balding: tough arms, pudgy fingers, all he lacks is a hairy chest under his scrubs. They work at the same multispecialty clinic—different departments in different blocks. Borya has a dacha not far away, along the same stretch of road, and their two careers are panning out the same way.

"Who made you turn out such a..."—he gropes for the right word—"an aristocrat? You were in the Pioneers as a boy, just like the rest of us. Were you given different books to read, or something?" Borya's not pleased with him. Another "Holy Doctor" Haass: "Make haste to do good!"[1]

What was the first book that Eric read on his own? He has to remember.

"*Little Lord Fauntleroy.*"

What's it about? Who's it by? Eric has forgotten. It had an inscription in it, in Mama's handwriting, which was still firm and beautiful in those days—you wouldn't even call it feminine. "May life never prevent you from growing kinder and better," and the date—his sixth birthday. He was brought up to be good. Why be good?—No one explained, it was obvious. But he remembers the inscription, and the book's title: *Little Lord Fauntleroy.*

He was offered half-pay, out of the hospital's private income. He'd never even thought about the money. But why not? He'd take it. How much would he want? After all, he was bringing along his own instruments... The instruments weren't actually his own; he borrowed them from his Moscow clinic, just small, portable bits of equipment, and took them back every Monday.

"Half."

The lady who is the deputy chief of staff smiles, though that's not done here. She wasn't surprised. There were plenty of reasons why a doctor from Moscow might want to come to their hospital. Scientific curiosity, whatever, we know it all. And money always comes in handy. Though admittedly, 50 percent—that's a bit steep.

"There's a woman who comes here, you know, dresses the ones who've died, makes them up, all that—she only takes 30 percent."

So there we are—this was his competitor. But now, it looks like he'll have a load of stories to tell—this isn't Moscow for you. Out there, of course, there's a lot of variety too—with twelve hundred staff for four hundred beds, each of which is occupied by some doctor's relative, or an active employee from somewhere else, or a paying patient. Of course there are stories to tell, but they're secret, confidential ones, and they rarely reach Eric's ears.

He's not to tell that woman anything, let's keep it all between us, *entre nous*, get it? Actually (and he makes an expansive gesture—Borya is obviously right to tease him for being an aristocrat) he'd do the work for nothing. Or whatever you like.

"For nothing?" Shouldn't have said that. He won't last long at that rate. She shakes her head from side to side . . . "All work ought to be rewarded."

Yes, that really had been a mistake. It slipped out by itself, somehow. He hadn't wanted to hurt anyone's feelings. And a parallel income really would be useful—even a small one.

"We'll sort it out as we go along," says his new boss.

Here's his passport, his qualification certificate, a copy of his work record. Oh, and his specialist diploma, and his postgraduate degree. That's the lot. He's in.

He crosses the yard, looks around: a number of separate blocks, security guards, just like a proper hospital. But now he's tired. Because it's hot, it's dreadfully hot, though it's only May. It shouldn't be like this in the countryside. No, but it's all tarmac here.

The medical staff are all gray and polite and walk about softly, saving their energy.

"Myocardial infarction. Take a look, if you like."

What do they mean—if he likes? They're too shy to ask, he thinks.

So he takes a look. No, this is no MI. Cancel every
patient home. Couldn't be better, could it? Everytl
to them, and sometimes things work out, but they'r
He's even been allocated a nurse—a hunk of clay, younger than ne
is, but looks older. Knows all about this place, looks at him attentively,
never smiles, and does all she's supposed to. People have bad teeth
here, that's why nobody smiles. Like in an old master picture, Eric
decides. He's trying to love everybody.

The yard is hot; he's come out here for a bit of solitude. He looks out
through the trees. People arriving, people leaving with wrong diag-
noses and random prescriptions. Never mind, he'll soon improve things.
He organizes a seminar, but he's the only one to open his mouth. Some
colleagues turn up, and they sit through it in long-suffering silence.

There get to be more patients, and sometimes he crosses between
the bollards on a Friday evening as well. Or even on a Sunday, if he's
called in. And it's gotten cooler—early June has turned out to be
colder than May.

"They just don't have any breeding, somehow," Eric complains
about his colleagues, and his patients.

What's so surprising about that? "Took part in the assassination
of Czar Alexander . . ."—he remembers that bit of paper. Even so, back
when he was a young man, you could sense someone's breeding from
the person's face. Not hereditary—the breeding that comes from
reading books. But how can you even talk about book learning nowadays, when people lack the most basic common sense:

"It's difficult, but not impossible," he tells a nurse. He's explaining
about transferring a seriously ill patient to Moscow. And now the
nurse hasn't a clue—does that mean it is possible, or not?

Actually, you need to look closer. There's life everywhere, there
must be nice people everywhere, and others who aren't so nice, and
doesn't his very use of the word *they* convey a moral error?

In the middle of June, the deputy chief of staff asks him to come in
on a weekday.

"Why, has someone important fallen ill?"

"No. The Security Bureau want a word with you."

"What about?"

"Can't discuss that on the phone, can I?" His boss is quite cool about it, no need for Eric to worry.

One of those massive gray blocks you see from the train: that's where the Security Bureau hangs out. At the desk there's a lieutenant waiting for him, a man of perhaps thirty, or even younger. Eric had long since realized that he's no good at telling a person's age. The man shakes his hand politely. An ugly, pockmarked face. He'll have a closer look at this lieutenant later on; just now they're on their way to get him a security pass. Everything's going by the book.

It's just a little bit scary. Why jump through all these hoops, if it's just for a chat? They could have talked at the hospital, couldn't they?

"No, that's not how we do things."

Finally he's shown into an office, which the lieutenant shares with another young man. This one is making his own cardboard folders, the sort you can buy quite cheaply anywhere. He carries on with this task throughout the lieutenant's interrogation. The office is shoddy, in fact worse than shoddy—it's an impoverished slum. Even the hospital is smarter and more up-to-date. There's a map of the world on the wall; lying on the windowsill are a newspaper covered with cigarette-ends, an electric immersion coil and some used tea bags.

"D'you smoke?" The lieutenant holds out a pack.

"No," Eric lies, for some reason. "Might I ask . . ."

He'll get everything explained to him later. For now, he's to listen to this. He's not obliged to testify against himself or his closest relatives. Understood? Then sign here. But just one more thing: Which close relatives specifically are included? Husband, wife, son, daughter . . . The end of the list is unexpected: grandad, granny. Eric laughs, a slightly ingratiating laugh.

"Does it actually say that—*granny*?"

"Yes. That's legal language for you." The lieutenant smiles too. An affectionate smile.

Is that it? No, now he has to read the article in the code that lays down his responsibility for any false statements. Or for refusing to give a statement. So does that mean he's been summoned as a witness?

"Oh, not really." The lieutenant dismisses the idea. Just that a signal has come through, and they're actioning it.

Eric looks at the book. What an odd way to print the criminal code—illustrated with cartoons. But the lieutenant likes that—it makes it less forceful. Finally he produces a paper—the "signal" he had spoken about. The writer's name means nothing to Eric, and he forgets it straightaway. Strangers have turned up in our home: that's the general message. And it's about him, Eric. And it concludes: We won't have it! We won't allow any of this—experiments on human guinea pigs, "transplanting our citizens for their organs." That was why the lieutenant had invited him. Does he have anything to do with transplants? No? We'll make a note of that. The lieutenant heaves a sigh and starts typing out his report, slowly, very slowly. Everything here is done in an antiquated, antediluvian way.

So what does he think about transplantation, anyway? It doesn't solve the problem, of course, but in some particular cases... If some of his patients were to get a heart transplant, it would prolong their lives a great deal. Only, we don't have any transplant surgery here. Though there are plenty of donor organs available. Look how many accidents and disasters there are. But you know how much organization there has to be—harvesting the organs, cooling them, delivering them, having doctors on instant call-out. We're short of the most ordinary things—forget about transplantation...

"Damn, the ribbon's worn out." The lieutenant heaves another sigh.

It's been a long time since Eric last saw a dot-matrix printer. He decides to have a smoke now. Looks out the window—evening is coming on. The lieutenant's colleague leaves. Somewhere beyond the dachas, the sun is going down. Eventually the lieutenant finishes his task and starts chatting about the successes their service is clocking up, their enormous technical advances, and what wonderful fellows they are. The only corruption-free organization around. Well now, who'd have guessed.

Looks as if he's allowed to go. Any minute the lieutenant will sign his exit pass. But suddenly he has another medical question:

"Tell me—a hiatal hernia, is that very dangerous?" He's all anxious now, even his voice has gone up a tone.

"No, no way!" Eric exclaims. He's off the hook. "Trivial. Don't lie down directly after a meal, that's all."

But it turns out that it isn't always trivial. The lieutenant's daughter died of it, when she was just two. They operated on her—and she died.

"Where?" asks Eric, in some bewilderment—it's hard to keep having to change his tune. "Not here, in our hospital?"

No, the girl died in Moscow, in the FSB's own hospital. They said the local hospital didn't do that kind of operation. Which was true . . . But recently the lieutenant had had another daughter, so what was the chance she'd have a hiatal hernia too?

The lieutenant has changed a lot over the last few minutes. Or is it a trick of the light? Anyway, Eric will read up on hiatal hernias, and ask around.

On Saturday, June 21, Borya goes to Eric's dacha in the evening, to watch the match: there's been a thunderstorm and his TV has given up. Eric couldn't care less about soccer.

"It's a terrific game," Borya explains. "The epitome of all that's virile. Kick—and it's a goal. Like sex." Hope the wife and child aren't listening. "Only soccer is even better. With a woman, anything can happen. You might not get it up, or something. But with soccer, you're on a high for ninety minutes solid. See?"

Yes, he sees, he sees it all.

Russia won, and Borya is on his way out, pleased as punch, tail in the air: the team is in the top four. "That's a good coach we've got, that Dutchman!" he grunts contentedly. He always said we needed a foreigner. What a shame Eric just doesn't get soccer.

"Be simpler," Borya advises him. "Then people will seek you out."

Does Eric want people to seek him out? Not particularly.

"An aristocrat, that's what you are, a proper aristocrat. Permit me to kiss your hand."

"Stop it," Eric tells him. "Stop clowning."

"No, but tell me—do they like you . . . over there?" Borya gestures over beyond the railroad station.

"Depends who. There aren't any *they*." And he tells him a bit about the lieutenant and his daughters—oh, bother, he never did read up about hiatal hernias. "Do they like me?" He thinks a bit. "To tell you the truth: No, they don't like me."

"So why bother with them? Conscience pricking you? The famous guilt complex?" Borya could be right there. A feeling of guilt toward everyone—first his parents, and now his wife, and his child—Eric has always had that. And then, toward some of his patients—he'll always feel guilty about them, as long as he lives.

"What about you, Borya?" he wants to ask. "Don't you ever have gnawings of conscience?" But no, of course his conscience never gnaws at him—he's too tough for its teeth.

"OK," says Borya, slapping him on the back. "Coke's the name— enjoy the game!" And off he goes. From out beyond the station, Eric can hear the chanting: "Olé, olé, olé, here we go, here we go . . ." Shouting and bellowing and singing, firecrackers exploding, car alarms going off . . . over here among the dachas, everything is still calm. "Olé, olé,"—yes, look how our language is growing. In those drunken, insulting, truculent tones.

On Sunday afternoon, June 22, the radio proclaims, "The grief of this day, the anniversary of the outbreak of war, is assuaged by our common joy at yesterday's victory." And next comes a phone call. "Yes, we do understand, but couldn't you please come over to the hospital at once?"

It's bustling in the emergency department. A gigantic fellow in his thirties, and a paramedic, and a policeman, and another somehow featureless man in a jacket; and lying on the couch, a thickset, muscle-bound guy, name of Poprov, seventeen years old. He's the one who's not well—his heart hurts. Was there any point coming over to see him? Eric examines him, listens to his chest, gets an EKG, does a couple of other things, and it's clear he's as fit as a fiddle. He's just very tense, and trembling a lot, causing movement artifact on the EKG. Otherwise he's fine. Eric has to write a report.

"What's your name? Popov?"

"Poprov!" roars the young giant for him. "Poprov, Alexey!" Hasn't he ever heard of Poprov? Left his brains at home? O-o-oh, not from around here . . . Just come down from the trees, have you, Mr. Not-from-around-here?"

The policeman shoves the giant out of the room.

What's he got to do with the boy? Eric wonders. He looks too young to be the lad's father. An "uncle," no doubt. But it emerges that he's some sort of assistant to the father, a minder, not anyone's uncle. "And what has the detainee done?" Eric asks indifferently, as though he knew his way around—otherwise you get nowhere. Well, nothing, he just pasted some Tajik with a baseball bat. Celebrating. "Why the bat? Where do bats come in? Do you have a baseball club here?"

Everyone howls with laughter—even Alexey, it seems.

"On his own?" Eric asks the paramedic, while Poprov is helped to his feet and allowed to dress.

"Who else was with you?" the policeman shouts at Poprov.

Is this any way to interrogate someone? Strolling around the room?

"As far as that question is concerned, officer . . ."

Listen to him, talking like a dictionary.

Poprov bares his teeth in a grin. He's not snitching on his pals. He's got principles. His teeth are hard and white, even tougher than Borya's. "If they pop him one, he'll sing," Eric suddenly thinks. OK, but he's only the doctor here, and the more repulsive his patient, the harder he has to try.

"Here are some tablets to calm you down." And he holds out a packet, from his personal stock.

A hand appears from behind Eric's back, and the featureless man takes the tablets.

"So, what's your relationship to him?" Eric asks again.

"My relationship is, I'm the warden of his isolation unit."

In other words, the prison. Oh, he'll remember that one.

"Look here, mister..." begins the prison warden. He wants to explain something.

"Doctor," Eric prompts him. "Call me doctor."

"Our system, doctor—don't get me wrong—it works slowly, but..." But—what?

Outside in the passage is his nurse. What's she doing here on a Sunday? She's upset. She's terribly sorry for Alexey, she knew little Alyosha as a child. "And what sort of a child was he?" Eric's question really startles her. All children are good. Alyosha has messed up his life since then; she's so sorry for that. He used to go to martial arts classes. Wanted to become a dentist. "And the other man, the Tajik, aren't you sorry for him?" Sure, of course she's sorry, he's human too. "Where is he, incidentally?" He's here, in intensive care, on a ventilator. Like to see him?

Why not, what's to stop him? Here he is, a thin Tajik, dark-haired, in a coma. How old? Twenty-two. He looks much younger, just a boy. No tattoos, dark skin, several bruises, gauze pads on his eyes. Eric removes them and examines his pupils. Gray eyes. A fly crawling on his shoulder—get the hell off! Looks at his arms—no bruising, no abrasions; he hasn't been in a fight. "Admitted here last night in a coma, with fractures to his facial skeleton and ribs. Not your field." His urinary catheter is draining outside the collecting vessel: put that right. It all looks very gloomy. The monitor, the ventilator, everything's looking more alive than this boy. Had a listen to his heart—all in order, so far. Is his brain alive? Who knows...?

So where's Poprov senior? "He's in Europe, supporting our team; the semifinal's on the twenty-seventh." Shouldn't someone rustle him up, this Poprov of yours? No, it seems—best not to bother Poprov.

Back he goes to his dacha, eats his lunch; when it gets cooler he'll be off to Moscow. But after lunch he falls asleep, and when he wakes, he thinks: So Poprov junior, Alyosha, the bright dental student, bought himself a baseball bat. There's martial arts for you. Alyosha watched the film *Brother* several times, he's a fan. The Tajik boy had something metallic hanging around his neck—not a cross, not a charm: Perhaps his name? His mama hung it on him before he came over. Why did he come? Because all his friends did. Everyone has the same idea. "Don't kill me, brother," begs the boy in the film. But Alyosha Poprov grins all over his face, and throws back: "You're no brother of mine, you black scum!" And lays into him with the bat.

How depressing. Lord, how depressing… Half asleep, he calls Borya. "Sporting greetings to you," he says. And waits. "Have you left the dacha already?" And waits some more. The noisy connection makes it obvious: Borya has left.

"What is it? Why aren't you saying anything?"

"I'm plucking up the courage to ask you something." Oh, please let this work… And he puts his question to him.

No, Borya has already left. Oh, fuck.

"Out of luck," Borya echoes.

But it worked, and suddenly Borya says:

"OK, I'm doing a U now. See you there." He's a good man, Borya.

Nearly two hours later, they're standing outside the hospital. Eric is smoking as they talk. It's looking bad, far worse than anyone had thought. Even so, they have to get the man to Moscow, get a CT scan of his head—there is some chance he could be saved. OK, Borya will get him picked up, we'll sort it with the lads. "Get me his case record, his passport, register my consultation. No relatives? What is he, a down-and-out?"

They have a coffee in the empty staff room, and talk about nationalities.

"The Tajiks are Aryans. Whatever that may mean."

"Really?" Borya didn't know. Thought they were *khaches*.

"Incidentally, *khach* is the Armenian for a cross." Eric has been reading about it.

"So they're little crosses. Not bad. Little noughts and little crosses." Borya is joking as hard as he can.

The transfer ambulance arrives at dawn.

He really is a good fellow, Borya.

"You're none too bad yourself, Little Lord Fauntleroy." They're both dropping with exhaustion. "Now you're their savior. Getting a patient like that transferred away, how about that! Don't worry, we'll get him there. Take no risks, get no champagne. Do you feel like some champagne?"

"They'll dream up some nasty story, just you wait." But he himself doesn't really believe what he's saying. Even *they* must understand.

During the week he doesn't think much about the Tajik business—can't pester Borya day after day. On Friday morning, driving past the sporting-goods shop, he remembers and goes in. Baseball bats? Sure, all you like. What about gloves and balls? No, we haven't got any of those. "You're not in Chicago, my dear." The words follow him out of the shop.

Summoning up his strength, he finally calls his friend. Borya is exhausted: it's baking hot again, and our boys have been knocked out. It's Germany versus Spain in the final—the Fascist axis. There's not much work to do—there never is, in summer.

"What about that young man"—Eric names the Tajik—"where did he end up?"

"Here and there," replies Borya in the most natural voice. "His heart went to Krylatskoe, his lungs to Sportivnaya."

In other words, they cut the Tajik up for his organs.

"They screwed up over his lungs—wanted to get them both, but they only got one."

Eric's holding the phone and saying nothing again.

"There's still his kidneys," he finally says in a dull voice.

"Seems no one fancied his kidneys," sniggers Borya.

Why's he laughing? That's not right.

"You're imagining things, doctor," replies Borya. "He was brain-dead. He had died, simple as that. We were examining a corpse."

Had Borya known that when he organized the transfer? He'll ask him, he will. Had Borya been expecting them to harvest his organs the whole time?

"When I did my U-turn on the highway, no; but later, when they loaded him into the ambulance, yes, I did think that. See, I'm a neurosurgeon. You did nothing wrong, nothing. Besides, Mr. Cardiologist, do you have anything against transplantation?"

Eric remembers: "Except a corn of wheat fall into the ground and die..." and "that a man lay down his life for his friends..." No, that's different, that's done by free will...

"And over here, we have presumed consent—ever heard of it? *Like it or not, miss, lie down in your cot.* Otherwise there wouldn't be any organs at all. Tomorrow some blind drunk in a ten-ton truck could knock one of us flying, and we'd be chopped into pieces for our organs. Though they'd screw everything up, as usual. One time we did everything right, and still you're... Supposing your Tajik had died like anyone else—would that have been any better?"

Perhaps it would. Eric doesn't know. Brain-dead... Borya did what he could, no question about that, but why...

"Why what?" Borya's obviously tired.

"Just the way you talk..." Yes, yes, it's all about the way he talks.

And what's Eric going to say to *them*, on the other side of the concrete bollards?

"Just tell them their Tajik may have saved two human lives. You have to take a broader view. We gained no personal gain from it."

Gain, gain—talk properly, Borya. And what's gain got to do with it? But we mustn't start quarreling now. One Tajik isn't the end of the world. Medicine is like that.

"We're not talking like professionals here, my friend," says Borya in a conciliatory voice. "No one knew it would turn out like this."

"Yes, that's the sad thing about our job."

"Well, brother, let's call it a day."
End of the call. Enough.

That evening he sets off for his dacha, without taking any medical instruments with him. His wife and child are expecting him. He has to chop down the maple trees that have run wild, and replace a water pump, and complete the title deeds for their land. Just like everyone else.

He never passed through the concrete bollards again.

August 2009
Translated by Nicolas Pasternak Slater

PIECES ON A PLANE

AN ENGLISH OPENING

THE AUTUMN years, their very beginning—seventy, seventy-five, life goes on. Many of the participants in this year's tournament will live another fifteen, even twenty, years, though of course these aren't their salad days: everything is already determined, realized. Still, they are the lucky ones: men of means, they get by without outside help—a comfortable life, secure. At some point the decisive loss will come: every life must end in defeat (or, more bluntly, must end)—but that much is fair, necessary even, no? Routine, in any case. Death is not discussed in their circles.

But in the meantime, why not get the gang together, move some pieces around a board? After much writing and wrangling, they had pooled together some funds for an annual tournament. '96—Philadelphia, '97—Providence, '98—little Williamstown, northwestern Massachusetts: frankly, none of the shabbiest corners of their *star-spangled* land for a gathering of aging chess-lovers. This year it was San Francisco's turn. One of the players arranged it all, from the accommodation to the venue. On their day off they all went out to the symphony hall together, took a drive around the town.

The games were played at the Marines' Memorial Club, the players the tournament's own spectators, arbiters, and organizers, too. Of course, the odd veteran would also stop by for a look—World War II, Korea, Vietnam: over the past century their homeland had had its fair share of wars. A great, powerful nation. Two rows of tables, sixteen players, everyone plays everyone; three rounds, then a rest day. In previous years there had been as many as twenty players; some fall by the wayside, but others appear, just pay your entry, and *welcome to the club.*

The muffled tap of pieces, soft lighting, the occasional quiet remark (chatter at the table is frowned upon); the smells of coffee and polished floors. Smoking is prohibited, of course, but no one smokes as it is—these men aren't enemies unto themselves. In the evenings they fill in the chart together, determine the day's most beautiful game, analyze it. The pleasant, understated world of chess.

But everything must come to an end, including the tournament, and its players fly their separate ways: north, to Seattle; south, to San Diego; to the East Coast. They part ways warmly, though this year's tournament proved rather...unusual, shall we say.

The flight for New York leaves with a slight delay. Coach is around seventy percent full, while in first class there are only two passengers, both ours, from our tournament: Albert A. Alexander, former ambassador to Norway (the title of ambassador is retained for life), and Donald, a businessman, *call me Don.*

Albert is wearing light chinos, a pink button-down shirt and a dark-blue, single-breasted blazer. A diplomatic bearing, the image of a peacemaker, he is elegant, handsome, even. Though admired and loved as a man, as a chess player he is decidedly average.

Don's life—or the first seventy-five and a half years of it, he jokes—was devoted to quite a different pursuit: selling ball bearings. We Anglo-Saxons love to make light of things, play ourselves down: in fact Don was king of the market, scourge of his rivals, with factories in Malaysia, South America, and other far-flung places besides. Retirees in his position have a tendency to strut around the citadels of European civilizations in long shorts and a baseball cap, visor flipped backward for others' amusement: clowns. Beefy Don is no such man. In addition to being one of the best players in the tournament, he is also its long-standing treasurer. And though his weight may be substantial, he runs every morning.

So what do these two men talk about? It is clear just by looking at them that on many matters (prayer in schools, same-sex marriage, gun control, what else? Oh, abortion, capital punishment, health-care reforms . . .) their opinions will diverge. As Churchill put it: *Democracy is the worst form of government, except for all those other forms that have been tried from time to time.* Both men are acutely aware of this paradox, the diplomat especially so. But what is important is that Albert and Don have both served their families and their nation well.

This year's tournament, however, had been pretty dispiriting for everyone involved. Two talking points, where to begin? First: Alzheimer's. Poor old Jeremy Levine, all-around nice guy and keeper of traditions, was in a terrible state. At least he could still remember how the pieces move, thank God. His openings were instinctive, confident, but after that it would all fall apart. His opponents, eyes averted, would propose a draw at the first opportunity. Ten, fifteen moves, and then—*Jeremy, what do you say?*

Jeremy had always been an affable man, but at the tournament he had developed a constant giggle—a shy, quiet titter. Honestly, it was uncomfortable being around him, a gray-haired child. Yes, he still recognizes some people, but everyone knows that that, too, will end, the only question being when. The progression of Alzheimer's is impossible to predict.

"He did recognize me," the ambassador declares.

Don isn't moved by such things: "That's beside the point."

What Don had found most galling wasn't so much Jeremy's presence—illness happens, what can you do?—as it was that of Carolyn, Jeremy's wife: chess is no infirmary. And there had been rather a lot of this Carolyn around, with all her *honey*s and *sweetheart*s. She was at Jeremy's side unrelentlingly, from the chess tables to his diaper changes.

"Her whole life she's zipped the man around like a radio-controlled car. Ironic, when she can't even use a computer! Just think, Al—I have to send her letters by snail mail."

Carolyn believes that reimmersing her husband in chess will slow his decline. According to her, Jeremy was almost back to where he had been a year before.

"The great fruits of our labor," Don chuckles. "Makes the whole long flight worthwhile."

Their meal arrives. The conversation moves on.

"But seriously, if you have no legs then don't expect to ski," Don says. "I'm opposed to all those cripple Olympics."

"You can say that to me, Don, but I wouldn't risk advertising those opinions to a wider audience."

In any case, it would be inhuman to exclude their old pal from the tournament. And besides—here the ambassador flicks his hand—what's interesting is the process, not the result.

No shit, thinks Don, with the form you've had lately...

"Don, you did give Jeremy a draw, didn't you?"

He did. In spite of his convictions.

In-flight conversations have their own stop-start logic. After the meal the old gents feel drowsy.

Would the ambassador mind if Don took a nap? After that they can hash over Ivy, the Russian: the second matter of discussion, and a serious one; something has to be done. Don will shut his eyes, lower his shade for a while, have some time to himself. There, internally, he will see pieces moving across a chessboard, capturing one another, clocks ticking. One winner, one loser: in the world Don wants to live in, everything is fair.

The ambassador dozes too. Below the plane lies America: land of opportunity, leader of the Western world—its tuning fork, if you will. Soon, the ambassador knows, other countries will start to catch up with her, and though that European charm that he holds so dear will inevitably become a thing of the past, life on this planet will be the better, the more humane, for it. Their tournament is a model of rational self-organization, more so than any political party, any social movement: such pure, conflict-free, from-the-heart undertakings are a rarity in today's world. The ambassador has seen a great many difficult, unpleasant things in his time. An awful lot of politics. His knowledge came at a cost.

If anything, the service in first class is excessive. The gentlemen are offered dessert, chocolate mousse. None for Don, thanks. Mousse? What's mousse? Is it like Jell-O? Don hates Jell-O; he can't stand anything that quivers.

"That's gotten me into trouble with the ladies before, believe me," Don chuckles.

Funny, yes. The ambassador, meanwhile, has loved one woman all his life: his wife. The same goes for Don, of course. But back in their college days . . . Oh, in college we were all polygamous.

The flight is bumpy, not conducive to sleeping. The fasten-seatbelt sign appears. There is a large river beneath them.

"Just the Missouri or something," the ambassador suggests.

"Not *just* the Missouri," Don grumbles, who lived in the Midwest for many years.

The ambassador raises his palms—elegantly, like almost everything he does. The Midwest is Don's fiefdom; the ambassador, meanwhile, has only ever lived on the East Coast—in Washington, New York.

So, how about that Russian? Matthew Ívanov, Ivy. Or as Carolyn, poor old Jeremy's wife, had taken to calling him, *Poison Ivy*.

"Been stung by the poison ivy yet?" she had asked every player.

Yes, they had all been stung, every last one of them. Matthew Ivanov, new kid on the block, had won the entire tournament: fifteen matches, fourteen victories, one draw. And no, the issue here isn't the prize pot—which the winner took outright—but the Russian's attitude toward the game, toward his competitors.

No one had been able to speak to Matthew, beyond the bare minimum required of the match: before each game—a handshake and *hi*, and then at its end—*that's it, I resign*. Matthew would nod, shake hands, and then leave. He never took part in the postgame analyses, not to mention the excursions. And at last night's dinner he had taken his check and framed certificate and ducked out with no more than a *thanks, everyone.* Where's that certificate now? Lying in a trash can, for all we know.

"Al, tell me, do you think he even likes chess?"

"The game certainly likes him, Don—more than it does you or me. Did you see our match?"

No, Don didn't see it.

Albert sighs: when playing a stronger opponent, you are forced to raise your game. But in the ambassador's head-to-head with Ivy, his hands were tied as early as the ninth or tenth move. In a bad position, any move is worthless.

"Where did the kid even come from?" Don wonders.

The ambassador shrugs.

"An immigrant. They like it here."

"Sure they do—we keep them fed." Don is annoyed. "America, the freest country in the world. Too free, if you ask me."

"There are free countries in Europe, too," the ambassador says, with a conciliatory tone. He flashes one of his best smiles—the one reserved for his cohorts, allies.

Don has never been to Europe. The ambassador finds this strange.

"You recommend it? What's the point?"

What can you say to that? There are wonderful places.

"But how about you, Don? How long did you hold out against Ivy?"

First off, it was the opening game of the tournament. Second, Ivy was playing white. And third, the newbie spent twenty minutes on his opener.

"So the clock's ticking, and I've got this kid I don't know just sitting there in front of me, thinking. His head's down, I can't see his eyes. I mean, what is that, some kind of joke?"

"I imagine he was being entirely serious. He was probably tuning into his thoughts, deciding whether he was in the mood to play aggressively or to beat you in a positional battle. Ivy's a master."

In the end the youngster had gone with c4, the English Opening. Don responded with e5.

"The Reversed Dragon?" the ambassador asks in delight.

Don nods. It all went by the book. He quickly recites the moves. "Know the system?"

"Oh, yes, of course," the ambassador nods.

Like hell he does. Back when Don was running his factories, his ability to tell when he was being lied to saved him from many a sticky situation. He is getting increasingly worked up:

"Look, I can take a kicking, but at least give me something to show for it! But no, he just bleeds you dry, squeezes you like a machine! I'm seventy-five—I can't compute like him! *A master*! I can see he made an impression on you . . ."

"Yes . . ." the ambassador says, as though searching for the right word, one clearly long-since found. "You know, he has a certain . . ." He is planning on saying *audacity*, but Don interrupts:

"Just say it straight: kid's a hustler. I checked, and there's no chess player by the name of Matthew Ivanov."

"Don, their alphabet is different. Remember those old sports jerseys, C-C-C-P?"

"Well I'm telling you, that CCCP of yours was in it for the money!"

"Money? What would he want money for?"

"Al, what does anybody want money for?"

Is this guy out of his mind? Don thinks. Like Jeremy?

Well if it's the money they're after, the ambassador muses to himself, then why did they sell their politics so cheap?

"Russians have suffered a great deal this century," the ambassador says contemplatively.

"So you're telling me *the kid* suffered?"

The ambassador continues:

"Perhaps I shouldn't be telling you this, but a few years ago the Russians sold their foreign policy for one million—yes, one *million*—times less than what we were willing to pay them for it."

They both sit in stunned silence. Don—at the size of the sum, *jeez, one mill, that's six zeros, what kind of money were we sitting on?* The diplomat—at having blabbed to Don.

"I understand," says the ambassador, breaking the silence. "We have to protect the spirit of the tournament. How about abolishing the prize fund?"

"We're not an infirmary, Albert. We're not against good players, God no. We just want them to behave properly."

"So," the ambassador sighs, "that means drawing up a code, some rules and regulations. And doing away with winner takes all"—he mimes a staircase with his hand—"but instead eight thousand, five, three. First, second, third."

"Yup, it has to be done," Don nods. "Because you can bet on it, next time we'll have three of those... Ivanovs showing up on our doorstep. Your beloved CCCPs."

Don is right, of course: their tournament, their great project, their brainchild, is under threat. All this having to lay down the law... it's everywhere nowadays, even in family life. Meanwhile, he and Don have done just fine with their old ladies without any such written binders. The four of them should meet up in New York sometime, go to Carnegie Hall or Yankee Stadium... then they could have them over, show them the collection. The ambassador collects owls—marble, clay. He even has a couple of magnificent taxidermies. The owl is a symbol of wisdom.

"The Don, that's a beloved river in Russia. Perhaps that'll redeem them somewhat in your eyes? *And Quiet Flows the Don?*" he says with relish. "It's a book, it won the Nobel Prize. Not that you, Don, could ever be called quiet." The ambassador looks out the window, squinting. What is he hoping to find out there?

At this point there is a minor disturbance. Behind them—where the first-class lavatory is—they hear a noise. A young man has slipped quickly inside and locked the door. The stewardess gives the passengers a guilty look, shrugs: *What can you do?* The other lavatories are occupied; someone has clearly had an urgent call of nature and burst into first class.

Soon—too soon, somehow—the sound of the flush is heard, and the young man steps out of the lavatory: none other than Matthew

Ivanov himself. On recognizing his recent competitors, the young man smiles. His teeth are a brilliant white, but the smile still comes out tense, sad.

Both Don and the ambassador make some bewildered movements, meanwhile Ivanov, who had almost recoiled when he first saw them, now takes a seat in the second row from the back, diagonally behind them. It is clear he hadn't wanted to run into the old men, but that running away from them would have also felt wrong. The only one who can muster a welcoming gesture is the ambassador—not Don, and certainly not the stewardess, who had been on her way to shoo the uninvited guest back into coach, but hesitated upon seeing that her wards clearly knew him. The young man, if he did show any aggression, initially showed it only toward her.

He preempts her: Is there really any reason why he can't enjoy a wide, comfy seat for a while? Because his ticket is for economy, the stewardess says. And? Is he disturbing anyone? Is he depriving the others of even a fraction of the comfort they have procured? Still, the stewardess says, it's unfair, wrong. Unfair to the others in economy, and especially unfair to those who have bought first-class tickets. Unfair and immoral.

"Immoral?"

What does this young man find so funny?

"Mr. Alexander," he says, addressing the ambassador, "do you also feel this way?"

The ambassador shrugs ambiguously.

"I get it, we're not supposed to, but *immoral*?" The young man is inspired: "Whatever happened to the parable of the vineyard workers: *Is thine eye evil, because I am good?*—know that one, Mr. Ambassador?"

Don—who has been strangely quiet so far—strikes his fist onto his table:

"You heard the lady. It's unfair and wrong." He is red and angry now, like he used to get back when he sold ball bearings.

The young man stands up. The ambassador says, stiffly:

"We respect your aptitude for the game, Matthew, and we should be happy to continue our acquaintance. However, as you can see, this is neither the time nor the place." He tries to smile nonetheless. "How I wish I knew Russian like you do English! You had excellent teachers."

The young man replies:

"Yes, outstanding. And the textbooks were first-rate. As I recall: *What is that noise in the room next door? It is my grandfather eating cheese.*"

Albert, experienced diplomat that he is, knows how to take a blow. He's thinking up a witty retort, but none is needed—the young man is already gone.

After the guest's departure, the old-timers try to piece together the conversation he ruptured.

Don asks:

"What fable was that—about wine?"

"A parable. From Matthew, I think. Yes, very on the nose! My goodness."

This latest incident has left them both thoroughly shaken. They're elderly men, after all.

"How did you come to know Scripture so well, Albert?"

"Diplomacy," the ambassador replies. "Like it or not, it makes a demagogue out of you." His charm is gradually returning.

The plane starts to make its descent. Soon after, the Statue of Liberty appears through the windows, a formidable woman holding a tablet and a torch. The seats are returned to their upright position.

"God knows who we're feeding," Don ponders, looking at the statue over his neighbor's shoulder.

The ambassador, too, is gazing at the giant sculpture: this lady needs no one; no part of her quivers.

Don asks:

"And you, Albert, what religion do you practice?"

The diplomat replies, a sudden sadness in his voice:

"I don't believe in God." Then, inexplicably: "*Sir.*"

*

I:I

"Anatoly Vladimirovich!" It takes me a while to realize who's calling. It's been twenty years since anybody used my patronymic, and even then it was mainly cops.

He says: Matvey. Gives a long-winded explanation as to how he got my number.

"Ah, so you're the son..." Yes. The son.

A confused kid—clearly somehow we've already fallen short of his expectations. When you emigrate, it's not your homeland you lose, but your image of your destination—that's just my own, personal observation. I ask Matvey how his old man's holding up. Not bad, he says, still alive.

I tell him to come over; he does.

We're sitting in my rented studio on Stanyan Street, near the park. There are boxes standing along the wall. We're all very mobile here, you know. Americans are a mobile people.

I had a book come out recently—*Art de Vivre: A Psychologist's Perspective*. I published it myself. It even got a few reviews, and a college came calling, with the promise of a permanent position. Not the most illustrious institution, to put it mildly, and I'm not big on spending my days with students, either, but you have to take what you can get.

Matvey's going to have to face up to the real world, too.

He gives a listless nod. That's one thing you could never accuse his father of—listlessness. So does he take after his mom, then? In any case, something about this Matvey kid catches my interest. I haven't been all that sociable lately.

He's a graduate, from the Moscow State Linguistic University. Sadly, languages won't impress anybody here, especially not English. But he does have a nice smile: that could help. I can't remember if his father was much of a smiler. His mom I can't remember at all.

A smile's a smile, but that'll only get you so far.

"Hey, Matvey, why not bone up on some programming?"

"I guess," he says, "I'll probably have to."

"I'll make a few calls for you."

He nods:

"Oh, just in case, my surname's Ivanóv. They pronounce it *Éye-vanov* here."

He took his mom's name? He shakes his head: nope. The plot thickens. He changed it. And where's he staying? Here, he says, in town.

"Where exactly?"

"Twenty-Fifth Avenue and . . ." he trails off.

"Twenty-Fifth is long. What, up in Sea Cliff?"

Ah, say no more. With Márgot-Margót? Amirite?

Not Margarita, not Rita—Márgot, Margót, Margosha: no single variant has yet been established. She herself prefers Márgot, stress on the first syllable. A luxurious woman: smooth skin, completely wrinkle-free. She wears her hair just as she pleases and has a striking sense of style—no one else here walks around like that. She is thought to be over forty, though (why not?) she could even be a whole fifty.

When she first arrived, with her husband, spiteful tongues (mainly female) called her a debauched Leningrad broad, nothing more. But no, Margot's no broad, or not *just* some broad—she's a phenomenon. She's helped a lot of people here. Supportive, but not suffocating, no clinginess, no guilt trips, she sets them all free—her very own *art de vivre*. I wouldn't mind getting to know her a little better myself, only the opportunity hasn't presented itself.

So how does Matvey know her? In the biblical sense? OK, OK, just kidding. But you get me, right? No reaction. He says: through mutual acquaintances, his mother's. An important clarification. Everyone needs somewhere to stay in the first few weeks. And Margot's is by no means the worst option—far from it.

*

There's a certain elusiveness, a looseness, about him. That won't do here: you've got to be a part of society. Go get yourself some opinions, defend them. Democracy's a godawful thing, but as it stands we haven't come up with anything better.

Health-care reforms, for example. What does Matvey have to say about that?

He shrugs:

"I'm pretty healthy. Haven't had any run-ins with medicine."

Or, say, Supreme Court nominations: What does he think? Same-sex marriage—for or against? Experiments using embryonic stem cells? For the avoidance of any doubt: America is the freest country in the world. The new Rome. The place where history is forged.

Actually, how *did* he get here?

"On a plane."

Well, obviously he didn't swim. No: How did he get the visa—for Jewish ancestry or something? His father had never been a Jew. No, he says, he won the green-card lottery. Let me explain: the green-card lottery is no lottery, not really: they take kids with a good education, Americans aren't fools. Sure, sometimes they'll take an old lady or two, just for optics. A lottery. It's important to know how things are done around here.

Anyway, the first step has been made, a very important one at that: he's here. Now it's time to hustle, to get moving.

"Read the papers, a range of them. This civilization of ours is primarily a financial project, then legal. Get to know the problems, otherwise you might as well be living in, I don't know, some kind of sanatorium."

Though if he's at Margot's, a sanatorium is pretty much where he already is.

He says, uncertainly:

"They throw some newspaper at our door."

I can imagine. No, seriously:

"You don't want to be some flunky or marginal. Mar*go*nal. Forgive the pun."

He waves it off: right now he's fine to be anything. So long as he can just be.

"Right now it's like I don't exist."

Romanticism, nonsense. We all exist.

So how does Matvey plan to earn a living? He shrugs, again. When kids don't know that at eighteen they go into medicine or law school. But Matvey's already—how old?—twenty-six.

By the way, does he keep a journal? It's a handy thing. Only don't write about your feelings. No one cares about them, we all have the same ones. Just some advice, seeing as that's my field. Hey, maybe he's thinking of becoming a journalist or a writer? Matvey doesn't want to talk about this, either. A strange young man. Of course, a father like his could never have a normal son.

I first wound up in their Leningrad apartment in '77, by chance: some girl, a careless being in all respects, needed some sort of reference or review for a paper. She had missed a deadline, was incapable of dealing with the paperwork herself.

Why his home? That was where he worked.

So anyway, the man of the house—let's try not to name names, OK?—sat me down in an armchair. He was relatively young, though with pretensions of a kind of noble decrepitude.

"Well?" he said, and held out his hand. Long fingers, no ring.

I handed him the paperwork, and he started reading. One leg wound around the other, like the thread of a screw. I could never do that myself.

There was a lot of old furniture—it was your average cultured Petersburg home. The usual volumes: burgundy-bound Romain Rollands, brown Bunins, green Chekhovs, gray Dostoyevskys. Their doubles still travel around with me in boxes. After the second or third move I stopped unpacking them.

He finished reading the papers, sighed:

"No, I'm not signing this."

"Why not?" I asked.

I mean, at the end of the day, they weren't my papers.

"I'm afraid."

"What are you afraid of?"

He sucked one of the tips of his glasses.

"What can I say...? Everything."

That encounter convinced me of one thing alone: professional snitch he was not. But rumor had it that that was exactly what he was.

How about a coffee? I'm afraid I can't offer anything else. Matvey isn't hungry anyway. I tell him about the first time I met his father. Omitting the odd detail.

"He can't do that anymore"—of his legs.

Makes sense. Old guy's coming unscrewed.

As for the delicate matter. Back then, everything revolved around one thing alone: the authorities versus the dissidents. Just bear that in mind. Plus, if you ask me, all this declassification, the opening of the archives, it's a dangerous thing. Many names will be ruined for nothing. I mean, the KGB did hackwork, too: it had a plan to meet. Back then they might call you in, say, and ask you: Are you a good Soviet?

"Did they call you in?" Matvey asks.

What does that matter? So they call you in. And you'll say: Yes, I'm a good Soviet. So then they suggest collaborating. You'll find a handy excuse to get out of it: I'm sorry, I'd be happy to, but when I drink I get chatty. There were little tricks you could use. They'll sigh. Then: but if you get wind of any acts seeking to undermine...? Of course, I'll be in touch. They'll make a note: verbal agreement to collaborate. No signature.

Matvey furrows his eyebrows, like a little child:

"Why are you telling me this?"

"No reason."

Psychology is an experimental science. It's interesting to get a live reaction.

I couldn't have cared less about the papers: If he didn't sign, he didn't sign. Besides, my thing with that girl had already started to crumble on its own. A few years later, I started going to his apartment independently of any girls. *It's not that the world is small, it's that the intelligentsia is,* or so we used to joke at the time.

It's hard to say what he actually did with his days. They said he had an encyclopedic knowledge. But what did he in fact achieve? He wrote a successful foreword. To some book of letters. It's not like the old Red Bear would have given him much free rein, anyway. Especially not in the humanities.

I remember him sitting at his desk, bloviating exuberantly: "I, a disciple of the academic sciences . . ." What sciences? Christ knows, go ask him yourself. There was a bottle of some tincture on the table: he brewed it himself, not the worst of his eccentricities. In Gorbachev's anti-alcohol days, his tinctures saved many a good man from thirst. I remember him screaming: "Faux pas!" when his wife slipped the wrong glass under his nose. But the man knew many poems, and could recite them well.

He had nervous, musical hands, a strong jaw: his stock was clear. We even nicknamed him Duke, in a nod to his noble descent. I can still picture him clutching the invisible bridle of an imagined charging steed—*the idol on his brazen horse*—yes, he recited a lot of poems. Nolens volens, whenever you talk about Duke, his high style rubs off on you:

"What an artist died in your father, Matvey!"

Another nervous smile:

"Well, not quite."

Not quite an artist, or not quite dead? Both, apparently. Duke certainly cut a conspicuous figure in Saint Petersburg. He loved anything antiquated, and I don't just mean poems—statuettes, china, you name it. His term for such objects was "transubstantiation of the soul." He had an uncle he boasted about with pride—the guy hadn't evacuated during the war, out of a fear of coming home to find his apartment looted: "I'm no advocate of this suitcase-phonograph culture," he had said. Well, the man starved to death, but he did save the family heirlooms.

He was a monarchist, obviously, and an anti-Semite—though in a broader, more whimsical way. Wait, scratch that, he was just ruffling a few feathers, an old man trying to make himself relevant. He had a Jewish wife, after all. Who, Nina Arkadyevna? No, Nina Arkadyevna isn't Jewish.

At the moment I'm struggling to remember this Nina Arkadyevna, his third and, clearly, final wife. Something effaced, apologetic. The tedium around us was such that we were drawn to bright personalities—people with a sparking, seething spirituality, if not without their moral defects. She was a quiet postgraduate. Word was that Duke had married her to make an honest woman of her, so to speak.

As for Duke, he once told me that for every stage of his life God had sent him a spouse appropriate for that age. Yup, he said it, the G-word. So that must have been in the '80s, just before the end. Before that we had never heard a peep about God from Duke. Not that that stopped him from making a song and a dance about his newfound faith. I'm no expert, but I think he picked Eastern Rite Catholicism. Or maybe it was the other way around.

And then that story resurfaced, that old one.

In '49, Duke was a graduate student at our local university, Leningrad State. Have I got the year right?

"What year was your dad born?" I ask Matvey.

"'25."

Yes, that must be it. The faculty of languages and literature was home to a group of poets, though *poets* is pretty generous, really—they were just students, boys, aged between seventeen and twenty. Linguists, philologists, or, as we called them back then, *grammarians*. The way these kids lived, dabbling in poetry, it was like they hadn't noticed the authorities we were living under. And the authorities didn't like to be ignored like that. No, they had their own whims.

Anyway, it all started with stupid things, small potatoes. The kids got some verses published in a wall newspaper in the department. With their tawdry desire to experiment, excessively so, the verses rubbed Duke and a few others the wrong way. And Duke did have taste. He was an imposing young grad student, passionate, good at public speaking, and eloquent. Not to mention his looks. So he spoke out—and not in some smoker's hangout by the stairwells, but publicly, at a faculty meeting. He used the term *group*: Group X, which he named after the oldest and most prolific of the kids. It just slipped out by itself. A group of young philologists. Six in number. He started showboating: "The Russian language is not a language of philologists, but of Pushkin, Gogol, and Tolstoy." The wall newspaper was swiftly removed, and that seemed to be the end of it all.

But then a year or so later, the kids were arrested, every last one. "Anti-Soviet Group X," they were dubbed, or "The Six"—as though our Duke had foreseen it all. At the trial the boys slandered themselves and each other, as is customary, and everything came down to a single testimony—Duke's. Apparently having his say at the faculty meeting hadn't been enough for him. Or he had gotten scared: by then, it was clear that he was afraid of everything. "Life's like a rhyme—you never know where it's going to lead you," I once heard him say. Seems like he had written to all the right places, kept that rhyme going long after the faculty meeting.

The boys got eight years each, but they were released after five. None of them became poets, so you could say Duke was right about the extent of their talents. The kids kept *schtum* about the circumstances of their arrest, for a while. But then in '90 one university newspaper dug up the whole story and printed it: dark days in the history of the university, that sort of angle.

Duke responded in a letter to the editor. He started it with an epigraph from the Bible: "I said in my haste, All men are liars." In the letter itself, he wrote that yes, he had been summoned, and that he had caved and confirmed the boys' confessions—as far as he knew, they had already confessed. Back then we didn't know what you kids know now. And yes, although the investigative methods had been unlawful, he fully acknowledged the role that he had played. His testimony was a mistake, a tragic mistake, but the little verses of the accused were in all truth pretty so-so—just see for yourselves. Yes, he had also mistaken a faculty meeting for a creative workshop, for he lived—and indeed lives—in a world of consonance, ideas, and rhymes. Besides, he was no stranger to persecution himself, having been thoroughly berated for apolitical conduct at another such gathering. But, most importantly: now that his eyes had been opened to the Truth, he judged himself through the courts of his own faith and conscience, both significantly harsher than common, public courts. He laid down his arms. It wasn't like he could do much else.

But then one of the erstwhile kids seized his chance. He got his hands on his old file, and a copy of the denouncement—the one sent to the authorities—started making the rounds. A beautiful hand, instantly recognizable. *Pushkin, Gogol, Tolstoy*—even here Duke had found some time for a discussion of the classics.

We were ashamed: he was one of us, after all. We stopped going to see him; even his tinctures lost their appeal. And then he upped and left for Moscow. Word was that it was for Matvey, his son.

In Moscow we met, once or twice, at the odd funeral. Duke was always up for a funeral, even those of acquaintants he hardly knew. Every time he had looked hale and hearty, smart. He would speak beside the coffin and at the wake, and would sometimes even go first, if others were too shy to start. I remember, at the funeral of a certain poet, he said something along the lines of grief being unnecessary—because poets always die at the right time, once their work is complete. "Hear, hear," heckled one half-wit, also from the writing fraternity: "Go on then, shoot, put us all behind bars!" The story may seem savage, but behind the iron curtain everything was beyond the pale.

It appears that was to be the last time I would see Duke. He invited me over, but I have a lot of friends in Moscow, ones I know a hundred times better than Duke. And then I moved to America.

Does Matvey know the story of the Leningrad boys? No doubt. Why else would he change his surname? Frankly, it was a more interesting surname than Ivanóv. He knows everything, the whole shebang. How does he deal with it? I'm curious to dig a little deeper, but it calls for some delicatesse.

It's getting dark, time to hit the lights. The light switch in my room is broken; my hands can't reach to fix it. So we move to the kitchen, where the windows are big, to catch the last of the daylight.

I don't know if our paths will cross again. So I cut to the chase:

"You have to forgive your father. It's all over, you know? We're all absolved by the very fact of our existence in our dear fatherland. We all had a hand in the cookie jar, at the very least."

Matvey looks up:

"Who am I," he asks, "to forgive or not to forgive?" And then: "Has anybody even asked anyone's forgiveness?"

He gets up to get his jacket.

"Your hell will never end if you don't," I call after him, "Will you even go to the funeral? I didn't bury my own father. I had no visa, no money. As the Bible says, 'Let the dead bury their dead.'"

By this point he's almost out the front door:

"Knowing Scripture comes in handy sometimes, right?"

Who is this kid? Un-pin-down-able. Still, he's right: enough digging around in this trash can. He changed his surname—let's move on.

But somehow I don't want to end things here. I never go anywhere, and people rarely come to see me. Matvey was once a pro at chess, right? In a past life, he says. Still so young, and the kid already has a past life.

I have a chess set lying around somewhere. Does he feel like slogging it out? You can't even call me an amateur: I play once in a blue moon. But with this kid I'm one up in our head-to-heads.

The last time we played he was eight years old, in the chess group at the local Pioneer Palace—all openings and endgames, desperate to beat a grown-up. I know how to beat suckers like these—once. It's all in the psychology. So that time I beat him.

He had immediately started setting up the pieces again, but I said:

"Stop. You can have too much of a good thing. The second, third, or tenth time around you might be able to beat me, but I won't be playing."

He had been on the verge of tears: chin wobbling, eyebrows arched. But he kept it under control, good kid. I tried the same trick on a couple of other kids after him.

I remind him of our match history, but he pretends he doesn't remember. I ask him:

"Don't you want to get even? I'll get out the chess set, brew some coffee, turn on the lights."

"No, Anatoly Vladimirovich, let's leave it at that."

And then he left.

THE VICTOR

Leningrad is the capital of Soviet chess. Matvey's mother takes him to the chess group at the local Pioneer Palace. This is where the greats trained—the world champions and grandmasters, whose portraits line the corridors and classrooms. Whenever one of them emigrates, or doesn't return from the West, the portrait is removed.

It was Matvey's mother who had insisted on chess, seeing it as a chance to get ahead, get out. Not that she had had to insist all that strongly: his father, wrapped up in his work, wasn't all that interested in his son, and because chess was a quiet pastime, Matvey wouldn't disturb him. Besides, chess could be played into old age, chess players were the first to be allowed out of the country, and hardly any of them then faced repression back home. These were the sorts of things you thought about back then—everyone knew somebody who was doing time. A doctor is still a doctor in a prison camp, a musician still a musician: they can get out of some of the labor by performing in camp productions. But Matvey had no obvious talent for music.

A smart, focused, diligent boy, he has an excellent memory. The coach teaches the students judicious placement: the pieces should be comfortable.

"Look after them as you would a close relative."

The only close relatives Matvey has are his father and mother. Plus some half brothers from his father's earlier marriages, though he only found out about them later. When he finally met them, they were already grown-up, with their own wives and children. He never felt any brotherly feelings toward them. Besides, he saw that they could hurt his mother. A certain inclination for rudeness, aggression—or he sensed as much in them, at least.

However, as it happens, intuition isn't one of Matvey's strong points. Openings, endgames—those can be taught, but when it comes to intuition you either have it or you don't. Matvey, however, does benefit from an unusually precocious ability to compute options. He is good at thinking from both sides, and always finds the most astute, intelligent moves for his opponents, something few are able to do. But he also thinks too much, which lands him in trouble with the clock.

"Not enough intuition, that's why," says his coach.

Perhaps the coach is right, or perhaps Matvey is lacking in something else equally indefinable, that special sort of chess genius. Either way, by the time he finishes school it's clear that there will be a ceiling to his development in the game, even if it has yet to be reached. Matvey, now a candidate master, is already traveling the country, winning prizes. But soon, soon, he will quit.

A good hack, that's what he is. Matvey will never be a grandmaster: for him that road is closed, even if he could hold his own in such illustrious company: grandmasters, unlike many other sportsmen, are people with taste. Matvey particularly likes seeing them stick around after the game, discuss, analyze, crack the odd joke, smile at the person who has been their opponent for the past few hours. What he would give to be one of the people on stage during those moments—the best, the very best, in their chosen profession! A remarkable community—one that transcends state and national borders. Like great musicians, mathematicians.

A mathematician, that's it! No, in that field a talent for mental arithmetic has long since lost its value. That would be the wrong move.

So, with school behind him and his chess pursuits nearing their end, all of a sudden there was Moscow—a long, tedious dream, at the end of which Matvey changed his surname, won the prospect of US residency, and left. Here in San Francisco he was supposed to wake up, come back to life, but he had ended up—as the old man so rightly put it—in a sanatorium, Margot's house. The dream continued, albeit somewhat more pleasant. But a dream is still a dream.

Margot comes to his bedroom every evening, to wish Matvey "sweet dreams." She has some exquisite creams that make her skin salty to the taste, which he likes. What he doesn't like is their domestic situation: her husband and his strong handshake—too strong, somehow. The two of them are practically divorced, he's no cause for concern, but can that really be true? He's away for long stretches at a time on "business," but such "business" is no source of contempt—Margot has no eye for business. Still, when the husband is at home Margot doesn't set foot in Matvey's room (and his dreams really are sweet). So are they still together? No, don't ask, it would only spoil their... the word is not said, but implied. There are different sorts of—what's the word?— *arrangements, commitments.* Life is long; you'll see yet, my dear.

Margot loves variety: a swim in the ocean, always cold, she's a strong swimmer—go on, don't be afraid! They'll take a dip, have a swig of cognac, and then she'll teach Matvey how to eat oysters: a touch of pepper, lemon, no sauce—an uncomplicated science.

Besides the suite of writers shipped over from Russia, the huge photography monographs, and the many objets d'art that are dotted around the house, they have a multitude of books personally inscribed by the authors. *Art de Vivre*—from the psychologist friend: *to she without whom my book would never have seen the light of day.* Matvey mentions this friend—the supposed specialist on the art of living, the strange man with the troubled gaze—is the book worth reading? No, of course not.

"He talked about my father."

Margot tells him to forget it: he's a man maimed by emigration, unhappy, maybe even dangerous if given half a chance. Forget it all.

Margot's father was a poet, by the way: he spent time in prison.

"Uh..." Matvey's request for her to recite something of his is met with a flick of the hand. He died a long time ago. They didn't even live together. She doesn't remember anything of his by heart—that's Matvey's department, memory. The past doesn't exist, nor does the future, all they have is what's here—the now. And that's not so bad, is it? Matvey, she sees, wants to achieve something, settle some score, but Margot feels no such pull. She isn't drawn to results—that's why she has no children, as those spiteful ladies say. Margot loves processes, the process of life. San Francisco and its surroundings are the ideal place for that. There's no history here—no endless weight pulling it back: its fortunes, once cobbled together on gold, are now made on computers, and there's the odd earthquake in between, but none of that can be considered history.

They stop in at that club, center, whatever—Memorial—their crab soup is unbelievable. A notice there catches Matvey's eye, about an upcoming chess tournament. What's the prize money? Only birds, as Chaliapin said, sing for free. Matvey often quotes others, though this is a habit he is trying to kick—he got it from his father. Margot, however, likes it: she sees his little quips as flirtation, as tenderness, part of his efforts to win her over. She is a living, breathing being, after all; she feels emotions as well as sensations. Such a shame he notices so little, wrapped up as he is in his thoughts of setting himself up in America, of his father, his past, his future. When will these kids ever realize there is no past or future: there is only the present, their crab soup (go on, laugh—their soup), but also—this evening, the lights from the bridge bouncing off the water, the smell of sea-weed—there, smell it, don't think about it!—just live, breathe!

He'll trounce them all, make himself some money. Pass him the phone. It just so happens that they have an odd number of players. No, no need for lunch, accommodation, or group activities. Margot couldn't lend him a thousand bucks, could she? The entry fee, for the prize fund. Of course. So he plays chess?

That evening Matvey locks the door, so that Margot won't come in while he calls his mother. It's morning in Moscow. How's his father?

Well, he just ate some broth. Matvey snaps at his mother—Who cares about broth?—as though the expanse between them obliges them to speak only of life-and-death matters. Well, what does he want to know? After the news, the big news—*surgery would be advisable, though no one will agree to perform it on a patient your age*—there remain a multitude of small blessings for the invalid and his near and dear to enjoy: he ate some broth; he went to the bathroom all by himself; he asked me to read to him.

"What, should I fly back?"

"No," his mother says, "not yet." His father will assume that Matvey has returned to bury him.

Matvey's preparations for the tournament consist in studying the games of recent years, a pursuit he never had any intention of taking up again. Shame—not even the library has any books in Russian: chess is that rare field in which we Russians are still ahead. Matvey has his suspicions about the level of those whom he is to play, but who knows, maybe some money-grabbing compatriot of his will show up. The only Russian, however, turns out to be him.

He is dealt a strong opponent in the first round. The clocks are started, the game begins, Matvey is playing white. He thinks for a long time, moves his hands under the table to calm his shakes: he hasn't so much as touched a piece in eight years. Brawny Don plays robustly, honestly, in the same spirit as Matvey. He is almost his equal: had he computed a little better, not messed up his options, he would have gotten a draw. For a long time white stood no better than black.

Matvey plays the first game without leaving the table. After his win he is exhilarated, famished. He hasn't paid for refreshments—not that anyone would object to his taking some, but he feels uncomfortable eating at their expense. Margot drives over to pick him up and takes him out for an early dinner; she has never seen him so energetic, so alive before. But in the second round he beats his opponent easily. He watches the games on the neighboring tables, feeling like a hawk in a room full of parakeets.

Romantic chess. The gentlemen's opening preparations are all done and dusted by the fifth or sixth move. One of the men—a certain

Albert A. Alexander, here called "the ambassador"—unexpectedly smells of home, somehow, of family.

"Hail, Caesar!" the ambassador exclaims before their game. "The condemned salute you!" In Latin, of course. *Morituri te salutant*—the sort of Latin that everybody knows.

The ambassador gets a drubbing. Matvey doesn't even have to try all that hard: the man starts pretentiously—the King's Fianchetto Opening—and within a few moves creates a position he can't sustain. Then, with a sly look at Matvey, he moves his pawn—go on, take it. The pawn is bait, Matvey wasn't born yesterday. Poorly thought through attacks here and there, challenges with nothing to back them up—none of it romantic so much as sloppy. The old big shot even has the nerve to suggest a draw. Finally, after completing his last, inane, move, the ambassador raises his hands, tilts his head to one side, and, in a gesture of capitulation, stops the clock.

Matvey doesn't go to the evening reviews: Oh, do it yourselves, I don't have the energy, posing as some kind of grandmaster.

With feebleminded Jeremy, Matvey's intention was to lose: to just sit and think for fifty minutes, then fifty more, run out the clock, but instead he proposes a draw—no need for him to outdo the others in everything. *Moderation is the best of feasts,*[1] as his father loved to say.

He's in a bad way, gasping for breath, it's time, his mother says—he doesn't even have the strength to cross his own legs. The thread of that screw has straightened, smoothed. Matvey could have gone straightaway—his victory is assured some rounds before the end of the tournament—but then what would happen to his prize? Those bastards might swipe his money. No, that's unfair, of course, Margot's right: What have they actually done to him?

There, it's over, Matvey has his money, and now tomorrow morning he'll be out of here. He already has an open ticket from San Francisco to Moscow via New York, bought long ago. Margot comes in to wish him one last night of sweet dreams, and even though her husband is home, she spends the night with Matvey.

Early the next morning she drives him to the airport. Kisses him longer and more passionately than people do when only parting temporarily. Oh, how Matvey will come to long for that Margot! She isn't going anywhere—come stay, eat, drink, live, experiment! Margot is eternal, always yours and never yours, no one's.

When he steps onto the plane—they board with a slight delay—he notices two of his recent opponents in the first-class cabin. Donald and that repugnant man, the ambassador. The plane accelerates and takes off. Matvey gazes at the bay.

Though he is leaving somewhat temporarily—his father's death and funeral, how long can that take? A week, a month?—he will not be coming back to California. He has lived here as though in passing, tangentially. He had planned to wash cars, make deliveries, spend a night or two on the streets, certain that some sort of anchor to life would eventually appear—but nope, he had landed up in that sanatorium. Next time he'll go to New York, or—even better—somewhere out in the sticks, become a pizza delivery boy and learn how to fight. Matvey has always wanted to know how to fight—though never wanted it enough to join the army, of course. The family line had always been that they had moved to Moscow to save him from conscription. Lies.

He recalls how, on the way to Moscow, his father had asked him, in true Gogolian form:

"Themistocleus, tell me, which is the finest city in Russia?"

Matvey had replied as *Dead Souls* demanded:

"Saint Petersburg."

"And what else?" asked his father, prolonging the game.

Matvey nodded: Moscow. Yes, his father really does love Gogol. But even then Matvey had suspected that their move was more of an escape—his intuition isn't so bad as all that.

Their Moscow apartment is smaller, of course, the standard of living being "higher" here (read: more expensive) than in their newly renamed hometown. Still, they do live in the center, in the Zamoskvorechye District: *One should always live in the center.* His father settles into the role of Moscow nobleman. The tinctures are redeployed to attract guests, but somehow no one is enticed.

Everything feels rotten to Matvey, dark. With time Moscow State Linguistic University materializes; languages always did come easily to him. He spends his evenings translating from English, a wide range of genres, mainly esoteric. Here and there groups of people emerge, flare up, and disperse; publishers are appearing and disappearing all the time. *Deadlines, deadlines!* His clients hurry him along. Don't get bogged down in the details! If something doesn't make sense, just use your imagination! They pay in installments—sometimes more than expected, sometimes not at all, sometimes with a year's delay.

Like so many people in publishing and translation, Matvey plays with words, writes funny little centones and palindromes. He dabbles in more serious writing, too, in an attempt to fill that hole, that emptiness within, though he suspects that this can be no real basis for writing. The serious texts don't quite come together. Luckily he's had the forbearance not to show anyone any of his masterpieces—he wouldn't have had anyone to show them to, anyway: he hasn't made any close friends. Never mind, maybe one day. For now he needs to focus on his languages, on his studies, on becoming a translator.

Languages, like chess, are also a chance to escape. His mother, in the early days especially, tries to make him brighten up: Look, Matyush, how beautiful fall is here in Moscow, it was never like this back in Leningrad! Remember when you were little, how you liked to stomp on the leaves, go *crunch*? The Moskva might not be anything to write home about, but the foliage here is different than in Leningrad—lusher, more southern, look! And there's more sun—you do like the sun, don't you? But he and his mother are rarely alone—here in Moscow she's almost constantly at his father's side.

Matvey's father is approaching seventy, with no successes to his name. Little by little he sells off his things—his paintings, his china. He loves objects that speak to the old way of life, an authentic material culture. He also gives lectures to young people at the All-Union Znanie Society, a vestige of the USSR.

New watchwords start appearing in Matvey's father's lexicon:

objectivity, exteriority—he wants to appeal to the younger generation. Surprisingly, some young people actually do go to his lectures, but their participation isn't exactly what the lecturer would have wished:

"Nina, to them I'm just a sentient fossil."

His mother also tries to earn some money on the side, takes up copyediting and proofreading for publishers.

"The Russian language," his father says in response, "is not a language of editors and proofreaders, but of..."

She quietly walks out, into the kitchen, where the television is. Soviet films, pre- and postwar, black-and-white in every respect. Matvey doesn't understand how she could watch this garbage.

"Don't turn it off," says his mother, "there's nothing to understand. If you don't like it then fine—good, even—but just don't turn it off, leave it."

And then, as the great changes roll in, his father becomes very devout. He has taken to professing his faith everywhere—in any company, often apropos of nothing, openly and immodestly. This is also when everything starts to shift, move, clatter around them; suddenly there isn't enough food to go around. With the same artlessness with which his father would always snap up the choicest morsel of food (Nina ate like a bird, after all, and Matvey was a grown man, while he was a hungry old gent) he speculates positively about the likelihood of his own salvation. Some will be saved, others will not.

In Leningrad his father had been a Catholic, but upon his arrival in Moscow he declared European culture to be inherently destructive, and defected to the Old Rite church. He pays a few visits to the Rogozhskoye community, the center of the largest Old Believers denomination—*communing with the community*, as he affectedly calls it. He also picks up the habit of adding "*sya*" to his words, in an earthy, southern manner—but it doesn't last: apparently his "objectivities" came more naturally to him.

At one of his lectures (Matvey is there to give him a lift home afterward—his father's health is already failing) a member of the audience asks if the man has any wishes for the younger generation. His father thinks for a long time:

"We have one life, be it long or short."

He had always had a penchant for little aphorisms. Matvey awaits the continuation with his usual shame, but his father calmly says:

"Don't be afraid. Fear nothing."

Do it, thinks Matvey—now, do it now! He already knows the details of the Leningrad affair. Speak! Say it badly, awkwardly, pretentiously, to these kids, to everyone, just say it! But his father says nothing. Only that: Fear nothing.

That hole, that emptiness, grows, expands. As is true for any alcoholic or addict, it will soon swallow up everything—the remnants of any love or compassion, any capacity for joy. That is when Matvey makes the decision to move away and change his name.

And so he rejects a surname that is supposedly princely, almost regal—a complicated history, one with roots in the Byzantine Empire. Put it this way: when noble lineages had come back into fashion in the '60s, especially in Leningrad, his father had been pretty well set up. Which is precisely why, when making that break, it is the surname that Matvey changes.

Doing anything via the legal route is impossible, and who needs that anyway? Wise people—a couple of his associates who know the score—tell Matvey that all he has to do is get a passport for international travel with a different surname. They have a guy who can help, we're all free now—the only question is what it's worth to you. Where's their guy from? The inside—they're all from inside the service.

So intelligence does that now too? You bet—*for whom nothing's a small matter*, if you catch my drift. You'll just tell the Americans your old surname changed; they're naive enough to buy it. Think about it—besides the documents, what *is* a name change? Or are you dead set on having it done by an old woman in a black cloak? Come on, man, just say yes, it'll all be fine. What surname do you want? Matvey gives the first name that pops into his head: Ivanov.

One month later he gets his passport. So their guy came through. Eight years after the dissolution of the USSR, they are still making passports with a hammer and sickle on the front. Who cares? What matters is that it has his new surname inside. Anything goes, so long as the customer's paying: that's Moscow for you.

Soon New York. Beneath them is water: cloud, and beyond that—ocean, rain. Beautiful but monotonous, lonely. Like hell, if there is one.

His father didn't do sickness with the same panache as health: he got weaker, swelled up, gasped for breath. One might have expected an influx of professors and luminaries to his bedside, a clash of varying opinions, but no, all they got was a middle-aged surgeon in a faded surgical jacket, who took one look at his medical records and said: multiple comorbidities; no one will agree to operate. For some reason his father just accepted it: Well then, we'll wait for the end. But they could get a second opinion, a third, even—find a surgeon who will take him on?

"Nina, please, I'm tired." He forbids her from even considering the operation. "Time to stop the clock—ask your son what that means, he knows chess."

There were, of course, episodes of pity, superficial intimacy—especially when Matvey knew he would soon be leaving for America. His father wasn't against the move: "They even put 'In God we trust' on their money"—one of his later bungling remarks, though to be fair, it was said with no ulterior motive. His father had no desire for money, he just wanted to be alone with Matvey's mother.

A day or two before Matvey's departure, his father asks him to teach him how to use a computer: he knows how to turn it off and on, but nothing else. No, don't click on that, it's an old chess program. You can delete it, if it's bothering you. And that one, too. His father pesters him with questions: How do I delete a program? How do I send a text to print? How do I make sure it doesn't get lost? Matvey will show him everything, write some instructions. And that, what about that . . . What's that thingy called?

The World Wide Web, the Internet. Matvey thinks: That's definitely no place for you. At some point you'll figure it out, type *anti-Soviet group, Leningrad University*. And your surname.

Matvey hits the armrest. It hurts, but not enough. Right now he would gladly headbutt something. Excuse me, he has to get up. And—ahead.

The stewardess steps to one side.

"Stretching your legs?"

And a few other things besides. He's going up there, beyond the curtain, to give that old snob a piece of his mind.

Ten minutes later, he's back. It went well. His heart is pounding, every beat resounding with pain. When they land he calls home. Is his father alive?

No, he died forty minutes ago.

ULTIMA FERMATA

Dead, his mother says, he's dead.

He took his medicine, and she read to him a little—he wanted old, eighteenth-century poems. Then she went to make him something to drink, and suddenly he cried: "Nina, I think I'm dying. Call Matvey!" She went to find the phone, but by the time she found it he said: "Don't call, I'm feeling better." After which he gave two deep sighs and then stopped breathing.

"He's been talking about you a lot lately."

Don't, thinks Matvey. It's too late. For everything. He had already started to feel his heart on the plane, but now the pain is even stronger.

She read to him a lot. Poems, he loved poems. Matvey's mother doesn't seem overcome, just focused.

"Matyush, we'll talk when...Where are you?"

In New York.

"We'll talk," his mother repeats. "I'm turning off my phone."

Her phone is ringing off the hook. Matvey hates that she's alone.

It's fine, she says. There's no getting away from people. His father loved company, after all.

"Your brothers are arriving tomorrow."

His brothers. They have been calling nonstop lately, demanding that she take action.

"There was nothing to be done," says Matvey, "I mean, we were prepared for this."

"Yes." His mother replies. "I'm going to sit with him."

Matvey might have made the flight had he run, but at some point the time just slipped by—plus his first flight had arrived late. The gate is closed until tomorrow—there's only one flight to Moscow per day. They did call him, made announcements. He still isn't used to his new surname.

"My father died today," Matvey says with shame.

They are very sorry to hear that, sincerely. They'll put Matvey up in a hotel. No—no hotel, not another night, he can't. He has to do something, keep moving, please, help him. They'll see what they can do. London, Frankfurt, Paris are all booked up. Now then, there would be the possibility of flying through Rome. They'll put him in first class, in light of... well, you know. No surcharge, here's the ticket, and the one for his connecting flight, no need to hurry, he can set everything down. How is he holding up? He's OK, thank you. He really appreciates it.

Matvey's biological, innate connection to his father had always been weak—nothing to break there. But it's strange, all the same: there one minute, gone the next. Plus the dread of the sight that awaits him: his father's cold, slightly yellowed body, a corpse. Or will they already have taken him away? That would be better—but no, his father was also no fan of "suitcase-phonograph culture," he would never have agreed to such a thing.

Matvey has seen dead people before: one of his chess coaches (nothing scary there, just crowds of people and, over in the distance, wreaths and a coffin), and his maternal grandmother, back in Leningrad. It wasn't so much that he wasn't close to her as that he hardly knew her: she had never accepted her daughter's marriage to a man practically the mother's own age. Both at home and in the church, Matvey's mother had been constantly adjusting her, touching her, patting her. Matvey wondered if this had almost been intended for him, to show him there was nothing to fear. He had stood there for a while, stewing in his own nonparticipation, before kissing the paper band placed across her forehead.

First class, New York to Rome. He'll be stuck there almost eight hours, won't get to Moscow till evening. Around him sit gaudily dressed Americans, a big group of men and women.

"Make yourself comfortable."

The pieces should be comfortable, yes. Matvey almost instinctively downs something strong before takeoff. Maybe it'll help him to sleep. He almost never drinks spirits, but when is it called for, if not now? He refuses any food.

Newspapers, a whole trolley: *Go get yourself some opinions.* His neighbors take a few, each one huge, like the portions in American cafés. The men and women dive straight into the columns of small-print figures. Stock quotes: *this civilization of ours is primarily a financial project, then legal.*

Matvey takes a paper too. To read it from cover to cover would take him a few days at least. Politics, local news, culture, sports. Out of (recently resurrected) habit he flicks straight to the chess section, but then stops: What's the point? But there, as he thumbs through the pages, he sees the obituaries. On the nose, one might say.

What unites all of the people in the stories he reads is their time of death: in April 1999—just like his father. Each article mentions where it happened, the cause of death, whom they are survived by, career milestones, and something nice they will be remembered by. Well, not always nice.

A Republican senator has died, at ninety-four, one who had major sway on the Senate Judiciary Committee. A vocal critic of violence and pornography in the media, he was a champion of capital punishment and opposed gun control. During Nixon's presidency he spoke in favor of a failed nominee to the Supreme Court—a man many considered gray and mediocre. "Even if he were mediocre," the senator declared, "there are a lot of mediocre judges and people and lawyers. They are entitled to a little representation, aren't they?"[2] He is survived by a daughter and two sons.

Another: Seventy-three-year-old Estelle Sapir, who won back her father's money from the bank some decades after his death at Majdanek. "You have to survive,"[3] he had told her. The last time they spoke was through barbed wire in the South of France, where he drilled her on the names of several banks in which he had savings. In '46 the British and French turned the accounts over to Sapir without a murmur, but the Swiss had demanded written proof of her father's death. Concentration camps not having been in the habit of giving out death certificates, Estelle had had to fight for fifty years to get them to return her father's money. She had no children—only nieces, nephews, and great-nieces and great-nephews.

The articles are coolly written. Understatement, reticence—it's everywhere, even in grief. Matvey goes on reading, sipping from his glass.

The owner of a baseball team who spent millions to help society; the vice president and governor Nelson Rockefeller's first wife, who bore him five children and danced the Charleston into old age; a judge from the Bronx, who had sentenced the murderer of a young woman and two girls to seventy-five years in prison—the maximum sentence. The courtroom, it states, had given the judge a round of applause.

Six times eight, Matvey calculates, plus two (the eldest had been given ten, not eight, years). Fifty: his father had doomed those Leningrad kids to fifty years of prison and prison camps.

Matvey takes a look around at his neighbors: some are reading, others sleeping. Will even one of them be honored with such an obituary?

A top-up, please. Oh, why not, just bring him the bottle—all of it. He has never drunk as much in his life as he has in the last three hours. You have to eat something, the stewardess says. She has to make sure none of the passengers get intoxicated. If he doesn't want a meal, she'll bring him a salad. Chicken Caesar or Greek. Fine, bring him a Caesar.

That's it, one last life story, and then he has to try to get some sleep.

A veteran of the First World War, Herbert Young, died at home in Harlem one week short of his 113th birthday. Just two months earlier he had been made a knight of France's Order of the Legion of Honor. At the ceremony he had saluted his flag, and later raised a glass of champagne.

In the First World War, Young had served in the Pioneer Infantry regiment. The regiment, which was made up of Black servicemen, remains a symbol of segregation in the United States Army. One month before his death, he had told journalists: "I enlisted because I was lonely. All the rest of the boys had gone to the service."[4]

In his later years Young's vision and hearing had deteriorated, but he still remembered the war keenly: "I was scared all right, and anyone who says otherwise is fibbing." He had wielded a bayonet against the enemy, and was poisoned by German gas. Of the 350 boys in his regiment, only 12 were spared—the majority died of disease rather than battle wounds. After the war, Young stayed on in Europe for nine months, burying the dead. On his return he repaired old cars, and at eighty-seven he married Grace, then in her twenties. *Complete information about survivors was not immediately available.* Young had given his French medal to his eleven-year-old great-great-great-granddaughter. When asked, one month earlier, what had helped him to live so long, his reply had been: "I stayed out of trouble."

Don't be afraid, Matvey remembers, *Fear nothing.* What would they have written about his father? The bottle the stewardess reluctantly brought him is almost empty, and Matvey feels neither sleepy nor particularly drunk.

A humanist, they would write, aged seventy-four. A repeated religious convert, he was fond of witticisms, not all of which could be attributed to him. A graduate of Leningrad State University, a versatile scholarly administrator, an advocate of academic purity and opponent of all manner of experimentation. A connoisseur of both Russian poetry of the eighteenth and early nineteenth centuries and grass-based tinctures and spirits, he earned the nickname Duke due to his blue-blooded appearance and noble descent. He is survived by a widow and one son—no, multiple sons. In 1949 he penned a political denunciation of six students, who were subsequently sentenced to a total of fifty years in Stalinist prison camps. Neither in private conversations nor publicly did he ever express remorse for his actions. An unrepentant snitch—grief would be misplaced. No, no need for that. Just the facts. Fuck the papers.

Matvey manages to lean back, heel back, until he's almost horizontal, finds a position in which his head doesn't spin. Rome, he's flying to Rome. All roads lead to Rome.

In the world ye shall have tribulation, so his father would often repeat in troubled times. *Knowing Scripture comes in handy sometimes*, yada yada yada. No, no tribulation here. Grief would be misplaced.

But he does feel something else. All his life Matvey has existed within a two-dimensional system of binaries, coordinates. First chess: black/white, win/lose, 1/0. Movies: good guys/bad guys, fascists/Soviets. Then new dichotomies appeared: authorities/dissidents, resilience/treachery. He got himself out of all that, got away, but even in America he had found similar oppositions: Black/white (again), Republican/Democrat, left/right. *The sum of these various vectors is what shapes one's vision of the world*, so say grown-ups, people with experience of life—those who have learned, Matvey suspects, to hide the hopelessness of it all, plug the void in their souls, stifle the pain somehow. Some have mastered it better than others. He remembers Margot: the lights from the bridge, crab soup, the smell of seaweed. Meanwhile, that strange old psychologist, his father's acquaintance, couldn't conceal a thing. Black/white, Russia/America: two beams, two directions, two vectors, each situated on a plane of their very own making. Matvey so desperately wants to see the world differently, but he knows that any attempt to find something else within it will simply splinter on contact with that depthless, heightless plane: a tablecloth, a TV screen, a chessboard. Left/right, forward/backward—therein lies the choice. *Ride to the left and lose your horse, ride to the right and lose your head*: a fairy-tale trope that the kids in chess club loved to riff on. Life/death. *Spurious infinity*—back and forth.

For a while he manages to drop off, and there, as he dozes, Matvey groans, tries to take a small step, move, up and to one side, but he is held back by figures jostling around him: a naked, ninety-year-old Mrs. Rockefeller—or is it Margot?—tripping the light fantastic to the Charleston; the ambassador with a blue, puffed-up corpse-face shoving a pawn into his mouth; the old man with Alzheimer's tittering, *he-he-he,* grabbing onto him, practically dangling from him—*go on, take it.* Margot's husband with his strange handshake, senators, judges, that passport guy—*they're all from inside the service*—and that psycho psychologist, flushed with excitement, bragging about his apartment: "We're going to furnish it properly, hang some pictures, I've got a feeling we're going to be very happy here. You know what I mean? No? Then you have a personality defect. How about a coffee?" Matvey is suffocating, he has to respond: it's not a matter of happiness or unhappiness, just let him loose, let him free, let him out! However, this is actually a response to other events—in his stomach, rather than his head. Luckily he manages to run to the lavatory in time—and it's free.

He throws up—undigested Caesar, alcohol, again and again—an abomination. Less the remnants of his feelings so much as that of his guts. After yet another bout, Matvey hunkers down between the pan and the sink and loses consciousness. Then he comes to.

Water, he needs a lot of water; he's dehydrated. The stewardess knows exactly what he means. He lets himself be watered, seated back in his row.

And so, his insides purged, Matvey lands in Rome. The current of people carries him through passport control and then to the exit, even though that isn't at all where he needs to go. Well, he does have seven and a half hours to kill . . .

"To Rome?" Matvey asks in English as he steps onto the train.

"*Sì, sì*," they reply. *Ultima fermata*: the final destination.

Matvey doesn't remember getting off the train, or wandering through the morning shadows, or that he then had sat down on a stone to clear his head. The stones are unexpectedly warm—they haven't lost their heat overnight—and Matvey soon finds himself lying down. Twenty minutes later he opens his eyes, props himself up on his elbow, and looks around: the outline of a large cathedral, no people; just pigeons and a predawn silence, one filled with a meaning Matvey can't place.

But he will later come to recall the feeling: like he was coming out of a lengthy freeze, the city wrapping him up in a blanket. The image, the metaphor, all of that comes later; for now he just feels a sudden sense of freedom. Like in childhood, when you have been sick for days, and then you wake up with a cold, clammy forehead and your pajamas and pillowcase are soaked, but nothing hurts anymore and your fever is gone; you feel good. Matvey lies back down again, bundles his jacket up under his head.

HOME

He is woken by the music. Or, rather, by it having stopped. It's light now; the sun has risen.

"Heads up," a boyish voice says in Russian behind him, in excited alarm.

He sees six or seven girls—violinists, violists—and a male cellist, all of whom are around fourteen. What was it they were playing so well?

So he actually slept—just a few hours, but everything around him has changed: a bustling Roman morning. He still has his money and his passport. His phone tells him: *Finito il credito*.

"Guys, chill," says one of the violinists, a girl.

In California he had tried to steer clear of his compatriots—these encounters almost always seemed to leave him with a sense of shame. But how could these kids have known he was Russian too? None of them asks him anything.

The cause of the kids' alarm appears—a carabiniere. He's tall, with a thick neck: a theatrical villain. He surveys the musicians, Matvey sitting on the ground, and a few beggars who have set themselves up nearby. Taxi drivers, smokers who have stepped out of their hotels, and, yes, pedestrians: the stage is set, full of people. The villain spots the jar of money, says something sternly, in full voice. A short man in a white apron comes springing over, picks the jar off the floor and points at the cathedral. The carabiniere walks on and the jar is placed back on the ground, there's already a nice collection inside.

There, the kids have been saved, so now they have to play. They flick through their music, confer among themselves. A taxi driver steps out of his cab:

"*Silenzio!*" He claps his hands, demanding silence—not that anyone was really making any noise.

The taxi driver, with his head shaved, would have looked very macho, were it not for the dark sunglasses with light frames resting on his forehead, and the similar coloring of his shoes: white with black toes.

The first violin nods—and *play*. Matvey has never heard music at such close range before, and the lack of stage makes a truly unique impression. Actually, no: it's more like Matvey is sitting *on* the stage.

Sadness—it's nice to feel sadness, a depth of emotion. Oh, shit— his watch is still on California time, or has he already changed it? Their final piece, bright, fast, passes him by, he's too wrapped up in calculations, in making sure he doesn't miss his flight again. No worries, he still has time—just over three hours till takeoff.

The listeners applaud, cast their money. Matvey stands up, empty and light inside. If anything, he's just thirsty. He pulls out a bill, one hundred dollars, a rich American: the girl who's keeping an eye on the jar gives him a curtsy.

The musicians take their instruments, hastily shoving the money into their pockets and cases. Suddenly they freeze:

"Abramych," says the cellist.

From the other side of the square, his head tilted slightly to one side, a man is walking toward them—their teacher, presumably. He stops by the children. Abramych's entire body reads like a question mark, but there is also a glint in his eye. He also happens to bear a horrible resemblance to that chess coach from Leningrad, the one who died—a certain weary calm. Though his hair isn't quite as gray—yet.

"And where might you be going, ladies and gentlemen—or, rather, gentleman?"

Where indeed—to wander Rome's streets, get out of the hotel, see the Eternal City! They can always rehearse back home—while they're here, can't they just see the Roman Forum, the Capitoline Hill, and the Colosseum? They already know the music anyway, let them have a day off from rehearsals. Or even better, let's all go together—Piazza del Popolo, the Spanish Steps, the Trevi Fountain...

The names alone...!

"Your curiosity is to be praised," the teacher, coach—Abramych—nods. "So then why the instruments?"

Because this is Italy, they can't leave anything lying around, it'll get swiped, *presto*.

"And the chair?"

The boy is clutching a chair—your average hotel chair. What else can he do? You can't play a cello standing up.

No big deal, they needn't expect any trouble from Abramych. End of scene, curtain.

Even though he didn't register it, that last piece of music, its tempo, has seeped into Matvey's bloodstream.

"*Più presto*, to the airport!"

"What music!" the now-familiar taxi driver exclaims, in a mixture of English and Italian: "*Bello! Bellissimo!*"

Matvey sits down in the passenger seat, in the Russian way. Let's go!

The driver asks Matvey when his flight is.

"Oh!" he then exclaims, "that's lots of time!" Fiumicino Airport is only half an hour away. They'll just stop off somewhere first: he has to say hi to his godson on his birthday, if Matteo doesn't mind? They've already introduced themselves: the driver's name is Vittorio.

Rome: not from paintings or photographs, but from some earlier time—before the languages institute, chess, before everything—it's as though Matvey already knew all of this, or, rather, sensed it.

That particular unpaintedness of the walls, the columns that line them, all different (they built with whatever materials they could filch from antiquity), a church corner jutting out, washing hanging from the lines—underwear and bras, hung out for all to see: you know exactly what to expect, but even when you're wrong and turn a corner only to find something you didn't anticipate, that feeling doesn't disappear; you saw it, you sensed it, you just didn't know the details.

Matvey remembers his maternal grandmother's apartment, which he had helped his mother to clear out. Sofas, armchairs, books, pictures, icons, and flowers everywhere, with no space in between, like how kids are taught to paint: fill everything in, don't leave any gaps.

What is his new acquaintance saying?

"You need to be careful, this is Italy." He must have seen Matvey giving the musicians all that money.

Here's a story for you: a Black American athlete, a sprinter (world champion and Olympic medalist), got robbed of a lot of money—fourteen thousand dollars, something like that—right there in the street, in plain sight. A little kid did it. He sank his claws into the champion's hand—or maybe he even bit it—and then whipped a whole wad of cash out of his pocket.

"Whoa, did they catch him?"

"No! He got away! From the Olympic champion! Because he was used to running straight, but the kid was running like this, zigzagging," says Vittorio, jerking the steering wheel back and forth, sending the car swerving from side to side. The Italian chuckles, seemingly delighted at the kid's feat.

Their conversation jumps around: So Matteo's Russian! Well, as it happens, Vittorio had (or has) a Ukrainian girlfriend. He holds the steering wheel with one hand, while with the other he points at parts of himself and reels off some mangled Russian words: *forest, clearing, hillocks, hole* . . . Basta, enough: Matvey can guess what body parts his Ukrainian has.

They stop at a typical Roman house: black shutters on the windows, partially stuccoed walls. They honk a few times. A disheveled woman comes running out with a half-naked kid in her arms.

"Vittorio!" She cries, kissing the driver loudly, and shoves the godson into his hands.

Vittorio shows the child to Matvey: Want to hold him for a minute? Matvey touches the boy's toes—all the same, as though his makers, lacking the patience for the trimmings, simply cut slits into the feet. There, the child is returned to the mother: Can't she see they're in a hurry?

Matvey only has an hour, he still has to change his money, buy credit for his phone, tell his mother he's alive.

"We're fine." No need for Matteo to worry.

"What are those whoppers over there?"

Turns out they are some Mussolini-era constructions: Italy, too, has seen all sorts.

Matvey needs some alone time, if just for a little while: he has had his fill of drama for the day. Vittorio senses this in some way too: he's going to take him to a place nearby—it's on one of Rome's hills, where there is a gate with a miracle-keyhole.

"Huh?"

Il Buco della Serratura, the holy keyhole, Matteo will see it for himself. And once he's seen it, he can walk down into the orange garden. Vittorio will change his money and top up his phone credit, and when he's ready he'll give him the signal, like that.

Drivers turn to look at them. Vittorio gives them a gesture—hey!

The taxi climbs the hill. If only time would pass a little slower. What trees! Red, white, everything is in bloom. He has never seen these trees and bushes before: bougainvillea, oleander (his mother will tell him the names later). If only he could stop, touch them, feel them—if nothing else.

A dark green door, and in it there is a keyhole.

"Then down, to the garden. And watch out for the cats," Vittorio warns.

It's no joke: Rome's gardens and parks are full of cats who are fed on tinned meat, at the city's expense! Is that really right? These cats are militant, ragged; they all but jump at the people.

The square is empty, framed by white stone. Inscriptions, many dates. I Value Xylophones Like Cows Dig Milk: I—1, V—5, X—10. Somehow the Romans got by without zeros.

Matvey is certain that Vittorio hasn't deceived him. But in order to see a miracle, you have to be open to it, right? Matvey, having neither the time nor the patience to open himself up, just looks through the keyhole.

He sees a corridor of hedges and, at the end, like a window, an aperture. And in it: the dome. San Pietro: St. Peter's Basilica. Of course Matvey recognizes it. Turns out St. Peter's isn't so big after all—in fact, it's pretty small. In photographs it looks huge, colossal.

The dome is light, translucent, almost spectral. Miraculous, truly. Matvey stares and stares, occasionally tearing his eyes away to check that there isn't a line behind him. No, he is alone.

The square in which Matvey is standing transforms into a room; a quiet, isolated room in the corner of a building. It has a window. And he is alone in this infinitely tall room, by this window onto the world. Matvey has never experienced anything like it before. *Exteriority*, one of his father's words. He would have gone on standing and staring, were it not for his phone, which suddenly bursts into life. Thank you, Vittorio.

His mother.

"How are you?" Matvey asks. "How do you feel?"

"Well, you know," his mother replies. "Have you landed?"

"I'm in Rome. I'm landing tonight."

Clearly she has no energy left for surprise.

Someone's buzzing again; she has to open the door.

He waits for his mother to come back, while he walks down to the garden. Now that it has appeared, the room he has discovered does not disappear back within him. Rome, the city-house.

His mother picks up again. Tells him who has arrived. No one he knows.

Moscow, she suddenly tells him, is still alien to her.

He had no idea. He thought that the leaves, the fall . . . That's to say, he didn't actually think anything.

"So where . . . ? Back to Leningrad?"

"Wherever you say, Matyush. You're the head of the family now."

They'll talk more, later. She doesn't have the time now. He should just focus on getting back, she's off to make some coffee—for the guests. Making coffee is all she has done all day.

"Just a minute. Wait." Matvey has to keep reminding himself that just there, by his mother, lies the dead body of his father. Otherwise he would tell her so much—about how he enjoyed the music, how varied the forms of happiness are here. And about the city-house.

She reads his mind:

"How could I ever be sad about what makes you happy?"

Slightly set back from the road is the entrance to the orange garden. There is a single gate, and on a seat beside it sits an old lady with gigantic dark-blue veins on her legs. Sleeping, apparently. Her face is sickly, something not quite right about it. What did she do in her past lives? Did she sit and keep note of people's comings and goings? Did she make collage portraits of Il Duce using buttons? No, she's probably too young to be a fascist. Matvey walks around her and into the grove.

There are oranges everywhere, on the trees and at his feet, whole and crushed. A boy of around four or five is throwing a ball into the air. Is he trying to hit the oranges? In any case, he can't throw it high enough.

Matvey shakes a tree. The trunk isn't wide, but it's extremely strong. A few oranges fall, and he takes two—one for Vittorio and one for himself. He tries to peel one, but the peel is thick, crumbly, difficult to remove. He squeezes the bitter juice into his mouth: ugh, inedible.

Paths, benches, grass. No cats to be seen: they must be hiding somewhere.

A small fountain, a stone construction with a metallic, lupine head, painted red. Matvey bends down to the she-wolf's jaws and takes a long drink. He splashes himself with water, then takes another drink.

An elderly woman, a matron dressed in black, waits for him to finish. Can she really bend over that far? No, the woman stops up the wolf's mouth with her hand, revealing another opening on top of its nose: the water spurts upward. She drinks, then walks away.

In contrast to the scene of an hour before, in the square—Piazza di Santa Maria Maggiore, that's its name—there is no theater here, no plot to speak of: the gatekeeper, the matron, the boy with his ball, even Matvey—they all came here, to the orange garden, for reasons of their own. *Live, forget*—isn't that what Margot wanted him to do? No, no, he has no intention of forgetting this. Quite the opposite: he wants to remember, to render, to embody it in words. Shame he still can't express anything right.

Matvey walks over to the farthest boundary of the garden from the street. A short stone barrier, beyond which there is a precipice. A view of Rome: the bridge across the river, green and narrow. *The Moskva might not be anything to write home about*, he remembers. The roofs of houses, domes. And St. Peter's—on the horizon, occupying a small part of it. Now, when it can be compared to the other buildings, it is clear that it is enormous.

Depth; height. And—a belonging, a presence, not just anyone's, but his, his presence in this world; himself as a part of it. It's strange, he's done so much—studied, competed, moved—but nothing has ever given him the same sense of presence that has come over him in the last hour.

Time has slowed down completely; it's practically stopped.

A car horn sounds: Vittorio. Coming, my friend, I'm coming.

When had he last experienced that feeling, not so much joy as clarity, plenitude, definition; a feeling so large that it felt impossible—dangerous, even—to keep it all inside?

Chess homework, a problem: white has three pawns, black two (one of which is making a break for the other end of the board), as well as a bishop and a knight. White gets a draw. After much reflection, a ten- or eleven-year-old Matvey suddenly sees what the problem is getting at, and solves it. Mama, look! He is even shaking with joy: I move here, there's no holding back that pawn, only I don't turn it into a queen, but a knight! Otherwise it's a fork—there. You move for black! Block him, block my king! Now you move the pawn, but no, don't change it for a queen—that would be a stalemate, can you really not see? Yes, for a rook. Meanwhile I have this little resource. What's so funny? And then what do we have?

"You win," his mother smiles.

"No, it's a draw! Look—two white knights against your rook! Completely different pieces from what they were at the start. Isn't it cool?" He is both overjoyed and annoyed: she should be looking at the board—but where is she going?

Nowadays chess programs can solve these problems in an instant. And besides, Matvey is no longer moved by their flat beauty.

Vittorio is beeping with all he's got. Quiet! *Silenzio!*

The sun is shining, on the city and on him. He turns his face up to its rays. Genuinely, it's as though someone is personally looking after him.

The beeps become one continuous signal. Matvey waves and runs over.

What is Matvey's occupation? Vittorio asks him on the way to the airport. He thinks for a long time before replying to this seemingly standard question. To his own surprise, he says: a writer. Good thing Vittorio doesn't ask what he actually writes.

On the plane, Matvey gazes out of the window. So he liked Rome, that's nothing strange. He could probably feel like part of a whole anywhere, right? Matvey covers his face with his hands. His palms smell of bitter oranges.

After the funeral service and the burial, after the ninth day of mourning, the relatives will leave, and just Matvey and his mother will be left. He will ask her: Did you know?

She won't ask what he means. Instead she will say:

"I knew. From the very start."

And what does she think—was Matvey right to change his surname?

She will nod.

"Although . . ." she will smile sadly, "it was a beautiful name."

2011, 2016
Translated by Alex Fleming

CAPE COD

"For paradise is a dead end."
                    —Joseph Brodsky, "Lullaby of Cape Cod"

I.

WHERE to take a girl if you're broke? To the ocean, of course.

They pick up stones, toss them at the water. Alyosha's bounce, skipping along the surface, but try as she might, Shurochka can't replicate his trick; hers go straight under. This frustrates her—though not seriously, of course.

Both are twenty-four, both on their first trip to America, the first time that either one has left their homeland: it's 1989, which means exit visas, state-ordained exchange rates; they each have six-hundred-odd dollars in pocket for the trip. Alexey and Alexandra—Alyosha and Shurochka—live in Moscow, and when it comes to what is happening in their country, their feelings are the same.

Shurochka is a young geneticist; advanced biology at a good high school, biology at Moscow State. Alyosha's academic background is more unassuming. His high school, granted, was also good, but it could only get him as far as the Moscow Institute of Oil and Gas, or *Kerosinka*—the kerosene stove—as it's affectionately known: even with his Russian name, in the early '80s Alyosha, being half Jewish, stood no chance of getting into Moscow State's Faculty of Mechanics and Mathematics. So Kerosinka it was.

Shurochka has a constantly sunny disposition, smiles most of the time. Alyosha, on the other hand, has more of a whiny look about him, eyebrows furrowed. No big deal: to her he has a brooding kind of appeal.

They first met not just anywhere, but at Harvard, by the library, the day before yesterday. And today he has borrowed his friend's car and brought her out to Cape Cod—yes, *Cape Cod*, they call it, not *Treskovy Mys* à la Brodsky, only rare cranks like Alyosha's dad would translate the name back into Russian. To be fair, how else would the old man know of Cape Cod, if not for that poem? It's not like it features in his prized prerevolutionary Brockhaus and Efron encyclopedia.

The scene is set: two of yesterday's children, both cultivated and attractive, meet abroad, in a beautiful country. She's a geneticist, he has genes: on his mother's side, Alyosha is related to a famous composer. Shurochka comes from a large family, with living parents and uncles and aunts, and she is also here in a more advantageous position: there's some (small) interest in her at Harvard, where they accepted her abstract for a conference. Alyosha is visiting a friend. Here, travelers like him are called *vacuums*—they suck up everything they can get their hands on.

Alyosha is smitten; he wants Shurochka, while Shurochka has yet to make up her mind. She also happens to be more experienced in these things; she was briefly married to a classmate of hers. Of course, Alyosha, too, has some experience of love. But love isn't what this story is about.

So they stand there, down at the water's edge, until Shurochka comes up with a game: they will name unusual stones after Lermontov's heroes.[1]

Long, dark, thin: Bela; fancifully speckled: Grushnitsky; a pair of light, semitransparent pebbles: Princess Mary and her mother, Princess what's-her-name.

"What about this one?" she asks.

"The Ossetian coachman."

Shurochka also remembers him from school, bit part though he has.

Maxim Maximych: rotund, slightly pitted, no arguments there.

Even the unnamed temptress from "Taman" is fished back out of the water. For every character they can think of there is a stone—one for Werner, and for Vera, and there! Lieutenant Vulich—but for the big man himself, Pechorin alone, there is nothing. In fact: Who is Pechorin, even? Stone after stone is flung into the water; they can't settle on a single one.

Did Shurochka ever have a crush on Pechorin? Of course she did, when she was thirteen, fourteen. All the girls did. Tut, tut—already finding someone to be jealous of.

The public slices of coastline give way to private beaches, all peppered with the same mix of shingle and sand. The place is practically deserted, but the young day-trippers still pass the odd person or two, nice-looking folk with dogs, books. A wonderful place, Cape Cod: to the left—trim, not intimidatingly grandiose houses; up ahead—beaches as far as the eye can see; and, to the right—the cool, placid Atlantic.

Wouldn't it be nice to live here, eh? Goes without saying.

The air is warm, the water cool. No one else is swimming, but—when else will they get the chance?—off into the water they go. Alyosha is a strong swimmer, but neither the motion nor the cold subdues his desire. He swims up to Shurochka, who is standing on a sandbar, and presses up against her. She follows his lead, at first because his forwardness takes her by surprise—as, in fact, does this sudden expansion of her horizons—but then, later, because it turns out she likes him, too. Prudish as America is, a boy and girl in an embrace just off the shore is quite within the bounds of acceptability, especially when the water isn't transparent enough to see what's going on beneath.

Afterward they swim back to shore. It's starting to get dark, but Shurochka still catches the happy look on Alyosha's face. Inwardly she is quite surprised by what has just happened. Social mores have yet to loosen up back home—in their circles, at least. But they aren't at home. They get dressed, gather Maxim Maximich and his cohorts and—away, back to Brookline. By the time they get to the car, the sky has darkened, sunk.

*

Shurochka is staying with her aunt; Alyosha with his friend, Lavrik, a short distance away by Moscow standards. Brookline is a suburb of Boston, though for all intents and purposes it's part of the city. Alyosha describes his flight from Moscow to New York. His plane had been empty—no one could get tickets, what an idiotic situation, an idiotic government he and Shurochka managed to wind up with. Then, in New York, he had had to walk a few sketchy blocks from Forty-somethingth Street up to the bus station: prostitutes, drugs, pornography—had she seen it? No, her aunt had picked her up at the airport. Well, he had sure gotten an eyeful. It had even made him start to wonder if old what's-his-name—you know, that fatso from the TV—hadn't been so very wrong when he described the horrors of this place. Shurochka doesn't know who he means, she doesn't watch politics on TV. But a huge Black guy on the street had asked her for a lick of her ice cream when she told him she didn't have any change. Alyosha didn't even have a TV until his mother died.

The conversation takes a turn: a lost mother, a sadness. Yes, his only living relation is his father, and he's already pushing seventy. Believe it or not, his grandfather was born well over a century ago, in the last years of Nicholas I's reign. In Alyosha's family they tend to have kids late, skip a generation. Not that anyone resents that, of course—they could just as easily have not had any. But hey, enough about that—would she like to move here? He would. She would too, like any sane person. Obviously.

They are sitting in the car outside her aunt's house, Alyosha's eyelids starting to droop from the jetlag. It's so nice here . . . Yes, very nice, but there's no point chewing on it. Stewing on it, whatever.

"Man, what a shithole you live in!" Lavrik had declared on Alyosha's first day stateside, after hearing the news from back home.

Theirs had once been a gang of three: Alyosha, Lavrik, and Rodion. But Lavrik had left, torn out of that place as soon as it was possible, and now, being already in a position to bring over guests, that's exactly what he does. He had invited both of the friends he left behind, but Rodion hadn't felt like making the journey. And, now that he's here, Alyosha doesn't feel comfortable as Lavrik's guest: Lavrik has taken to lecturing him for petty reasons, settling old school-day scores from back in Moscow. Plus Alyosha has six hundred dollars burning a hole in his pocket—he has to spend it wisely, make the trip worth his while, so to say. Plus his mother died recently. Fine, maybe not so recently—a year ago, give or take—but it's only when it's someone else's mother that that could seem anything but recent. Still, he has to be grateful: for the food, the place to stay, for lending him his car to take some girl out to Cape Cod. A horrible feeling, to feel like you're using a friend. But he does indeed make the trip worth his while: for months afterward, he and his father, and then Shurochka too, live off the money he makes from what he brings back. It has to be said, at this point in time everyone in this story is wanting for money, very much so. Except, perhaps, Alyosha's father.

As for Lavrik, he gets by teaching programming courses, but mainly lives off casino winnings. He'll slip on an expensive watch (rather, an imitation) and, in the company of Russians of his ilk, travel to some distant venue to play. Nothing complicated, just keep a tab on the cards that have been dealt and you have a minor advantage. Beyond that, a few simple rules to play by: when to buy in, when to hold off, when to raise the stakes, when to walk away. No guesswork, no attempts at intuition. Whole books have been written on the subject. But this, of course, is no stable income: players like these are already being booted out of casinos.

One day, while both eat instant noodles at the table-slash-desk in Lavrik's studio apartment, Lavrik, face down in his bowl (big ears, small head), runs Alyosha through the ins and outs of the stock exchange. The securities market is the most promising right now—everyone is scrabbling around for a strategy that offers stable success.

Alyosha hems:

"The philosopher's stone, huh? The power to turn anything into gold?"

Lavrik tells him to wipe that smirk off his face, stop putting on airs. These are serious matters—statistics, probability theory, linear algebra—this ain't alchemy, pal. Linear algebra, however, he mentions with a certain caution: in math, just as in music or gym, no one forgets the old school-days standings.

Shurochka returns to Moscow the day before Alyosha. She packs her bag under her aunt's guidance, Alyosha helps her to weigh it. Every pound counts. While her aunt isn't looking, Shurochka stuffs the last nooks of her suitcase with the stones from the beach—Bela and Kazbich, Werner and Vera, the younger and elder princesses—the entire company.

Alyosha says:

"Let me take something too."

"You take the Ossetian coachman."

Shurochka smiles; white teeth, black hair. She brings all manner of things back with her from America: gifts, the paperwork for a grant on genetics, a VCR. And—in the form of either a blastula or gastrula (the early stages of embryonic development) her future son, Leo, conceived in the cold waters of the Atlantic. It is also possible that Leo came into being a few days later, in Brookline, while Lavrik was out, but Shurochka finds herself leaning toward the more romantic, aquatic version. Mother knows best.

The Moscow of '89 is rife with social tensions, as people discover the manifold varieties of truth. Attention has shifted away from minor, private concerns to matters of civil and public importance. There is no time to waste, and Shurochka and Alyosha's lives come together quite effortlessly. Even the question of where they should live—with her parents, or with Alyosha's father?—is hardly fraught: the real answer is in the U.S. of A.

Until then, however, it probably makes more sense for her to move in with Alyosha: the apartment is big, with an unoccupied room that used to belong to his mother, even if, yes, it's a mess, dominated by a grand piano apparently used by Scriabin himself. On the other hand, the entrance to the building reeks (Can Alyosha really not smell it?), and then there's the father, a man unenthusiastic about the prospect of new lives appearing alongside his own.

The death of Alyosha's mother brought father and son no closer together. Hers was a slow death, almost five years from the diagnosis. Her room is still heaped with books and records, which grew uncontrollably in number with the progression of her illness. They would do well to throw out the ones that no one will listen to or read: keep the precious books, those Brockhaus encyclopedias—it's rare to find a household with all eighty-six volumes—and throw away or sell whatever's left. But who will actually do it? Alyosha's father long since stopped noticing this accumulation of objects around him, one accompanied by a loss of people. He has quit all of his jobs, turns down any requests for private lessons, and is now entirely immersed in his textbook on harmony. He has been writing it for as long as Alyosha can remember.

Day and night, the radio hums in his room—Deutsche Welle and the BBC are no longer blocked—but it's as if Alyosha's father no longer hears the set. In any case he doesn't pay it any attention. He's too busy with his textbook.

"All of these strict rules on doubling and suspension have their own kind of beauty," Alyosha tells Shurochka, who nods and asks no more. So much the better—he would have struggled to explain it. Alyosha made it only as far as elementary music theory, and even that he has forgotten.

Alyosha dropped music at fourteen. His parents had asked him what would make him happy, and he had given them an honest reply. Presumably he lacked any talent for playing, otherwise they wouldn't have allowed it. Still, that ever-elusive happiness hadn't followed.

"His textbook will be completely different," Alyosha continues. He needs Shurochka to respect his father. "The others get students to solve problems, but they don't look like actual music." Yes, now he remembers what his father used to say: "This book gets them to study one composer, and then another—what one would have done with a melody, and then the other. Harmonize in the styles of different eras, genres. See what I mean?"

Yes, Shurochka sees, but there is no way they can live with Alyosha's father. Not that she's opposed to domestic life, no: despite her youth, she knows how to make a home. But living in an apartment that stinks of everything—mold, the trash chute, yesterday's meals—is neither pleasant nor healthy for their future child, nor for Alyosha, nor for herself.

"If you could just have a word with him, Alyosha..."

About what? About him having to make space for new life? There's no changing an old man. Especially one who is so particular. Alyosha tries to remember the last time he and his father had a serious conversation. It was probably just before Alyosha started university. Things were already so hard at home, he might just as well join the army, he had thought.

At the time there were rumors (later confirmed) that after the first year of university, service-age boys were being rounded up and shipped off to Afghanistan. So Alyosha's father had found an aged nephrologist who agreed to give Alyosha a suitable diagnosis, teach him how to deceive the draft board.

"Are you afraid I'll get killed?"

"Not only that," his father replied.

He didn't want his son to have to open fire on people; for every soldier or officer killed in Afghanistan, almost a hundred civilians were thought to have died. Back in those days his father still actually listened to Voice of America et al.

"Can we even call it war? Genocide, carnage, punitive action—take your pick. I should say, Alyosha, that I've seen my fair share of sadness, even shame, in my time—most of us have, especially in this country. But in such acts we can have no part."

That was the conversation.

These days Alyosha and his father lead an almost wordless

coexistence. One has a young wife and plans to move to America, the other—easily guessed: a slovenly old age, an unending textbook on harmony.

The evening that Alyosha returned from Boston, he, Rodion, and his father shot the breeze together in his father's kitchen. *Have you been missing Russian food?* The locals in America had kept asking Alyosha. *Nope,* he would retort: *We miss it enough in Russia as it is.* Alyosha recounted his anecdote with a laugh, but the other two listened stone-faced. Alyosha, worn down by the wine and lack of sleep, let rip:

"If only you knew what a shithole we—"

"Just what we've been waiting for you to tell us," Rodion cackled through his almost toothless grin.

Even back in school, Rodion had always exuded a sense of self-righteousness. But it was only then, on his return from Boston, from Shurochka, that Alyosha realized what this self-righteousness was built on: a sense of being shortchanged. Rodion, incidentally, had never been able to complete his studies; he had actually done his military service.

"Tell me, do many Americans call Lavrik?" Rodion asked. "'Cause at New Year's he said *Hello* in English when he picked up the phone."

No, Lavrik only gets calls from Russians.

"It's just . . . it's so nice there that you want to feel like you belong."

His father had said:

"Emigration is a disaster, a mental illness."

How would he know? He had never even been abroad.

"And staying here, is that not an illness?"

"It is, just a different kind."

(Why can't Rodion put those teeth away?)

"You still need a homeland for something."

For something, yes. But what?

Such was the lead-up to their departure: pointless conversations, paperwork, an intensive study of English; the flurry of Shurochka's pregnancy; loans of weighing scales, baby baths, and other hard-to-procure items.

Finally, a child is born. He is registered, no quibbles over his name. Leo, his name will be Leo—a beautiful name, short, international.

2.

Much happens over the next decade: Leo's first tooth, also the first to be lost; his first words; his christening in Moscow, held the day before their emigration at the insistence of a great-aunt, who also steps in as godmother. The godfather, naturally, is Rodion. But this is all common, and therefore uninteresting; at that time in Moscow every child was being christened. What are interesting are those singular, private moments, those stones gathered on the beach. Upon their arrival in America they have Leo circumcised, for good measure; it's the done thing, the Americans have their own medical views on the matter. Let him be like the rest of them, they think.

As for Maxim Maximych and company, ten years on they find themselves on a bookshelf—next to Lermontov, as luck would have it—in Alyosha and Shurochka's very own home. Less than a decade has passed since their arrival, and already they have their own home. Alyosha is no longer Alyosha, but Alex, in the local manner, while Shurochka is Alexandra or even Alex, too—who needs all those extra syllables, anyway? Of course, at home she remains Shurochka.

There are many ways to acquire a home, ways of owning property without attempting to actually own it outright—just pay the interest, sell it off later. When the time comes—once Leo's grown up and their house is worth more—they'll sell it and find themselves a place back in Cape Cod, something small but by the water. This is their plan.

Shurochka-Alex has a job in a small genetics laboratory, though almost all of her paycheck goes toward a nanny for Leo. Over the years Leo has had a succession of nannies, invariably Russian, none of whom he has developed an attachment to. Alyosha-Alex is a middle manager at a company that writes software for playing the stock market. The company's financial results are outstanding; the programs work. Stochastic process theory, linear algebra, nothing magic.

For them, family life consists in a shared evening meal (supper, dinner, whatever they call it here), in Alex and Shurochka sleeping in the same bed each night, in ferrying Leo to and from school and extracurricular activities, in a pleasant, odorless everyday existence, in family celebrations, and in certain public holidays—albeit without the enthusiasm typical of many new arrivals. They have been to Italy (twice), to Spain, to France—more Shurochka's interest than Alex's, but good for the boy, too. Alex doesn't feel the need to travel. He's happy at home, in Boston.

Many want to get to America, but no one's in a hurry to get to heaven, Rodion says after casting them a glance. *Though I guess you hardly feel the need for heaven when you live in such harmony.* He comes to visit them once, but doesn't stick around for long: he has other things to see in America—a couple of old monasteries, typical Rodion. Alex and Shurochka hadn't even thought they had Russian Orthodox monasteries here. Rodion is very religious nowadays. Fine. But before returning to Moscow he mentions something about procreation, suggests his friends ought to "beget" more children. He also thanks them, yes, praises them, but it still leaves a nasty taste in the mouth: What, is he judging them?

"He's a hypocrite, your Rodion," Shurochka says once he has gone. "Leo didn't like him either."

Leo is six by this point. Two days earlier Rodion had accidentally spilled hot soup on his legs.

"Leo's a trooper; he didn't cry. But your Rodion is a piece of work, he doesn't even know how to shake a hand."

This much is true. Rodion has always struggled with handshakes, produces limp, flaccid things that he gives with a titter, as though doing something unseemly.

"Like a wet fish, yuck."

It is Shurochka's firm belief that a man with such hands couldn't possibly have knowledge or truth on his side.

"Please, don't get worked up," says Alex, his eyebrows furrowing. "Rodion promised he'd check in on Dad for me."

"A normal thing for a friend to do." Then she puts the boot in: "And what an idiotic name."

"You wouldn't happen to be pregnant, by any chance?"

"Not by any chance."

As for the name . . . Alex laughs:

"Not everyone gets to be an Alex."

Rodion has indeed promised to check in on Alyosha's father, find him a woman to help out around the apartment. But it's not so simple as that: his father doesn't want any strangers hanging around, and where do you find these women, anyway? It's not about the money, or not only about that—no one wants to work. That's rich, coming from Rodion.

At the same time every Saturday, Alex calls his father and a short, more-or-less unchanging conversation takes place. His father is alive. The money that Alex sends him is enough. He is happy to hear all is well with Alex.

"You shouldn't feel guilty," Shurochka tells him.

He shouldn't, so he won't. Besides, this isn't a matter of guilt. His father doesn't even want to visit. There's no dragging an old man over by force.

His father's sole remaining interest is his textbook. But then, once he's finally finished it . . . he'll have to get it published. Strange, his father says, how few people care about something as important as harmony. No, not that he's complaining, but hasn't Alex noticed how nowadays people generally seem less interested in knowledge, in truth? His father doesn't want to cause Alex any unnecessary trouble, but it's clear that he's going to have to get the textbook printed at his own expense.

On no account is this anything to worry about. Shurochka's right, he shouldn't feel guilty.

Week after week, year after year, identical conversations. He should fly to Moscow, visit him in person, show him Leo; this can't last forever.

Leo, now almost ten years old, attends an expensive private school. He loves to win, and is one of the best students in his class, but never quite the best. Second or third, as a rule. He isn't the only one who loves to win.

Much of his education is devoted to foreign languages and sports: the country's best universities take note of sporting achievements above all else. Leo isn't a tall boy (in this he takes after Shurochka, who in gym was always last over the line), so for these purposes that rules out tennis, swimming, and basketball. For exercise—sure, knock yourself out, but what Leo needs is tangible success. And so, with his combination of ambition and self-restraint, one-on-one combat is the discipline for him. Boxing isn't for white boys, so wrestling it is.

Between his slim build and white teeth (also from his mother's side) and his hazel eyes and long fingers (these from his father's), Leo takes after both Shurochka and Alex in appearance. In character, however, he is hard to pin down.

Alex asks Shurochka:

"You're the geneticist, you tell me: What shapes a person more—nature or nurture?"

"And what shapes a rectangle more—length or width?"

A smart one, his wife.

Sometimes Leo scares his parents. Recently, to impress the girls (and the boys, too, presumably), Leo opened a third-floor window and did a handstand right there on the sill, until the teachers came running. The other kids had called them; in schools, snitching is the norm.

"Even when you tell him off or shout at him, he digs his heels in, never backs down," Shurochka says, not without some pride.

"He'll go far," say her aunts, "If only he'd been born in America, then he could have become president someday."

Is there anything people won't say about kids? For the moment, Leo's life is school and extracurricular activities: Russian, French, wrestling. Conversations with his parents.

But these conversations become more complicated. Although Leo is fluent in Russian, he has taken to responding to his parents only in English. All emigrant families go through something similar, which is why they bring in teachers.

"But he spoke it so well as a child!" says Shurochka, upset.

They recall the funny hybrid words Leo used to make. *Pictureskny*— of a flamboyantly dressed man. And? It might not exist, but the word is completely convincing in Russian. Or when he said his nose was *wetting itself* instead of *running*. Any parent will have similar stories of their kids.

Leo's birthday is coming up, so they invite his friends over to celebrate, including, for the first time, girls. Leo clearly has a crush on one of them, Yulia Karavayev-Schulz, who, as her partly de-Russified surname suggests, is also of Russian descent. Karavayev and Schulz are both violinists, who had Yulia in Spain before moving to Massachusetts, to play in one of its best orchestras.

Yulia is top of their class; her parents have trouble paying her school fees but are given concessions, so talented is she. And it was for this very same Yulia—the best student and, one would think, also the prettiest—that Leo stood on his hands in the open window.

Some of the details of that incident have since come to light: while the kids next to Leo froze in horror, and those slightly further back ran off to fetch a teacher, Yulia had walked up to him, closer than anyone else, and Leo had said to her, in French: *Tais-toi et ne bouge pas*. Why wouldn't he say it in Russian, *molchi i ne dvigaysia*?

Alex asks Shurochka: Had boys ever tried to impress her like that? Oh, yes, she's seen all sorts of overtures, including the most idiotic. Now, however, she's stuck watching this boyish idiocy from the inside.

What should they give Leo for his first round-number birthday? What does he want?

Leo wants to stop learning Russian. He has no need for Russian anymore.

He makes his announcement, then goes up to his room. Alex asks him to come back downstairs.

Leo asks: If they were immigrants from any other second- or third-world country, what would Alex say then?

"Can't you see...Culturally, it's top-rate," says Alex, gesturing at the shelves of books. "And in science too, once upon a time. Though for science you can get by without it, of course..."

That's it—Alex has it, a surefire way to make his son see, once and for all, why he does in fact need Russian:

"*But what I love—for some strange reason,*"[2] Alex proclaims, "*is the cold silence of her plains...endless forests,*" Oh no, he's forgotten it. "*Her rivers as wide-spreading as the sea...*" All Alex can do is butcher Lermontov's poem. "Well, in any case, forests, plains, and rivers," he concludes, with an awkward chuckle.

Alex thinks back to when he gave up music. A powerful thing, genes. Leo's teeth flash, bright white, as he smiles at his dad. Nothing malicious, just a smile.

One Saturday, Alex's father doesn't pick up the phone. Nor the next day. Alex only manages to get hold of Rodion as evening falls, Moscow time. By now Rodion is some sort of palm reader, psalm reader, it's all Greek to Alex.

"Sinner that I am," Rodion says, "I confess, I haven't visited or called in a while—I was on a pilgrimage last sennight..."

Sennight?

Rodion hasn't called the man in three weeks.

Another day passes. Now Rodion has been to the apartment, but no one opened the door. The spare key was there, under the doormat, but for some reason the door wouldn't open. Perhaps the lock is broken. Or his father bolted the door.

"What bolt? We never used to bolt the door."

"Well maybe in America you can leave your doors unlocked, but life is dangerous here."

What a chump, Shurochka was right. So call the police, have them break down the door.

"No point," says Rodion, suddenly showing some resolve: the police only follow up if the family files a report.

"Were the lights on in the apartment?"

Rodion doesn't remember. On, off, would it change anything? It makes no sense for him to go back and check now. *I have needs too*— that's what Rodion's tone is saying.

"And the neighbors?"

"What about them?"

Alex knows full well: his family's endless music had never put them in their neighbors' good graces.

But the phone does work. Rodion has checked, called the exchange—if Alyosha can believe he had enough brain cells to manage that. Please, let's not argue, Alex asks.

"Prayer is what is called for here," Rodion says firmly.

Alex has to get to Moscow, urgently, but urgency isn't in the cards: he needs a visa. He hears word that all emigrants' citizenships have supposedly been reinstated—they emigrated from a country that no longer exists, after all. Alex tries to explain this at the consulate, he writes to them in Russian, but the reply comes in English: You need a visa.

His only hope is that his father is in the hospital.

"Or on a composers' residency, or something," Shurochka says, trying to reassure him.

A composers' residency?

Eight fraught days later, Alex lands at Sheremetyevo.

He passes customs, changes some money, gets in a cab.

A squat, stocky driver—now the prevailing type of man here—takes him to his father's building. Rodion didn't manage to make it out to

Sheremetyevo, got waylaid by some "infection." The streets are cold and dark; in October, the sun sets earlier here than in Boston.

Alex has trouble recognizing the building, despite having lived in it from 1965, from his birth, until emigration. A light is on in his father's windows, probably a bad sign. If his father had gone to the hospital he would have turned it off.

The key is where it always is, under the doormat. Alex puts it in the lock. His hand is trembling, his pulse racing. He turns the key, but can't get the door to open. The taxi driver—who has been waiting downstairs—comes up to help. No luck.

"Bolted. My grandma always . . ." the driver mumbles.

Alex doesn't hear. The door is bolted from the inside. He starts to shake, a tremor—now stronger, now weaker—that will accompany Alex throughout the entirety of this trip.

At the police station he takes a seat to fill out a report. It's slow progress. He's written almost nothing in Russian in years, let alone by hand.

The police officer sees the ordeal he's having:

"Call EMERCOM, they aren't such pains in the ass." By which he means there are fewer formalities.

Back on the front steps of his father's building, Alex waits for EMERCOM, whatever the letters might stand for: the word didn't exist in his time. At the police station he had been too shy to ask, and back in the taxi it had slipped his mind. He feels terrible, alone. His American cell isn't working. And those shakes—internal, external, everywhere.

They pull up. Two guys around twenty-five. Vladimir and Stas.

They don't ask for any documents, just follow him inside.

"You said it was the second floor."

Alex realizes his mistake: in America they number the floors differently.

"Sorry, misunderstanding." He hands them the key.

"Right," says Vladimir. "Right. Got any bills?"

Alex hands over the first thing to hand—a hundred-rouble bill.

Vladimir shoves it between the door and the frame, then yanks it back, trying to flick the latch. Still nothing.

Alex hazards a guess:

"Might one hundred dollars do the trick?"

Stas smiles: No.

It's just that Alex had thought those bills might be stronger, that's all.

The guys get it. It's fine. No offense taken.

"But I will owe you something, right?"

"We never say no," says Stas.

Vladimir presses his ear to the door:

"Voices."

Alex rushes to the door, listens. The radio. His father's radio is always on.

The three of them go back down to the street, look up at the window.

"We'll have to call the switchboard," says Stas, patting his pockets. "I'm out of smokes. Got any, Vlad?"

They say they need some sort of special ladder. Please let them find it. Please don't let them leave him here.

"What are we freezing out here for," says Vladimir. "Let's go inside."

Alex has managed to calm his shakes a little. He scans the space around him. Did it really always look like this? What's that bowl doing in the corner? It's all so sad, somehow. Stas is back: the truck will be there soon.

Alex listens to their conversation. Stas is planning to join the army, or maybe both of them are. As contractors: they've already long since finished their mandatory military service. They want to go to the Caucasus. What's there for them to do here? Nothing.

"In what sense?"

"Like, er, there's nothing to do."

Eventually they say: Community, that's what they have out there.

But not here. Here it's every man for himself. This is all too much for Alex to take in. Still, he asks:

"But who's the enemy?"

"Whoever's shooting at me, that's the enemy. And in the morning, who knows, the same guy might be selling me lamb for my shashlik."

Well there you have it. A while since he was last in Moscow? Yes, it's been a while.

"You could get killed," says Alex.

In 90 percent of cases the guys who get killed are the ones who go looking for top-ups, if Alex catches their drift. As if he could miss it—his Russian hasn't gotten that bad.

"But the officer will still write to the mother and say *your son died a valiant death.*"

"What else would he write—*your boozehound son died looking for booze*?" Stas chuckles.

Vladimir gives his colleague a stern look. They both know what awaits them inside the apartment.

The truck pulls up. Let's go.

Alex and Stas make their way up the stairs. They have barely reached the third floor when the apartment suddenly bursts into life. The sounds of glass shattering, footsteps. The door opens. Vladimir is standing on the threshold, blocking the doorway:

"Stasik, the police. Alexey, you stay there."

Over the course of that night, many others come and go. Someone eventually helps Alex to get to a hotel.

And so Alex becomes the eldest in his family.

3.

More years pass without incident; Alex is already forty-two, as is Shurochka. Of course, they can rustle up stories to tell to company: how they missed that flight, or mistook you for that famous violinist; how Alex broke his ankle while skiing, and what one of Shurochka's relatives drew on the cast when they visited him at the hospital. Or how they once drove back from Cape Cod to Boston in heavy snow-fall (a rarity here, invariably a nightmare), and spent half the night sandwiched between two trucks, and Shurochka's temperature was over 100 degrees, and they almost ran out of gas, and then Alex had a panic attack, but Shurochka somehow managed to find the right words to say in spite of her fever, made Alex breathe into a paper bag.

On the work front, too, there is much to tell: Alex could recount how he left his company, taking a few colleagues with him; how he set up his own business, got taken to court but won; he could also touch on the thrust of his work, his search for the philosopher's stone—Alex uses his old metaphor with relish—but here, he can never tell the whole story. In fact, he shouldn't talk shop in general: for success in this game, secrecy is of the essence. And if the conversation should still happen to wander there, he can't afford to give away any details, show his hand. Just laugh it off, shut it down with metaphors.

The stock market—the world's biggest casino—lists a few thousand companies. What exactly they produce is irrelevant, all that matters is this: their stock will rise or it will fall; the market swells and contracts like an ocean. The rules that govern these fluctuations are mysterious and demand study, but the fishing goes on, whether the waters are rough or calm, and always in small numbers, so as not to reveal one's presence, scare off the fish.

It is becoming increasingly common to see dapper gentlemen nearing sixty who, with their trained voices and elegant attire (the sort that young Leo would have termed *pictureskny*), have spent their whole lives at the exchange. Once upon a time these men would have sold futures contracts for orange juice, corn, or copper, but nowadays their abilities to shout down their peers, pull off a sharp suit, and catch the essentials from a column of figures are no longer needed. What can Alex say to them when they come knocking at his door for work? There's no mastering linear algebra at their age.

Alex is now CEO. Every day his company closes deals worth 200, 300, 400 million dollars. These figures have long since ceased to represent what they invoke—the equivalent of goods or services—though try explaining that to anyone who hasn't dealt in such sums.

When it comes to the normal money, however, the stuff he finds in his pockets or his checking account, Alex is still just as careful as he was when he was a boy, when it was always in short supply. For him, the big money—the stuff he withdraws and invests daily—is but an abstraction, absolute terms in a mathematical equation. Which means the short-term loss of a few million dollars riles Alex no more than an unexpectedly expensive ice cream at the airport. He loves his work: it would be impossible to write algorithms for life's every occasion— no, you have to clean them up, perfect them. Plus, nowadays he can work without even having to get dressed, from home—or, rather, one of their homes: he and Shurochka now have two.

The house they call their "old" house is in Newton, near Boston; the other, unsurprisingly, is in Cape Cod: their dream came true. It is next to the water, modest from the outside but enormous inside. With a double-height living room. Upstairs, overlooking that space, run the master bedroom, Leo's bedroom, a guest room, and Alex's study. They could afford an apartment in Rome, Milan, or Venice besides, probably even in all three at once, but wherever they are, Alex misses New England, its two-story homes, its rectangular green road signs, its easily intelligible kindliness, from a predictable personal distance.

At the moment Alex and Shurochka pay only short visits to their new house, but once Leo has finished school and gone to university they will make a more permanent move. For now, however, Shurochka has moved her collection of stones there: Maxim Maximych, Bela, Grushnitsky—Shurochka still remembers who is who. Family celebrations and meals with her relatives also gradually move here. Everyone loves Cape Cod.

With her husband's success Shurochka hardly needs to work, and so, gradually, she has let it go. Family life keeps her busy enough. She had planned to devote some time to philanthropy—she is told she has good organizational skills—but that time never seems to materialize. Now that Leo is older, her main interest is travel.

Shurochka loves Europe, especially Italy. One year she goes there with an aunt, the same one she stayed with in '89. The aunt had never been to Italy before. Shurochka couldn't stand by and let her miss out on seeing it.

Shurochka is just as attractive as she was in her youth, and still looks well under forty. When she's off on her travels men make their moves—some of which by no means idiotic—but she stays faithful to Alex. He does love them, after all, her and their boy. And though perhaps lacking in a certain imagination, if you could call it that, that spontaneity that, as she sees it, alone could have led to Leo's conception, he does give his all to make them happy, right?

After one of her trips to Italy, Shurochka shows Alex her snapshots. A cemetery, the Russian section. Well-kept graves, the transliterated names of nobles, GALITZINE and TROUBETZKOY, and then, unexpectedly far back, the neglected, slanting ВЕРА ГОЛУБЕВА. A photograph cannot convey it all. This grave, this Vera Golubeva, had affected Shurochka a great deal. The Cyrillic. She has missed Cyrillic. Alex sees this as no great misfortune.

While Shurochka was away, Lavrik had come to see Alex again. Every one of his visits turns into an ordeal, but when you have a lot of money, endurance becomes a necessary skill.

"Could us simple Moscow boys . . . ?" Lavrik begins, shoveling food into his mouth. He is, to put it delicately, already on the sauce, forgets what he was going to say. "Cheers, anyway!" Lavrik drinks much more than is allowed here when driving. "Hey, old buddy, old pal, remember all those Chinese noodles I fed you?"

Alex has forgotten nothing. Lavrik's ears are going red—it's either the drink, or he's in need of "advice" again. Any minute now he'll say it: I need your advice. *And then my money*, Alex will want to reply, but he would never say such a thing, no, he'll just hand it over.

"I'm pretty left-wing nowadays," Lavrik declares.

What does that mean, exactly? A contempt for personal property? Nonrepayment of debts? Alex needs to lose Lavrik quickly and go back to work, but their conversation keeps getting sidetracked; Lavrik's nose keeps getting out of joint:

"Clearly your money makes your opinions more valid. . . ."

Yes, he must endure this, too. But Lavrik's remarks are unpleasant: Alex has always been a mathematician, it's his thing. A good, applied mathematician, yes.

Lavrik finally gets to the point: He's in a bit of a jam . . . It's stupid, he doesn't want to get into it, but in short, he could go to jail. Lavrik hopes to avoid having to do time inside, on medical grounds. He's deeply disillusioned with America, by the way.

What medical grounds are these? Psoriasis.

"I know some specialists, our compatriots, they'll do the certificate." And he promises never to bother Alex again, never to come here. Once the check's in his hand, Lavrik's mood improves sharply: "I'll owe you to my grave."

Alex lets him step out of the house ahead of him:

"Not quite so far as that, I hope."

He watches Lavrik pull away—last time he knocked over the trash can—and then it hits him: never again will he have friends like Lavrik and Rodion. Schmucks that both turned out to be.

Suddenly he is reminded of an episode from a few days after his father's funeral.

He and Rodion had arranged to meet in the center of Moscow (predictably, by some church) and then walk to his father's apartment to go through his things. Alex didn't like the idea of going there alone and, however much it pained him to rely on Rodion, he had no one else to ask. Alex had arrived early and, feeling cold, slipped into the nearest store to warm up. The store was a supplier of religious paraphernalia, and there, inside, was Rodion, trying on a cylindrical purple hat by the mirror. So engrossed was he by his own reflection that he noticed nothing—and no one—around him.

"I'll try that little kamilavka there, too, please," Rodion told the shop assistant.

The hat in his hands was clearly not the first he had tried. Behind the counter hung many different clerical hats, including round, extravagantly embellished ones.

The sales assistant started to ask questions in a cutting tone of voice.

"It's a surprise for the priest!" Rodion cut her off. "His head is identical to mine! Exactly the same size!"

Rodion's face flashed with the very same expression that Alex, as it happened, remembered from elementary school: it was the face that Rodion made whenever he was lying to the teacher. His rotting teeth, his self-righteousness—all of that had come later. Alex stepped back outside and waited on the street. At the time he was in no condition to dwell on such things, but now—how many? six years later?—the memory suddenly came flooding back.

Leo is disappointed in his parents.

Their English isn't great, for starters; both have an accent. Look at it this way, Alex jokes, our accent just makes our speech more expressive. Leo, however, doesn't like it when a language is mangled. At school he is taught in a British accent, and—would you feast your ears on that—sometimes the way he pronounces his words leaves his parents scratching their heads.

Secondly, Alex and Shurochka are hardly sports enthusiasts. When Alex broke his ankle, Leo, as Shurochka put it, expected them to strap on their skis and head back out to the slopes as soon as it had healed, to prove something. Leo was fourteen at the time.

"The only thing you'll prove by that is your own stupidity," Alex had quipped.

Few parents manage not to annoy their children.

Alex and Shurochka also have their own complaints about Leo. Specifically, Shurochka is upset by the stunts Leo pulls with Yulia. Shurochka doesn't want to see anyone but Yulia at Leo's side, however much she tries to remind herself that matchmaking is a hopeless pursuit.

She had taken a liking to Yulia on that very first, historic, day, the birthday on which Leo gave up Russian. Yulia, the best student in the class and, yes, a pretty girl, too, had told Shurochka that she laughed like her horse. Shurochka had been playing Monopoly with the kids, and when the luck started going her way, she had had to try to fudge her way out of winning. She and Alex had been knocking back their wine, and Shurochka genuinely had laughed a lot.

But on the matchmaking front there may be some hope after all. When the time comes for the kids to start dating (at fifteen, sixteen), the parents on either side have to drop them off at the movie theater, for example, or at the park: there's no way of getting from one suburb to another without a car, and kids only start to drive at sixteen. The parents will go their separate ways, and pick the kids up again at the end of the date. Some of the parents even sit and wait together in a neighboring café, but such rapprochements are neither to Alex's nor Shurochka's, Karavayev's nor Schultz's taste.

One evening, Yulia, kindred spirit that she is, invites Leo to see an Italian film. Shurochka drives Leo to the theater. As they approach, off drives Yulia's parents' car—their family only has one car, and it's easily picked out, thanks to its broken right taillight. And there is Yulia at the entrance, wearing narrow glasses, looking around—where's her friend? At which point Leo—in the front seat—suddenly slides down in his seat and commands Shurochka: Stop, let me out. He jumps out and hides in the shadows: Go on, turn the car around and go away. His plan is obvious: to keep Yulechka waiting a while, look-ing out for him.

"You said it yourself, Shurochka: boyish idiocy." If anything con-cerns Alex about Leo, it is only his academic progress.

He needs to do well on his exams, forget about sports. In their inexperience, they had overestimated its importance.

Not that Leo's wrestling successes aren't good; they just aren't good enough to count for much. Leo has suddenly shot up and bulked out, so he has had to move up into the middleweights, two categories higher, where there is some serious competition. The smart move would be for him to focus on his studies and drop the sport—it won't help him get into a good university now—but Leo doesn't want to leave his club.

"What does he get out of all this wrestling?" Alex has been to a few matches. Sweaty guys pressing and squeezing each other, trying to topple their opponent, continuing their rumpus on the floor.

Shurochka doesn't like the wrestling either. And what, one might ask, is the point of carrying on? As she understands it, for Leo it's all about the moment when you've held out and held out all you can, or you're even on the back foot, and then you sense it—there, he's done, your opponent's drifting; now you'll be the one to do the pinning. A strange sort of pleasure.

"Fine, fine, let him," says Alex, as if anyone were asking his opinion.

Their boy has grown: he now has his own car and his own income, first as a lifeguard in the park, then as something else. Therein lies America's strength: even the children of the rich start from nothing.

Leo is already in the twelfth grade, the last year of high school. Many of his peers have jobs as waiters, librarians, tennis instructors, while in his evenings Leo keeps the peace in some café bar, twenty dollars an hour. Strange that they took him on—he won't even be eighteen until May. The clientele are a fairly docile crowd—the most force Leo will ever have to employ is a handshake, a firm stare. Shurochka pictures the scene: the night sky, the moon, a pub; Leo leading a troublemaker out to a poorly lit street. Good thing he's almost finished with school—hopefully he'll be off to university soon, then a new life can begin. It would be good if he didn't hurt Yulia. Incidentally, the school is putting in a recommendation for her for Harvard, but not for Leo. How will he ever get over that?

School is ending in a few months, but Leo clearly hasn't decided what to do next. Perhaps he'll wait a while, get his bearings first.

"At least here we don't have conscription to worry about," Shurochka says.

Leo has neither a propensity nor the capacity for natural sciences, or for the humanities, at that. He'll probably go for something technical. Or else legal. Worst case: business school. His SAT results weren't spectacular.

Alex gives a sober assessment of the situation:

"Harvard isn't Leo's bag; a Kerosinka's more for him. The Kerosinkas here are perfectly fine."

There are hundreds of universities that could take him, but where has he applied? Leo locks himself away in his room and sends off emails. To Harvard, another five or six flashy names. All on his own.

"Why would no one tell him how stupid that was? Does he even have any friends?" Alex is confused, upset.

"Yes, he does. Either from wrestling, or that . . . establishment where he works." Shurochka is also upset.

Yulia, by the way, was accepted by Harvard, they found out back in February. Many other places besides, if not everywhere she applied. Shurochka is delighted for Yulia, sincerely. Leo needs to learn how to lose.

Still, where will he go? He'll tell them when the time is right.

"Let's leave him to it," Alex suggests, "Let him figure it out for himself. He won't let us help him, anyway."

And, without waiting for Leo's answer, Alex and Shurochka move out to Cape Cod. It's May, after all, and the trees outside their windows are already in bloom—magnolias, and others, too, Alex never can remember their names.

4.

There are some things that Alex can never forget: that dip in the Atlantic in '89; the search for his father in 2000. And Leo and his friend's intrusion into their Cape Cod home in June 2008—that, too, Alex will always remember. But first, two or three weeks earlier, Yulia appears out of the blue on their doorstep.

A crunch of wheels on their gravel drive; Shurochka looks out the window. Oh, Yulia! She had been expecting Leo.

"Is Leo coming too?" Yulia asks, trying to play it cool, but she always was an earnest girl.

Yulia speaks to them in Russian. She had actually just driven over to say goodbye: the day after tomorrow is the prom, and next week she'll be leaving for Spain, to visit her grandmother and great-grandmother. Her great-grandmother is very old, she hardly recognizes anyone anymore. And then—Harvard, a new life. School, childhood: they're over now.

It's touching: Yulia has driven this whole way—an hour and a half in all—just to see them. But yes, Leo will be here soon; he's coming for dinner.

A miserable, pleading look appears in Yulia's eyes. Of course—it was naive to think Yulia would be here just for her and Alex. Yes, Leo's coming to pick up his tux for the prom—Shurochka has had the trousers rehemmed. And Yulia—what will she be wearing? Does she have any pictures?

Has Shurochka put her foot in it again?

Turns out Leo isn't taking Yulia. He's asked Joan to go to the prom with him.

Joan has a limp—one of her legs is much shorter than the other.

"No one wanted to ask her," says Yulia. Her voice quivers, then breaks. "Very noble of him, no?"

Best leave her alone, let her take a seat. Would she like any juice, any water? No, thank you, she's fine just waiting.

Yulia steps into the next room, walks over to the bookcase. She had never dared to ask before, but what are those stones about?

Those aren't just stones, they represent a very precious memory for Shurochka. For her and Alex. She shows her:

"This is Princess Mary, and that's Dr. Werner, and here's Yanko the smuggler..."

Yulia doesn't get what she's talking about. Surely she must have read it? No? How could such a thing happen? Let's fix that right now.

Shurochka hands her *A Hero of Our Time*: Make yourself comfortable, you're in for a treat. Seeing as they're waiting anyway. Meanwhile Shurochka will get started on dinner. How does risotto with beef and mushrooms sound?

A half hour passes, then an hour. The evening starts to draw close, Alex comes down wanting some food. Leo must have been held up.

"Shh, quiet, don't disturb the girl." Shurochka will give Leo a call.

Luckily she has the good sense to do it upstairs.

Ugh, Yulia's there? Shurochka thinks she can make out the screech of brakes through the line. No, Leo isn't coming today. He'll pick up the tux another time.

"Any news on college?" Shurochka shouts.

Soon; they'll find out very soon. Dial tone.

Now what can she tell little Yulechka? There's nothing for it but to tell it like it is.

Yulia claps the book shut, gets up. Red splotches appear across her forehead.

Alex asks how she's finding the book—does she like it? Of course she couldn't have finished it in an hour—she should take it with her. They would be happy to give her the gift of Lermontov.

No, no, Yulia couldn't accept a gift.

"Say," she asks, "is it a valuable book?"

Alex doesn't understand what has happened. Why is she crying?

Shurochka gives her a prompt:

"It's her grandma. I mean, great-grandma. Yulia, Yulechka, everything's going to work out for you."

Yulia jumps into her car, drives off.

Is the book valuable? Strange question.

That year's heat wave comes in earlier than normal. When Leo and his comrade step into the house, the first thing they do is ask for a drink. Ice water. Plain water.

Leo says his comrade's name, but for Shurochka and Alex, it goes in one ear and out the other. John, they think. Or George. It's awkward to ask again. His head is shaved, his ears stick out.

They drink their water, and then: Attention please, can everybody sit down?

"Ooh, drumroll," says John or George with a smirk.

Leo appears to be nervous. No, not one bit, it's too late for nerves. So, they wanted to know where he's going next? Well—pause—today he enrolled at the United States Military Academy. West Point.

On hearing this news, Alex and Shurochka bow their heads, afraid to look at one another.

Jug Ears is the first to break the silence:

"Well would you look at that, they're so happy the cat's got their tongue!"

Why is this boy even here? Whose idea was this? And why West Point, all of a sudden?

All of that is irrelevant now. Leo has made his choice. It's his decision. Alex and Shurochka look at their son and his comrade: if anyone holds the power here, it's Leo.

Besides, it's a free education. Only if Leo leaves the army will he have to pay the tuition back.

What does money have to do with this? Has this—the academy—just happened today? The final decision, yes.

Leo turns his head in profile and looks through the window. He looks illuminated, bright. His decision has been made. Money doesn't decide everything, it's neither here nor there, truly. Leo made it through all of the entrance exams.

Exams?

Jug Ears pipes up yet again:

"Eighteen pull-ups, seventy push-ups, seventy squats . . ."

"Squats," Alex repeats, dismayed. He doesn't know what to latch onto, what to ask. "In how much time?"

Leo nods: that's a reasonable question. Supporting his father, as it were.

"One minute." His comrade is undeterred. "Cross-country running . . ."

Alex clears his throat:

"And you? May we congratulate you, too?"

No, Jug Ears hasn't entered the academy, but they can still congratulate him. His fate has been decided. Certainty, that's the important thing. And after today, he knows he can get through anything. After meeting his interviewer.

"Thirty years in the army! Blown up seventy-five times! You got that? Seventy-five! Everyone he enlisted with is dead!" Jug Ears seems genuinely impressed. "But what really matters is how he gives you his undivided attention. When he's next to you, he's yours—all yours! There's no evasiveness, no slyness with him. It's like, *bam*," here he points at his chest, "and you realize that he sees everything, he can read you like a book. Even the things you didn't know about yourself!"

"But who is this, your..." Alex asks, "some sort of general?"

Oh, the daggers in Leo's eyes!

His friend, however, isn't letting up anytime soon:

"That's just it—he's not even an officer! A sergeant major! It's a rank."

Leo turns to his comrade: his parents probably aren't too interested in the details. But Jug Ears rattles on effusively:

"He entered the army as a recruit. Just think of that career path! Private, private first class, corporal..."

Alex covers his eyes.

"Are you OK?" Shurochka asks him quietly in Russian.

Yes, it's just the light. The sun is very bright.

"Sergeant, staff sergeant, master sergeant..."

Shurochka gets up, flicks the Venetian blinds.

"First sergeant, command sergeant..." and finally, triumphantly: "Sergeant major of the army!"

Alex flinches; he has the impression that this sergeant is about to burst in through the door, complete with medals and prosthetics.

Shurochka asks Jug Ears:

"So, how was your fate decided?"

The sergeant major told him he should enlist as a private.

Well isn't that something. And Leo? What did he tell Leo?

For Leo he predicted untold successes. And not just in the army. Leo has what it takes to become commander in chief, that's what he thought.

"No, no, no, no, no!" Alex suddenly bursts into life. "Anything but commander in chief! Leo was born in another country! Boys, who's been feeding you all this?" Alex suddenly feels limp. He laughs, but he does it alone.

Oh, no, these aren't hysterics. The words came out well—about the commander in chief, that is. But in today's conversation this is his last success.

The tension starts to subside.

The academy has a lot to offer. Girls even study there, by the way. Granted, not many, but some. Anyhow, it has lots of different stuff. Cinema, philosophy, water polo. A Jewish choir.

Alex tries to remember: is there even polyphony in Jewish music? Whatever, that's not the point. They sing in unison.

"Fine, Leo, but it's not like you'll be joining any choir. They could send you somewhere. Afghanistan."

Jug Ears replies yet again (who's asking him?).

They could, he says, you bet. And as it happens, personally he's hoping to be deployed. He wouldn't want the operation to end before he's had a chance to see it.

"But that means you'll have to . . ." Shurochka has never touched on such topics before. "You'll have to shoot, kill people?"

Perhaps she means to say the army isn't necessary? Jug Ears, quite forwardly, takes a long look around their home:

"So you'd prefer it if they whacked you out here, instead?"

Does she even follow politics?

Shurochka gets up: no, she doesn't.

Leo touches his comrade's hand. His meaning is clear: go have a smoke.

They should pardon his friend, he's very right-wing.

Once Jug Ears has stepped outside, and Shurochka into the next room, Alex puts it out there:

"Just remember, that if anything…We can pay for a year, two, however much it takes to go to a normal university. This idea of self-sufficiency, independence…" Alex is sure that if he just puts his mind to it, he'll find the right thing to say.

He, Alex, dreamed, still dreams…Of what? Leo's too lazy to even ask. Of something else. Alex needs to paraphrase the talk his own father had with him. What year was that? '83, probably? Everything works so well here—even the propaganda, he suddenly thinks. Alex's temperament isn't one for changing minds, even if this is his own son.

Meanwhile Shurochka stands at the bookcase with the stones, catches her breath. A horrible thing, to debate someone's choice. Typical demagoguery, she thinks, male, obtuse. Totally incompatible—with their lives, with everything.

Her breaths are returning to normal now. She must give Leo something to remember them by when he leaves. Here—Maxim Maximych. Dappled, pockmarked—if she can have a narrow hole drilled through it, he'll be able to wear it around his neck. Shurochka knows exactly what Leo will do with Maxim Maximych: without even asking who it is, he'll laugh, fling it off into the ocean as soon as he's out the front door.

Shurochka hesitates, then returns to the men in the living room.

"No luck?" she asks Alex with her eyes.

Leo intercepts her gaze, smiles at his mother: no.

After Leo and his comrade leave, Alex and Shurochka sit in silence for a while. Then Shurochka says:

"We didn't have enough children."

"And had we had more," Alex replies, "They'd have run off to Afghanistan too."

Other than Shurochka, Alex has no one left. He knows this is how it will be until the end—his, hers, it's all the same.

We'll have to nurture his taste for travel, Shurochka thinks. Or else what lies ahead won't be life, so much as a continuous epilogue.

5.

Just over two years have passed. Leo hardly ever calls, and he doesn't like it when they call him. Students at the academy accrue points for every excellent grade, which they can exchange for various perks: the right not to cut their hair or clean their room, a leave warrant. Leo's hair is short and he has always loved order, so his accrued capital is probably spent on leave. Perhaps he'll come for Thanksgiving. Not that he came last year. Either he must have been sick or he was being punished. Or perhaps he just went somewhere else. They don't know the details. It's Leo's life.

But in theory they hadn't even quarreled.

Alex listens to a lot of music now. He has bought a grand piano.

"There are worse ways to cope with a midlife crisis," that's what he says about his hobbies.

"You'd be better off getting a mistress."

Come on, is his playing really that bad? No, it isn't bad, but Shurochka can take the liberty of joking: she has nothing to fear.

Truth is, even for an amateur he's so-so. He complains that his fingers don't obey him. The pieces he once knew are, of course, beyond him now. He has to study the music for a long time, struggles to learn it by heart, but perhaps he did once have some talent, after all? Yes, some, everyone has some sort of talent. In any case, he has no cause for regret: What else would he have become? Someone like Yulia's parents? They were certainly more naturally talented than he.

He has positioned his grand piano so that he can see the water while he plays. He should be looking at the music and his hands, not admiring the ocean. Oh well, it's not like he's a professional. The most he can aspire to is learning "the sheep" well enough to play it to himself and Shurochka. "Sheep May Safely Graze" is one of his favorite pieces. He looks at one part, then another. A complex thing, polyphony. Alex remembers his mother playing this chorale, his father listening to her, both so old—they had always seemed old to Alex. Once, while moving boxes of papers, he had found a photograph of his mother at the piano, his father standing behind her. Alex probably took it himself. In it his parents don't seem so very old.

Now that Alex has plenty of time and money, and his body hasn't started to make any grumbles, he spends more and more time pondering the bigger questions. What is each person responsible for, and for what are their parents? Are we accountable for anything at all? If so, then to whom? But he is incapable of coming up with an answer, and once these thoughts rear their heads they only spoil Alex's mood. Nowadays when something upsets or angers him, he makes a terrible frown. His entire face furrows—his eyes, nose, mouth; all of his facial muscles participate in the process.

"I can't look," Shurochka says, if he falls into thought in her presence.

One day in late September (the air warm, the water cold) they walk out to the ocean.

Alex asks:

"Do you realize who we made, you and I?"

Oh, yes. Has Alex only just figured it out?

"You *did* have a crush on him as a girl."

Shurochka takes off her shoes and steps onto the warm stones, turns them over with her toes.

March 2013
Translated by Alex Fleming

LUXEMBURG

I NEVER liked funerals (who does?), but when a childhood friend calls, there's no getting out of it. As a med student I'd seen more than my share of corpses, especially among the leadership (if only they'd do us a favor and all croak at once). Back in the early '80s we were herded out to mourn for Kosygin, then Suslov, then Marshal Grechko—is that right? I forget the exact order...The truth is we kind of enjoyed it. Other citizens were forced to wave their little flags on either side of Leninsky Avenue in the sweltering heat or the freezing cold, greeting the visiting Gustáv Husák as if he were the fifth Beatle, but all we had to do was to line up in the Pillar Hall of the House of the Unions, look dour, and listen to Chopin or Tchaikovsky for a grand total of fifteen minutes. Then we were free to go. The main thing was not to disrupt the hallowed proceedings with some nasty jibe or a chuckle. The leaders were dying off in droves back then, sometimes several a semester, so it became a kind of tradition with us to stop off somewhere on the way to the Pillar Hall and grab a bite—say, at the kebab place near the Conservatory on Herzen Street (still love that place) or at the glass-fronted café across from the Kremlin, where they've put up that horrible monument to Vladimir the Great (oh well, at least his namesake's happy). One time we dallied too long and missed our chance to bid farewell to Comrade Pelše. It was a big loss, and we knocked back a few too many drinks, in memoriam...But not to worry, they managed to bury him without us. Anyway, this isn't about Pelše or our senseless Soviet youth, with its monotonous pastimes. It's about Sasha Levant. We first met at school, Sasha and I, when we were both twelve, and though we can go years without seeing each other, he still considers me a friend—otherwise I wouldn't have been invited to attend the funeral of his mother, Maria Ilyinichna.

Her death came as a shock to me only because I had no idea that she was still alive. The quality of one's life is measured by how many people come to pay their final respects when it's all over (voluntarily, I mean—if it's a boss, the number doesn't count), but Sasha's mother lived to the ripe old age of 101, so good luck finding any of her old friends or colleagues among the living. What you will find is this: the morgue at the town hospital, a funeral parlor, a priest mumbling something or other, and Sasha and me, candles in hand. Sasha crosses himself from time to time (a new development), while I mainly look down at the floor, kneading the wax between my fingers. Why fill in the picture? We've all been to these funerals: dead old woman, dead flowers, dead everything. The priest—half our age, but also half dead—suddenly bursts into a homily, laying into us for ten straight minutes. According to him, Maria Ilyinichna passed away because Sasha and I didn't attend services often enough. Can't argue with that—but what was I to do? I'm an unbaptized atheist and have worked all my life as a psychiatrist at Kashchenko Hospital, where I've seen all kinds of things that prevent me from believing in the immortality of the soul. Sasha shoots a glance at the priest and whispers in my ear: "Unspent didactic potential." All right, time to go.

We load her onto the bus, with a little help from the guys at the parlor: "There you are—don't say, 'See you.'" Thanks for the tip, angels of death, but I know your rules of etiquette well enough. What I didn't know was that the deceased had converted, so I ask Sasha about it. "No," he says, "Mom was Russian." Her maiden name, it turns out, was Kotov?, and her first husband—Sasha's biological father—was a Gusev. She got the name Levant from her second husband. And all this time I had assumed Sasha was half-Jewish . . . Maria Ilyinichna had always looked Jewish to me. But then again, many intellectuals acquire Semitic traits as they age, and Sasha's mother was already quite old by the time he and I met. I'm a fairly broad-minded, liberal type of person, but I just can't turn a blind eye to the question of nationality. It's a matter of conditioning, and it starts in early childhood: you may be a genius three times over, but they still won't admit you to this or that college; your ethnicity is noted at the top of your report card; and even the word *Jew* itself is made to sound indecent. You begin to pay attention to these things, whether you want to or not.

No need to describe the crematorium in all its wretched luxury; if you haven't seen one, you haven't missed much. Besides, soon all of Moscow will be done up in similar fashion.

Having gotten rid of the deceased, we flag down a taxi and head— faster, faster—to a restaurant on Pyatnitskaya Street. I'm overcome by the desire to feel alive—to drink, eat, talk, move. I try to conceal this liveliness from Sasha, but he himself, it seems, doesn't plan to grieve expressively. I look at him, and he's in his prime, as they say: half-gray but still handsome. I don't have much of a gift for physical description; frankly, I don't even remember the color of my wives' and children's eyes. But I do remember other things—Sasha's hand-writing, for example: he wrote with his left hand (which was unusual, because they used to force lefties to switch over) and wrote very quickly, in small neat letters that looked like newspaper print, as if he were trying to make it easier for others to crib off him (which he always let us do). An excellent student across the board—had he been in the Komsomol, he would have received a medal with his diploma— Sasha had a special aptitude for the hard sciences. Not genius level, but very, very capable: enough to try for Moscow State's Faculty of Mechanics and Mathematics.

At our school, that was a kind of national sport for us Jews: first you try for Moscow State or some similar institution, like the Institute of Physics and Technology or, I don't know, the Engineering Physics Institute—they all held their entry exams early, at the start of July— and only then do you apply where, if they aren't exactly happy to have us, they at least accept us. "You won't get in, of course, but it's your duty to ruin their day," our advanced mathematics teacher used to tell us; he was later arrested for anti-Soviet agitation and given the max-imum—seven years in the camps, five in exile. To go where no one wanted you (at Moscow State they'd undermine us with particular cruelty) was considered perfectly normal. Pride wasn't really a thing in the '70s. And so the following scene would play out, time and again: a clever, curly-headed boy facing a team of anti-Semitic examiners and solving problems drawn from past National and International Mathematical Olympiads. The boy solves them all. The problems keep coming, but they aren't new; the walls of our school were plastered with them in the spring (take a good look, kids—last year's oral exams). Outside the lecture hall stand the boy's parents and teachers, ready to help file an appeal. Others—like me, for instance—had just come to watch, to cheer our fellows on.

In my case, the path to the mathematics department was foreclosed, and not because of the ethnicity in my passport—not only because of it, anyway. "Don't disgrace our people." No one came out and said it, but the message was clear. Be that as it may, I remember some funny incidents. A confused black-haired fellow, one year older than Sasha and me, checking the list of admitted students three times, still not finding his name, and, with tears in his eyes and his voice, complaining, "But I'm not a Jew!" What can we say, old boy? You have our sympathy—appearances can be deceiving, and as Comrade Stalin used to say, if you want to make an omelet, you've got to break some eggs. "I'll appeal to Lev Semyonovich Pontryagin!" he whined. "He can sniff out a Jew like no one else." Who's Pontryagin, you ask? A great scholar—algebraic topology, calculus of variations. He was blinded in childhood, which might account for his heightened sense of smell. An outstanding individual in every respect. The black-haired gentile gained admission.

No, Sasha didn't go to Moscow State. Didn't even try. He fed us some cock-and-bull story about being late with the application, forgetting his passport—none of us believed it. Now, in light of what he told me about Maria Ilyinichna, it also turned out that, biologically, he was a cross between a Gusev and a Kotova. Who would have thought? Alexander Yakovlevich Levant, registered as a Jew, but not a Jew—you might not find another case like this the whole world over... And the main thing is, he looks like a Jew. I must admit, I got a little agitated: Why hadn't he said anything? He could've appealed to Pontryagin. But I understand: some people just don't care to be put to a blind anti-Semite's sniff test. And so Sasha graduated from some obscure university, which had one thing going for it: a reserve officer-training corps that would keep you out of active duty. He learned several languages—English, German, and even Latin, I think—and made his living as a translator. Throughout all this, what moved him wasn't the spirit of the times, but rather—I don't even know what . . . I'm not sure anyone else noticed this, but I did. He seemed to lack passion, but then, none of us was particularly passionate, except for that math teacher. The life experience we gained in the Soviet Union prepared us only for life in the Soviet Union: Yes, we learned a lot of unflattering things—about ourselves, about people in general—but what use was it, all this knowledge?

I remember how our history teacher, a totally daft ideologue, reacted when Sasha, at fourteen years of age, said that the theory of Marxism was devoid of anthropological content. Her face fell. We, for our part, didn't even try to figure out what he could have meant by that. We'd consigned Marxism to the grave—who could possibly take that crap seriously? And a final note on the question of nationality: when Jews behave with dignity, there's always a hint of defiance in their stance—people hold that against us. And that's precisely what my friend lacked: defiance. Now I know why.

We order food and drink to the blessed memory of Maria Ilyinichna. Sasha drinks little—less than I do, anyway—and doesn't like to curse, which also hinders communication. My own lifestyle choices, on the other hand, were even noted in my school record: "Can be influenced by strong-willed classmates." Sounds silly. Who can't be influenced? But what it meant in Soviet-speak was: smokes and drinks, at the very least. I still got into med school; they paid no attention. I say to Sasha: "So you're baptized? I didn't know."

It turns out that Sasha got baptized right before graduation but didn't tell any of us. The question is tactless, of course, but I can't help it: what the hell for? Read too much Bulgakov? Listened to Andrew Lloyd Webber one too many times? (In ninth and tenth grade we all loved *Jesus Christ Superstar*—gorgeous women, hippies, lanky, handsome Blacks—a window into the free, non-Soviet world.) Sasha shakes his head: don't ask. He told his mother about it and got an unexpected response: "What a fool." Then she told him that when he was still an infant, his two nannies, both village women, had each managed to get him baptized in secret, and both later confessed to Maria Ilyinichna. A thrice-baptized Levant—wonders never cease ...

We eat heartily, without forgetting, however, the purpose of our gathering. Sasha tells me about his mother, shows me a few photos. The woman was a great beauty in her youth, and her face really did look Russian—even noble, I would say. Her biography too was heroic, especially in its opening chapters.

Take this scene: she's thirty years old, flying out of Leningrad at the height of the blockade. They keep sending her back, over and over again, to prepare the evacuation of yet another factory or scientific institute. It's a military aircraft, of course, and she's the only woman among a dozen men. The antiaircraft guns are thumping away, knocking the plane this way and that, and one of the officers loses his nerve: after the plane lands, he panics and takes off running toward the German line. Another of Maria Ilyinichna's traveling companions pulls out a pistol and executes the defector. And what does she do? Gets ready for the next assignment, as if nothing happened.

Throughout the war, says Sasha, his mother smoked strong tobacco mixed with hashish, so as to work round the clock without relaxing or falling asleep. Strange—doesn't hash usually have the opposite effect? Anyway, that's what Sasha remembers her saying. Maria Ilyinichna would spend all day at the Sverdlovsk railway station, an unloaded revolver in one pocket, and in the other, a license to confiscate building materials from passing trains. The evacuees had to construct a munitions factory from scratch by a certain date. If they managed to do it, she'd be awarded the Order of the Red Banner. And if they didn't—well, no need to spell out the consequences. That's the wartime economy for you. The factory must have been built, otherwise Sasha wouldn't be here.

But he is. And this is how he appeared: in the '50s Maria Ilyinichna was working in East Germany—hence the old heavy furniture in

their apartment and her knowledge of the language. She had a little
fling (or so she thought) with one of her subordinates, a man named
Gusev. This Gusev, however, took their romance seriously—so much
so that he officially denounced himself and his beloved for engaging
in extramarital relations, which was unacceptable for Soviet officials,
especially abroad. An interesting way to propose to a woman. Definitely new to me. I thought it was only jilted women who did that
sort of denouncing.

And yet Sasha's mother saw this as the best period of her life. East
Germany was nice, relatively prosperous—not like its western coun-
terpart. These were the good Germans, who had for some time fallen
into the hands of the bad ones. The Russians came and liberated
them—end of story.

Meanwhile, marriage to a subordinate, pregnancy, and, soon there-
after, a divorce (which, for a party member, was worse than extramarital relations) stalled Maria Ilyinichna's career. Some ministries
and committees, a couple of work trips to the Baltics (no farther),
and retirement with a supplementary pension. Besides, in the '60s,
she'd become a Levant—just you try to get promoted after that...
She was also given to grand gestures, and as the years wore on, the
gestures grew grander. For example, one time, trying to prove to her
husband that in the USSR, Jews were treated just like everyone else,
she crossed out the word *Russian* in her passport and replaced it with
Jewess: Just you watch, nothing will change. She used that passport
for several years.

Any sweet, touching memories? It's a wake, after all. Sasha gives
it some thought. "Mom could sneeze on command. Before leaving
someone's house, especially if she didn't like them, she'd announce—
loudly—'Let me go and have a sneeze.' Then she'd hide in some back
room and start sneezing... Twenty, thirty times." No, there wasn't a
whole lot of sweetness to Maria Ilyinichna.

I ask him what he plans to do with the ashes.

"I'll take her to Luxemburg."

Now that I get—a grand gesture! But it turns out I don't get it at
all. He didn't say Luxemburg; he said Luxemburg—a small town east

of Moscow, about two hours by train. It was named, of course, in honor of the fiery revolutionary Rosa Luxemburg (a Polish Jew, by the way). I'd never heard of it, but that doesn't mean anything. Sasha says it's nice—that he likes it, in any case, and is thinking of moving there. Oh, how I fear "going to the people," especially with surnames like ours (watch your back), but I wish Sasha luck.[1] For what it's worth, my circle is more eager to head in the opposite direction.

Fine, Luxemburg it is. "Is that what she wanted?" No, Sasha's mother had never expressed any desires on that score. She never spoke about death, never thought about it. As far as the afterlife goes, it's not so much that she didn't believe in it as that she had no interest in it. Luxemburg just happens to be the resting place of Yakov Grigoryevich; no one else in their family had died, really.

We drink again—this time to the memory of Yakov Grigoryevich, Sasha's stepfather, a pleasant fellow who was, clearly, nothing like Sasha's mother. And then we drink to the memory of our dead teachers, and to the school as a whole, which, thankfully, never tried to become our second family (that happens with schools for the gifted, and not only with schools).

It often happens that people at wakes suddenly lapse into levity, for no particular reason. Our waitress (amazing ass, by the way) says into her phone, very clearly: "What did she see in him, anyway? No sport, no body, no education." So we laugh, making no effort to hide it. She turns to us and asks, "How'd you like the beef stroganoff?"

"Bit too much salt," I tell her. "But not bad."

She shrugs, says, "I've had it. Seemed kosher to me," gathers the empty plates, and walks away.

We burst out laughing again. I wave her back over and ask for brandy.

Sasha receives a long text message and sinks into it. His phone is on the table and I, poor sinner, sneak a peek: "Only after a mother's death does one truly become an adult." Sasha isn't exactly five years old to be in some great hurry to grow up. That sort of thing could only be written by a woman, of course. Nonetheless, sympathy, however unhealthy, is still preferable to the healthy absence of sympathy. Speaking of, Sasha had a wife at some point—where is she? He doesn't mention her, and I'm too ashamed to ask.

I step outside for a smoke and look at what they've done to Pyatnitskaya Street: neat little curbs, even tiles, giant lampposts—an imported, un-Muscovite standard of beauty. But I still love Moscow; I haven't got a Luxemburg of my own. Then I look through the big window at Sasha: he's put down the phone and is just sitting there, lost in thought—a typical state on a day like this. Sasha notices me looking at him and offers a helpless smile. I go back inside.

"Do you remember what *fetus papyraceus* means?" Sasha asks, out of nowhere.

It's something to do with obstetrics, but I forget. What do you expect from a bottom-shelf domestic psychiatrist? My obstetrics exam was administered by my aunt.

"Fetus papyraceus, also known as a vanishing twin, is a twin that dies in a multiple-gestation pregnancy," Sasha rattles off, as if he's reading from a textbook. "That happened to me in utero—I mean, to my brother."

In other words, Maria Ilyinichna was carrying twins, and Sasha crushed his brother, flattened him against the wall of her womb. While Sasha was growing and gaining weight, his brother was weakening, dying, turning into a piece of parchment, a mummy. He says all this quickly, as if hurrying to get it off his chest. If the two of us—me especially—weren't half-drunk, Sasha wouldn't be sharing it. It scares me: such confessions can be the death of even the strongest friendship.

How did he find out? The midwives told Maria Ilyinichna; she, for some reason, told Sasha's nannies, and then they told Sasha—who also heard it from his mother's friends, colleagues, and just about everyone else. No one went into detail, of course, but from their hints and meaningful glances he guessed that it wasn't only Cain or Grand Prince Sviatopolk (and let's throw in Vladimir the Great, too—also queer, by the way) who were guilty of fratricide. Much later, about ten years ago, when Maria Ilyinichna started telling the truth and nothing but the truth, God help you, Sasha got a real earful, the nitty-gritty about her fetus papyraceus included.

He must have assured himself hundreds of times that he was blameless—there couldn't have been any ill intent, or any intent at all. But no one wants to live with that kind of stain in one's biography, to be marked from birth, literally. Now I know why he wanted to be baptized. A lot of good that did, I'm sure . . . If my friend were more naive, I could have loaded him up with some therapeutic crap—"you must learn to forgive yourself," or whatever—but he wouldn't buy that for a second. A goddamn shame. Really, right out of a Greek tragedy. Sasha waves a hand: no point in talking about it. As for Maria Ilyinichna and her truth-telling, I've been around enough old women of that type and I know the routine. They may not be senile at all, but they're old enough to be, and they begin to see the upside: now they can prattle on about anything that pops into their heads and no one will say a word.

Sasha and I keep chatting, drinking, but soon we both realize we can't stay up much longer. While Sasha pays the check, I ask the waitress to pour the remaining brandy from the decanter back into the bottle, so that I can take it home—why let it go to waste? She gives me a look, but does it.

Once we're outside, I can't hold back the question I wanted to pose earlier:

"What happened to . . ." What an idiot—I've forgotten his wife's name. In my defense, I'd only seen her a few times, briefly. Olya? Yulia? I remember she laughed a lot, and always covered her mouth when she did. Her cheeks and forehead would turn red too.

Sasha responds as only he can, brilliantly:

"She got divorced."

The dearly departed must have broken her down. But I won't pry. I'm sure Sasha's already said more than he'd wanted to say. We part with a hug (new for us).

"Come on, Sasha—you don't thank people for this kind of thing."

He smiles and shrugs: "I don't see why you wouldn't."

And then we go our opposite ways.

I.

In the beginning, the rose disappeared. Rather, first he planted it—after burying his mother, that is, and renting out his apartment in Moscow, moving to this wretched Luxemburg, and ordering a headstone. Then he planted the rose.

His plans for the move took shape in the few days preceding the funeral. Before that, he hadn't allowed himself to think about what might come "after." Some time ago he had been commissioned to translate a book of conversations on moral themes, in which he had read that to love someone is to say to them: You will never die. From then on, he had refused to construct a picture of the world in which his mother did not exist. Luxemburg—more precisely, a small house on the edge of town (two rooms, a kitchen, an anteroom, and a cluttered attic with a window)—was his inheritance from Yakov Grigoryevich Levant, his father. Or stepfather. Sasha never knew what to call him, so he usually avoided specifying the relationship. Maria Ilyinichna, who had never respected the man, used to call him Yashka ("Yashka hasn't worked a day in his life"), but she wasn't jealous and didn't stop Sasha from growing close to him.

One didn't need advice from a book to love Yakov Grigoryevich: he was a cheerful person, and believed that cheerfulness was almost a universal duty—it was just that not everyone succeeded at it. He bumped into Maria Ilyinichna at a concert, or maybe in a tram or just on the street, and fell in love with her right away. He took her from Gusev, which wasn't hard to do: the fellow had cooled long ago. But why she'd agreed to marry Yakov Grigoryevich is not so clear; he claimed it all came down to his surname—has there ever been a more beautiful one than Levant? They lived together for a few years, constantly quarreling, then divorced, just as nonchalantly as they had gotten hitched, and Yakov Grigoryevich went back to his communal apartment. He would see his stepson on Sundays, at the Cosmos ice cream parlor on Gorky Street. Yakov Grigoryevich loved music, especially the piano—not only Chopin, like everyone in his generation, but also Scriabin and Medtner. He also loved opera, and even jazz, smoked a pipe, took photos, dabbled in drawing. He regarded his Jewishness ironically, as an amusing handicap, which, luckily, exempted him from a number of obligations—in particular, from climbing the social ladder. And he regarded anti-Semites with similar irony: "Two things never cease to amaze me . . ." he started to say once, and Sasha, who had read about both the starry heavens and the moral law, hurried to finish the quotation. But Yakov Grigoryevich laughed: "I have another two things in mind: why they like vodka so much and like us so little." (He himself drank vodka only occasionally, preferring rum.) Under "profession," Yakov Grigoryevich always listed "inventor," but he never took much interest in his work. Although he had, in fact, invented something important during the war—so important that he wasn't sent to the front. But his most important invention was actually located right here in Luxemburg.

In the early '70s, Yakov Grigoryevich secured a place for himself in the old cemetery (there were already two at that point) and began to make trips here—much more frequently than one would expect of a relatively young, happy-go-lucky man. He ordered a white slab—limestone, locally sourced—and had it engraved with his name, surname, year of birth, and a frivolous epitaph: "All's well that ends well." The invention was this: below, at the foot of the slab, was a hidden button—you click it, move the slab aside, and descend into a little bunker. Protected from moisture and even from extreme cold, this bunker held an entire library, ranging from works that were officially classified as "defective" (Gumilyov's poems, Sinyavsky's *Strolls with Pushkin*, typescript translations of Orwell) to those that were out-and-out anti-Soviet (*Gulag Archipelago* and issues of the *Chronicle of Current Events*). When Sasha was in seventh grade, he and Yakov Grigoryevich stopped meeting at the ice cream parlor and started taking trips to the old Luxemburg cemetery. This led to the happiest moments of Sasha's youth.

He'd sit at the table, reading Bunin's *Cursed Days*, and in front of him would be tea, rum, leftovers—what little they'd managed to cook—and Yakov Grigoryevich (his father, yes, father) watching the changing expression on his face, or reading something himself (Sasha never asked him about his means of expanding the library), or listening to Voice of America. Then, when it was already dark, they'd go back to the cemetery, return the books, and take the train home to Moscow. One time, in the train, Yakov Grigoryevich began to sing, loudly, attracting the attention of other passengers. And Sasha, feeling uncomfortable, wanted to move away, change seats. "*In fernem Land, unnahbar euren Schritten* . . . Citizens, " Yakov Grigoryevich announced, "this is my son. Where are you going, boy? Sit down." A tipsy elderly Jew in a half-empty suburban train on Sunday evening: no one aboard objected to his behavior—you can't choose your fellow passengers. What's more, one of them actually took a seat opposite him and said, mixing Russian and Yiddish: "*Azelkher yingele*—a nice boy, a blessing from God." This seemed to touch Yakov Grigoryevich, deeply. "Jews are a terrible people," he used to say. "It's just that everyone else is worse." They didn't come out to Luxemburg all that often, but Sasha will remember each of those trips as long as he lives.

Yakov Grigoryevich died quickly, either of stomach cancer or simply an ulcer, which was, in the words of Sasha's mother, to be expected, considering his lifestyle (poor food, rum): an inappropriate remark, and, as science has shown, a dubious one. His room in Moscow went back to the state, while the place in Luxemburg went to Sasha. All the deceased's belongings were brought there and stored in the attic, while Yakov Grigoryevich himself was laid to rest beside his favorite banned books. The snide epitaph looked awful, of course—one could only hope that it would eventually wear away to nothing. Sasha ruminated for a while, read the Bible, and, less than a month later, got baptized. When he told Eva, his wife, she asked: "Looking for another father, are you? Up in heaven?" He winced (why the elevated tone?), but nodded. Did he find one? Best not to ask.

A story: Yakov Grigoryevich had a neighbor—a single woman with a flat, featureless face. One time he brought over some heavy boxes and asked her to hold on to them; he was having repairs done and didn't want the workers to make off with his things. The repairs were never done, but a couple of agents did show up to conduct a thorough search; they turned the place upside down, and even brought in the neighbor (the very same one) to act as a witness. The agents didn't find any compromising anti-Soviet material, and soon Yakov Grigoryevich came to pick up his boxes. "You can count on me when it's time for more repairs, Yakov Grigoryevich," the neighbor told him. It's impossible to say for sure whether any of this actually happened. Nor can anyone truly vouch for the sequel: apparently, he wanted to reward the woman—a box of chocolates, brandy, something practical of his own invention—but she refused to accept it. "You think you've got a soul, while all I've got's a balalaika?" the neighbor asked. Again, we only have Yakov Grigoryevich's version, and he could well have made the whole thing up, or combined several characters into one (Maria Ilyinichna always insisted: "Yashka's a liar"). Apocrypha, tall tales … But something must have happened—otherwise, why would he have built the grave-bunker? That wasn't just a product of his quirkiness, like the epitaph. And that epitaph, by the way, was all wrong: nothing ended. Our relationships with our parents aren't severed by their physical deaths. The last thing Yakov Grigoryevich said to Sasha was: "I want you to smile every time you think of me. Might be difficult at first, but you'll get used to it. It'll become a habit." And so it did.

What a wise choice Yakov Grigoryevich had made all those years back, too. Cemeteries were the freest of public spaces in Soviet times. They were sites of artistic expression: put up a Star of David, a cross, a monument, write whatever you'd like, visit whenever the spirit moves you. True, the cemeteries in the big cities were always locked up at sundown, but here, in Luxemburg, it was all yours, day or night.

For a long time after Yakov Grigoryevich's death, the neighbor (she taught music, by the way) looked after his house, and even his garden. She didn't ask for anything in return, just did it; maybe he used to let her read his ill-gotten books—it's unlikely there was anything more to their relationship, besides their shared love for Medtner and dislike of the good old USSR. But the neighbor, too, was dead and buried.

And so, from his father Sasha inherited Luxemburg, while his mother left him her apartment in Moscow. It was big, and stuffed with old furniture—"trophies" from the victory over Germany: a turquoise-and-gold bedroom set, a bureau with a plethora of hidden drawers, a mahogany writing desk, a coffee table trimmed in marble, an antique mirror, etc. But Sasha no longer liked Moscow; he could even point to the exact moment when he stopped liking it.

One sunny morning, in the midst of the May Day celebrations, Sasha had to pick his wife up from the airport. He drove to Yugo-Zapadnaya station down traffic-free streets and stopped at the turn toward Leninsky Avenue. Everything seemed so cheerful, and he noted this cheerfulness: the calm of the city, the calmness inside him, Eva's return . . . Even his mother, uncharacteristically, hadn't managed to say or do anything to ruin his mood. He smiled as he waited for the light to change, imagining that once Eva was in the car, he'd convince her to go for a ride somewhere outside the city, wherever she'd like. (She regarded Luxemburg with total indifference: Paradise lost? Hardly. An ordinary village with its ordinary gray existence—no movies, no plays, no art shows. Well, yes, there was the river, the fields, the woods—that's all very nice, probably.) While the light was still red, a motorcyclist threaded his way between the cars, stopping just ahead of Sasha. There wasn't anything at all unusual about him—leather jacket, helmet, boots. He had also tied a black bandanna over his face, as motorcyclists often do, which made him look like a devout Muslim woman. Their eyes met for a split second. One time, in the Paris Métro, Sasha found himself pressed against a woman who was almost completely covered; all he could see were her bright, piercing eyes—that gaze was hard to bear. The light changed and they turned onto Leninsky. And then the motorcyclist rode up to a parked car—Sasha was watching him out of the corner of his eye, but saw it all clearly—and took out a handgun (large, not a toy, glinting in the sun) and pointed it at the driver. The car was expensive, black—that's all he can remember. It moved up a few meters, hit a fence, then stopped again. Sasha didn't hear a shot. What was it: a murder, a threat? No chance to examine the scene in detail—the flow of traffic kept carrying him onward. He didn't tell Eva any of this. Nor did they go for a nice drive out of town.

Eva (full name Elvira—Elvira Levant sounds good, doesn't it?) did a little film reviewing, a little translation from French. Sasha used to correct her translations, though he didn't know French, trying to inject a degree of logical sense that might well have been absent from the original. "The fog, someone likes Brahms, goodbye again..." Psychological, even pathological content. Her Russian didn't easily accommodate French texts.

"'After many years, this girl became my mother-in-law'—Eva, you should change that: *mother-in-law* sounds ominous."

"But that's what it says, *belle-mère*."

"Well, then write: 'Many years later I married her son.' I'm telling you, that's far more natural."

À propos: Maria Ilyinichna hated her daughter-in-law with such a passion that, in her last months, when her mind was completely gone, Eva was the only person she remembered and recognized—in photographs, because by that time Sasha was divorced. Maybe the gun had been a toy after all? That evening and the whole of the following day he'd looked through all the crime blotters and news reports he could get his hands on but found no mention of a murder at Yugo-Zapadnaya. Be that as it may, this thing he had witnessed, this totally peripheral occurrence, marked the beginning of a series of unpleasant developments at the very center of his life.

It began with his reluctance to drive, and all the ensuing inconveniences, and it continued with Eva signing up for driving lessons with a lanky blond instructor, a certain Oleg Zvezdaryov, twelve years her junior; Sasha and Eva had roughly the same gap between them, only in the opposite direction. She was intrigued: Oleg was a simple person, but just as critical of the people in power as Sasha. He was a fan of acoustic guitar music, liked some of the newer singer-songwriters ("Don't be a snob, Sasha..."). He was a big reader, too. ("Then why does he say things like 'should of' and 'irregardless'?" Sasha once had the pleasure of speaking to him on the phone.) As for his dislike of those in power, driving instructors, like waiters and hairdressers, tend to say whatever the client wants to hear. Was Sasha jealous? Turned out he had every reason to be. At some point Eva stopped talking about the instructor altogether, but then, just after she got her license, she found out she was pregnant. It was Oleg's. How could that be? She'd always claimed she didn't want children. Rather, she'd always said "later," and it was clear when that "later" would come—after her *belle-mère* was no more. In any event, Sasha helped her load up the car, and off she drove.

The pregnancy wasn't planned, but the infidelity was. Sasha later learned that Eva had been spending what little she earned on therapy sessions. This therapist determined that her discomfort arose from the fact that Sasha was much stronger than her, mentally; he recommended that she pursue her desires—for starters, take a lover. That, in any case, was how Eva understood the psychologist's recommendation.

Bad days followed. His mother could barely move and needed caregivers day and night. In politics, there was nothing but nastiness, both at home and abroad; he didn't really pay much attention to what was happening, but it was no use holding his nose: the nastiness had permeated the air. He'd also had to leave the publishing house where he'd worked for nearly twenty years: in the spirit of the times, the old guard had been supplanted by people "with an alternative sense of propriety," as one of his former colleagues put it. This, he came to feel, was only a minor link in the chain of unpleasant developments. Still, he had to admit that parting with the job wasn't easy. One might think that technical translation (of books on philosophy, sociology, even psychiatry) was a boring chore, and that in five or ten years it would all be done by computers. But no computer could ever write like Sasha Levant. "Nonsmoking alcoholics are few and far between, especially in the city"—his translation from a mind-numbing American textbook, in which the authors had inflated this observation into a flabby paragraph: you could open a novel with a sentence like that. Many considered Sasha to be the founder of an entire school of translation: avoid synonyms and pseudoscientific terms; don't use *practically* (a calque from English) in place of the perfectly good *almost*; to hell with *empathize*—show *pity* and *concern*; and who needs *lower extremities* when you have *feet*? Now, of course, this kind of thing is of concern to no one, not even the founder himself, but for many years it was a significant part of his life, perhaps the main part. All right, enough *frustration-lamentation*. He left, and that's that.

Sasha also had some experience with simultaneous interpretation. One time, when the authorities had just begun to let people travel abroad, he'd accompanied a certain physicist to a symposium in Stockholm. But whenever this fellow was asked a question, he'd respond with total nonsense—you couldn't make heads or tails of it. The other attendees kept scowling at Sasha: What a useless fool of an interpreter! When they were on their way back home, the physicist explained himself:

"I didn't want any of them to know what I was working on."

"So why did you agree to come?"

"What do you mean?" the physicist said, then sighed. "Why miss my one chance to visit Stockholm?"

The last few years were entirely devoted to his mother: earning here and there, hiring and firing caregivers, buying medicine and diapers. He lived day to day, and somehow managed it—didn't even have to sell Luxemburg. Now he needed some time to familiarize himself with the laws governing the disposal of property; he'd rent the apartment (there was a tenant waiting, a journalist for one of the major German papers) and receive a regular income, enough to live comfortably in Luxemburg—more than comfortably. A solid plan. And there was some justice in the fact that the apartment would now be in German hands; Sasha himself was afraid to move even a single item of trophy furniture, as if he expected his mother to reappear and give him an earful. Eva would call from time to time, taking his unconditional love for granted, as if he were Schnier, Böll's "clown"; they even met in person occasionally. She named her son Philip. Sasha saw him once, asleep in his stroller, and thought he might be able to bond with him. Oleg (surprise, surprise!) started hitting the bottle pretty hard—or, in Eva's elevated terms, began to "suffer from alcoholism." Imagine that! No one drinks, but he does...Was Sasha making fun of her? She took offense, hung up, but then called again.

When he's in bed, he remembers her full thighs, her knees, the birthmark beneath her shoulder blade, or funny incidents from their trips to Europe: how one time, back in Paris, in the middle of a heat wave, they were sitting on a bench and eating ice cream when an overdressed, heavyset woman came up to them and pleaded in a jumble of languages: "*S'il vous plait*... Eiscreme," and then, in Russian, "Where?" They quickly pointed her in the right direction, and she wasn't at all surprised that they had understood her perfectly.

Such was his past—all shuffled up, yes, but who remembers things in perfect chronological order, day by day? There was no need to replay his whole life in his mind, like a prisoner awaiting the gallows. A lot of things had come easily to him—granted, they were later taken away. But he wasn't tired. And despite the fact that he had fewer years ahead of him than behind him, he didn't feel that the end was nigh. There were still two, maybe three decades left to go; his genes were good. Patience, patience: put the household in order (home, garden), order a headstone for mother's grave, get Eva back—and adopt the boy, of course. Philip Levant would sound better than Philip Zvezdaryov, and there would be symmetry to it, a rhyme with Sasha's own childhood: stepson, Luxemburg. Maybe he'd even write something of his own, and if it didn't pan out (most likely it wouldn't), he'd just admire the trees and the birds, teach English or math at the local school.

A hot day. He walks around the house, opening the windows, and, while he's at it, straightening, dusting, and rearranging the pictures on the walls. Sketches, études... Yakov Grigoryevich wasn't one to sit on his hands, and when he lacked the resources or imagination to invent, he devoted himself to drawing—wonderfully, for an amateur—in pencil or charcoal. A naked woman lies on her side, facing the viewer, but has no face. Who is she? The neighbor? Mother? The knee and the curve of her hip remind Sasha of Eva. He hangs this one above the bed.

The radio is on, Rachmaninoff's Third Piano Concerto—he couldn't make out the pianist's name—a beautiful, very Russian first movement. One of the owners of the publishing house had once promised the employees that he would play this concerto, although he hadn't taken a single piano lesson in his life, and possibly didn't even know how to read music. They all laughed at him, didn't take him seriously: he was a warm, sentimental person, who had, as it were, taken the back seat all his life, and here was his romantic (or is pathetic the word?) dream. And then he robbed his partners—probably to his own detriment—and took everything into his own inept hands. No more talk of Rachmaninoff. And no more scientific texts—all church calendars. Ever since then, for Sasha, the Third Concerto elicits not light melancholy, as it ought to, but pity for the publishing house.

Another musical memory: their beloved neighbor, who had lived a quiet, inconspicuous life, suddenly spoke up for herself at the end. She willed that she be buried to the sounds of a string quartet, and even specified which. Of course, she meant a recording; where would you find a string quartet in Luxemburg? That's what the townsfolk remember: what a show-off—didn't want to be buried to live music, to Andante (that was the name of the local funeral orchestra—trumpets, trombones, tenor horns, cymbals, a bass helicon—frightful stuff), no, always had to be different, not like the rest of us.

Sasha switches stations: "In our country," a recently disgraced billionaire justifies himself, "the choice is simple: you're either a revolutionary or a conformist. If everything goes to hell, you hightail it to London. Me—I'm a conformist." Yes, with that kind of money, earned in that manner, the range of possibilities is indeed limited. But Sasha's no billionaire; he'll find something to do.

Of the things he'd planned to get done, all he'd managed to do was to bury his mother and to plant a rose on her grave—the first flower he'd ever planted.

2.

"It's disrespectful to cover slate with plaster," says Svyatoslav, the contractor. What he actually says is *disrespeckful*—that's how they pronounce it where he comes from. Svyatoslav is finishing up the veranda, repairing the porch. He's been working on Sasha's house for nearly a year.

Svyatoslav is a citizen of Ukraine; every few months he has to go back, to keep on the right side of the immigration laws. He has a huge lower jaw, thick hands, and is astonishingly strong. At first he lived with Sasha, but then he acquired something of a family in Luxemburg; his real family stayed in the Chernihiv region. He introduced himself as Svyatoslav, and that's what Sasha still calls him—no diminutives, nicknames. Svyatoslav, meanwhile, calls Sasha "Professor" (though he hasn't earned a PhD) or Alexander: three- or four-syllable names without patronymics sound strange, but that's how it's done now, especially in the provinces. The Tajik Gastarbeiters are an exception to the rule; the men almost always take the name Tolik, and the women are all Mashas. It's like Leskov's *Enchanted Wanderer*, with those endless Kolkas and Natashas, Sasha thinks with a smile. The unaccountable happiness that overcame him upon his arrival in Luxemburg had not yet faded.

He came down in the early spring, which turned out to be a long one, containing many movements and a huge number of details he'd never noticed before. Sasha kept nature at arm's length, and knew about the "sticky little leaves," the "colonnades of groves," and the "velvet fields" mostly from books. "It's so quiet here," he wrote to Eva one night, "that you can hear the snow melting." To which she'd responded with a smiley face—better than nothing. He wanted to learn the name of every bird, to say nothing of the trees and shrubs, so he downloaded all sorts of identifier apps: here's a *Sitta europaea*, the Eurasian nuthatch; on this side of the fence, you have long-leaved violet willows and wild sunflowers, on the other side, chives. The apple trees don't bear fruit, but how they bloom . . . They say he can graft them, but no, he'll never ascend to such heights of gardening. The electrical wiring, though, he can handle, better than any professional: easy, just follow the directions—everything "by the book," as the Americans say.

"Hey, Professor, could you have a look? Is it all right?" Svyatoslav holds out a piece of paper with printed text.

"What is it?"

Svyatoslav shrugs. "Hebrew. Don't you all speak it?"

Sasha doesn't want to disappoint Svyatoslav on any account. He goes to his room, photographs the text, opens the computer: OCR, transliterate, translate. "Detect language?" Yes. Turns out it's Yiddish, not Hebrew. *Undzer foter, vos du bist in himl...* But that's Our Father—the only prayer Sasha knows by heart! Letter by letter, he carefully compares Svyatoslav's text to the one he's found on the web: it seems to be correct. The only question is: What's it for?

"You'll see, Professor. Yiddish, Hebrew, doesn't make a difference." He even winks as he says it.

Svyatoslav returns from another trip to Ukraine looking very satisfied—here, take a gander. He removes his shirt and shows off a tattoo on his right arm: אונדזער פֿאָטער, "*Undzer foter*," from beginning to end.

"Wanted something about God—but not the stuff everyone else has."

Had Sasha known what Svyatoslav was going to do with it, he would have found him the Aramaic version. Or the Greek. But really, the imagination on this guy... He asks Svyatoslav for permission to take a photo, then sends it to Eva: now, here you have a simple person, not some pathetic fan of amateur singer-songwriters. By this time Eva had left Zvezdaryov and moved in with her parents. Sasha had asked her to come visit him in Luxemburg; she said she'd think about it. Go ahead, think away—just as long she was doing her own thinking.

Sasha's relations with his next-door neighbors can be characterized as episodic: he greets them, and they greet him, occasionally pilfering a little of this and a little of that—lumber, sand. He would never have noticed if it weren't for Svyatoslav. But it's no big deal, really: the losses are minor, and Sasha's far better-off than they are. There are two of them, brothers, who had either inherited the house from Yakov Grigoryevich's female friend or had simply moved in. The rumor is that they have a wife—that is, one wife for both of them. In general, they're an impractical pair: in June they try to sell last year's potatoes—however many they haven't eaten—and get upset when nobody buys any.

One of the brothers is heavy, slow-moving, and likes to stand by the fence and watch Svyatoslav work. He never offers help, only advice.

"Professor, should I tell him to get lost?"

Sasha shrugs, goes back to his room.

Home improvement is an engaging activity; people have been doing it for centuries. And even though, in these times, private property can't be regarded as entirely private, because some powerful set of hands could, at any moment, take it away from you (*snatch it* is the popular term), these powerful hands are unlikely to reach all the way to Luxemburg.

And so Sasha keeps acquiring things. On his last visit to the cemetery, by force of habit, he peeked into the bunker and immediately spotted a familiar little red booklet: his old Soviet passport. How did it get there? A mystery. Now just you try and disprove the existence of the subconscious. Sasha examines the yellowed photograph, taken over forty years ago: the frightened face (a reaction to the photographer, who had told Sasha to shut his mouth when he'd tried to smile), the hair cropped short, so as not to annoy the military instructor at school, a certain Colonel Dumbasky (he remembered nothing about the colonel himself, but he'd never forget the name). The fields were filled out in a calligrapher's hand. Name: *Alexander Yakovlevich Levant*. Place of birth: *Moscow*. Nationality: *Jew*. The loss of this passport had allowed his mother to insist, till the end of her days, that Sasha was always losing things, although he hadn't actually lost anything since.

The cemeteries in Luxemburg are overseen by a sallow faced, ghoulish fellow just shy of retirement, whose name happens to be Gulin—straight out of Gogol (he mustn't forget to tell Eva about him). They met when it came time for Sasha to bury the ashes.

He'd gone over to the cemetery, urn in one hand, shovel in the other, and was all set to start digging, but, at the last moment, thought that it might be worth asking someone's permission first. So he went up to the city council (used to be the "city executive committee" in the old days). There he found Gulin, hunched over a keyboard.

"What? Oh," he said and waved his hand, never taking his eyes off the screen. "Here we just bury 'em, no need to make it official. I'll get you a coupla lugheads."

He meant Tajik laborers. Sasha turned him down.

Gulin looked up at him, tearing himself away from his game of solitaire.

"You know what? Maybe you should fill out an application. I mean, you ain't burying a dog, after all." He slid a piece of paper toward Sasha. "You can do that, can't you?"

It had been a long time since anyone had asked Sasha whether he could write. He went out and buried the urn, scattered grass seed on and around the plot, and, the following spring, after he had already moved here—for good, he'd assumed—bought a rosebush ("Israeli garden rose"). He planted the rose and started visiting the cemetery regularly: he liked how quiet it was, and the plant needed watering—particularly, in the saleswoman's words, during the period of budding (it's always nice to acquire a new lexicon). He'd have to call on Gulin again when the headstone was ready, which should be fairly soon. The sculptor—who had come highly recommended by the illustrator at the publishing house and, by sheer coincidence, spent his summers in these parts—had showed Sasha his sketches: beautiful and austere, somewhat Protestant, with no laser-etched portrait. What photo could he have suggested, anyway? A lovely young official? That's not how he remembered her. A decrepit old woman? Sasha still had no integral image of his mother.

It's strange that she's gone, nothing more—no need to deceive oneself. Heroism and eccentricity, along with the wish to influence: those were her dominant traits. Once, when their relationship was in deep crisis, he read an American booklet titled *How to Deal With Difficult Parents*. It opened with the warning: "You won't change them. Put that in your pipe and smoke it." Then came a detailed questionnaire, with points for each item. His mother got the top score; it appears the American authors couldn't have even conceived of a more difficult character.

It's a pity he couldn't dredge up any touching memories back there on Pyatnitskaya Street, because there were things. For example, right at the end, one of her nurses boiled some potatoes and put in a few prunes; she examined the dish thoughtfully and said, "This is how my mother used to make it for me." Nothing special, it seems, but touching, no?

And so, the rose is planted: scarlet, two flowers in bloom, four buds ready to burst open. Sasha is sitting on the little bench at the cemetery, looking at a bush. He has to make a decision about his brother—not the flattened one. He doesn't even know why he ever brought that up—it's not like the story haunts him or anything. The fetus papyraceus had probably served to distract himself from Eva's high-minded condolences ("You have truly become an adult," "an era has passed," etc.)—how could he have explained that, at heart, Eva was actually a kind, decent person? In any case, Sasha's thoughts are now occupied by his other brother, the real one, whose surname he doesn't know. All he knows is his first name, and then only approximately, as well as his year of birth.

Five or six years ago, when Maria Ilyinichna was still in her right mind, she'd told him that she had given birth to a son during the war, in '42, between assignments, and had immediately placed him in an orphanage in the city of Kirov. The father? Evidently, she suggested, Sasha had little idea of what those times were like. She spoke in a calm tone, secure in her sense of righteousness. She had given the boy the rare name of Yeremey, or maybe Yermolay. She'd been picking over folksy Russian names and had forgotten which one she'd finally chosen. Hashish? What does that have to do with it? In seventy years of living, you forget plenty. The boy had been given a new surname, of course, and she didn't know the orphanage's address, but she was sure Sasha would track down his elder brother without much difficulty. After all, he had that—what's it called? Internet. The subject never came up again.

Let's imagine, Sasha says to himself, that you could in fact trace Yermolay (he prefers the name Yermolay to Yeremey) through the orphanage (there can't be that many of them in Kirov). And say you find him: an elderly man—over seventy, if he's still alive—a complete stranger with a made-up childhood and fictional parents (heroes who'd perished in the war or in Stalin's camps). And he, Sasha, is supposed to destroy the illusion that had comforted Yermolay all his life. And what if Yermolay had a mother and father whom he'd believed to be his birth parents? What was Sasha to offer him in exchange—some "trophy" furniture and an apartment in the capital? What was this, *Oliver Twist*, with him showing up and revealing the man's noble origins? Yet another memory: When the extremely chatty notary had certified his right of inheritance, she'd said, "It's a lucky thing you're an only child. I can just see my two loafers squabbling over my place when I'm gone," and started cackling. Sasha's heart is heavy: he knows he should be looking for Yermolay.

It must have rained overnight. The mud clings to Sasha's boots, but the air is clean, easy to breathe. Sasha walks along the path, looking at the headstones and crosses, reading the names, some of which are rather amusing. One of the nearest graves belongs to "Yevstolia Afrikanovna Smoochkina": a frightened old woman, not so ancient—just a bit older than Sasha, in fact—but in the '60s, when the picture was taken, people aged quickly, especially in the countryside. She reminds Sasha of his nanny, the last one. What was it that had spooked her, he wonders—also the photographer? Inside the spacious fenced plot (one of the graves is fresh), there are other headstones and markers, bearing other, less unusual surnames, but the one he'll remember is "Smoochkina."

Oh, and another touching recollection. Before his mother took to her bed for good, she had asked him to fetch a folder from the bottom of one of the bureau drawers. It was embossed with the words *USSR State Planning Committee*. "This folder is lucky," she had told him. "Whenever I went to the higher-ups, I took it with me, and they never refused my requests. Don't lose it." Sasha had smiled and nodded; he didn't believe in lucky charms. Nevertheless, he kept the folder.

"Mishura!" a woman's voice brings him back to the present. And again: "Mishura!"

A fat man of indeterminate age approaches the Smoochkin plot, holding utensils and bags of food. Mishura (the full name is likely Mikhail) stares at Sasha, somewhat bewildered. Then the woman appears—also large, untidy, a good match for her husband. The man takes out a bottle and an assortment of snacks, laying them out on the bench: marshmallows, a can of sprats, marmalade, cucumbers. Madame Smoochkina (as Sasha has dubbed her) observes the process without blinking, her mouth slightly open, as if she were collecting her thoughts. An awkward moment.

"I beg your pardon," Sasha says and goes back to his mother's plot.

He sits down on his bench and is no longer visible to the Smoochkins—between them are low fences, trees, crosses. But his loneliness does not last long: after about five minutes Madame Smoochkina walks up with a plastic cup filled with yellow liquid, setting it down beside Sasha.

"Needs a new coat," she says, picking at the fence with a fingernail. "That's homemade," she points to the cup. "Drink with us. To the memory..."

The liquid looks suspicious. And why should he drink to the memory of some stranger? Sasha decides to lie: the doctors have told him to stay away from alcohol.

"Eh..." she says with a dismissive wave. "They told Stepan Timofeich the same thing."

Stepan Timofeich is her father-in-law—the one to whose memory they're drinking.

"He was seventy-seven. Long enough, right?" she continues without a pause: "You wasted your time planting that rose. They steal them around here, even fake ones." She bends down so that her neck and chest, beaded with sweat, are right in Sasha's face.

"My name's Svetlana. What's yours?"

A mix of smells: sweat, hangover breath, perfume... He has to get away.

He rises and offers his name, which unexpectedly excites her:

"Alexander! What a fine Russian name!" She stops, looks Sasha in the eye: "Russian, right?"

"Yes," he replies. "Russian. The name is Russian."

Greek, to be precise—ἀλέξω means "to defend"—but he understands full well what she's really asking.

"Well, I should go."

He gulps down the "homemade" liquor and walks away. Near the cemetery gate he runs into Mishura and says, also unexpectedly:

"We should make proper paths. I'll bring the gravel."

Mishura nods: We'll go in with you.

Later, Gulin's "lugheads" will scatter the sand and gravel along the paths between the fences and charge him a surprisingly large amount. Closer to the fall, Mishura will see Sasha in town, come up to him, and announce: "Talked it over with the old lady. We can't go in with you on those paths." Fine, so be it.

Sasha was somewhat prepared, then, for the loss of the rose, but its actual disappearance—the sight of that hole in the ground—still upset him: a rose from a grave means more than some lumber or sand, after all. He imagined an old, decrepit alcoholic, no longer able to collect even empty bottles, much less scrap metal—imagined him digging the bush out of the ground with gnarled, trembling hands, anticipating how he would sell it at some dacha and take that first sip. Should Sasha plant another one? He remembers their neighbor—the woman with a soul, not just a balalaika—and how she'd put a note on her gate every time she left town: "There's a spell on this house. Anyone who robs it will grow sick and die." She had a way with words, that's for sure.

He complains to Svyatoslav: First thing he ever planted, and look what happened . . . The Ukrainian shakes his head, and the very next Saturday (such a stand-up guy) comes back from the market with a rosebush—by all appearances, the very same one that had been stolen. How did he ever manage to find it? Some things, Professor, are better left unexplained. Sasha pictures it: Svyatoslav the Brave walks up to an old man half-dead from moonshine or "fanfuriki" (a new word for bottled hooch he'd recently learned), who's selling a lone rosebush at the market. He grabs the old boozehound by the shoulders, lifts him up off the ground . . . No, it's true, better not to know. They replant the rose by the veranda, and Svyatoslav, a devotee of all things holy, surprises Sasha once more: before lowering the bush into the ground, he says, *Bismillah ir-Rahman ir-Rahim*"—in the name of Allah, most merciful, most compassionate. It seems some Tatar friends taught him the words; they'll ensure the plant grows better.

Eva asks Sasha why he goes to the cemetery all the time. Is that really healthy? They talk almost every day now. First of all, with Svyatoslav at the house, hammering and sawing, it's nice to get away to a quiet place, and second, Sasha's been going there for ages—doesn't she remember him telling her about the bunker? Plus, he has to prepare for the arrival of the headstone—his last obligation to his mother. Pour the foundation, etc. Svyatoslav, for all his innumerable virtues, refuses to help; he's afraid of the dead, even when they're underground. Was Zvezdaryov afraid of the dead? Who the hell cares what he was afraid of, she replies. Zvezdaryov is yesterday's news, *past indefinite.*

And besides, Sasha adds, it isn't like he spends all his time at the cemetery. Yesterday, for instance, he went to the café. Or maybe that was the day before yesterday? His days are filled with insignificant events, as if he were on some long train journey or staying at a sanatorium. Today he'll go to the café again. His household consists of one person, and it somehow feels silly to cook for himself—not that he knows how to cook. He tried, and even bought a book (*Dinner for Dummies*—heck of a title, right?), but when he came to the words "simmer" and "add as much as needed," he cut his losses. Eva laughs: "add salt and spices to taste," "cook until done"—she'll teach him. And he rejoices at this *simple future.*

What draws him to the café isn't so much the food (he knows the menu by heart) as the view of the river and the opportunity to observe people. The river has grown narrow and shallow. There used to be buoys all along it, and in the spring a huge vessel would come through, deepening the fairway; it doesn't come now, but the river's still a river. In the days of his youth, the buoys would light up in the evenings, and in the summertime a ferry would take people back and forth. There was such music and power in those nautical terms: "floating jetty," "pontoon bridge" (a few kilometers upstream), and, Sasha's favorite, "dredger."

It's the middle of August, with a foretaste of fall in the air. Sasha is seated outside, under the canopy, looking at the water and waiting for his food. Occasionally he strikes a match (someone has left a box on the table), blows it out, and inhales the smoke—he used to love that smell. He recalls the name of Yakov Grigoryevich's favorite tobacco. The other day Eva had asked him about the schools in Luxemburg, whether there was a decent one—an auspicious sign. She'd changed a lot over the past few years. "Men grow old and women change..." Who said that, Goethe? Eva herself studied at a perfectly first-rate Moscow school, but, for all that, can't even add fractions. What goes on in the head of a person who can't add fractions? Then again, who cares about fractions? Just think of all the things he himself doesn't know—the rudiments of music theory, for instance. True, Eva is just as ignorant of music theory, but... His attention is drawn by a cry—or rather, a whimper—at the neighboring table:

"What? A Tajik's gonna drink from the same cup as my child?"

Sasha sees a small group of middle-aged women, all fairly good-looking (though none of them can hold a candle to Eva, of course). There's a bottle of champagne on the table. The cry is followed by a discussion of whether one should allow Tajiks to use the bathroom inside the house; is that a lesser evil than having them relieve themselves on the property, under some bush? What if the children should see them? And what if, God forbid, one of the kids plucks a gooseberry off a shrub soaked in a Tajik's piss? Summer people from Moscow—soon they'd go home to the capital, while he, Sasha, would stay. He's no summer resident: this is where his parents are buried and where, he hopes, his stepson will go to school. Sasha imagines a boy plodding along in the murky morning, with a backpack that's far too big for him; even the name fits—little Philip, like the Tolstoy story.

Sasha decides he'll also have some wine. Today is a special day: the headstone was installed. A white stone cross, bearing symbolic images of the Evangelists (lion, angel, eagle, ox) and the inscription "Maria Ilyinichna Levant, 1913–2014," elegant and strict. The sculptor, Anatoly Vasilyevich, was satisfied—with both his work and the fee. He's a wizened, quick-moving old man; if it weren't for the bone calluses on his hands (evidence of injuries), he'd look more like an accountant than an artisan. Sasha likes old men of his sort, and likes his hands, too. Even Gulin, the director of cemeteries (he sent his workers, who turned out to be Kyrgyz), approved—"Good option"—and was impressed by the years of Maria Ilyinichna's life. It's a shame Anatoly Vasilyevich couldn't stay longer, but he promised to come back now and then: "Curious to see how the stone will behave" (whatever that meant).

"We've got Tsinandali by the glass now."

The young waitress's face is impenetrable. Last time he was here he'd noticed a bottle with a portrait of Stalin on the label, with a fake quote: "When I die, they will dump a lot of garbage on my grave, but the wind of time . . ." and so on. The paranoid Generalissimo would never have said, "When I die"—he planned to live forever, as they all do.

Sasha had asked, as calmly as he could: "You wouldn't happen to have one with Hitler on it, would you?"

The waitress caught his drift: "What have you got against Stalin?"

"Without going into specifics, let's just say that he murdered millions of my compatriots."

"Ah, I see . . ." she drawled, as if he'd told her that he was allergic to chocolate. At least she didn't ask him to say who, exactly, his compatriots were. In any case, Sasha won: they started serving Tsinandali by the glass.

Now the renovation is over, the headstone installed: his last debt to his mother, except for Yermolay, has been paid. He'd even planted a few things. September is coming. It's only eight and almost dark. The main drawback of life in Luxemburg is the absence of streetlights. Sasha turns on the spotlights at all four corners: *Mehr Licht!* He sits down on the bench, takes out his phone, and writes to Eva: "A good day, unmarred by inconveniences. I worked on my German a little, freed the gooseberry shrub from the rose brambles, wild grape, and weeds that had been choking it for years. I bet that people who don't keep a diary must think they'd never spent a whole day doing so little."

"How's life outside Moscow? All OK?" Eva responds.

"All OK here. Come see for yourself."

Hours pass before he hears back: "*Pourquoi* not? Phil and I are thinking of driving over early next week. If you'll have us."

At last . . . Sasha is seized by unrestrainable joy, the kind of joy he remembers from youth: you rack your brains over some difficult equation and then, all of a sudden, the solution comes—go ahead, write it down! When is she coming, early next week? He's lost track of the days. An almost unbearable happiness: soon he'd have his people at home, his family. All was not in vain.

That night he can't get to sleep for a long time. He wanders through the house, which isn't so very small, seeing it through Eva's eyes, remembering her body and her hands, her mouth, always ready to laugh—he missed her, how he missed her! Eventually he climbs back into bed, tosses and turns for a while, gets back up, straightens a slightly tilted picture (the silhouette of an unknown woman, charcoal on cardboard), and finally falls asleep at dawn. In his dream, he wins some unusual, very short distance race at the Olympics. The track is straight at first, then veers to the left, zigzags uphill, and there it is: the finish line. Sasha is only an average runner, but, this being the Olympics, he makes a special effort, and he triumphs. His success leads to complications and red tape: gold medals must be handed over to the Ministry of Sports, in exchange for a gold-plated duplicate—but he's not an athlete. He just happened to win, once, and he decides to keep his medal, refuses to surrender it. Sasha usually doesn't remember his dreams and has no interest in interpreting them, but this one he likes, and so he stays in bed for a while, going over the details in his head.

He will remember this lying in bed, this blissful loneliness, which for the first time in a long time brings him pleasure, because he knows it will soon be over. He'll remember the faint smell of fresh paint, the sunlight filtering in from under the door, the funny, senseless dream—the last happy morning, the last peaceful moment of his Luxemburgian existence.

The telephone rings. Anatoly Vasilyevich, the sculptor, is gasping for breath:

"Alexander Yakovlevich, the cemetery—come, come quick."

Undzer foter... he takes off running.

3.

Near the entrance to the cemetery, leaning against the fence, stands Anatoly Vasilyevich, pale-faced, gasping. The old man is having chest pain, but he refuses the offer to call an ambulance or even a taxi: It'll pass, it's getting better—you go on, Alexander Yakovlevich, and look at what they've done to the grave.

Approaching the plot, this is what he sees: enormous footprints everywhere, especially in the right corner, where his mother is buried, human excrement, and on the headstone—both on the back and the front, over her name—black swastikas. On Yakov Grigoryevich's marker, he reads the words DETH TO YIDS, spelled phonetically.

A long time ago, back in the 1990s, when Sasha had just learned to drive, some guy had grabbed and squeezed his face, really hard, right in the middle of the road. Apparently he didn't like the way Sasha had changed lanes, so he cut him off, blocked him, walked over, thrust his gross, meaty paw through Sasha's window, and wrapped his fingers around his face, pressing down on his cheeks, his nose, his eyes. As soon as the pain subsided and Sasha could see again, he stepped on the gas. He had no idea what he might do if he caught up with the bastard. Of course, he never did catch up. It was this same fury, and even a similar pain in the eyes, that he felt now—only there was no one to chase.

"Don't you worry, Alexander Yakovlevich, we'll clean it up, wipe it off. It's just coal, not paint," Anatoly Vasilyevich assures him.

No, not until the police arrive. And Sasha will go file the report by himself: a person with chest pain has no business hanging around a police station. Not that Anatoly Vasilyevich wanted to go. He'd prefer to stay right here, fix everything up, and put it all out of his mind—that's what he'd do. He didn't like the police, anyway. But this isn't about liking them, is it?

An hour later, Sasha is sitting in the dimly lit reception area of the Luxemburg police station, waiting for the detective, who needs to send an urgent fax (who sends faxes nowadays?) before they can drive back to the cemetery. Or walk: it's not very far. The detective's surname is Grishchenko, his rank unknown, likely not very high. For now, Sasha observes Grishchenko at work, rummaging through a pile of papers: he's lost the document he needs to fax. That's a stupid way to do it, picking up random documents and throwing them right back where you found them; it would be better to lay the discarded ones to the side. How many documents does he have there? Say two hundred. Three seconds each, and you'll be done in ten minutes, tops. Otherwise, what's the probability of coming up empty-handed after two hundred random attempts? Let's think: one minus one, divided by n, close the bracket, to the power of n. What's the limit? Intuitively, one over e. Sasha works it out: yes, that's right, $1/e$, nearly 40 percent—fairly high.

Sasha perks up a bit, thanks in no small part to the success of his calculation, and he begins to scrutinize the detective. Sad sight: an ill-fitting uniform that looks like a hand-me-down, skin ruined by chickenpox (they always warn kids not to pick at the scabs, but this one didn't listen), and, on his upper lip, a semblance of a mustache. There, he found it! Only took him about twenty minutes. Grishchenko places the document in the machine and dials a number—but he forgot to take out the staples; the machine does it for him, ripping the paper. All he can do now is scrunch up the remains and toss them away—but he misses the basket on his first throw. A pained, defeated look settles on his face. He must have worn the same expression when he would find himself at the blackboard, listening to his classmates throw out suggestions: some were accurate, others deliberately false—he always chose the wrong option, and everyone would laugh. The school from which Sasha graduated didn't admit boys like Grishchenko, but there were plenty at the one near his home, which he'd attended up to fifth grade. They used to give him an awful time, though he'd always suggested the right answer.

Well, sir—Mr. Detective? What's the proper form of address these days?

"I'm not a detective, I'm an investigator," Grishchenko says plaintively.

Whatever he is, it's time to get down to business: a crime has taken place—the desecration of both his parents' graves, vandalism. While he sat there waiting, Sasha had time to look at the law code, so he now cites the relevant articles and requests to file a report.

The look of pain on the interrogator's face intensifies. Stammering a bit, Grishchenko asks Sasha to hold on just one more minute, leaves, comes back, performs a series of obviously meaningless actions, flips the lights on and off, then, out of the blue, offers him water. "No, thank you, I'm not thirsty." Sasha repeats that he'd like to file a report. To whom should he address it?

"You are a cultured person..." says Grishchenko.

Perhaps—but what does that have to do with anything? This: the desecration of a grave is news of not municipal, or even regional, but federal significance. It's nationwide news. You won't hide it from the journalists—they have their people everywhere.

"The newspapers will get hold of it and use it uh in the interests of..."

In whose interests might feces and a swastika be used? Apparently, as a cultured person, Sasha ought to know the answer. In any case, Grishchenko asks him to put off filing the report.

Grishchenko's choppy, muddled babbling does reveal an intriguing fact, though: the Luxemburg police are in trouble with the FSB. In the process of (difficult word) "counterterrorism" training, someone planted a plain, nondescript bag at the station. There were wires sticking out of it. The cops took one look and just tossed it out, without informing the proper authorities—but why should they have? It was obvious that the bag had been planted by FSB agents —"we haven't got any other terrorists around here" (Sasha will remember this unexpected wording)—and who's dying to talk to the FSB? Now all the stations have to write explanatory memos. Sasha

still feels wretched, but Grishchenko's story does cheer him up
a bit.

"Do you suspect anyone?" Grishchenko asks with a sigh.

Why the sighing? A perfectly normal question. No, he doesn't.

Grishchenko turns to the window.

"Looks like it's gonna rain. They said it'd be sunny." Poor Grishchenko—they'd tricked him again.

Sasha suddenly realizes that the rain will wash away the footprints—they have to drive back now, no time to waste. But there's
nothing to drive: one of the police cars is out on patrol, the other is
out to lunch. Sasha should go ahead, and Grishchenko will catch up.
He's working for three these days: one of his colleagues just quit and
two others are on vacation. "So for four, then?" He doesn't get it. At
this point the witlessness triggers no irritation, only sympathy. In
any case, Sasha has to hurry back to the cemetery—why did he even
bother going to the police?

It's already drizzling, so it's important to measure and photograph
everything before the earth turns to mud and the tracks are washed
away. Sasha examines the evidence, snapping photos of every dent in
the ground from every possible angle with his phone. It appears there
were two people involved, both of whom had huge feet: all the prints
are thirty-three centimeters in length, but they differ in width. A
doctor friend had once told Sasha that watching an autopsy is far
more unpleasant than poking around inside the body yourself, and
now, having inadvertently become a detective, Sasha keeps his mind
on performing his job as well as he can. He photographs the swastikas on the front and the back, as well as DETH TO YIDS—with and
without flash. What's to be done with the biological material? Photograph that too, then pick it up with a shovel, take it outside the
fence, and drop it: naive to hope that the police might search for
human DNA in feces.

Several times he walks back to the cemetery gates to see whether
Grishchenko has shown up. Sasha is soaking wet, hungry, but he still
has to go back home and print out the photos—can't very well take
these to a photo shop. Black-and-white will do. He'll also consider

creating a national news story himself, maybe even an international one. He could call the German journalist who's renting his apartment. *Ende gut, alles gut*—all's well that ends well. Readers are sure to get a kick out of it. But no, he can't allow this to reach the public. He wouldn't be able to keep it from Eva then. He hadn't thought about her all day, and even now he doesn't think about whether he ought to tell her. Fortunately, she isn't coming for another few days.

Later in the afternoon, Sasha returns to the police station and hands the photos to Grishchenko, who apologizes for never having made it to the cemetery: he got tied up at work. He praises the quality of the pictures: a scale is indicated on each page.

"Now I don't have to go…"

"Is that a question or a statement?"

Grishchenko nods obsequiously. He'll find the perpetrators (the "evildoers," in the police parlance), he promises. His chipper tone reminds Sasha of the lies people hear on their deathbeds.

"Maybe you suspect someone?"

No, Grishchenko has already asked. Possibly… But no, Mishura isn't tall. Neither he nor, especially, Mrs. Smoochkina could possibly have such large feet. What if they had on galoshes? But all this was too wild, too deranged an act for their sort. The old drunk—the one who'd stolen the rosebush? Impossible. Think of how carefully he'd extracted it from the ground. Sasha shakes his head: he has no enemies.

Grishchenko carefully examines a photo of Yakov Grigoryevich's marker, probably reconstructing the proper spelling of "death."

"So why do you think your plot was singled out for… uh…"

Sasha helps him: desecration. Probably because they couldn't find any other Jewish surnames in the vicinity. He fears, and anticipates, a foolish response (that some of Grishchenko's best friends were Jews, for instance), but the investigator takes it coolly and calmly: a case of Article 282—incitement of hatred or enmity on the basis of nationality. Then Grishchenko explains, in a perfectly humane way, that his own great-grandfather's name was Moisey, even though he came from a peasant family. His grandmother was bullied, called a Jewess, and even had to change her patronymic. Sasha feels the need to reassure Grishchenko, tell him that Russian sectarians often gave Old Testament names to their children, so his grandmother was bullied in vain.

Sasha has to admit, however, that the investigator has made a somewhat different impression on him this second time around—he seems less simpleminded. Maybe he'll really find them ... "Not something the cemetery alkies would do," Grishchenko says. Sasha had never heard of this category of citizens. "They grub around cemeteries—at Easter, especially, when people leave shots of vodka for their loved ones." Sasha hadn't known of this custom, either. "Probably one of the youths," Grishchenko offers. So how many people are there in Luxemburg between the ages of fifteen and thirty? Let's say a thousand. We can rule out females. Some of the young men are away—either serving in the army, or living in Moscow, or already locked up. The number of suspects shrinks to, say, two hundred. How many of these have the right shoe size? These are the thoughts that occupy Sasha as he makes his way home.

Yes, things were different after that road rage incident, with the fat hand in the window: he'd blown off some steam, cooled down, and driven on. It's cold, damp, almost dark. What should he do? In one of the psychiatric textbooks Sasha had translated there was a chapter on how to provide assistance to victims of rape: advise them not to clean up, not until they've been thoroughly examined and all possible evidence has been collected. But how can one fight this powerful, perfectly natural impulse? He gathers a rake, a flashlight, a sponge, soap, and a bucket and goes back to the cemetery. An hour later, order is restored: the ground is level, the stones clean—all traces of violence are wiped away.

My strength faileth me. Sasha is home now, sitting in the kitchen with the lights off and weeping bitterly. He hasn't cried this way since he was a little boy. "At all costs try to avoid granting yourself the status of the victim"—easy for Brodsky to say. Sasha washes his face, looks out into the yard. What's he waiting for: a storm, falling trees, howling dogs? For nature to react in some way to today's terrible, unimaginable event? There's no reaction. All is quiet. Luxemburg is asleep.

He doesn't feel like eating, but a drink wouldn't hurt. There's a bottle of Riga Black Balsam in the sideboard—it's been there for at least forty years. He takes it down, peels off the sealing wax, and, sip by sip, downs a full glass of its fairly strong, nasty, sticky-sweet contents. Then he climbs into bed, his heart pounding. He knows he ought to try to get some sleep, but he only manages to drift off briefly, toward morning. Another vivid dream: an unfamiliar, frightening old man—his brother, Yermolay—is noisily defecating on their mother's grave. Absolutely clear. Nothing to analyze.

4.

"A woman takes a man seriously only under the following circumstances: when he's puttering about with his car or with another woman," Yakov Grigoryevich used to joke. Like any gem of universal wisdom, this wasn't always true. Eva took Sasha's misadventures very seriously. She drove down without Philip and they walked for a long time, had dinner, and spent the night together. They didn't go to the cemetery: she didn't ask to go, and Sasha didn't offer. Nor did she speak about their plans, or cry, or express morbid pathos. She did, however, compliment his domestic achievements. In the morning she drove off. She was his wife, and they needed to find a way out of this situation together; she was sorry—sincerely so—that Luxemburg had not lived up to his hopes.

They had never officially divorced. Neither of them attached much importance to such formalities—and it turns out Philip was a Levant from birth. As for his hopes, it may be too soon to give up: a misfortune occurred, an accident, but if the culprits were found and properly, legally punished, then why cross out Luxemburg? (A choice of words, *cross*, but so be it.)

"Sasha, my dear, but your—what's his name, Nemchenko, Demchenko?—won't find any culprits. I bet he'll end up announcing that you made the whole thing up. Or, worse, that you went and did it yourself."

There's a good deal of absurdity and stupidity in the provinces("the idiocy of rural life," as the *Communist Manifesto* puts it), but it doesn't reach this degree. Why would he paint a swastika?

"Darling, why are you explaining yourself to me? Don't worry, they'll think of a reason. 'To destabilize the situation'—that's their go-to. You don't watch TV, but I do, every once in a while. Mom and Dad always have it on."

No need to continue. But one can't just leave it like this, either. Eva nods: No, one probably can't. Still, rape, in her opinion, is not an altogether accurate metaphor.

"Sometimes a car rolls over, lands back on its wheels, and drives on," she offers—but this seems more applicable to their relationship.

Sasha kisses her: Drive carefully. He's grateful to her—for coming to see him, for understanding, and for leaving, too.

The Internet reveals that a 33-centimeter print corresponds to a size 47 shoe. "Russian feet are generally a little wider in the ball, where the bones are, and higher in the arch—one might say, more fanned out": an interview with an Italian director of a shoe company (not a bad translation). And here are some statistics: only one in one hundred males has a shoe size of 47 or larger. What are the chances that two Luxemburgers wear that exact size? If he were to concentrate, he might figure it out, but he's finding it hard to think.

Sasha wanders around town, looking at people's feet. He even glanced at Svyatoslav's shoes when he came into the house to pick up a tool: they were big, no denying it. He's a little scared to go back to the cemetery. It would be good to install a camera, preferably one that works in the dark. Could they launch another attack? No, Grishchenko insists. Sasha sees him regularly, asks how the investigation is going.

"Some rock bands spell 'death' that way"—that's Grishchenko's latest discovery.

Sure. Conduct a search at the radio station. What's next? Might Grishchenko discover that the swastika is an ancient Hindu symbol for the sun, or luck, or whatever? Their conversations turn ugly: Sasha threatens to publish photos, while Grishchenko complains about his intolerable working conditions and stammers out stories that he's unlikely to have invented—he doesn't strike Sasha as a particularly imaginative fellow—but that often strain credulity.

For example, in one of the neighboring districts, some bigwig's son shot four people and tried to get rid of the bodies by burning them, was caught in the act, and now the investigators are getting calls from people in Moscow, who are asking them to put themselves in the young man's place: he made a mistake, got mixed up.

"What are you driving at?"

"Alexander Yakovlevich, in your case, there's no murder, not even a raping." That's how Grishchenko says it, "a raping."

One time he also says: "We've got to live here." Or maybe: "You've got to live here." So similar, those phrases, yet so different in meaning. Sasha will hear both multiple times, along with comments about destabilizing the situation: "We're reviewing various possibilities." Eva was right, as was Anatoly Vasilyevich—they'll never find who did it.

Sasha mows the lawn, rakes the clippings into a pile, and sets them on fire. Ash is the ideal fertilizer for a rosebush, and in the winter it's best to cover the roots with oak leaves: they don't rot, and they keep the soil warm. Knowledge of this sort used to give him pleasure, helping him feel connected to life (to "real life," as they say), but now the routine—trimming the lilacs, draining the outdoor pipes before winter, turning over the watering barrel, plugging the vents in the semi-basement—bring him nothing but dull pain: Why is he doing it, for whom? He's given up on German, too. But he needs something to occupy his days: all his life he's consumed alcohol only occasionally, in small quantities, and he has had only one bad habit—chess on the Internet, which he plays until he feels sick, as if he were gorging on potato chips or cotton candy.

It was Yakov Grigoryevich who had taught him to play, of course— who had showed him the moves. He himself had been especially good at checkers, and had even dreamed of becoming a master of the game and being sent to an international tournament, where he'd defect— but he never quite reached that level. When he was still a schoolboy,

Sasha had attended the Moscow State University chess club, solving problems, studying openings and endgames. He had witnessed the game between Karpov and Korchnoi, both contenders for the world title (Fischer was champion at the time). It was held at the Pillar Hall of the House of Unions, and Sasha was one of the few people there rooting for Korchnoi, who was older and kept losing—one could sense he was on the verge of a breakdown. Just as, in the words of one of his school friends, the life experience you gained in the Soviet Union prepared you only for life in the Soviet Union, so too does chess teach you nothing but how to be better at chess: if you seriously devote yourself to the game, you'll never become a mathematician, a poet, or, least of all, a sensible human being—though you might increase your willpower. Fischer, for instance, had all his crowns and fillings removed, believing that Jewish dentists had installed listening devices in his mouth—a total nutjob, but you can't deny that he had the courage of his convictions.

One time, when Sasha was in tenth grade, Botvinnik came to their school. "Mikhail Moiseyevich," someone had asked him, "how do you feel about what Korchnoi did?" (What Korchnoi had done was to realize Yakov Grigoryevich's dream: he'd defected.) The grand master replied, "I feel the same as you do," and the boys—a number of them, but a large number—applauded for a long time. Later, during the simultaneous exhibition, Sasha almost played Botvinnik to a draw.

In short, Sasha had a gift for the game, could have taken it further, but instead, here he is: lying on his big bed or sitting at the table, playing speed chess for days on end against opponents from all over the world—there are tens of thousands, possibly hundreds of thousands of them on the web.

Time control: three minutes, five max. Each player suspects the other of dishonesty, of using software that's far more capable than Fischer ever was. Opponents are chosen at random, according to one's rating, and Sasha's is quite high, over 1,900. His first challenger is from Libya, the next from Albania—what's going on over there? Sasha would gladly enter into dialogue with each of them, but that's just not done. Only Ukrainians, when they see a Russian flag next to his name, sometimes write: "I don't play with occupiers." What can he say? Sasha is firmly against what the state is carrying out in his name, but has he done anything about it, besides burying himself in his private life? A "good German"—that's what they call his kind in English.

When Western Europeans and Americans find themselves in a losing position, they usually surrender right away, though some play on to the bitter end, with a bare king—very unsportsmanlike. Worse are the Arabs, Indians, and Greeks, especially those with lower ratings: they come up with all sorts of tricks. But again, if we accept that only individuals can bear responsibility, it's best not to think in terms of national character.

Sasha is in the kitchen, partly dressed, sitting in front of a plate of half-eaten eggs, a cup of cold tea, and, on the screen, an opponent from Syria. Sasha plays White. The pieces zip across the board. Damn, the Syrian got disconnected: in thirty seconds he'll have a loss on his record. Let's break off the game, then, since the fellow's position isn't so bad. The Levant, by the way—that's Syria, Canaan. He's back, writes, "thx," and offers to add Sasha as a "friend." Is he in a trench or something? "No (smiley face), in Germany. Again?" Sasha makes a wish: if he wins, the police will find those who did it. He loses. Two out of three?

When he gets a call from Eva, he responds to her questions monosyllabically and she hears the clicks that accompany each move. He promises to call her back, but forgets, and she feels hurt. She hates his habit, and Sasha himself would be glad to kick it, but how else can he fill the void? "You don't even find pleasure in the game, just oblivion," she says. "There has to be a way out of this situation—it's abnormal, pathological." The way out is to find them. "Enough already, it's been a month, they'll never find them," she says, losing her patience.

Grishchenko also grows impatient when Sasha pesters him with questions: Has he examined the graffiti around town? Talked to the principal at the school, the teachers? Looked for people with large feet? Monitored the social-media chatter?

Does Sasha really have nothing better to do than to bother him?
"And what would you do in my place?" Sasha asks.

"Me?" Grishchenko stares straight ahead, thinking. "I'd go to
Israel." It comes out quietly, without malice. Plain and simple: What,
you've got a homeland, Alexander Yakovlevich, might as well . . .

Coincidentally, the same thought occurs to Eva. "Great minds
think alike"—what's the French phrase?

Eva doesn't go in for jokes:

"There are agencies out there that can help you put together the
documents, fill out the forms—all very quick, no red tape—get the
Absorption Basket." My, what fancy terms. "And if you don't like it,
you can just come back," she continues. "A lot of people do it." Nobody's going to take Luxemburg or his precious Moscow apartment
away from him. Yes, Eva knows that Sasha doesn't like arguments
that rest on what "a lot of people" do, never mind "everyone."

Emigration is too serious a step.

"So, take it seriously! Please. And stop with the goddamned chess!"
She hears the hated clicks again.

He feels sorry for Eva. She has it tough over in Chertanovo, raising Philip in an apartment with five other people: her parents, sister,
and two nephews. Though she says it's OK, even cheerful. He'll look
into those agencies, see what the options are.

The weather is clear, no precipitation expected. Sasha is sitting out
in the yard, breathing the cool air and trying to concentrate. For a
start, he should try to wake up: he's still half asleep, can't shake his
drowsiness. It isn't emigration, she says, it's repatriation, a return to
his homeland. A paradox of material implication—that's what they
call it in classical logic. All consequents stemming from a false ante-
cedent are true: "If two plus two is five, then snow is white"—correct,
but so is "snow is red." If Israel is his homeland, then . . . what?

Reflections of this kind don't help him to wake up, they only drive
him deeper into the realm of dreams—someone else's dreams. Over
the past few days his chess rating has fallen to 1,700. People ("a lot of
people," in Eva's words) make decisions in something less than the
full bloom of rationality. His whole life, Sasha has tried to avoid do-

ing that, but now, instead of waking up, he submits himself to dream logic and searches the web for the phone numbers of various agencies, rummages through his documents, calls. As it turns out, he can arrange almost every detail of his departure without getting up from the computer.

The man who handles these things is named Zvi ("Grisha, in Russian"). He has a quiet, friendly voice, and though Sasha asks him the same questions over and over again, he remains absolutely calm: Why get irritated with a person who's only now understood that it was time to leave? Will he and his spouse need help filling out the applications? No, he and Eva know how to write. Then all Sasha has to do is gather up the documents that testify to his Jewishness and then, as they say, it's full speed ahead. Grisha will help with the logistics: transportation, insurance, one-way tickets, and so on.

"Will my old Soviet passport do? It says 'Alexander Yakovlevich Levant, Jew.'"

"The consul will be glad to see the passport, but he'll need the birth certificate."

Sasha only has the adoption papers. He explains that he can look for the birth certificate, but it's unlikely to please the consul.

"I see... Well, unfortunately, according to the laws of Israel, you aren't Jewish."

Sasha sighs—almost with relief.

"Wait, it's too soon to give up," says Grisha. "Let's poke around on the other side. People make unexpected discoveries, and one grandmother is all you need."

Come to think of it, Eva did mention a relative with a surname ending in "-ich," who managed to get registered as a Belarusian.

"You see?" Grisha says. "Just do a little digging." He'll also try to talk to people close to the consul about Sasha: it's an unusual case, which may spark the consul's interest. Some luck he had—while Grisha, in Soviet times, was registered as Russian, although his surname is Malkin. A nice, amiable chat.

Sasha is scrolling though some points of advice for emigrants, gathering up his courage to speak with Eva, when he suddenly comes across the following warning: "Faithful Christians need not bother. They are immediately sent away with no right to reapply. Israel has no need for such 'Jews.'" Oh no, that can't be … And even if it is true, why be so rude about it?

"No one's going to stick needles under your fingernails, Alexander," Grisha-Zvi says, as unperturbed as ever. "Tell them you're an atheist. We've all done our time in the Communist Youth, haven't we?"

Actually, no. Sasha wakes up, comes back to life: Eva, we're not going to Israel. It doesn't matter what kind of Christian he is. A very bad one, pitiful. Nevertheless. And he'll find them a place to live. In Moscow. They'll evict the German. Sure, it would be undignified, embarrassing, and the newspaper paid in advance, but the decision is made: if the police manage to find the criminals, then their family would live in Luxemburg, if not, then in Moscow. As Peeperkorn said in *The Magic Mountain*, agreed and settled.

As it happens, they wouldn't have to offend the German. This was done for them, by what are now called "specially trained individuals" (a repulsive turn of phrase). At the end of November, Sasha receives a letter: his tenant, Martin, informs him of his imminent departure— he must leave the country within five days. A correspondence unfolds: the reason for his expulsion, Martin thinks, is a series of articles about the church, in part covering the case of the "sagacious elder," Father Pavel (one of the most effective operations the KGB ever launched within the Russian Orthodox Church), but the straw that broke the fairly fragile back of the authorities' tolerance was his piece on a seemingly innocent topic—the "methodological movement" and its influence on the Kremlin. The article carried an epigraph from Dostoyevsky's *The Possessed*: "Starting from unlimited freedom, I arrive at unlimited despotism." The official pretext for the expulsion is a violation of immigration laws. There's no point in even trying to appeal the court's ruling, and so, dear Sasha, writes Martin, please do come to pick up the keys the day after tomorrow, and while you're here, attend a friendly party in honor of Martin's departure and the closing of the correspondent office. Sasha's place suited Martin very well—it's a pity he couldn't stay longer.

The question is resolved. Farewell, Luxemburg. Let's not deceive ourselves: the experiment failed. From now on we'll come here as so many others do, in the summer months, to get some fresh air, pick berries and mushrooms, discuss the merits and deficiencies of the hired help, and admire the scenery. Sasha loads up his backpack with all the necessities (his clothes, the computer), cleans and prepares the house for the winter (shutting off the water and gas), and now here he is, walking with Eva from the Kurskaya station. They're heading toward the apartment where he was born—where, it appears, they'll spend however many years they're fated to spend there. Here's Yakovoapostolsky Lane, and here's his native Lyalin Lane. In his youth, Yakovoapostolsky was called Yelizarova Street, after Anna Ilyinichna Yelizarova, Lenin's elder sister, who had tried unsuccessfully to share documents establishing their family's Jewish roots with the public. These roots, Sasha tells Eva, weren't especially strong (one grandfather, named Blank), yet they'd be enough to secure Ilyich's emigration— that is, repatriation—to Israel.

The party's in full swing. Martin is a tall blond Berliner with a slightly childlike face. His plane takes off at six fifteen in the morning. He's grown attached to Moscow over the course of his assignment, feels at home here. Sasha is sorry that things ended this way, and he himself, as Martin understands, is no fan of . . . An eternal question: To what extent are we responsible for the actions of our government? Martin shrugs: as a German, he's familiar with the problem.

Sasha walks through the apartment. Everything seems to be where he left it, but the place looks lighter, more spacious: some of the furniture is in storage and the pictures on the walls are less densely crowded—the family photos have been taken down. He recognizes and at the same time does not recognize the home in which he's spent his entire life, with the exception of the last year and a half. Whatever the apartment had been, comfortable wasn't it, but now it feels comfortable, *gemütlich*—Sasha likes it.

A tall, skinny woman approaches them and takes Martin by the hand: Will they just go on standing there in the hallway, then? She praises Sasha's German: comfort—*Gemütlichkeit*—is the most important concept to grasp if one wishes to understand the Germanic spirit, which is in essence a bourgeois, burgherish one. The woman's name is Edyta and she works at the German embassy. She's a devotee of Dostoyevsky, Shostakovich, all that terrifyingly Russian stuff, and is pretty far left: It was she who'd suggested the epigraph from *The Possessed*, says Martin—but it's time to get back to the guests. An assortment of foreign correspondents—European, American—and several diplomats have come to bid him farewell. They're gathered in the big room, where Sasha's mother had lived.

Eva is perfectly at ease among these strangers—she misses socializing. Her cheeks and forehead are rosy from the wine. There are a few women here, but Eva is more beautiful than all of them. An elderly diplomat from Austria—a rotund, crimson-faced fellow—is speaking about a certain eminent individual best known for calling journalists morons.

"He's clever," says the Austrian, "subtle, perceptive, but he has no control over policy."

"So he's a cynic," someone retorts.

"We diplomats are all alcoholics or cynics."

The other guests laugh, and one of them says, "Clearly, thou hath chosen that good part."

The old fellow laughs too: "One doesn't preclude the other. The two qualities often go hand in hand." He tops off his and Eva's glasses.

They drink to Martin's health and wish him success back home:

"Home is the place where, when you have to go there, they have to take you in," Edyta says, quoting Frost. She's the only person in attendance who seems truly sad.

Exactly at midnight everyone leaves—except for Edyta and Martin, who try to help clean up, despite Eva's objections and the fact that Edyta can barely stand upright. Eva and Sasha finally manage to expel them from the kitchen, and another half hour later a car pulls up at the entrance.

"Alone at last," Sasha says, having seen Martin off, and he embraces Eva, pressing her close.

"Shh…" Eva whispers, moving away from him.

In the big room, with both feet on the coffee table (one stocking torn), Edyta is sleeping. Not sleeping—only dozing. Give her fifteen minutes and she'll be good to go: Could Sasha and Eva make her some strong coffee and call a cab?

"Your problem," she says, without taking her feet off the table, "is that no era ever ends around here. One of my German friends said that—she's lived here many years."

Interesting. Sasha would like to go on discussing this idea—he misses conversations on abstract topics—but Eva interrupts him. Seeing as Edyta works at the embassy, Eva takes the opportunity to ask her a burning question: Can she, Sasha, and the little one immigrate to Germany on the basis of Jewish descent—and if so, what proof will the Germans need? Will the nationality field in Sasha's Soviet passport suffice?

Really, Eva dear, so inappropriate … Nevertheless, Sasha digs the old passport out of his backpack.

"Any proof of origin will do," Edyta responds indifferently. "Especially this. History has been teaching us a thing or two."

She's more sober than she seems, and her Russian is superb—just an occasional error in tense:

"The number of people who are wishing to leave the country has quadrupled over the past few years. 'For the sake of the children,' as you all put it," she says, ironically or not—impossible to tell. The queue is long, but Edyta will see what she can do. She asks for Sasha's number.

It's the middle of the night. Sasha and Eva are lying on a narrow couch for two, holding each other. They've spent many happy and unhappy nights on this couch.

"Maybe that's the solution? Germany?" Eva asks him.

And what's he going to do there, become an electrician?

"Live, for one thing," says Eva. "A long happy life." Casual, semi-inebriated pillow talk.

"In order to live, one has to exist. And I don't feel that I do."

What does he mean, she asks—here he is, in the flesh: healthy, bright, knows several languages. She laughs: he even knows how to add fractions.

5.

Tá ta-ta-tá tá-ta—right? Or is it: *ta-tá ta-tá tá*? *Home is the place where…* Those damned diphthongs—how many syllables, one or two? Sasha had never tried to translate poetry before. It's so infernally difficult to fit the simplest words, placed in the most natural order, into a metrical line while retaining the rhyme and that double "have to." The problem is more interesting than any someone might encounter at a math tournament, if for no reason other than the fact that it has no single right solution. Eva has gone to Chertanovo to get Philip and gather their things, while Sasha lies around on the couch, assembling words.

He hears a noise. Back home in Luxemburg, Sasha had come to recognize every sound: the neighbor sliding his car into the garage or cursing out his bees; the attic window flying open and clapping against the frame; the snow falling from the roof. Now he would have to get used to a flood of indeterminable sounds, to the chaos of urban life. There's that noise again: it's his phone vibrating on the floor.

"Alexander Yakovlevich, I tell you, it's harder to reach you than the Kremlin."

"Who is this?"

"Grishchenko. Didn't recognize me?"

The voice is deep, weighty. Sasha senses it: they've found who did it.

"Alexander Yakovlevich, I think you deserve a commendation from the Ministry of Internal Affairs." Sasha hears another man laughing; Grishchenko isn't alone. "You've helped expose a cell of extremists."

"Really?" Sasha's mouth is dry and his tongue is heavy. "You've really got them?"

"Yes, got them both. What's so surprising about that? We have a good clearance rate. Stop by the station after lunch." Dial tone.

Stop by—easy for him to say. Within fifteen minutes, Sasha is in a taxi. He looks himself over: unshaven, wearing yesterday's rumpled clothes—doesn't matter. He texts Eva: "found them," with three exclamation marks. She replies: "congrats." A restrained reaction: she'd been counting on Sasha's help today, and she doesn't like his suggestion that they delay the move to Lyalin Lane a bit. She also thinks the police can handle this perfectly well without him.

"But I haven't given my statement."

"Ah, yes, all right. Has Edyta called, by the way?"

No—but why would they need Edyta now? Everything's working out fine.

The cab arrives quickly. Less than three hours later, he's in Grishchenko's office.

"Please be seated, good sir."

On the other side of the desk from Sasha is a person completely transformed: his handshake is firm, his speech is smooth, and even his uniform fits him better. His mustache shines and bristles. No, this isn't Grishchenko, the lowly investigator—it's the brilliant detective Hercule Poirot.

What was that he said over the phone—a criminal cell?

"Grishchenko was joking," says a man sitting in a dark corner behind Sasha's back. Sasha hadn't noticed him when he'd come in.

Grishchenko introduces them:

"That's Mishukov, a lawyer—he defends the rights of detainees." Then, to Mishukov: "I was joking, was I? And if we send a task force over to their place, what do you suppose we'd find? Flyers? Weapons? Ammunition? I'm not talking about planting stuff, either—I mean on the up-and-up."

"Without 'planting stuff,' you'd find empty bottles of cheap beer," Mishukov replies with an air of distaste. "Klinskoye, maybe Arsenal Strong."

Sasha takes a closer look at the lawyer: a short, plump man in his forties, with a pointy nose, a low forehead, and slicked-back dark hair. He could play a pimp in the movies.

"Besides, you don't have a task force," Mishukov adds.

Mishukov and Grishchenko might have been classmates. And maybe Mishukov was one of the ones who had deliberately offered the wrong answers when Grishchenko was at the blackboard.

The latter rattles off article numbers:

"Article 214—vandalism. Article 282—incitement of hatred or enmity on the basis of nationality. Article 244—desecration of burial places." He's obviously done his homework. "Alexander Yakovlevich, did your parents take part in the struggle against fascism?"

"Yes, my mother even received the Order of the Red Banner."

"Oh," Grishchenko exclaims, "Part 2! Up to five years!"

Mishukov twists his lips:

"Two at the most. For incitement it's two at the most."

"Did your father receive any medals?"

No, Yakov Grigoryevich had no medals. Was Sasha imagining it, or did Mishukov really mutter: "The First Tashkent Front"? No one in his family was evacuated during the war. But that's what a lawyer is supposed to do: issue provocations, inspire antipathy—like in *Judgment at Nuremberg*. Sasha's reservoir of patience is still quite deep. He asks for details: How were they found?

"In the course of the ongoing investigation," begins Grishchenko, but Mishukov interrupts him:

"They were taking a shit in a driveway."

Both of them? At the same time?

"A neighbor called the police. They took a huge dump and drew a swastika on the wall."

"We will subject the handwriting to analysis," Grishchenko says, undeterred.

"What analysis? They've signed an honest confession. Petrakov has," Mishukov interrupts him again, then turns to Sasha: "Would you like to meet our guests?"

What—they're here? Grishchenko and Mishukov laugh: Where else would they be? Sure, back there, in the cooler.

"You can deck 'em if you want, Alexander Yakovlevich. We wouldn't stop you." Sasha doesn't understand Grishchenko's proposal. "I mean punch them, with your fist—like this. Or with your elbow, if you want. Or kick them. Just not in the face."

"Be careful, Grishchenko—it's bad luck to demonstrate on yourself." Mishukov clears the way. "After you, gentlemen."

Behind grimy white bars, on a wooden bench facing the door, sit two lanky, miserable-looking young men with huge limbs and disproportionately small heads. Their feet, encased in huge boots, nearly reach the bars. They stare at Sasha. No, he's never seen them before. He looks away.

"On your feet, Petrakov!" Grischenko commands and kicks the first—the one closest to the entrance—in the shin. "Morons!" he shouts. "Went and shit on the grave of a Red Banner recipient!"

One of the detainees jumps up from the bench, while the other falls to the ground from the force of the blow. Grishchenko approaches the second, who's groaning in pain, and knocks one of his boots off with a kick, then pushes it toward Sasha.

"As you requested, Alexander Yakovlevich—size 47."

"Stop it! Just stop!" Sasha hadn't known he was capable of taking such a decisive tone.

For a moment no one speaks or moves a muscle. Mishukov is the first to come to his senses.

"Things are heating up, eh?" he announces. "Ready to sign the confession?" Mishukov asks the young man on the floor, then sits down on the bench and leans forward. "What? No, buddy, them's the breaks—you can't unfry an egg."

Sasha needs air. He goes out to the yard—if he only knew how to smoke, he'd gladly light up. But he isn't alone for long. Mishukov comes out too—to take a break, stretch his legs. He complains about how stuffy it is inside, then sweeps his hand around the snowless yard:

"Pretty as a picture . . . Eight degrees. End of November, right?"

"Listen," Sasha tells him. "I'm the victim of a crime and you're a lawyer for the accused. Regardless of how conscientiously you plan on doing your job, let's not discuss other topics."

Suddenly—Sasha doesn't even understand where she could have come from—a woman wearing a black headscarf falls at his feet. He bends down to help her up.

"Father, dear father, don't do them in!" the woman shouts and wails, frantically crossing herself and trying to hand him money: "Here, buy yourself some candy!"

Sasha finds this impossible to endure. Sheer bacchanalia, straight out of Dostoyevsky. "I don't need your money."

"Everybody needs money," she tells him.

"Use it to hire a good lawyer," he says, still trying to pull the woman to her feet.

Mishukov drives her away with a barrage of foul words, and she huddles in the corner of the yard, continuing her hysteria from a distance.

"It was Volodya who put him up to all that nonsense, knocking around the cemetery at night," she says, and then: "I know where you live, you bastard!"

"The classic formula is request-threat-bribe. Petrakova has the last part ass-backward. She's a familiar sight around here," Mishukov explains. "Worked as a matron up at the hospital. Swiped some linens—what else was there to steal? Single mother. Judge took pity and gave her probation."

They return to Grishchenko's office.

"Would you like some water, Alexander Yakovlevich?"

Yes, water. Sasha turns the glass in his hand, gathers his thoughts.

"I don't know which is harder, for you to hear this or for me to say it..." No, that's not right. "I had hoped against hope that the offenders would be apprehended, but now..."

So? Is he ready to give a statement?

"To confine them to our prison system..."

Mishukov breaks into a smile:

"Which prison system would you prefer? The Dutch?"

"Uh..." Grischenko grunts and appears to wilt, to become his former self.

Mishukov comes to his comrade's aid:

"Alexander Yakovlevich, the guilt of the detainees is established not by you, by me, nor by the police, but by the court alone." Grishchenko nods to the rhythm of his smooth-flowing speech. "The only thing that is asked of you is to write what you saw at the burial place of your parents"—he looks at the photos—"dear Yakov Grigoryevich and dear Maria Ilyinichna, on what day at which hour. If you wish, you can note that you incurred extreme hedonic damages and declare a claim for reimbursement—in any amount you deem fair. After that, it's up to the court." Mishukov smiles again, broadly.

Sasha finds the strength to smile in response:

"Under normal circumstances, that's exactly what would have happened." He gets up: it's time for him to go.

"Make sure to mention the Order of the Red Banner!" Grishchenko shouts at his back.

When he reaches the main entrance at the end of the corridor, Sasha cautiously cracks the door open and peers out. There's a person out there, but, in the dusk, it's impossible to tell whether it's Petrakova or some other woman. He doesn't want anyone falling at his feet again—better wait. He stays in the half-darkened corridor, breathing quietly, listening closely to every footstep, trying to make out every voice.

"Why the fuck did we even call the clown down here?" Mishukov asks.

"All that running around, and now we'll probably have to charge them with petty hooliganism," Grishchenko says with a sigh.

"Don't piss your pants just yet," Mishukov tells him. "We've got the photos. You can dial up Gulin and take his statement."

Silence. Grishchenko must be considering the idea.

"Where did he come from, this . . . Lohengrin?"

Lohengrin? Sasha might have misheard. He jerks open the door and, concealing his face, hurriedly crosses the yard to the street.

"Laws are like sausages. It's better not to see them being made"—Churchill, Bismarck? A low, repellent truism, worthy of Mishukov.

Sasha enters his house. It's chilly. In twenty-four hours without heating, the house has gone completely cold. And it smells of mice—

one would expect that in the winter, but as long as he lived here, he never noticed the smell. He hasn't even been gone two days, yet the house feels strange, foreign, though he knows every object in it by heart.

Calls, calls, calls—from Eva, from numbers he doesn't recognize: Grishchenko, Gulin, Edyta? Best to turn off the phone.

He sits down at the table and pulls out a stack of paper. He hasn't written anything by hand in a long time. Beyond the window is darkness. Sasha feels no hunger, no pain, nothing.

"*Statement.*"

Sasha smiles, recalling the clerk at the publishing house—a young woman who began every letter with the word "*Letter.*"

He crumples up the paper, takes out another.

"*In the beginning, the rose disappeared ...*"

POSTSCRIPT

If his number hadn't been in my phone, I might not have recognized Sasha's voice, though I was just about to call him myself. I had news for him—really good news. Great news, even. And here he was, inviting me to go out and "get a beer."

To get a beer—a strange proposal, coming from him. In American films it can connote anxiety, mental discord. He says he didn't know how long he'd be in Moscow, that he might have to go soon.

"Back home to Luxemburg?"

"Not clear yet. Maybe to Germany"—all this in a washed-out, colorless voice.

Preparing to meet our German fascist brethren, eh? Anyone who considers himself a Jew has no business going to Germany. And besides, drinking beer isn't a required skill, even for them. I'm not too fond of the stuff, by the way: a senseless drink, beer—doesn't get you drunk, like vodka or cognac, just dulls your mind.

"But OK," I told him. "I know a place on Tatarskaya. Belgian beer on draft, good food—decent portions at reasonable prices, by Moscow standards." I gave him the address.

"I can take the tram, I think," Sasha said.

Yes, Sasha, dear boy—you can take the tram.

Sasha's tone put me on alert, as did the odd beer proposal, but it was the comment about Germany that worried me most. As long as I've known him, Sasha has been opposed to emigration. My hope was that he hadn't decided to harm himself—an undignified gesture toward everyone you leave behind, like saying, "I know how this one ends, but you all keep watching." Incidentally, we've got the third-highest suicide rate in the world, especially among the rural population—and this despite decrees from you-know-who, which force us doctors to fudge the numbers.

The news I had for Sasha was truly fabulous. Natasha (my aunt Natalya Israelevna, my dad's sister) is a well-known ob-gyn, who almost had a job in the maternity ward where Sasha was born—in any case, she could easily give them a call: although she's ninety now, her name still carries weight in professional circles. In fact, I suspect I only got into med school because she pulled a few strings—it certainly wasn't thanks to my grasp of biology and chemistry, which, let's be honest, was pretty lousy—but she's never fessed up. But enough about that. Sasha's mother, of course, gave birth in the Kremlin Hospital, as it was then called, in the maternity ward of the Fourth Chief Directorate of the Soviet Ministry of Health; now it's the Central Clinical Hospital of the Presidential Administration of the Russian Federation. They kept trying to transfer Aunt Natasha over there—which says a lot about her level of expertise, considering the "Israelevna" in her name—but we in the family will never forget her famous response: "I am used to treating the proletariat." That sure shut them up.

Anyway, I told her about the fetus papyraceus: What rotten luck, right? Fate, destiny. Then I forgot all about it—but Aunt Natasha remembered, the clever old girl. Suddenly she rings me up and says, "You can tell your friend that his Greek tragedy is canceled." They couldn't dig up the full birth record, of course, but they did find an entry for the event: "Maria Ilyinichna Guseva, elderly primigravida. Term delivery, no complications." No fetuses flattened against the wall—none of that, likely, happened. (In telling Sasha, I drop the "likely.") "Midwives," Aunt Natasha had added, "like to run their mouths. You can't do anything about that."

"What does 'elderly primigravida' mean?" Sasha asks. "Never mind, I get it."

Yes, a first-time mother is old at thirty, elderly at thirty-five. Now they say "mature," in the spirit of tolerance, sensitivity, etc., so as not to traumatize anyone.

Sasha turns the glass of beer in his hand and says, "So I never had a brother either." Then he pushes aside the menu. "I'll have whatever you're having."

Frankly, I had expected a more emotional reaction.

In the two years that we hadn't seen each other, Sasha hasn't exactly declined, no, but he seems to have faded somehow, dimmed. He's no longer in his prime. I mean, I'm sure I haven't grown any younger myself—plenty of booze and nothing to lose (sorry, couldn't resist the rhyme)—but I'd always thought of Sasha, whatever his condition, as more rational and responsible, and I still do.

"Getting a beer" is a euphemism for having a talk. The waiter brings our food and I dig in, while Sasha starts his tale. Turns out Luxemburg, as one might have expected, was no *jardin d'Éden*.

For me, the desecration of graves is, as it were, a familiar plot—and so is the subsequent desire to flee. I remember the state my dad and Aunt Natasha were in that time they came back from Malakhovka, where they'd seen approximately what Sasha had discovered in Luxemburg, only on a far larger scale: half the Jewish cemetery had been wrecked. "That's it!" Dad declared. "We're getting the hell out of here!" Poor Aunt Natasha arranged for an immigration invitation from Israel, which nearly ended her career, but Dad never followed through, and neither did the rest of us. This was back in the '70s. I had just done the deed for the first time, with an actress who was much older, and I felt it would have been unthinkably cruel to aban-

don her (what a dope—as if I were her one and only). Now Dad is in
that same cemetery in Malakhovka. "God rest his soul," I'd add, if I
believed in any god even a tiny bit.

I find it difficult to say whether life would have been better for us
in emigration—whether there would have been any kind of life at
all. As for Sasha, if I knew what he wanted, I could give him some
sort of advice, one way or another. Jewish graves get desecrated all
over the place. Take France, for instance...

He nods.

"If it happens in France..."

And what, I sometimes ask myself, keeps me here? The force of
habit? Inertia? Not just that. It's a matter of mutual understanding—of small details, brief glances, indirect remarks. I call over the
waiter: "Young man, can I smoke on the patio? It's too cold in the
street."

The waiter looks at me for a while:

"Not officially."

See, Sasha? That's what I mean.

Sasha nods:

"Sometimes it's better not to understand."

Now, as to the evildoers, it's a miracle that they found them in the
first place. I, of course, would lock them up and throw away the key:
if all those laws about blasphemy, incitement, etc., apply to anyone,
it's to them.

"So it's off to prison for a swastika, but what about Stalin on the
Tsinandali?"

Tsinandali? I don't get it. Has he written a statement?

"Written one? Yes..." An ambiguous answer.

Sasha asks whether there's any hope, even the slightest, of reha-
bilitation in prison. What does he think? If you beat a person's head
with a stick for several years in a row, would you expect that person
to grow wiser? We can guess what it's like in there. They'd been
preparing us for the camps ever since we were kids—and I don't mean
summer camps, either. Of course, even those were a dry run for
concentration camps. That's why I went to med school—"a doctor is

a doctor even in prison," as they used to say. And also in wartime. That's what they were preparing us for: prison and war.

"Good for them," the young waiter says, bringing me another beer.

I'm taken aback and fall silent for a moment—in which time the waiter, who's either drunk or simply loose-lipped, walks away. His impudent quip seems to have slipped right past Sasha's ears.

"I'd just like to know what they make of themselves, what goes on in their heads."

Honestly, nothing much. Difficult childhoods? Sure, probably. I've seen my share of their kind, and not only at Kashchenko. We're used to feeling guilty before the slower-witted, the uneducated, but there has to be a limit.

"When they watch movies, do they sympathize with the positive heroes, or with characters more like them?"

No, in the movies they sympathize with the heroes, like they're supposed to. That, dear boy, is what makes the movies the movies.

"What about the Jewish characters? Pharmacists? Violinists?"

Not so much, Sasha, not so much. There, I've managed to cheer him up a bit.

And what sort of piss-poor anti-Semites are they, really? Amateurs... Aunt Natasha was a nurse at the front. One time they brought in a wounded soldier with one foot—hell, two feet—in the grave. But still conscious. She was all ready to start a blood transfusion—one needle in his arm, one in hers—when he starts to howl: "Get that Yid bitch away from me! I'd rather croak than have one drop of Yid blood in my veins!"

"Did he die?"

Well, yeah. As for the freaks in Luxemburg, if Sasha's itching to show mercy, he can forgive them, on the condition that they ask for forgiveness. Only they still won't learn—won't understand a damn thing.

Out of the blue, Sasha asks:

"Do you play chess?"

I know the moves, but no more than that. A game with me would bore him silly.

"In a bad position, there are no good moves, which is why it's bad."
A maxim, it appears, that lurks in the hearts of chess players. "Yet
you have to make a move," Sasha continues. "The clock is ticking.
You could also admit defeat. But it's too soon for that: a lot of pieces
still on the board."

I ask a rather awkward question: Is Sasha depressed?

"What does 'depressed' mean? And which one of us is the psychiatrist?"

Without going into professional designations (psychiatry is a
bunch of blank spots—its track record is pitiful when compared to
other therapeutic disciplines), I need to establish whether Sasha can
benefit from medication. I wouldn't want to prescribe them just like
that. I ask about his sleep habits, his appetite, whether he feels suicidal
or has any unpaid debts. In the end I still can't decide whether to give
him something or to talk it out. But what can I say? It's easy to have
such a talk with people of a lower caliber, but I look up to Sasha.

He takes out his phone and starts scrolling through his photos.

"Have a look at this—from the Luxemburg bus station."

A sheet of instructions of how to behave if you're captured by
terrorists. Blurry, but I can make it out. Point one: "*Get hold of yourself.*"

"Funny, isn't it? Just get hold of yourself." Now he's gloomy again.

We chat about this and that. For no apparent reason, I begin to
complain about Freud: that bastard delayed the development of our
field for decades, and he still keeps us back. He should have written
novels, if he was so damned observant. Now you just try clearing away
that rubbish—slips, dreams, the unconscious—when bimbos of every
gender have grown so attached to it. Why did I lay into Freud like
that? It's ridiculous and tactless to lament how difficult my job is.
There you have it: the effect of beer on the organism.

I go to relieve myself and when I come back, I see a folder of antediluvian vintage on my side of the table. What is this?

Sasha chuckles:

"Fetus papyraceus number two. Look through it, when the spirit
moves you. It should help you make your diagnosis."

I hate to diagnose an old friend: Could Sasha really be in the grips of graphomania? Nothing to be done. I shove the folder into my briefcase.

A waitress comes to clear the table. Sasha hasn't touched his beer or eaten much. She asks:

"Will you be eating the rest?"

I guess they encourage the staff to adopt a rude Soviet manner—part of the charm of the establishment. We shouldn't have come here. And then I too put my foot in it:

"Sash', buck up. What happened isn't so terrible—nothing that can't be fixed." Then, trying to make up for that foolish comment, I come out with another: "It's just that, like I said, no prophet is accepted in his own country."

Sasha raises his eyes—I'd never noticed how green they are:

"So it was *you* who said that?" And then adds, as an aside: "Except there's no country, and no end of prophets."

That's the side of Sasha I love. Although I love all his sides.

He asks for the bill: the beer will have to stay, but he'll take sausages and other snacks home with him. We promise to meet up more often, though we know it's unlikely. In the end I make him swear to keep me abreast of all the latest developments, external and internal, wherever he finds himself—Moscow, Luxemburg, Germany—and walk him to the tram. We stand at the stop for a long time, freezing, not speaking—each in his own head now. Then I make my way through courtyards back to Pyatnitskaya: not a person in sight, the roadway narrow, the sidewalks impossibly wide. And the frigging bike paths—for whom? It's winter from November till March. Whatever—we'll get over the paths.

In the subway car I take out Sasha's folder and examine it closely: old, with snap buttons, and made of cracked leather—leatherette, more likely. And it smells of something forgotten, prehistoric, like regional libraries back in the day. *USSR State Planning Committee*—I'll be damned... Imagine the orders, reports, denunciations it must have held. Photos: I look them over and nearly drop them to the floor. "DETH TO YIDS," I catch in passing. Some girl sitting next to me snorts and sniffs. I stare at her attentively—stupid-looking, all done up. She turns and scoots away a little. A desecrated grave, footprints, shit, and—black on white—a swastika.

"*In the beginning, the rose disappeared . . .*" The letters are even, almost as if they were printed, entirely clear, correct—a handwriting long familiar, from early youth. I become so engrossed I nearly miss my station. How did he put it? In a bad position, there are no good moves. Depression? No, dear boy, you aren't depressed. Just sad.

December 2019
Translated by Boris Dralyuk

BIG OPPORTUNITIES

OPPORTUNITIES, you understand? Soon he'd have enormous, almost limitless opportunities. He kept insisting on those opportunities—opportunities that would open up for him soon, that lay just around the corner. She should know, though, he added, that he was doing just fine as it was, better than fine, better, in any case, than she could imagine. She, of course, hadn't the slightest intention of imagining his current opportunities, much less the ones at which he was hinting. All she needed was for him to deliver her as quickly as possible—who can remember where, after all this time? The editorial office, a party, the theater. So what, she doesn't want to hear who he is? Oh, she knows well enough, but she won't say it: another annoying, chatty driver, a *grdonchik*—one of a handful of words of Armenian slang she'd picked up from friends. Despite the cluster of consonants, *grdonchik* was still, in her opinion, far more euphonious, more affectionate than the Russian *bombila*, although it meant exactly the same thing—an unlicensed cabbie. This is Moscow in the nineties, every other car is a cab. Raise your hand and someone's right there: "How much?" "How much can you spare?" No, he's no *bombila*, the fellow yammers on, and this isn't his car—he gets this one through his job. His own vehicle's totally different, of a whole other order, and he isn't about to ruin it on these roads. He didn't pick her up for the money, either—pronounced "*eee*-ther," with a kind of Jewish intonation, though he clearly isn't a Jew. Then again, he also doesn't look Russian: maybe Komi, Chuvash, Udmurt? A small man, but with enormous, in his words, opportunities ahead of him; a rapid, choppy manner of speech, matched by a rapid though generally careful manner of driving; a face that isn't exactly ugly, just expressionless. He's entitled, he says, to a personal driver, but he prefers to do everything himself. For the sake of encounters like this, maybe? But what's it to her? "Stop over there." So that's it? Maybe she'd like to have lunch or dinner, "get a meal" together? Oh God … Have you looked at yourself in the mirror? No, she doesn't want to offend him. His courtship, let's call it, wasn't arrogant, but rather naive, automatic, terribly foolish. He tried to seduce her not with a show of prowess, of wit, or of talent, but with big opportunities. The only appealingly human thing about him was his speech impediment, a childish one: his *s*'s sounded like *sh*'s. She had tried to leave him two hundred, or maybe twenty thousand (she can't remember what the money was worth back then), but he refused to take it. Instead he handed her a card with his personal number, saying he never gave this number out, to anyone, hardly ever, so if she happened to change her mind … Oh, certainly—*merci*.

Victories of this sort don't bring even a hint of joy, and she would never have remembered the pint-size *grdonchik*—considering the number of men who had hit on her before and after, although seldom quite so clumsily—if not for an incident, an occurrence that changed her life forever. They showed up at her door early in the morning—six men and a dog—put her eighteen-year-old daughter in a car and took her away, and then they turned the apartment upside down. She was having the place renovated and it had seemed to her that it couldn't be made more of a mess than it already was, but apparently it could. She was afraid for her daughter, felt all this was happening to someone else, not to them, not to her, and was ashamed—embarrassed by the piles of underwear, old letters, photographs. She also knew she needed to fight, of course—to call lawyers, say nasty things to these goons—but her life seemed to be over. "What are you looking for, gentlemen?" Gentlemen, right. "Listen, on what basis are you searching my apartment?" On the basis of an order—see for yourself. Extremism, terrorism, anarchism, social-media records. When the time comes, she'll hear all about it. The dog alone behaved itself more or less decently: walked around, sniffed a few things, then plopped down.

She gave it some water. "What's this?" the one in charge asks her, sounding, for the first time, the least bit interested. A real professional: he had found a card in the lining of an old purse—name, surname, number, that very card. "Give it here!" she snatches it from his hands and, without giving herself time to figure out what exactly she wants to say, makes the call. "Yesh," with the characteristic *sh*. Their conversation hardly lasts two minutes, and she's the only one talking: tears, vows, pleas—not the moment for shyness or discretion. He finally says, in the same dispassionate tone in which he'd told her about his opportunities, "Pass the phone to the one in charge." The man goes out, then comes back: "All right. We'll lock her up for a long time if she doesn't leave the country by Tuesday. Never call that number again, got it?" He grins: "Go over to the station and pick up your darling. Caesar, come." They leave. "Life's fucking sense...": a half-finished inscription on a fence, author unknown. The good things, the best ones, are often anonymous.

A number of years passed—quite a few years, because her daughter had since managed to graduate from the university in Lille, while the daughter's Moscow friends and acquaintances, boys and girls from good families just like hers, had managed to serve out their sentences in prisons and camps—they were given from seven to twelve years—while after numerous adventures and travels she herself had ended up in her own house in the South of France. And, of course, all these years she'd been following, peripherally, out of the corner of her eye, the career of (it must be said) her benefactor, the *bombila*, the *grdonchik*—following it with horror, since here and there, in Africa, Asia, and even at home, he was invariably to be found at the center of some unthinkable, unimaginable evil, in violation of all divine and human laws. Until finally she comes across an announcement that he's been awarded a hero's Gold Star, his second—this time, however, posthumously. "In an attempt to save the crew" and so on, and so forth—implausible nonsense, without even a single believable detail, which is of course never the point—"he died a hero's death," along with some number of people. And to her, as to all commentators, it's perfectly obvious that all this official chatter is intended only to conceal, to drown in itself the shameful, disgusting truth of what had actually happened—a drunken death while out hunting, a political murder, or something of that sort. How strange, she thinks: he's lying there in a deluxe coffin, powdered and made-up, with his enormous, limitless opportunities, waiting to be buried in the best cemetery next to writers, artists, and composers, all to the sounds of beautiful music that he probably never liked. And would she want to find out that the announcement of his death was false? No, better not to ask oneself such a question. He had done her a favor, been good to her, while to everyone else—judging by the terrible things they write and say about him—he had been exclusively bad. All right: Does she feel sorry for this little man with his childish speech impediment? After all, she owes a very great deal to him, if not her own life: her daughter's freedom, this South of France. Maybe she does feel sorry. A little.

September 2021
Translated by Boris Dralyuk

THE WHILST

"Something new had come into my soul,
and had poisoned the life I had lived up to that hour."
—Leo Tolstoy

I.

DURING the night, KP, head of the Department of Ancient Languages and Cultures, didn't so much dream of hell as see it. Hell appeared before him. Not someone else's hell—not Dante's, not Tolstoy's (white, red, square), not a bathhouse in the country with spiders in every corner. No, this was his own personal hell, the one to which he would soon be confined. The arrangement was so simple that it gave off an overwhelming aura of authenticity, of absolute truth: nothing but naked consciousness, eternally imprisoned within itself. Perfectly silent, perfectly dark, impenetrable to all sounds and sensations. Cry and shout all you want (to yourself, of course, as you have no lungs or mouth), no one will hear you. And there would be no end to it, no distinction between night and day, no break for sleep, no power to turn it off—this everlasting consciousness—and no chance to beg for deliverance, or even for a brief respite. Remember, compose thoughts, torment yourself—no way out. Are you living or dead? Doesn't matter. Nothing matters any longer. You are and are not, forever. In such circumstances complete annihilation, actual nonexistence, seems an unattainable blessing. This kind of torture is impossible to endure even for a few minutes, but you must bear it forevermore.

"No, not that . . ." He'd shake his head, get up, drink some water, then lie back down and close his eyes—and there it was again. Hell refused to be dispelled.

In his youth he had suffered from bouts of terror at the thought that, someday, he'd no longer exist. Perspiration, palpitations. Tonight was different. Tonight he had come to realize what *would* exist. Never before had the future revealed itself with such terrifying clarity.

In the morning he told his wife about it, trying to make it sound like a meaningless trifle, a silly dream—rubbish, right? But he couldn't bring it off. The vision had been too real.

His wife said, "The Chinese have that, I think. They've thought of everything." She didn't like the Chinese.

A beauty past her prime, she was essentially unkind, but cultivated and observant—one of those women who consider themselves smart and, in fact, are quite smart.

A legitimate question: What had he done? The punishment should in some way fit the crime. Not once had he hit anyone in the face. He had led, if not a righteous life (who among us is without sin?), then at least a clean one—in a broad sense, not just with respect to bad habits, to say nothing of vices. He hadn't hidden his talents in the earth, though perhaps those talents weren't so very outstanding in the first place. Nevertheless, he had built up his life like a magnificent building, stone by stone, and that also took talent, didn't it—building a life? He was the head of a department, which, for all intents and purposes, he himself had created. He took good care of the faculty and staff, even of the most insignificant secretaries, and he had never gotten involved with any of them or with the students, hadn't fu . . . (He didn't care for foul language, even when talking to himself.) Hadn't messed things up, hadn't squandered his life, like so many of his peers. So why, then? What had he done?

"To deserve hell, you mean, or the dream?" his wife asked. "Hell doesn't exist, but the dream . . . Payback for Seryozha, probably. Anyway, it's only a dream. Now, what should we order for dinner tonight—duck confit with brussels sprouts?"

Strange that his wife should mention Seryozha. Especially since it was she who had brought him the news about the money and the European Court. KP himself had always taken pleasure and pride in Seryozha's academic accomplishments, and he had written him a friendly letter in parting ("Believe me, you will be missed"). He had probably even saved him from serious trouble: yes, that would-be Ajax might have made a very big mess indeed. Seryozha understood, in the end, and silently left for Estonia. Tartu, Pärnu—a province by the sea. No better place to sit out turbulent times. So what did Seryozha have to do with any of this? Nothing at all.

Half vision, half dream—the same thing happened the next night, and then again and again. And even throughout those days and months when hell didn't appear before him, he continued to sense its reality. It would never let him go, would stay with him forever.

2.

We who work under KP's leadership find it painful to watch our department fall apart. There is no other department of its kind in Moscow or, as far as we know, anywhere else. Now it's transforming from an object of superior value (KP's phrase) into a mere subdivision of a school of higher learning, a quite ordinary element of the system of graduate education. On the surface, little has changed in recent years: the dismissal of a couple of colleagues (out of more than eighty), the expulsion of a handful of students (neither the worst nor the best, but the quickest, most nimble). Yet something did break—irrevocably, it seems, although it's hard to say what, exactly.

As for KP himself, even now, at seventy-five, he cuts a most impressive figure. He's gone gray and grown a bit stout, but his voice is every bit as beautiful as before, and he wears his extraordinary erudition lightly, with no intent to oppress his interlocutors—wishing only to surprise them, maybe. Of course, in those well-known, widely circulated photographs taken some half a century ago, depicting him with his gorgeous young wife (to whom he is still married, by the way) and the man who would become poet laureate of the United States—well, you simply can't take your eyes off him: the spitting image of Jean-Louis Trintignant in *The Conformist* or *A Man and a Woman*, an actor of great masculine charisma. Actually, it was from the poet laureate that he copied this manner of his, this way of both being with us and not quite there—as if he were in a different dimension inaccessible to us, a little to the side, a little higher. You could imagine him too glancing absentmindedly at a portrait of a member of the politburo and saying, "Who is that fellow? Looks like William Blake." He had always dreamed of mastering the art of posing such questions, and master it he did. As time wore on, however, his graceful manner grew a bit rusty, and he began to insert old-fashioned phrases into his speech, to correspond more firmly to the classical image of a professor of humanities. The truth is that KP, in contrast to the poet laureate, lacked genuine prowess—wasn't really cool, you might say—and he knew it. He also knew that he couldn't learn to be cool, and that that was fine. Instead of worrying about coolness, he was constantly helping those around him, many of us, deal with everyday practical matters—finding a part-time job, a good dentist, etc.—and without expectations, without falsity. People feel that. He never stooped to vulgarity, never called our department "one big family": family is family, departments are departments. By the way, some of us are far more accomplished, in terms of scholarship, than KP. Until very recently, we had Seryozha here, teaching ancient Greek—talk about a world-class specialist in classical tragedy. KP describes himself as an administrator par excellence. Much to his honor, given his opportunities, he never did become a full professor. He specializes in late Byzantine literature.

Seryozha used to laugh about that. "Perfect job for a Byzantinist, heading a department. Bureaucracy is in your blood."

Their pseudoscholarly skirmishes were really in jest. Seryozha—an aging adolescent, half-gray, seventeen years younger than KP—represented antiquity, ancient Greece, while KP took the side of Byzantium. Seryozha would go on the attack: "A living culture, born of a living language, invents something new at every turn. And what have you got? Classification, systematization, carrion flesh in place of fresh ideas. All you do is copy, protect, preserve."

And KP would smile and respond: "Who would have even heard about your Greece, were it not for us Byzantines?"

Colleagues, senior and junior, two Russian intellectuals, both classical philologists—what else could they quarrel about? Yes, those were the golden days of our hallowed department.

Now, what KP didn't like were political arguments. He'd simply offer, in a low, deep voice, "for there must be also heresies among you" or some other bit of Scripture (he knows it quite well), then turn and walk away.

One day, however, he did lay out his views.

"I'm not afraid of anything, needless to say. At my age, after many a summer"—typical—"I have nothing to fear. As to politics... Events transpire, ladies and gentlemen. If everything went your way, would not the history of mankind itself come to a close? An aircraft was shot down, a person was poisoned, locked up... Unfortunate? Perhaps. Almost certainly, yes. But was there ever a time when the situation was markedly better? Under the emperor Justinian? Under Peter III? Nicholas II?"

No, we did not think that the situation was better under Nicholas II.

KP continued: "Change is needed, even necessary. But let's do without revolutions this time. 'For a change,' as the Americans say." Then he turned to Seryozha. "Following the youngsters off a cliff, are you? You yourself have declared that, in modern history, we are the losers. Remember, the father didn't whip his son for playing cards, but for trying to win back his money..." He quickly corrected himself: "I definitely do not mean to call us losers. Just look at the department we've created. But to interfere in the course of history, at our age, would be indecent, unchaste. Leave youthful undertakings to the young. On some issues, one can afford the luxury of not having an opinion at all."

He also said that the improvement of morals ought to be our only concern—it was our only hope. He reassured us that everything would be fine, and even quoted the poet laureate: "as if life will swing to the right, swaying left." We didn't need KP to recite that one—we know it well enough.

3.

"Folks, today we'll be learning Latin. You'll learn your Greek when the prof gets sprung from the clink."

The young Latinist N. uttered these words as he entered the auditorium, and the report to the administration revealed that students greeted the announcement with a standing ovation, shouting approval and stamping their feet.

It wasn't only the ancient period that occupied Seryozha's thoughts, but also the modern one, and he presented his opinions on the latter before the cameras of one "undesirable" TV station—energetically, with ample quotes from freedom-loving ancient poets. He spoke as he moved through the city center on his way to a protest, a march. There were young people all around him, shouting slogans offensive to the authorities. In the background some of the marchers were being rounded up and shoved onto buses. Seryozha's gray hair and beard fluttered in the wind—a hardened agent of the opposition. The footage is easy to find on the internet.

"The suicide of Ajax," KP's wife commented.

KP frowned.

"How utterly tasteless. What's the matter with him—diarrhea of the mouth?"

"A hemorrhage of courage," his wife retorted.

He repeated her joke often.

During the demonstration Seryozha was dragged off to the police station: a night on the cement floor, the next morning in court. He recounted it often, cheerfully: how they wouldn't let him go pee-pee, how the cops would change their tone depending on whether the scales of justice were tilting toward a fine or toward prison time. It's funny, they let him out for a smoke near the courthouse, phone and passport in hand. Seryozha managed to call both a lawyer and some friends. They all advised him to leave: the court would issue a fine, in absentia. If he stayed, they might send him to prison. But Seryozha went back in. He felt bad for the cops who'd trusted him. In any case, he got off with a fine and twenty-four hours in jail. Seryozha would tell his tale, gesticulating, laughing, inserting unexpected phrases, and we would reflect on how quickly this vocabulary (and not just the words) had entered our lives—"busted," "locked up," "sprung." It was as if it had been there all along.

A little while later KP went to the administration to inquire about the students slated for expulsion (quite a few of ours were detained that day, more than a hundred, especially mathematicians, and many could not be defended), and also asked about Seryozha. How do we know all this? We have our ways. Both KP and the administration have their secretaries, after all.

"What do we do?" KP asked.

Perhaps he didn't come right out and ask, but just raised his eyebrows.

"That depends," the rector replied.

Our rector doesn't really know English, but he likes to use these borrowed phrases—"doesn't work that way," "have a nice day."

"Take care of yourself," he told KP at the end.

This phrase—another borrowing—could not by itself have served as the cause of Seryozha's dismissal. But then KP received another bit of news about him from the Internet, again via his wife (she liked to stay on top of things).

"The European Court of Human Rights has made the state pay out some serious money to your Mandela, that noble prisoner. Look, they've written him up in full regalia: professor of the Department of Ancient Languages and Cultures..."

That was the final straw. KP summoned Seryozha to determine what kind of threat all this posed—not to KP himself (after many a summer...), but to the department. Seryozha shrugged it off:

"That money was for my detention in 2014, after that Crimea thing."

Then he flashed a smile—a rather impudent one, we must admit—and explained that the ECHR worked slowly. There was a huge backlog of cases, all tangled up in red tape, so it would still take time to get his payout from the motherland for this latest stay at the police station. He even gave KP a wink, apparently.

The department and its safety: the superior, sacrosanct value. And so that very evening KP sat down and began a letter to Seryozha: "I am writing to you on this sad occasion ..." In essence, he had invented a new genre: dismissal in the form of a friendly letter.

Personal correspondence is usually subject to public airing only with both the author's and the addressee's consent, which is why we didn't immediately learn of the letter's contents. But at some point Seryozha just couldn't resist. He was no longer working with us—not working at all, actually, just living off the ECHR money—and forwarded the letter to two or three colleagues. They showed it to several more, and it began to pass from hand to hand. So now, in the smoking room (no one smokes anymore, but we still call it that), we gather in a group and read our favorite passages aloud.

"My age-old compeer," one departmental joker starts us off. "You must not suspect me of approving in any wise current developments."

Another picks up from there: "The blessed days when one might combine teaching at an institution of higher learning with criticism of the authorities have, alas, fled. Whether they come again is a wholly separate and rather painful question ..."

"Is the chief totally off his rocker?" the young Latinist N. cuts in. "Who does he think he is, Pushkin writing to Chaadaev?"

Laughter all around.

"Upon whose side shall a greater share of truth be found—yours or mine?" the second reader asks in a gentle tone, then answers, lowering his voice: "Such things are unknown to me. Yet I am convinced that no one possesses the truth in its entirety."

"B-r-r-ravo!" shouts the first. "Wait, this is the part that gets me. Check it out: I am perfectly aware of and to a large extent sympathize with the arguments that may be mustered against my conclusions, yet—and this is of utmost significance—we are all free, whilst we are indeed free, to make our own choices. And then suddenly, bang: Believe me, you will be missed."

"Whilst!" the second reader repeats. "Lord, that's good...We are free to enjoy, whilst we're employed."

And so the entire department went over the letter. For the sake of objectivity, we must note that Seryozha's exploits divided the opinions of his colleagues: another person's boldness may cheer and excite some, but it angers others. Seryozha left for Estonia and found a new position. Judging by what we hear through the grapevine and by his growing list of publications, he seems to be doing well. He hasn't kept in touch. And KP, they say, has bad dreams at night.

4.

He couldn't find a job in Moscow, so now he teaches Greek to Estonians and writes his articles about ancient tragedy. He maintains his links to the broader world mainly through the Internet, but the number of these links is shrinking. Some of Seryozha's compatriots condemned his departure: stay where you're put, bear your cross. Emigration and how people feel about it—that too, as KP would say, is a separate and rather painful question.

Seryozha learns what day it is—*esmaspäev, teisipäev, kolmapäev* (Monday, Tuesday, Wednesday)—from the inscriptions on the pillbox he bought at the local pharmacy. He isn't so young anymore, takes medication. The Estonian language is neither Greek nor English, triggers no associations, but he's managed to get a handle on it. Days are more difficult to tell apart.

You couldn't call his life a living hell, but it's no heaven either. Seryozha doesn't consider himself a Christian, but his nanny did teach him one prayer when he was little, a prayer he had always recited mechanically at difficult moments—before exams, say, or when loved ones fell ill. He recites it now, from time to time. When he reaches the words "as we forgive those who trespass against us," Seryozha stops and remembers KP. No, he hasn't forgiven him, hasn't even tried—but no one had actually asked for forgiveness. Now it occurs to him that he had dealt with his dismissal in only an outwardly Christian manner, had accepted the loss of his beloved job and of his native country with only the appearance of humility. In doing so, he thought, he would rise above and defeat both KP and the anger that welled up inside him as he read "The Whilst" (the title he gave to KP's letter). But in fact Seryozha had achieved no victory, because—it was clear to him now—he had acted only as a polite civilized person. And what is a civilized person in the face of history, of eternity? Nothing. Zilch. He should have raised an uproar, filed a lawsuit, or smacked KP in the face, right in front of his female colleagues—lightly, with the back of his hand (we're talking about an old man, after all). He could at least have said, "You really shit your pants this time, didn't you, Trintignant?" He lies awake, sober, his mind reeling with variations, but it's too late: the time for slaps and insults has passed.

He has no nightmares, but every morning—before washing his face, brushing his teeth, and taking his pills—he reaches for the laptop. What earthshaking news does he hope to encounter? It's obvious, and one could even predict how it would all play out. Some unrestrained young woman will comment, in capital letters, "YESS," with three exclamation marks, and the Russian TV stations will play Chopin's Scherzo No. 2. The official announcement will no doubt contain the words "has departed from life." Such people neither die nor even pass away, they depart from life. The Internet will be abuzz with speculation about the appointment of the chairman of the funeral committee. And then, who knows? Seryozha might go back, emerge from the extended sleep of emigration, even though his position at the department was filled long ago. Hard to believe, but maybe ... Losers—that's what Seryozha considers himself to be, in the historical sense, along with everyone in his circle—need something to believe in, just to keep from going mad. For now, it's this: the gray sky, the cold sea, the frigid Baltic landscape. And, as they say in film credits, any similarity to actual events is purely coincidental, though inevitable.

November 2021

POSTSCRIPT

At the end of February, it wasn't only KP waking up in the middle of the night and gasping for breath, it was half the country—or perhaps a little less than half, according to the polls (but who believes the polls?). The Anglophilic rector added his name to a collective letter in support of the war, but KP escaped that fate: So far only the rector has been asked to sign. KP's wife is of course horrified by what's happening but tries to keep her opinion to herself, at least until they find themselves in safer circumstances.

The real Seryozha and I sit drinking coffee in the heart of Yerevan, on Pushkin Street. So far we haven't managed to reach Estonia or any other European nation. We exchange a few words, but are for the most part silent: However great our difficulties may be, they pale in comparison to those of the young Latinist N., who stayed in Moscow with his ailing parents, not to mention the plight of the people bombarded by our rockets and shells. Today is the fifth of March—a major holiday, in the circle to which we belong. The young people at the next table over make a toast: "That one croaked, and so will this one." Seryozha and I raise our cups, signaling our approval.

Yerevan
March 2022
Translated by Boris Dralyuk

KILOMETER 101

Essays

MY NATIVE LAND

I.

N. IS THE principal town of one of the regions next to Moscow, and I've been working here as a doctor for a year and a half. It's time to sort out my impressions.

The first and most dreadful one is this. The two most obvious feelings in the patients here, and many of the doctors too, are a fear of death and a dislike of life. They don't want to think about the future. Everything ought to stay as it is. Not life, just living out one's days. On vacation they have fun, they drink and sing, but if you look into their eyes you don't see any merriment there. Here's an acute case of aortic stenosis, needing urgent surgery. If he's not going to have it, no point lying in a hospital bed. "So what's going to happen? I have to die, is that it?"—Yes, so it turns out: he's going to die.—No, he doesn't want to die, but he doesn't want to travel to the regional center either, with all the fuss and bother of appointments and the rest. "I'm already fifty-five, I've had my life."—So what is it you want?—Retirement on health grounds. A sickness certificate. He doesn't believe in the possibility of getting well, what he wants is free medicine. "Doctor, am I going to live long enough to draw my pension?" (People who don't live to draw their pensions are failures; so long as you do get that far, it makes your whole life worthwhile).

Second: power is split between money and alcohol, i.e., between two manifestations of Nothingness, emptiness, death. Many people think that problems can be solved with money, but that's hardly ever true. How can money help you to awaken an interest in life or love?

And that's when alcohol takes over. Here's an example of what it does. Not long ago, a two-year-old child named Fedya fell out of a first-floor window. His drunken mother and her live-in boyfriend got Fedya back into their flat and locked the door. Luckily the neighbors had seen it all, and called the police. When they came, they broke down the door and the child ended up in the hospital. The mother, as mothers do, was standing hollering outside in the corridor. Ruptured spleen, splenectomy. Fedya lived, and even pulled out his airway himself (no one was watching—all busy with another operation). Then he pulled out his intravenous cannula too.

Third: practically every family has had a violent death in the recent past. Drownings, exploding firecrackers, murders, disappearances in Moscow. All this contributes to the background against which our own family life is played out. I have often had to deal with women who had buried both their adult children.

Fourth: I have scarcely ever met anyone deeply involved in their work. It's just that sort of feeble-spiritedness that makes people incapable of focusing on their own medical treatment. All those drug names (trade names, generic names) are another problem, and so is dosage. In order to take 25 milligrams, you have to break a 50 milligram tablet in half, or a 100 milligram one into quarters. That's difficult, and no one wants to bother. Weighing yourself daily and doubling your diuretic dose if your weight goes up—that's simply unrealistic. There aren't any scales at home, and the idea of buying one never occurs to them. It's not about the money. People are just *practically illiterate*—they know how to join letters up into words, but they don't apply their knowledge in practical terms. Their usual response, when I ask them to read the recommendations I've written for them in large print, is: "I haven't got my glasses with me." But if you've come out without glasses, that means you weren't planning on reading anything today. And that's illiteracy. Here's another test: "Do you understand where you have to go? Do you understand that you need to say you were referred by me?"—"Yeah, I suppose so."—"So what's my name?"—Angrily: "How should I know?"

Fifth: it seems that friendship is an experience restricted to intellectuals. So-called ordinary people don't have friends. I haven't once been asked how a patient was getting on by anyone other than a relative. Mutual help doesn't exist—we're the biggest individualists you could ever imagine. Our nation doesn't seem to possess the instinct for self-preservation.That's just our lot: it's easier to die than to ask your neighbor for a ride to Moscow."So, no wife, but what about friends?"—None. "I've got a brother, but he's in Moscow. I've got his phone number somewhere."

Sixth: men are almost always idiots. A man with heart failure, if he doesn't have a wife trailing around after him, is bound to perish before long. This idiocy begins in adolescence and progresses steadily, even if the man grows up to be a chief engineer or, say, an agronomist.

A man who cares about his relatives is a rarity, and those who do, inspire respect. One such, Alexey Ivanovich by name, is a patient of mine. He's managed to arrange for his wife to get a kidney transplant: he sold everything they had, and spent forty thousand dollars on the operation. It's not usually like that. Mostly it's "the Lord gives and the Lord takes away," a funeral and a memorial.

Self-made people are revolting. One of them came to see me the other day with a recent anterior myocardial infarction. Thanks to her husband's thievery, she'd built herself a big stone house next to ours. She regards me as an equal, or almost, so she starts by complaining about being jolted around in her car, although "it's a good one, a Volvo." And goes on to say "I've got to send my grandson off to Cyprus now, to stay with my daughter—she's studying there. You know, Cyprus has really gone downhill—too many gays." And more in the same vein. Incidentally, the clinic atmosphere is generally a nonsexual one—not like some Moscow clinics, where the sexual tension pervades the air.

And another thing: old people barely get treated here. This one's seventy, what do you expect? Well, why not the same treatment as a twenty-five-year-old? I remember a tottering old woman in a shop, grunting to herself as she picked out bits of cheese, butter, or sausage—the "best bits," as people say, meaning the cheapest ones. A line had built up behind her, and the assistant, a fair-haired young woman, said with feeling, "I'll never live to be like that!" The old woman suddenly looked up and announced firmly, "Oh yes, you will. And very soon too." In Sparta they had an even more rational approach to their disabled people. And what's left of Sparta now, beyond a few stories? You get the impression that we're somehow saving up our resources, or manpower, to treat the young; but it's not like that. People do try to treat an old person, if he's *socially significant* (the father of the electricity grid manager, say, or the mother of the deputy head of the local government).

Actually, old women are the most interesting people of all. Not long ago I spent half the night inserting a temporary pacemaker lead. When everything worked out OK, I shook my assistant's hand; and then the old lady, who had been gasping for breath a minute earlier, held out her hand to me too. "What about me?" she said, giving mine a firm squeeze.

One thing I'm constantly hearing is: "Easy for you to say, Maxim Alexandrovich!" What that actually means is—it's easy for you, Maxim Alexandrovich, you don't mind the trouble of doing…

The part played by the church in the life of the hospital and its patients is negligible. There aren't even any outward signs of piety, like icons on bedside tables. But everyone is baptized, everyone wears crosses around their necks, even a terrifying man named Ulrich. Ulrich has personally shot and executed sixty-eight people (Ukrainian nationalists, gangsters following the 1953 amnesty, miscellaneous others); he's a driver, veterinarian, faith healer, and freelance operator for the FSB, the State Security Service (that one's probably a lie). He has a service pistol, a Stechkin (unless that's a lie too). He can punch half a ton; just the other day he knocked out his eldest son's front teeth. There's got to be discipline. There's got to be discipline, and if anyone doesn't go along with that, he'll be pulled up with a fist or, if need be, a bullet. Pension, a mere twenty-seven hundred a month. What about the FSB, don't they help? No, he's a volunteer. Talking to Ulrich is scary—any moment, he could reach for his Stechkin. And his craziness (his ex-wife works black magic from a Moscow office, jinxes him, all that sort of thing—karma, breathing machines, magnets)—all that is a result of his pure evil, not the other way around. But that sort of patient is a rarity, most are peaceable enough.

Nobody even talks about how stupid the authorities are—the regional authorities, or the Moscow ones; all that people talk about is how to fool them. That gives rise to stories that would need a genius like Petrushevskaya to relate. Here's one: there's a regulation that says that amputated limbs are not to be destroyed (incinerated, for instance), but have to be interred in a cemetery. Irresponsible one-legged citizens don't bother to collect their amputated limbs, so that our morgue recently accumulated seven severed legs. They had to wait for a homeless man to be buried (at the state's expense, no witnesses) and hide the legs in his grave.

So what do I see that is good? The freedom to help lots of people. Even if the help isn't accepted—just the opportunity to offer it is good. And the lack of obstruction by doctors and the authorities. If you want an intensive care unit—fine, have one. If you want to bring in medicine and distribute it—also fine. If you want to admit a patient in order to rescue him from his alcoholic mother—go ahead. The lack of traditions is a good thing: unlike other provincial towns, N. doesn't live on its traditions.

We don't suffer from xenophobia either, really—although the other day I pulled a printed leaflet off a shop door that said "Keep N. a White town." But as far as I can see, the only people who want to do anything for our hospital are people from outside. We're very tolerant—we'll put up with anything; sadly, including things that we shouldn't put up with, like heroin dealing. No one complains that something is intolerable—all Moscow people are thieves, and that's just how it is.

People respect books, and knowledge, and experience out in the wide world; but no one is envious. What does it matter if a patient refuses cardiac surgery—who wants to go through that anyway? And there'll be some bright spark locally who'll explain that it's best not to do anything. Whenever that happens, it comes across as a medical failure, a defeat, a comedown. That's why we have to plaster our walls with diplomas—and do our best, and try hard, and get deeply involved in conversations with patients.

It's cheering to see hopeless-looking people who are at least prepared to do something active, even if they're not exactly thirsting for it. And another thing—the feeling of continuity about things that happen (since everyone ends up in the same hospital). You can follow up how any particular story turns out, and that gives you more of a sense of responsibility.

And there are some encounters that give me pleasure. Not long ago I treated a cheerful, skinny ninety-year-old lady named Alexandra Ivanovna: her father, a priest, died in the Gulag, her mother starved to death, she herself never had any education, and worked as a kindergarten assistant. I've never met anyone closer to sainthood. It's the same with genius—you can sense these things, but you can't really recount them. I told her: "You've got a dangerous illness (a myocardial infarction), you'll have to stay at the hospital." And she chirped back: "Bird flu, is it?"

The other day I got a nod from my great-grandfather, who died soon after I was born. I commented to a patient of mine that she had an unusual and beautiful name—Ruth. "Ruth, the foreigner," I said, and she replied: "There's only been one doctor that noticed my name, and he liked me a lot for it—and I went to his home, too." That doctor was my great-grandfather. When he'd done his time in the Gulag, he lived and died at Kilometer 101, in the town of N. Nowadays they don't send people to Kilometer 101 anymore—you have to get there under your own steam.

Another thing I like, of course, is the feeling that this is my town. I like it when people greet me in the street. A real man among mice? Maybe—but that's better than being a mouse among mice. Particularly when another real man might turn up anytime, and, before you know it, more still.

From what I've said, it's clear I'm happy to be working in N.

April 2006

2.

Another year of my provincial life has passed, and much has changed, largely thanks to the "real man" I mentioned above—my young colleague and friend. We manage everything so well between us that we're beginning to run out of patients. Mortality in our hospital is half what it was. There are more and more opportunities to help people. Nobody interferes with our freedom. It's a sin to complain. An anonymous oligarch has given us a splendid instrument. Our work is growing more professional, closer to the ideal, though still a long way from it. There's less sentimentality around, less of being treated as a great and good benefactor. If that hadn't happened, we'd have had to regard the town of N. as surrendering to entropy, Doctor Zhivago's last resort. Not everyone who withdraws from Moscow is another Field Marshal Kutuzov. On the other hand, that joy I felt in my early days here—the joy of meeting people and just being in the town—that has gone; I haven't had any more nods from my great-grandfather, and I'm looking more objectively (and hence more gloomily) at everything around me. As we try to extend our activities to the surrounding districts, I'm having to meet up with the authorities more and more often—district, regional, or Moscow authorities. That doesn't exactly make life easier. Unlike bad events, which trigger a positive feedback loop (fear—shortness of breath—worse fear—and so forth), good and rational activity lands you in worse and worse difficulties.

Medicine. Medical help in Russia is as easy to access as ever; but it's not all that effective. "Believe me," says the doctor in Gogol's tale, in a voice neither loud nor quiet,—"I never treat anyone for financial gain...Of course I could reattach your nose—but that would be much worse. Best leave it to Nature. Keep washing your face in cold water, and I promise you that even without a nose, you'll be just as healthy as if you had one." That's more or less how things are still done today. In a single decade Russia changes a lot, but in two centuries—not at all. Doctors and patients still suit each other perfectly. But then we turn up, and away we go. One man takes a lot of warfarin without any tests, just because he's feeling off—and suffers a serious bleed. Another one with a prosthetic heart valve gives up taking warfarin, and develops a thromboembolism of his femoral artery. You might say he'd lucked out. The cause in both cases is the same—alcoholism plus male idiocy. Here's how it comes across. If a man consults you and you ask him what he's complaining of, nine times out of ten he'll reply irritably: "They told me to see a cardiologist."

The chief problem with Russian medicine is that we don't have primary care physicians. The patient follows the advice of the last doctor he saw—if he follows anyone's advice at all, that is. The hospital prescribed one treatment, the polyclinic prescribed another, the regional hospital yet another, and in Moscow they said he needed surgery. Who's he to listen to? The one he liked best? The one who was most reassuring? The one who charged most? Or the one with the grandest title? How could a professor (or an academician, or a chief specialist, or a top consultant) be talking nonsense? I remember my horror as a child when I first discovered that grown-ups could be idiots. Many of my patients still haven't realized this, and that gets them into difficulties.

The doctor himself doesn't know what part he's supposed to play. Is he deciding something—or is he there for no particular reason, just to air an opinion? In theory, the primary care physician is the precinct doctor; but the main role this person plays is writing prescriptions and sick notes; he's often a drinker, despises his job, and despises himself. (Chekhov wrote in his notebooks that precinct doctors were "hypocritical seminarians and Byzantines," which is rather cryptic.) These doctors have long lost the habit of making any decisions ("Don't say it's wrong, don't say it's right, put nothing down in black and white!"). This is how they talk to a patient: "You get heart pains when you walk fast? So why hurry?" Oddly enough, patients will settle for that kind of answer.

We're not short of hospitals or medicine—we just don't have standard procedures, there's no single system for consulting our sources of scientific knowledge, no system for proving anything, and no requirement for any such system. Of course, some people succeed in providing help—by accident every time, or so it seems. The important thing is to turn an art into an everyday craft—that's what progress is all about. Of course, all sorts of things do get done in our country. In St. Petersburg, not long ago, a woman received a lung transplant. Does that mean that "this country *does* lung transplants"? In some respects, the situation here is even more hopeless than in equatorial Africa. Out there, where they have nothing, you can bring them something—medicine, or equipment, or doctors—and those things will become established, and there'll be some benefit. But here in Russia we have an advanced legal system which is growing ever more effective at protecting us against any change for the better. Questions such as "How long should a person live?" or "Should disease be fought by every single means available?" are resolved not by people, but by the authorities. (For instance, one official contraindication to calling out the neurosurgical team is "age over seventy.") And then everyone yells, "What's the State thinking of?" But "the State" means the police—and what do they know about medicine? They don't even have any way of assessing it, beyond numbers of visits, duration of hospital admissions, numbers of high-tech investigations, and the like. As a matter of interest, before the revolution, the province of Tula contained just a single writer, while now there are three thousand—but that single writer was Tolstoy.

"Who needs us, anyway?" one woman asks. She's not old, but she has stopped taking the diuretics I prescribed her, and now she's got bad edema. "You do—you yourself, and your family too." She makes a dismissive gesture. "Of course, in Soviet times..."

It's not only in the district town, but in the regional capital too, and even in Moscow, that one feels the lack of anyone who can follow a consistent line, in either conversation, or treating patients, or private study. My colleague and I recently found ourselves visiting two of the main regional hospitals. We quite liked one of them—a rather impoverished institution, where the doctors worked hard, and took the trouble to read medical textbooks (sadly, only in Russian). The other one we didn't like at all. Both of them, incidentally, were *judenfrei*, which isn't a good thing in a place where patients are treated. (That was the beginning of the end of Russian medicine—the "Doctors' Plot." All the rest—mass emigration, the brain drain of active staff to Western Big Pharma—all that came later.) Dr. Lyuba, a little beauty with superlong fingernails ("We're clinical cardiologists," she says, meaning "we're no good at anything") is expecting to be taught catheter ablation of arrhythmias next year. One minister finds himself quoting Stalin without knowing he's doing it: "No one here is irreplaceable." I suggest to him, as meekly as I can: "Some of us are." But I'd have done better to remember that "everything is decided by the cadres." I'll never learn to play the Mephisto Waltz, not even if you buy me a new Steinway, and no more will Lyuba ever cope with any arrhythmias, not even if she files down her nails. But our bosses will never understand that. "We'll teach them," they say, "we'll send them to Moscow, or Europe if need be, or America." It won't work. You can't grow roses on an ice floe. No one in America is going to bother to learn Russian so he can tell Lyuba all about arrhythmias (she "took some English classes at college"). Once my colleague and I were driving along an empty, snow-covered road, everything was achingly beautiful, and my colleague was telling me about genetics, or rather molecular biology, while I looked around and wondered— what were the disasters lying in wait for us? What are the disasters awaiting that drunken woman, standing idly by the crossroads? Hard to say, but they're certainly out there. Might she ever pull herself together, sober up, and go home to her children, or meet a good man somewhere?

Money. The main myth, which practically everybody subscribes to, is that money is the decisive factor in all things. Gossip, the engine of provincial thought, is monotonous and boring and all focused on money. My presence in the town of N. is the subject of many unflattering rumors, all centered on some supposed "economic activity" on my part (which doesn't exist). In Soviet days, there would have been different rumors—unpleasantnesses in Moscow, or a desire to perform experiments on people, or links with the secret police (an even more frightening accusation), or with "abroad," or a desire for fame, or family problems. No one is interested in that sort of thing nowadays.

People are driven by more than just greed for money: there's vanity, too, and sex, and lust for power; but nowadays all those vices are forgotten. The main rumor making the rounds is that the hospital has been bought by people from Moscow, and soon everything will be charged for. When you stretch out your hand to help others, however benevolently, they always suspect your hand is groping for their pockets.

The idea of money in people's minds, especially for men, is highly destructive. Money can achieve anything—you can cure yourself, cure your child or your mother. That attitude leads to a lot of mute despair. Someone dies, but no one says why. Mother died because there wasn't enough money for her treatment. And the despair is ramped up by television ads: "Toyota—Drive your dreams." But look at you, you loser, you couldn't manage to earn enough (or even steal enough—stealing is OK, if it's to cure your mother). Real men drive their dreams, they've always got Tefal thinking about them, and "Dirol with xylitol and carbamide" looking after their teeth for them. (Carbamide, incidentally, is normally known in English as urea, a perfectly ordinary substance.) Of course, we all need money, and don't have enough for a lot of things; but money isn't the chief problem.

Emptiness. Olya M. was admitted to the hospital with poisoning by vinegar essence, causing esophageal burns. (That fall our hospital had turned into a sort of branch of the Hotel Angleterre, where Esenin committed suicide. One person had hanged himself right in the ward, another had thrown himself out of a window, and a woman had made two attempts to hang herself—all over the course of two months.) Before that, Olya had tried to slash her wrists. She's twenty-eight, looks fifteen, and works as a cleaner in a cafeteria. Grew up in an orphanage in Lyudinovo, Kaluga province. Lives in a two-room apartment with an alkie husband, an alkie father-in-law, and a clean seven-year-old daughter who came wearing a hair ribbon to see her mother after her first day at school. And a mother-in-law who's obviously very fond of her granddaughter. I tried to have a conversation with Olya, but it wasn't a great success. I told her husband to give me her passport, and I locked it in the safe. That was the only sensible thing I did. I suggested she might move out (I had no idea where to, but I'd have thought of something); but she refused. She just lies there bored stiff, doesn't read anything, though she says she can read. I gave her a copy of the New Testament, which she handed back—she probably read the first words, "The Book of the generation..." and gave up. I fixed it up for her to talk with Father K., a wonderful man, a priest who had come from Moscow to consult me; but it was a waste of time. He was the only one to speak; I wished Olya could at least have cried. We got some clothes together for her, then a different man turned up from heaven knows where. She's going to live with him. She discharged herself, happy as a lark.

Two months later she was back. She'd been drunk (claimed to have had nothing but beer: it didn't look that way), and had slashed her abdomen open. Badly. They stitched her up. She looks coarser than before. Groaning with pain. "Shit! I coughed." She looks like a victim, but over time she could commit practically any dreadful deed—cut her husband's throat, or her girl's, or mine. The simplest thing would be to declare Olya mentally ill (though she's not delirious or hallucinating, and psychiatrists find it rather improper to ask what's meant by the mind). And anyway, would that explain anything? If you look at Olya, it's obvious that evil isn't an inherent part of human nature; it's something that gets into it, penetrates it, to fill up an empty place, the intercellular space. Evil and good are different in kind, and emptiness has an affinity for evil. (The saga of Olya M. recently acquired a further installment. Her drunken husband was admitted with a knife wound to his abdomen, and injuries to the small bowel and common iliac artery. His story was that the handle had come off a meat chopper, and he had fallen against the table on which the blade was lying, and so on.)

Some encounters are less tragic. The inhabitants of the town of N. are much kinder to people in desperate straits, particularly the homeless. In a recent hard frost, the emergency team went out to pick up a "criminal cadaver." "Looks like Sasha Terekhov has finally gone to meet his Maker" was how the paramedic put it. But while they were on their way, this living corpse hailed a cab and took himself to the hospital, where he pretended to be gasping for breath. He was admitted into a "social bed," and the next morning he was gone. Another homeless man, a Russianized German with severe aortic insufficiency, has been living in the hospital for three months, because there's nowhere to discharge him to. He's transformed in appearance from an alcoholic vagrant to a decent-looking man with a little beard and a stick, and he's stopped drinking. During this time his ex-wife came to the hospital too, and he asked for her to be admitted; their children together have been visiting her. He was given seventy rubles to pay for a letter to Germany—he's a German, after all; there are people he could write to. Some Moscow hospitals have a different attitude: after three days' admission, vagrants are bused far away from the hospital. They have staff responsible for carrying out this policy.

There's still some humor in the situation, though it lessens as the same thing is repeated time and again. Some days ago, a patient of mine brought me a present—a three-liter jar of gherkins. She told me how good they were, and I thanked her. And then: "Maxim Alexandrovich, what are we going to do about returning the jar?"

I never see any real, active evil. Just emptiness. In the hospital latrine you find torn scraps of crosswords (patients and staff do a lot of crossword puzzles). "Disorderly crowd," six letters. And in a woman's neat hand, the word "PEOPLE." (The crossword composer was thinking of "RABBLE.") Even before I arrived in N., I've always tried to avoid the words "the People"; but often I've been wrong, for any number of reasons. Brodsky, for instance, said of Solzhenitsyn: "He thought his problem was communism, but his problem was people." You can't treat the so-called "people" like small children—in most cases, they're adults, and regard themselves as responsible. When you get to know them well, you don't perceive any sense of loss or of unfulfilled possibilities. True, they're looking forward to a life span of fifty or sixty years, not the long lives seen in the West; true, "there never had been a bridge, and no bridge was needed"; and true, they do prefer cheap pop music to Beethoven. When we organized a charity concert, the audience consisted almost exclusively of vacationers

206 · MAXIM OSIPOV

from Moscow. (I have to say that our loathing of classical music, despite our enormous success as performers of it, is quite inexplicable. A musician friend of mine who spent time in a mental hospital wasn't allowed to use his portable stereo—this was to prevent him from listening to classical music, in itself a form of schizophrenia. The other patients were allowed their players, because they listened to "normal" music, i.e., *unts-unts-unts*.) The most relevant Chekhov tale today is "The New Villa," not "In the Ravine." When they are genuinely free to choose among members of their own social group, people like to associate with the Lychkovs.

The Authorities (the people you can't say no to). A plain Soviet citizen and a plain Soviet district committee secretary used to be very different sorts of people. And that distinction holds today. Lychkov ate up everyone who got in his way; yet he was legally elected, though of course extremely stupid by the standards of an intelligent person (are there any other standards?). But in some respects he's acutely perceptive. I'm talking to him, but my eyes are saying: "I need your signature so badly, I'm even prepared to have a drink with you." He has no objection to a drink, but not on those terms.

I've had a great many dealings with the authorities. Not one has been a pleasure, but two have surprised me. The first: I asked a big Western company to send us an invoice for a CT scanner (which some benefactors had promised to buy us), quoting its actual price— half a million dollars—rather than one million dollars, to include a cut for us. People spent a long time trying to persuade me—if we charged more and took a cut, we could buy other instruments with it (well, yes, and of course those would come with a cut for us as well, and so on, right down to pillowcases and surgical needles). That's how the Russian language acquired the extremely versatile verb *pro-platit'*, "to pay something through," meaning lubricating everything with money. Then it transpired that buying the instrument without someone taking a cut was impossible, it would have put our bosses in a difficult position. In other words, you're not allowed to drive through a red light, but that's the only way to get anywhere.

The second episode happened when I asked some influential

medical friends of mine to protect me from our bosses. "No problem. Tell us whom to call, and we'll sort it all out." I asked how exactly they were going to do that. "To be honest, we usually threaten people with physical violence" (enlisting the help of grateful gangsters whom these doctors have treated). So I rapidly changed the subject and started discussing heart attacks, strokes, and other pleasant topics.

I found all that very depressing, but then I started looking at things in a different light. The problem isn't that "you can't do anything in this country" (after all, we did manage a few revolutions); it's the fact that the language I talk is as opaque to them as theirs is to me. A textbook of psychiatry quotes a patient being asked: "What's the meaning of 'Don't bite off more than you can chew'?" He replies: "Who says I bite off more than I can chew?" And it's the same between us and our bosses. "You're a State personage," I tell a top politician, to which he replies: "The State—that's a relative concept."

There are two ways forward from here. The first is to learn the new language. That's difficult, and I don't feel like doing it, particularly as it's so close to my own that I might get confused. It's not only all those weird new expressions—there's a whole different structure of concepts and techniques of argument to be learned. It seems to me that the things I say bear no relation whatever to what I hear back. And I guess the authorities have the same impression of me. The second approach is to press all the buttons in turn, as one does with an unfamiliar computer program. That works often enough—so that looks like the way to go.

March 2007
Translated by Nicolas Pasternak Slater

A SIN TO COMPLAIN

"THERE can't be too much work, like there can't be too much love."
So said Father Ilya Shmain, who also lived and worked in our town.
"Well then, let's try it: an enormous, ponderous, / creaking rudder-
turn."[1]

Six months have passed, and things seem much improved, but
sometimes I'm still gripped with despair, as powerfully as ever. It
would be fine if we were talking about growing new organs in the
lab, or constructing an artificial heart, or some other medical revolution—but everything that happens is ordinary, though it takes a
phenomenal effort to achieve it, and success seems to be a matter of
luck. "O Lord, deliver me from the man of excellent intention and
impure heart," our enemies would say, if they had read Eliot's *The
Rock*. And I can understand them. We've heard more than enough
from loudmouths with impure hands and thoughts. A man of action
is suspect; a compassionate observer is far easier to understand.

But dreams have proved very effective. By way of dreams alone,
we get equipment, and medicine, and whatever else we need for our
work. Friendship—a concept restricted to the intelligentsia (and only
in that sense a Russian concept)—has done its bit, and now we have
almost everything we need and can cope with. Well then, let's try it.

If you want to have a life—not in an abstract, national sense, but a
life of your own—you need space; and in Moscow there isn't enough
of it. "I've surrendered this town," says an artist friend of mine. In
Moscow nothing is on a human scale—and that's not in the sense of

a great cathedral, but quite the opposite. Far better to live in the provinces, if you have something to keep you busy. Two minutes to get to your place of work—a minute and a half, if you hurry. On a moonlit winter night you can see for miles around; and central Russia has many more seasons than four. The main thing that poisons the life of the provincial dweller is the lack of choice. The view from your window will stay the same to the end of your days, and you already know your final resting place in the cemetery. There's no way out. If you haven't tried living in a great metropolis, you'll never be reconciled to this unchanging world. At least we no longer see those funeral processions that used to scare us as children, with men carrying an open coffin through the streets while the brass band murders Chopin.

Moving to Moscow from the provinces is something that feels right and proper, it's a kind of mass phenomenon. In our town there are almost no people between ages twenty and forty, except the ones nursing their bottles of beer in the middle of the road. But moving out of Moscow to the provinces is an individual act, which is hard to emulate—and that's the problem with it, from the point of view of a Westerner, for whom being on the fringe of society generally means being a failure.

Looking at Moscow from outside, you begin to notice all sorts of trivialities. The closer you get to the city, the shorter the distance a man walks from the road to urinate—nothing to do with the Old Testament's "him that pisseth against the wall," just that they have nothing to be shy about. No one knows anyone else, everyone's a stranger. From a distance Moscow gives the impression of a gigantic polyp (whatever happened to "Moscow the beautiful"?), with some areas showing malignant transformation. But on closer examination you can find people there who will give time, effort, and money to help our hospital become the one we planned.

Pressing all the buttons in turn was a mistake. In an instant our gentle, wordless way of life was disrupted and lost all its piety and purity. Everything started from my conversations with a certain progressive journalist. "In Russia," he tells me, "everything is better than it looks." Aha, good to know. He smiles at me—after all, he and I are the same, the elite. Soon we'll have the State on our side. And then officials begin turning up to see us, either to carry out unwanted checks (how else can the State remind you of its existence in peacetime?), or for no reason at all, just to show their faces.

For reasons of its own, the administration has decided that if the regional center doesn't possess some resource or other, then we shouldn't have it either. One government minister said to me, "I'll take you to Region!" I have to say that our small-time administrators are still very scruffy and physically unattractive. What were these men doing when they were young—torturing animals? Working as army warrant officers? The pinnacle of human evolution is a unique biological species—one that couldn't care less whether life has any meaning. Words, glances, handshakes—they're all pointless. Officials, especially feeble ones, reckon that life could hold no greater happiness than to have their job. In this schizophrenic, fictitious world, they talk about nonexistent things, which—by virtue of being talked about—acquire a sort of demonic half-existence. One good thing about the present day—there's none of that damned ideology. (On our local Lenin monument, someone has scrawled in charcoal "Misha, this is Lenin." No one has bothered to clean it off.) They're not trying to control my thoughts anymore.

One top boss (now an ex-boss—they're always being changed) liked to shoot off his mouth. He'd talk about himself in the third person ("So-and-so can promise you . . ."), as if being a boss was his very essence. A long way from Blok's Hamlet, "And I die, a prince, in my native land." You can assassinate a prince, but you can't fire him. In contrast to Soviet-style rhetoric ("the feats of ordinary working people," etc.), that boss now talks of the "people" in accents of disgust or patronizing contempt. "This granny turns up at the polyclinic . . ." Look here, young man, what sort of a granny is she to you? The chief physician of one of the hospitals in the neighboring region was fired and given a conditional sentence. Why? There was a deranged old woman who kept turning up at her hospital, making a nuisance of herself and getting in everybody's way. So this physician asked the local police chief to do something about her. She didn't know that this old woman wasn't a "nobody." The policemen drove her off into the woods and left her there to be savaged to death by feral dogs. The men got six to eight years each.

There is one group whom the authorities are happy to recognize and take seriously—gangsters. They're scary and repulsive to write about. "Gangsters are people too"; "Gangsters have laws of their own": yes, and a cancerous tumor has its own laws too, laws of growth and metastasis; and it, too, consists of living cells. But when it kills its host, it dies too. Theologians assert that this is the devil's own dark purpose—to destroy the world, and himself with it.

So far I've managed to avoid direct confrontation with gangsters. Violence in our town has more of an ad hoc character. "Citizen A, born in such-and-such a year, in town B, came to the home of citizen C, born in town D; there he encountered citizen E, and inflicted two knife wounds to his thoracic cage." That's how the investigator sees it. But locating a gangster when you want one is as simple as moving from a decent Internet page to an indecent one. All it takes is a couple of clicks. Getting a gangster to help sort out any problem you like—that's the great temptation of our age. In the old days, you'd have gone to the KGB—just as ubiquitous and all-pervasive. Getting them to help you, if you were a respectable person, was regarded as out of order. But with gangsters, it's different—and now here's a very sweet elderly lady recommending that I apply to a certain rich peasant, if I need funds: "He's not a gangster anymore, though he might have been one..." And he donated a set of curtains to the library, and a local bigwig recites poetry at his birthday party. And it isn't that the bigwig is telling himself, "Hold your nose; look the other way and kiss the villain's hand"—he genuinely feels friendly toward this man of action. So what does it mean—"he's not a gangster *any-more*"? Has he undergone some grand spiritual conversion, repented, done his time? Or does he simply no longer need to kill people? "Yes, but his children are studying at Oxford…" Children, as Gogol wrote of Chichikov, are such a sensitive subject! What happened to "visiting the iniquity of the fathers upon the children, and upon the children's children"? There's enough evil there for years to come, but lady intellectuals are easy suckers for a man of action.

Several times I've found myself treating one of these "brothers," with their dead eyes. I ask, in all innocence, "Where did you get those tattoos? What do they mean?"—"What's it to you, doctor?" So why do them, then? It's some kind of professional symbol (like an anchor or a swallow), and we're supposed to bow our heads and hold our tongues. Making us complicit in their loathsome secrets. Once on a flight I was sitting next to a psychiatrist who'd done four years inside, and he told me a lot about how to survive in a modern prison or camp. Mostly it was all very boring.

Luckily the things that fill our provincial lives are very different. Often unique, often touching. You set off to work in the morning, dawn is just breaking, and you overtake a tiny little boy trudging off to school with his huge satchel. Tolstoy's little Philip to the life. You won't see that anywhere else.

Or—on a good day—you've managed to do something new. New for us, I mean. And it worked out OK, and then you did it again, and then suddenly you're surrounded by all kinds of lucky coincidences and everybody needs you, like Evgraf Zhivago. Or else a patient (especially if he isn't too sick) tells you something so amusing that you instantly find yourself wondering how to tell it to a friend, or write it down, and you can't wait to do that. I was taking a history from a film director—very mediocre, I suspect, but very successful—and I asked him, "Do you smoke?" He waves his hand expansively and says, "No, but go ahead, light up, I don't mind."

It's a joy to learn and to master some skill—to do something no worse than they do in the West. That's what our profession is all about—behaving professionally. Gogol's doctor, incidentally, behaves professionally: he tells a lie, assuring the patient that he can reattach his nose (in those days doctors were constantly lying; that's why Chekhov called them "Byzantines"), and then advises him, "Keep washing your face in cold water." That was how people were treated. Hydropathy was one of the advanced treatments of the day. Nowadays, professional behavior means acting according to Western medical textbooks, which protect a patient from his doctor's strokes of genius. We aren't saviors and healers, like the sailor in the old Soviet cartoon ("What good deed shall I do today?")[2] "Tell me, fellows, are you doctors by inheritance or by vocation?"—"By education."

Incidentally, the experts tell us that Gogol wasn't really talking about a nose at all, but quite a different part of the body. I think they're wrong. That's because my experience of Russian officialdom has totally convinced me that everything Gogol wrote about it is literally true.

I come across lots of different people, and each one of them represents a sort of Russia of his own.

Here's a thirty-year-old programmer from the neighboring town. He's thorough, uses educated language, remembers when things happened, and what treatments were given in the past. Has a firm handshake. Asks to read up about his illness—he can handle that. He makes a very pleasant impression: you can see his needs are the same as ours, freedom and order.

Of course sad things happen, but they're comforting too, in their own way—because they're genuine. Alexander Pavlovich, a tough, sly seventy-year-old peasant, has died. I never managed to persuade him to have his aortic valve replaced. Or rather, I did persuade him, but too late. Neither kind words nor threats did any good. When we met in the street, he'd give me a sly wink ("Wasted your time, trying to frighten me, doctor—I'm still alive!"). Then, when things really got bad, he went to China for some Chinese medicine. And once pulmonary edema had set in, he agreed to have the operation, but then I had his daughter from Magadan assailing me rudely and frantically—"Who's going to be looking after him? What guarantees can you give us, supposing we agree?" Well, there we are, it didn't work out.

There's a retired colonel, very seriously ill, living in the country. He's had a major infarction, treats doctors with well-founded suspicion, but can be made to listen to reason. My colleague and I were examining him together, exchanging brief comments in English—naively thinking our patient wouldn't understand. Then, as we were withdrawing the probe from his mouth, our colonel suddenly asks, "How did you manage to get such a piece of equipment?" In English.

Once they even brought in a real American (married to a local girl, has lived here for several years). He was unconscious after drinking antifreeze. No one drinks antifreeze for kicks—it's for committing suicide. Judging from his tattoos, he was just an ordinary guy—and a Trotskyist. Later it turned out that he didn't speak any Russian. Why had he wanted to die? Found himself living in the wrong century? We never did discover. Treated him with ethanol and sent him for dialysis. That's another Russia too: apparently there are seventy thousand Americans living in Moscow.

I had a melancholy Russian yuppie come from Moscow to consult me. Nothing whatsoever wrong with him. "What's your occupation?"—"Business." Probing any further seemed embarrassing.

We also have very wealthy people living in our town, and sometimes they too fall ill unexpectedly. I got into conversation with one of them (who turned out not to have had a heart attack). He was scared of dying; and it wasn't the adrenaline-fueled panic that wakes you in the night and makes you feel you can't breathe. It was a perfectly rational fear—that he'd never, ever manage to take his favorite little toys with him. It's people like him, I think, who have their bodies frozen after death—the height of tactlessness toward the Creator: "Thanks, I've got it covered." I got mad at him, and when he asked how he could help us, I nearly served him the classical reply "Get out of my sun"—but instead asked for another little bit of equipment. A fat, greedy boy in fancy glasses—it's hard to beg someone like that for a piece of candy or a bike to ride. "Don't give them fish—teach

them how to fish"—but is that Christian? Did the Savior teach
people to fish, or did he give them fish to eat?

On the other hand, there are some people whom everyone relegates
to the bottom of the heap: Tajik laborers. You forget that we used to
share a country with them, and at school they were taught the same
things we were. You try to remember that this is part of the price
paid for the comforts of our life today—but it doesn't stick: they're
Tajiks, strangers, not our kind.

A neighbor of ours keeps animals and takes an interest in world
events, in her own way. She's watering her vegetable garden. "We need
one of those hoses they use in Europe for breaking up demonstra-
tions." When the coup happened in 1991, she commented: "Look
what's going on in our country, and here's poor Mikhail Gorbachev
taken ill." She's sorry for everybody—for Gorbachev, or any other
sick person, and for the calf or piglet that she's going to sell. She ad-
dresses it as "Borya, little Borenka," and in her next breath, "Wouldn't
you like some of the meat for a nice kebab?"

This neighbor remembers a little of the war. No one at all remembers the '30s. Recently I heard at second hand how they eradicated
Trotskyism in our town. The chairwoman of the kolkhoz had an
interesting biography, and a well-deserved reputation as a witch.
(Local legend describes this woman as extraordinarily beautiful.
During the First World War her fiancé was an airman—one of the
elite, not in today's sense. But he left her for her own sister. So the
woman decided to get rid of the sister. She placed candles upside
down in church and wrote prayers for the repose of her sister's soul,
according to an old folk custom. It worked, the sister died, but the
woman never got her fiancé back.) And now she received a government
order: name five Trotskyists. She consulted the local peasant women,
and named five members of the Communist Party, which was all
there were. They were driven to the nearest town and shot. Then she
was ordered to hand over another five. The local women named the
village drunkards, idlers, and no-hopers. They were shot too. When
an order arrived demanding another five names, the chairwoman
said there were no more Trotskyists in town. She was warned that if

she didn't come up with five names, fifteen would be taken. So she
wrote the names of all two hundred men in the kolkhoz on bits of
paper, and pulled out five at random. The five peasants were driven
off, and that was the end of the battle with Trotskyism here. (That's
the pattern of our Terror's victims: one-third communists, one-third
no-hopers—including Mandelstam—and one third picked at random.)

Our hospital janitor is sweeping the front steps with a homemade
birch broom. We're standing nearby with our friends, who have come
up from Moscow in several automobiles. The janitor is trying to sweep
the dust in our direction. When we move away, he follows us, still
sweeping and muttering hostile obscenities. The first to give way to
his nerves is this janitor. He's drunk. "Tell me—you're the boss here"
(because I'm in a white coat) "did you have to eat wood chips after
the war?" That's all he needs us to take in: his past sufferings, perfectly
genuine, and his no less genuine alcoholism.

But the easiest to understand, and probably the most pleasant type
of patient is the intellectual. Of course, a conversation with an intellectual takes two or three times longer than with anyone else. If you
ask, "What's your occupation?" he'll tell you that he belongs to six
different creative organizations, and if you ask him when he began
suffering from shortness of breath, you'll hear that in the early '80s
the Armenian Composers' Union invited him to visit their Creative
Center in Dilijan. Never mind, I've been to Dilijan too, and what's
more, I remember the film he made with Schubert's "Unfinished"
Symphony, and I remember what Mravinsky said about the way the
second movement was played. After a conversation like that, you can
be sure that your intellectual will stick to your instructions. And
there's no need to ask him if he smokes—of course, he smokes cheap
Belomors.

What is it that unites all these different Russias? What saves our
country from falling apart? At your worst moments, you tell yourself
it's nothing but inertia. A friend from Boston writes, "It has occurred
to me, paradoxically, that the Soviet system perpetuated many of the

weaknesses of prerevolutionary Russia." We're scrambling back into the nineteenth century, even in our spelling: give us back our old orthography! In the family of nations, we're the pupil who has to repeat a year. He's finishing up the year with his classmates, but you can't expect anything much from him. Everyone else is subject to discussion, and, if need be, to condemnation, but we aren't. Here's this beanpole sitting behind his desk, the tallest in the class—but what's he thinking about? No answer. A meaningless dream—that's the feeling we sometimes get about our own history. There's no line of direction in it, no vector. Our language? Well, yes, but because of the abrupt lowering of standards, it's becoming more and more the language of the bargain basement, a collection of hand-me-downs and parasitic words. And now our free newspaper (where our citizens find out about everything in the world, since there's no bookshop here) tells us that "Natalia Goncharova was the wife of Alexander Pushkin." How is one to explain that you can't refer to the poet without "Sergeyevich"—that "Alexander Pushkin" will only do as the name of a steamship?

The Scriptures say: "Wilt thou also destroy and not spare this place for the fifty righteous that are therein?" Well, never mind the righteous—do we even have enough decent people? Or have we really "loved darkness"? "Russia is done for," said Father Ilya, after taking confession in our local church. "The husband drinks and beats his family, the son drinks and beats his family, and the grandson drinks and beats his family"—that's what he heard from his luckless women parishioners who came to confession. So what's wrong with a fight against our own alcoholism, as a national idea? There's too little of a boyish atmosphere, excitable, creative, and genuine, if clumsy; and far too much of the masculine, mature, even overmature sort. Men sit stripped to the waist, their heads fuddled with drink and smoke. They're not enjoying each other's company anymore, and should have gone home ages ago; but there they still are, tearing bits from a cold chicken carcass that looks like a human fist. That's a festive meal for you.

Next morning, the man's wife or daughter—or perhaps a hospital nurse—will pat him on the back and say, "You're looking OK today." This time he's coped, hasn't gone off on a bender. Alcohol is our battlefield. Love, hate, attraction, revulsion, all together. We aim for coexistence. Alcoholism—not picturesque, not ascetic like Venichka Yerofeyev's, not like a sign recently seen in the Moscow metro: "Donate 10 rubles to promote Russian alcoholism."[3] No traditional male amusements in the hospital: no televised football, no dominoes—all that has lost its interest. Alcohol is everywhere. It plays a part in the life of practically every family. And we acknowledge, and yet deny, its power over ourselves. The cardinal virtue, as with the ancient Greeks, is not sanctity but moderation: so-and-so "knows how to drink." If he goes on a bender, it's the alcohol that's the winner.

This is how a bender begins. Someone drinks himself into a stupor, switches off (and I mean switches off—he doesn't fall asleep and then wake up feeling guilty), regains consciousness after two or three or four hours, still drunk; hunts for another drink, always manages to find one, drinks some more, all he can handle (all there is), switches off again, and so forth—until the cycle is broken by some external force (he's taken into custody, or locked up at home), or until he's so ill that he can't even lift his arm, let alone drink. Then he's brought to the hospital and tied down to stop him jumping out the window when he develops delirium tremens.

The problem isn't only with people going on benders, the harm to their health, the loss of a great part of their lives. It's also the constant, unremitting dialogue with alcohol, which absorbs a person's whole life. It's like a dialogue with one's own fatigue, lethargy, laziness, depression. But there's no possibility of a victory here—the best you can hope for is to remain stable. "And men loved darkness rather than light . . ." It's a dialogue with the abyss—and the abyss is getting wider and wider. Work, love, and every single human attachment—everything tumbles into it. It's like living through a blanket of cotton wool. You're not dealing with the present time, or people, or life, but with death, and the abyss, and alcohol. Perhaps we ought to abandon the great Russian literary tradition, and give up looking for Dostoyevskian depths in everyone (if you dig a bit, you're sure to find that). Shouldn't we instead make a simple medical diagnosis—the man's an alkie, a slob, and an idiot?

What do my patients think about? That's a puzzle. It's not a question of how educated they are. Here's a man sitting in front of me, listening and not listening to me as I anxiously explain, as I always do, how he has to lose weight, move around, take the pills, go on taking them even when he feels better—when all he wants is one thing: for me to shut up and let him go home. Sometimes he might vaguely mention a disability certificate or a sick note; then I reply, "Who are you going to show it to? Saint Peter?" He grins, even if he doesn't understand. What's he thinking about? Probably the same as I am when I'm in the electricity-supply offices being told off for not paying my bills, because I don't understand anything about tariffs or late payment fines or why I need to pay before the twenty-fifth, and all I want is to get away. There we're talking about electricity, here we're talking about life: but you can understand the man. I've never had such an interesting job.

Here's how it all began. Two and a half years ago, late in the morning on a gray April day, I was just arriving in the town of N., carrying with me a small suitcase containing a portable ultrasound machine and a lot of little bits of medical equipment. I had traveled that road dozens of times, hundreds of times, but I'd never before felt such a sense of elation. The melancholy beauty of early spring, the poor wooden houses and the rich brick ones, even the slippery, potholed road—everything filled me with joy. I felt like shouting aloud, "Citizens, bring me your hearts!" I'd never before experienced such a primal joy in doctoring. There had always been some ulterior motive: learning, impressing my professor, defending my thesis, finding material for a book.

My new colleagues gave me a friendly welcome. I got a modest consulting room of my own, with a couch, two chairs and a one-legged table. (The other legs had fallen off of their own accord, but this one had become firmly attached; I had to borrow an axe from the hospital carpenter to amputate it.) I covered my peeling walls with charts I had brought with me, showing drug doses and prices. The biggest hole, I covered with a political map of the world. A nurse asked me shyly whether a map of the region wouldn't have been more useful (she was right, of course). I answered arrogantly that I had been looking for a star chart, for such was my ambition, but hadn't found one.

Consultants are first introduced to the *socially significant* individuals in the area—not necessarily sick ones. Even before that, they meet the litigious ones. My first patient was seventy-year-old Anna Grigoryevna, who had written to Putin to complain about the poor treatment she had received, and her poverty and loneliness. She sent her letter to the Kremlin. The president's office faxed the hospital: sort her out! Anna Grigoryevna was reckoned to be crazy—what an idea, complaining up there! I told her, as offhandedly as I could, that Vladimir Vladimirovich had sent me to see her, and I asked her to undress. It turned out the old lady really was ill, and hadn't been properly treated, but she wasn't crazy—just depressed. When we get involved with our patients' souls, we ought to confine ourselves to those parts of them that are short of serotonin. "How much can you afford to spend on medicine?" I asked Anna Grigoryevna. Nothing at all, it turned out. She had stocked up on kasha, but her pension wouldn't come in for another ten days. "What do you mean, depression? It's just sadness," our university psychiatry lecturer used to say. I checked the prices of the drugs I'd prescribed, and told my patient: "Vladimir Vladimirovich asked me to hand you a hundred and fifty rubles."

Then I worked for the rest of the day. That evening the surgeons looked in. "You're out of your mind, putting in all this effort . . . Even the Tajik immigrants don't work that hard." And off we went to celebrate my first day at work. "Let's just check if the traffic police are out on patrol," said the surgeons, and made a phone call. "No worries, doctors, have a nice evening," they were told. I asked them to share the secret phone number. "Nine-one-one," said the surgeons, "don't forget."

I never again gave money to my patients. But Anna Grigoryevna turned up a year later to say goodbye. Her brother was taking her to live with him in Simferopol. And she handed back my 150 rubles.

> Rustle your leaves, you oaks in springtime!
> Grow tall, you grass-shoots! Lilacs, bloom!
> There are no guilty, all are righteous,
> On this blessed, all-forgiving day!

So wrote the poet Severyanin,[4] and that was the mood of my first day at work. And I think it has kept me going to this day.

Of course, there's been a lot of grief and darkness since then, and sometimes I wake at five in the morning and can't get back to sleep—probably because my own serotonin stores are running low—and then there comes a very timely call from the hospital: I'm wanted. It's cold and foggy out there, but ten minutes later I'm hurrying into my office, plugging in the machinery, things start to hum, I slip on my white coat, look at the velvety gloom outside, and tell myself: (1) this is as good as it'll ever get; (2) this is what happiness is.

September 2007
Translated by Nicolas Pasternak Slater

A NON-EASTER JOY

IT'S NOT easy being the chief of staff of a hospital. First, you have to manage people, which isn't pleasant—particularly if you have a soul, and particularly in a district hospital where there's no one to choose from. Second, all sorts of things go on in a hospital: patients drop cigarette ends and set fire to their mattresses, jump out of windows, pilfer from the nurses, write complaints, or die; roofs leak, chimneys get blocked, all the lights go off. Third, the rules of the game keep changing and you have to adapt, making sure that the staff and patients don't suffer—whether the changes are bad or good. Fourth, you have to deal with the authorities, not to mention agencies like the Fire Service, Sanitary and Epidemiology Service, and the Drug Control Service. And you mustn't let all those considerations make you forget what you're there for: you may run the hospital as an enterprise, but you have to remember that it's more than an enterprise, more than a business entity.

Our chief of staff is a woman of fifty-six who wants to change things for the better—and not only via official channels. This has caused her a certain amount of unpleasantness, and one such issue came to the attention of people all over Russia. We (three doctors and a number of supporters of the hospital) tried to help—to help both her and ourselves. Since I took part in these events, it is incumbent upon me to tell you about them.

I.

On leap-year day, Friday, February 29, we inaugurated our cardiology department—a new one, serving a number of districts. And on the very next working day, the following Monday, our chief of staff was fired, with no reason given. During our morning conference we were visited by our mayor's tipsy deputy, who read us the order. That caused an uproar in the papers, on the radio and TV, and online—our friends started the response, and it carried on under its own steam. The following Tuesday, we received an order from the police to hand over our financial records. That was when we discovered that we had been indulging in fraud on a massive scale. But we soon ceased to fear a criminal prosecution—the document sent to us turned out to be a fake. The official government newspaper played a decisive part here. That Thursday, I was summoned to meet an Important Personage. Without changing into women's clothing, as Kerensky did when fleeing from the Bolsheviks, I set off for Moscow as Lenin set off for Petrograd, in a light armored car provided by one of our benefactors.

I won't enter into the details of my interview with the Important Personage. All I will say is that the position of a district hospital cardiologist (as low as you can get on the professional ladder) turned out to be a very advantageous one. I talked about our chief of staff, an honest person who (most importantly) identified with the other doctors, rather than with the administration. "*We* saved so-and-so!" she says. The outcome of our interview is well known: the mayor was invited to take early retirement, with his professional fate and that of the chief of staff to be decided by the elected district council. Even the Important Personage couldn't oust a democratically elected mayor.

That was a tempestuous week—not even a week, four days, during which the phone rang nonstop. It calmed down only at night. We were so carried away by our lust for battle ("We've got to win!"—and don't even ask "What for?") that we forgot the reason for our existence—our patients. "Now you understand public officials," said our benefactor; "their lives are like that all the time. That's why they can't be bothered with people." You get the same sort of feverish activity between a death and a funeral, when you go through a lot more in the course of two or three days than you normally would. People turn up, express their sympathy as they must, one person goes off for the death certificate, another prepares the funeral feast.

Sympathy can express itself in different ways. But even unhealthy sympathy is better than a healthy lack of it. So, thank you, a big thank you to everybody, including S. At one time I used to regard him as a friend; but we hadn't met for eight years. He'd been a great success, but sometimes he has a drink too many and writes me affectionate letters full of quotations from Wittgenstein and Saint-Exupéry. Here's a letter I got on Wednesday morning, March 5: "I have been watching the events unfold with pain and sadness. I'd very much like to help you to look at what's going on from an entirely different viewpoint . . . Just call me. That would be a great victory for you, in a metaphysical sense. But if that's not possible for you at present, then please accept this pattern as a gift. If you take a look at it, even just occasionally, it will bring you success. Since giving up my work almost completely three years ago, I have spent my time designing patterns. Hugs from . . ." and his signature. The attached file contained a pattern of stripes and stars—quite a pleasant one. I asked my colleague to suggest a diagnosis. He decided against a psychiatric disorder and said, "This is some sort of spiritual ailment."

"What a mess!" enthuses my American coauthor, after reading all about us in the *Washington Post*. He'd been out of contact for ages, editing and finishing some chapters for the American edition of our book. But now he had emerged from hiding and gotten in touch.

Sometimes you get unexpected suggestions. My former neighbor from Moscow, a biologist who also owned a small grocery store but now apparently lives on Sakhalin Island, writes: "Sooner or later you'll realize that all your efforts are a waste of time, and you'll go off to treat Ethiopians or Filipinos. They'll be far more grateful for anything you do for them. I've spent a long time living in both places—they're full of wonderful people."

*

A "non-Easter joy"—the expression came to me almost at once—is not the joy of meeting someone or receiving a gift, nor the joy of contact with a superior power. It's probably what Napoleon felt on entering the empty city of Moscow. The absence of resistance—like a knife through butter, or, better yet, through sunflower oil. The hand outstretched to inflict a blow, or receive a handshake, is left hanging in empty air.

On Friday, the day after my conversation with the Important Personage, when all the journalists had left and the phone had stopped ringing, that emptiness became frightening. No one brought us the keys of the chief of staff's office; all the female members of staff got black-and-white copies of a card with good wishes for Women's Day (March 8), signed by the mayor; while the man himself had left for who knows where. There was no official news about job losses ("please call after the holiday"), but it became clear that these brothers weren't giving up the fight. Any minute they could declare me insane and forcibly hospitalize me at the Bushmanovka, the regional psychiatric hospital. "This doctor has had an attack of schizophrenia or whatever—sort him out. Despite his condition, he's been meeting up with presidents and ministers, and giving press conferences, and getting officials dismissed."

But then we were lucky enough to get a fax (it wasn't easy—March 7 was a half day): a reply from the Important Personage to the government newspaper; things had gotten a bit easier, and I wasn't going to be carted off to the Bushmanovka. Instead we landed in a state of terrifying emptiness. That's the state we're now living in.

The emptiness takes on substance, and figures emerge from it. Several businesspeople, very ordinary ones, and the spiritual leader of our town, the mayor's confidante, whom we've known for a long time. She owns a number of enterprises, and her bookshelves carry volumes of spiritual instruction side by side with *Business Accountancy* and

Laws of Local Self-Government. This Confidante has lived through some very hard times. She has pleasant manners and the voice of an angel, and is fond of using religious jargon: our history "leads her into temptation" and prevents her from "making her peace." I tell her "You have no fear of God." And it's true, she doesn't fear Him, she feels He owes her: for all she has suffered, for the fact that she reads such a lot of religious literature, spends hours standing in church, and observes the fasts. The store of evil within this Confidante is staggering. It was she who invented the stories about us performing experiments on people, administering banned medications, and rehearsing for an Orange Revolution ("I've read up about those techniques"). The journalists have played their part too. Our enemies probably don't remember Dostoyevsky's *The Possessed*, if they ever even read it, but journalists are bound to remember the young people who descended on a peaceful provincial town in order to blow it up. We too have got the charity balls, and the domineering women, and the bombastic man of letters, and even an aristocrat—our own benefactor ("An aristocrat is irresistible when he goes in for democracy").

We get talked about on TV—the ward is Chekhov's Ward No. 6, the people are silent, the court has been bought. It's easiest to ignore the interesting bits—that our chief of staff has twice taken the mayor to court, and won both times; that the local inhabitants have written a petition in favor of the hospital and are collecting signatures. That's what the party press is like—in our case it's far worse than the government newspaper. We get compared to George Soros, or Yukos Oil—what a wealth of material to attack us on! It's like a passage from *One Day in the Life of Ivan Denisovich*: "Only after the war the British admiral took it into his blasted head to send me a souvenir, a token of gratitude, he called it.What a nasty surprise, and how I cursed him for it!"

It's a well-known fact: if you set a million monkeys to type on a million typewriters, sooner or later one of them will produce a masterpiece. The monkeys have one advantage: they hit the keys at random. "How am I supposed to understand everything?' demands the female journalist. Well, yes, indeed, if you plan to write about *everything*.

Some papers suggested we should explain the situation in our own words: "You're so good at writing." That's very convenient for the person making the suggestion—like "You're tall, please change the light bulb." We always refused. Not out of arrogance—we just didn't have the strength.

A lot of nonsense was written about what went on. But the whole thing was simple. We weren't fighting "the forces of evil" in general, nor "high-handed officialdom"—we were just fighting against the people getting in the way of our work. What were we fighting for? To have our chief of staff reinstated. She let us do what we wanted—which was to treat the sick. There's no politics in that, and hardly any economics either. One can't say no to the authorities, but she did. Why do they appear not to be afraid of anything? They are afraid, they're very afraid—but they're fighting for the same thing as we are: the right to live their own lives. The hospital has become the battlefield. It was their Borodino: a little village of no importance to anyone but us, its inhabitants.

The list of people who supported us online begins like this: Abramova, Aizenberg, Akimova, Akulova, Albaut, Aldashin, Alekseyev, Altova, Amelina, Andreyev, Averkiev, Avilova, Azarova . . . Signatories from Moscow, Lisbon, Washington, Chekhov, Kursk, Saint Petersburg, Beersheba. Engineers, doctors, teachers, entrepreneurs, students, scientists, writers. A thousand signatures. Did it all work? Who knows? But it gave us a great deal of comfort and inspiration. However fast you can run, however hard you can hit, the fans are always a help.

What are all these people up in arms about? Was it worth raising such a ruckus over a woman of retirement age who was fired? The answer came from a friend of mine who works at the Russian State University for the Humanities. She wrote: "I spend my time explaining four different verb forms in Hebrew, and I know you're spending your time examining patients. It seems to me that you and I are doing the same thing." So the answer's a simple one: those people are fighting for themselves. Of course it's frightening to fight against emptiness personified—but this is one of those rare occasions when we absolutely have to win. That emptiness is doing its best to swallow us up, to bend us to its will—like "gaffers" in the army, or "brothers" in prison; and we rookies and newbies are sticking up for ourselves. We've got to win—win on the bottom line, get the right result, not just do well and show that we're tough. That's what'll decide the rest of our lives, from now on.

There are a lot of side questions. For instance: If we manage to win out, but only with help from the very top—can we regard that as a victory? Of course we can. The hospital belongs to the state, so who better than the state to help it? People ask: What about the local people, your patients? That doesn't bother me. We're doctors, not marshals of an army of patients. "So how do ordinary people react to what you're doing?"—They're dying less than they used to. An old lady comes to see me. Some months ago we sent her to Moscow for an operation, and now she's much better. "I hear they're closing the hospital. Could you let me have some pills before they do?" She's right. She's small and we're big; who's supposed to protect whom? Take your medicine and lead a healthy life—that's all we ask.

Our professorial colleagues stood up for us too, although some found it uncomfortable. They spend a lot of time at all sorts of meetings; we don't, that's why we got ourselves down here, to fight for our freedom to arrange things the way we see fit. Medicine has always relied on authority; in the old days, that was all there was. Whereas in math, for instance, authority isn't that important. That's all right, medicine is going the same way now.

And there's another group of people supporting us: "Heroes of Russia." One of them, who was actually awarded a Gold Star, Hero of the Russian Federation, bursts into our office: "We'll show them!" He's already had a few drinks this morning. "We'll bend them, we'll break them, we'll put them where they belong." "What on earth was that?" asks my colleague. "That was a Hero of Russia. Benya the King, not one of us pansies, with glasses on our noses and autumn in our hearts." Anyway, the heroes, and the journalists, and the professors, all did their best. Don't think I'm not grateful. I am.

2.

Things have been happening. On March 14, there was a meeting of the regional councillors. The chairman—so trim and bronzed, he didn't seem to belong here at all—proposed a compromise: the mayor could be reprimanded and the chief of staff reinstated. The chairman and his wife are good people; they've put themselves out for the hospital before, collecting money for it and sharing our concerns. But the chairman had only just returned from skiing in the Alps, and his flight had left him tired and jet-lagged; he failed to talk to the people he should have, and the upshot was that six of the fifteen councillors voted in favor, and the rest against. The chairman keeps saying, "Our trouble is that we're too honest." He's lost a kilogram and a half in a day.

Those bullheaded fellows had won the day. What is it that makes them so intransigent—do they see any move toward reconciliation as a sign of weakness, a signal for mounting a counterattack? All we were proposing was a reprimand for the mayor, and the reinstatement of the chief of staff; no winners and no losers, in fact. But the chairman—it was ages since he'd been living in real time, where the situation actually changes depending on what you do and say.

A sense of real time: that's when you discover that the past imperfect tense has become the past perfect, in other words, the past in which you can't put anything right or change it. That was in the air when I met with the Important Personage, as it was when Kitty and Levin declared their love. The passage of time is suspended—your presence of mind is needed right now, right here. The fact that you're generally perceptive, or well informed, or decent, or whatever—all of that belongs to the past. It improves your chances of acting intelligently now, in the present situation, but it doesn't guarantee anything.

We're on the losing side again. So should we leave, or stay? If we see ourselves as benefactors of the human race, we ought to hang on till the end, so we get streets named after us. But as it is, we're free to make our own decisions—all we are is doctors who wanted to improve their working lives, and we nearly brought it off. We indulge in fantasies of drafting a letter; we're surprised that we never got an answer to the first one; and we remind ourselves that the unit of time in provincial Russia is a week. One of the top bosses, right at the top, will surely help us.

"Thanks to such and such improvements," we write, "total mortality in our hospital is down by half, while deaths from myocardial infarction have been reduced to one-sixth of what they were." That's the truth, though we're sick and tired of repeating it. What are we going to boast about in a year's time, when there'll be more patients, and they'll be more seriously ill? But for now, while we're in this mess, the patients have almost stopped falling ill. The ones we do have look out of place in our freshly refurbished wards—as Grand Duke Konstantin Pavlovich once observed, "War dirties uniforms and creates disorder." You have to make an effort to get people to look right in such splendid surroundings—new tiles, smooth walls, big bright windows. My colleague has a certain amount of work to do, while I have our Major and Minor Cardiology Labs to sit in, making phone calls and writing petitions.

An elderly woman turns up with an attack of arrhythmia of unknown duration—at least a week. I need to pass a probe into her esophagus, check the heart for thrombi, anesthetize and defibrillate her to restore her normal heart rhythm. Over the past year we've done all that dozens of times, perfectly happily. But today... what can we do, when the woman who is our new chief of staff would be delighted to see us fail? If only the patient's rhythm were to return to normal while we're fussing over the apparatus. And for once, this is what actually happens. Sinus rhythm. "Look—Somebody up there must have heard us!" "Don't blaspheme," says my colleague. Yes, sorry. We're very tired—not a huge price to pay for independence, but it's almost all we're prepared to offer.

We come out of the hospital and suddenly notice that in our subdued state, we match the landscape better. And our fear levels are lower. Where could we go, anyway? Tutayev, Kirzhach, Boldino?

Wherever you go, everything's the same. It's easy to see why we have such miserable lives and such a wonderful literature.

Well, never mind, it'll all work out. Someone needs us here. This town doesn't belong only to officials and their confidantes—there are spruce little old ladies too, with their grandsons and granddaughters; it's the town of Richter, Zabolotsky, my great-grandfather Mikhail Melentyev, and the plump hypochondriacal little woman from the drugstore, and the nice schoolteacher with something odd on her aortic valve; it's a town of artists, and of a quiet, pious alcoholic with congenital heart disease; the town of Father Ilya Shmain, the town of Tsvetaeva.

3.

It had to happen. On March 19, suddenly all hell broke loose. A ten-man inspection committee arrived at the hospital and, at the same time, fifteen auditors descended on the administrative offices. The ensuing storm brought down the mayor, and even the poor chairman. And more or less incidentally, it seemed, someone turned up to read out a decree: "The chief of staff is to be reinstated." Once again, the emptiness had been driven out into the intercellular spaces. Alas, it will still exact its revenge; but our First World War is over. Il faut travailler. Back to work.

In his final speech to the regional council (reproduced in the local paper) the mayor said: "Strangers have entered our home and wrecked it . . ." What sort of a "home" is he talking about? When we first arrived, it didn't even possess a defibrillator. There might have been a "home" here, with KEEP OFF THE GRASS! in front of it—but there wasn't any grass, just beaten earth, and had anything ever grown there?

The emptiness went in for high-flown rhetoric. A long, anonymous article appeared, titled "Practicing Genocide on a Regional Scale." It opens with some moving words: "We Russians have always been re-proached for not sparing our own lives in the name of succoring other nations. Such is the primordial nature of the Russian soul, nurtured in us by ancient tradition and Christian love ..." And before long— little wonder—a passage about us, the strangers: "These crafty new-comers have become expert at exploiting the generosity of the Russian people for the furtherance of their own mean and selfish ends." That's the central message.

So here we are, at last. "What's it like being a Jew in Russia?" asks a little lady from an international Jewish organization. That's all they think about. So I tell her—difficult, but still legal.

"For their own avaricious purposes, these outsiders skillfully exploit the power and wealth of our state—a state created from the labors of Russian people over thousands of years." A whole column in the same vein. And then—another three columns about the hospital, with numbers, order dates, incoming and outgoing consignment numbers, detailed cost breakdowns, disingenuous lies. Everything jumbled together, like the authors in the Confidante's bookshelves. Warm words for the mayor ("grandson of veterans, son of a soldier"), and—modulating into a remote key—warm words for Chekhov too. A section on "Why the prosecutor's office was blind," and a bit about me and my colleague ("the cardio-investors," "the two cardiac failures"). And when it gets to the Important Personage, it talks about his motivation—"anti-Russian, anti-People ... what drives him is free-masonry."

"They're just primitive, ignorant people," good folk tell me. I'd put it differently. They're bad people. They're primitive because they're bad, not the other way around. Some jerk executes a risky maneuver on the road, tailgates you, and flashes his headlights—out of my way! Is he primitive too? "You're more clever than he is, take no notice ..." OK, I'll take no notice. But as for being clever—if I have a higher IQ, does that mean I'm cleverer? The Third Rome is far closer to the Second one than to the First; here it isn't a question of intelligence. And a frightening thought occurs to me: Supposing it was just this bloody-minded obstinacy (not driven by ill will, but by the desire for wholeness), this infinite willingness to sacrifice oneself and others, this belief in words, that defeated the Poles, the French, and the Germans? Anyway, everything now needs to calm down; there's a lot of work to be done; we need to live together. Let's regard all that happened as an initiation. (Some years later, a new minister arrived from the regional center to open our refurbished surgical department. Afterward he and I stepped out into the street, and he looked me up and down. "You don't look like a fighter, not one bit." I named the ex-mayor and said, "That's what he thought too." We gave each other another searching look, and went our separate ways.)

"Our lives will never be the same again," I tell my colleague now. "We can't go into the cheburek joint—you know who we'd see there. Never mind, we can eat dumplings instead. We won't leave, of course not, but we need to insure our houses. Houses get burned down. They forged a paper, didn't they? So what other tricks have they got up their sleeve? Don't go into that pharmacy; just don't go there, simple as that. The municipal one is closed? All right then, go tomorrow. It's cheaper there anyway (and there's no real difference). You can protect your house, build a fence. There's no need to go for riverside walks along the Oka; if you have itchy feet, why not go to Drakino? That's a different district, only fifteen kilometers away—it's a pretty place too, and you won't meet anyone. But who needs to go out, anyway? Just open a window—the air's good anywhere. What are we doing here, after all—spending the summer?—No, we're here to stay. We've earned our place. We belong now."

March 2008
Translated by Nicolas Pasternak Slater

THE CHILDREN OF DZHANKOY
A Documentary Tale

To the town of N.

I.

THE LATEST incident in the town of N. began like this: early one morning, a Volga of the kind used to transport fair-to-middling public officials rolled up to the hospital and deposited a handful of bureaucrats from the regional center. They were seeking donations to benefit the children of Dzhankoy—give what you can. Dzhankoy, in the north of Crimea, is home to a major railway station; many people passed through it in Soviet times. Our visitors couldn't tell us how many children there were in Dzhankoy, or what these children needed, but it was clear that the money, if it ever reached them, would do so not in the form of crumpled rubles but of cobbled paths, say, or of an opulent monument, like the one recently erected in the hospital's courtyard—the bust of some foppish state councillor bearing a pompous inscription, in prerevolutionary spelling: "The greatness, glory, and benefit of the Fatherland are the proper goals of the learned, active, experienced Physician."[1] The hospital received this curious old fellow instead of medicine, catheters, dressings—instead of salaries for nurses and assistants, some of whom, in fact, had to be fired. That's a clever way to improve the stats: raise the average income of the medical staff by dismissing its poorest members. Then, at the bust's unveiling, things almost came to a head, as it were.

"The state has given you everything," the authorities said, sounding offended, as usual.

"What has it given us, exactly? Doctor Who, over there?"

"Electricity." And, after a pause: "Heating. Water."

"Maybe we should chip in to help the children of California? Since we haven't annexed them yet..." That joke went over like a lead balloon, with both the visitors and the other doctors. Well, if Dzhankoy is in need...The total came out to over fifteen thousand rubles.

That evening, an image, a metaphor suggested itself: "It's like a heart attack. The patient is hooked up to the monitor, hoping that the machine's monotonous beeping will tell him something, anything. All he can think about are household chores, little errands, and the physical well-being of his loved ones. Can't read, can't listen to his favorite music—not because of the pain (there's no more pain), but because books and music belong to the past, while the present...It's as if there is no present. There's only the beeping of the monitor, only the other patients, who are just as confused as he is, and the sense that life will likely go on, but that it won't be the same. Life will be different. But in what way?"

It was then that a new element appeared in daily life: an important, depressing element, like father's death or mother's illness (that same year she had to be moved from Moscow, for the last time, to be here, closer to the hospital)—like undeniable knowledge about one's neighbors.

This fund drive for Crimean children took place in March 2014. The powerful, positive emotions that flared up long ago, in a different era—"Citizens, bring me your hearts!" and all that—are still there to keep one going, like any real (if not altogether sober) feelings. Ten years have slipped by, almost unnoticed, since that first day in the town of N. A lot can change in ten years.

N. is old (only younger than Moscow by a century) and small, but it's a proper town nonetheless; it has a hospital, two secondary schools, two cemeteries, two Orthodox cathedrals, a police station, a prosecutor's office, and a courthouse. There are also two libraries—one for children, the other for adults. The first, thanks to the efforts of philanthropists, is going strong. The second is declining rapidly: no subscriptions to the big journals, and the only new donations come from two local members of the Writers' Union (both unabashed anti-Semites). There's a music school (an accordion and a piano); a vocational school (a college, as they now call it); an art school; a House of Children's Creativity (up for auction); a palatial House of Writers (big mosaic, concerts, readings); an employment office (invariably empty); two traffic lights; tons of pharmacies; a few retirement homes; a dock; a twenty-five-meter pool; until recently, a bowling alley (went belly-up); a nightclub called Through the Looking Glass (land of imagination: Alices of all sorts—black, red, bald—a Mad Hatter, a White Rabbit, Humpty-Dumpty, but very few visitors); a registry office; an art gallery; government buildings—municipal and regional; a fountain; a statue of Lenin on Lenin Square, which lies at the end of Lenin Street (but no corresponding avenue—the only avenue is named after Pushkin). The town paper is called *October*; it publishes all the local death notices, which is the only reason doctors read it. And, of course, there are fields, ravines, forests. In terms of water, there's the river Oka—navigable by ships, dredged and deepened every spring—as well as a shallow little stream. There's also a pond at one of the rest homes—"stocked," as the ad promises. The Oka isn't rich in fish, but one time a patient managed to pull in several kilograms of sterlet. There's no bridge, and who needs it? This region maintains no relationship with the one that lies on the other side of the river. Since the brick factory closed down, most of the men have been driving taxis or working security at the town's innumerable shops. There's no industry to speak of.

The main problem with small towns is the lack of choice, but here there's almost always a choice (the hospital is an exception), what the Brits might call "the other club"—a place you wouldn't be caught dead in. Teachers don't live on Resurrection Hill. Why? Just because—for a similar reason that those who are loyal to the local hospital would never go to the cheburek joint.

Wine isn't in great demand among the locals, but there are also two wine shops.

"Do you drink every day?" the young saleswoman asks the gray-haired artist. Behind his back, the girls at the shop call him Don Ramón—his favorite label.

The saleswoman isn't judging the artist, she's just curious.

"No, not every...well, yes."

And a follow-up question, posed just as courteously:

"Do you just sip it, or chug it down?"

She doesn't know how else to ask; he understands and takes no offense. Incidentally, the locals are drinking less: for example, they've stopped bringing the doctors moonshine. And they smoke less, too, and drive more cautiously; all the daredevils have either come to their senses or gotten themselves killed. People don't beat their children as frequently. Yes, despite it all, the town of N. is moving ever closer to the West—and much more quickly than Moscow is, too.

There you have order: even tiles, wide sidewalks, not a single stall or kiosk. Here you have less by way of order, but at least no one torments you: no concrete barriers, no boom gates across every driveway, no forced resettlement, and the lesbian couple, though they stand out a bit, are treated pretty much like everyone else—in contrast to the state, the residents of N. have come to respect privacy.

Concerning the name of the town. It's a well-known fact that writers are inferior to pigs: "A pig doesn't shit where it eats, doesn't shit where it sleeps...A pig would never do what Pasternak did" (Vladimir Semichastny), and that's why the landscape of Russian literature extends only to Moscow, Petersburg, and, very tentatively, to Voronezh, Taman', Mtsensk, exotic Abakan ("Where the clouds roll on," and where they've even established a cloud museum), Magadan, Orenburg, while the rest is all Yuriatin, Skotoprigonyevsk, Kalinov, Glupov, Goryukhino—in a word, N., so as not to upset Semichastny.[2]

"The world doesn't break, no matter what you throw at it": stories happen (or rather, anecdotes), but one's ability to observe them is dulled by excessive proximity to the subject. To witness and be surprised—that requires the right balance between the old and the new, the familiar and the unfamiliar. While even a superficial, momentary acquaintance is sometimes enough to arouse sympathy.

Olga L., thirty years old, came for a consultation from a neighboring town in the company of another woman, the head of a kindergarten:

"Will you see us, Doctor?"

Olga doesn't need a cardiologist, her heart is fine, but she has severe type 1 diabetes. "Have you got a glucose meter at home?" It burned out.

How can a glucose meter burn out? It runs on batteries. The truth is it burned *up*—in a fire set by her alcoholic neighbor. Olga managed to save her children (she has three), and now they live in a back room at the kindergarten. No husband.

"Did the neighbor survive?"

"The hell he did." In a cheerful voice: "Burned to a crisp, like a buffalo wing!"

There are fires in N., too. A one-story house burned down in the center of town, killing one woman. She handed her children to her husband through the window but couldn't get out herself. The husband suffered burns to his body and there was serious damage to his eyes; he's hospitalized in the surgical ward. The children are fine; they're in the children's ward, naturally. Word arrived that public officials of a very high order—the type that travel in Mercedes and BMWs, not mere Volgas—would take this matter into their own hands. What does that mean? Would the family be rehoused? No. Would the victim like anything else? To be left alone—and to be given antibiotic eye drops. That last request is, apparently, too trivial for the officials to deal with, and besides, there's no way to satisfy it: medical purchases are planned far ahead of time.

The governor wants a tour of the hospital. He puts on a robe over his jacket, shoe covers (senseless measures, if you think about it—pure optics):

"How're they treating you, Gramps?" he shouts at an octogenarian. "Doctor let you have a tipple when you need one?"

"I'm not an alcoholic," the man replies. "And I'm not hard of hearing."

The governor takes a more respectful tone, asks the man about his life. The man complains that his pension barely covers his rent and utilities, to say nothing of his medications, food...

"You've got rights and entitlements, you just don't know how to use them," the governor interrupts him angrily.

"An island is a piece of land which is entirely surrounded by water," Chekhov's poor "darling" repeated meaninglessly, with conviction. One patient—an architectural restorer—tells a story: one particular public official—the highest-ranking in the country—took a liking to a monastery on Valday Lake. He's fond of monasteries. This one was on an island—probably for a reason. The public official ordered a bridge to be built to connect the island to the mainland, and the construction destroyed the island, with the best of intentions. The authorities can bomb just about anything, and this earns them attention, like any dangerous thing. But they can't provide a hospital with pills or nurses, and so their power—as another patient, a Georgian, once put it, before being gently corrected—isn't worth a hill of bees.

The public officials in the town of N. can't build a bridge, much less bomb anything. They're sturdy fellows of medium height, running to fat, who never part with their leather murses—even on their yearly visit to church, on Easter Sunday. When the previous mayor moved out of the apartment he was occupying—and out of town—he left behind a dozen fire extinguishers. Nothing else. And now that's all he's remembered for. The only thing the public officials of N. fear are public officials of a far higher standing:

"The general came around, gave Pavel Andreyevich hell..." This is the man's secretary, who's run into a hospital to request some document or other. She's relishing the story, going into raptures. "I tell you, he screamed and screamed—scared Pavel Andreyevich so bad that..." All of a sudden, in a falsetto, for the whole ward to hear: "He shat himself!"

An example of the attitude one should take toward various authorities was set by a surgeon from the neighboring region. At the end of the working day he was surprised by an inspection team. "Hold on, I'll be with you in a minute," the surgeon told them, then went into the next room, changed, and quietly left the hospital. They waited and waited, then left as well.

"Don't try and put yourself in the authorities' shoes," the head of a major scientific institute in Moscow advised Mother when she worked there. This man served as the prototype for Anton Yakonov in Solzhenitsyn's *The First Circle*. Neither under him, nor under subsequent heads of the institute, when she herself was put in charge of a laboratory, did mother participate in "mandatory volunteerism"— no picking potatoes, no construction work on Saturdays—and she never faced any consequences for her refusal. "Don't want to," and that was that.

Aunties (water, electricity, gas), summer people, foreigners, Tajiks ("Got any work here, boss?"), artists with one foot in N. and the other in Moscow (or maybe even Paris), entrepreneurs, local scientific intelligentsia (Space Research Institute): each group has its own hierarchy, its own distinct estates, which sometimes comprise only a handful of individuals. There are also the lower depths, cheek by jowl with the rest: an orderly whose husband, recently back from prison, regularly beats her in the face; a single woman from Moldova who rejoices whenever she's allowed to bring her five-year-old daughter along on cleaning jobs—she usually isn't, and then the girl stays home alone all day. In this circle—where people struggle just to survive, where there's no running water, no electricity ("you've got rights and entitlements"), and where one might see a toilet in the kitchen—amazing things happen.

Volodya Z. was released early from prison and sent to the hospital in N., so as to die on the outside (that is, "receive treatment at his place of residence"). Of his forty-two years—hard to believe—a full twenty-six were spent behind bars, serving eight separate terms ("bids"). When asked if this was true, the police chief, who frequently visits the hospital for both professional and personal reasons, said: "They always exaggerate. Nineteen years sounds about right…" The last time Volodya went up, the charges had been pressed by his own sister, from whom he'd nabbed some piece of furniture or other. (Is there a hospital in Moscow that treats both the police chief and the people he's put in jail?)

Volodya was wheeled from the elevator directly to the Major Cardiology Labs and diagnosed with severe aortic and mitral valve disease. He eyed everyone warily, and was prone to brief outbursts of rage: doctors are people in uniform, after all—not Volodya's preferred company. But he made sure to take his pills. Soon he stopped gasping for breath and his edema disappeared. Then he went to Moscow for a valve replacement—the only real way to improve his condition.

Volodya was operated on by the flamboyant Father Georgy—colonel general, professor and member of the Russian Academy of Sciences, priest of the Ukrainian Orthodox Church (Moscow Patriarchate), defendant in the famed "case of the nanodust" in the House on the Embankment (where the plaintiff was none other than the Patriarch of Moscow and all Russia),[3] former health and social development minister, chief of the Kirov Military Medical Academy, and so forth and so on, many colorful details: in the institute he heads, they say, everyone must confess to the director. "Now, don't you fret. If something goes wrong under my scalpel, you're headed straight for heaven." That, according to Volodya, was how Father Georgy comforted him before the anesthesia was administered. But everything went smoothly. Volodya received two mechanical valves, and returned to N. sober, ruddy, and full of gratitude:

"I'll do anything you want."

What, for example?

"Pound someone's face in, maybe."

No face comes to mind.

"I can serve a term for you."

Well, well, well. Go ahead, steal a cow or a goose, or smash the front window of the café (they call it "Stalin's," because the owners have put up the pockmarked Generalissimo's portrait), and Volodya will take responsibility for the crime.

242 · MAXIM OSIPOV

He died a few months later, but not before fate smiled on him one more time. Volodya had found a job at a mortuary, picking up the deceased. One day, as he was removing a body from its former home, he got to chatting with the woman who'd just become a widow. They took an immediate liking to each other and, before you know it, filed a marriage application with the registry office. Although Volodya had been warned about the dangers of combining warfarin (which he was taking to prevent valve thrombosis) with alcohol, this was his wedding—and what's a wedding without a drink? He couldn't deny himself the pleasure. And that was the end of him: cerebral hemorrhage.

The town of N. owes its relative prosperity—cultural, medical, architectural—to non-natives, be they summer people or those who have come to stay. Like the United States, N. was created by immigrants. It was the summering intelligentsia that rebuilt the church on Resurrection Hill (in Soviet times, it had served as a bakery and, later, as a warehouse for consumer goods). It is they who put on the concerts and the annual art exhibitions, they who give jobs to the locals and eat at the café. The mild aversion the locals feel toward them is perfectly understandable: the French resent America, the Greeks resent Germany—dependence on others is a heavy burden. But even among the teenagers of N., there's no real opposition between natives and non-natives.

The children play make-believe, pretending they're coquettes, ladies from Moscow. They plop themselves down on sunny spots on the floor and intone, "Ah, a tanning bed!" But coquetry is not the exclusive domain of the young:

"I think I ought to tell you," an eighty-year-old lady from Moscow sighs, "that when I was a sweet little three-year-old, my parents had a terrible quarrel."

Does she understand that this is a doctor's office?

"My father grabbed me by my tiny little arms and dangled me over the railing of a bridge, shouting to my mother that he'd let me go if she didn't listen to him. Ever since then, my left ventricle has been dilated."

Her left ventricle is not dilated. No, this finding didn't suit her at all.

The hierarchy of the summer people is established independently of their relative wealth or, shall we say, the architectural merits of their dachas. The most important determining factor is an individual's accomplishment—but not in Moscow. If a person's book came out in America, or her painting was purchased by a museum in Berlin, or his tour in Japan was met with success—that counts. Go to the head of the table, say a few words. The natives, too, respect international success: at the funeral of a wonderful painter Eduard Steinberg, who was a friend to all (he lived in Paris but was buried here), the police donned their full dress uniforms and blocked off traffic, although the drive from the church to the old cemetery only takes a minute, and there are never that many cars on the road.

Great-Grandfather, on Mother's side, wound up in the town of N. not entirely by choice, like many political prisoners (he was sentenced in 1933, one of fourteen doctors accused of poisoning Maxim Gorky). He came here after a stint in Butyrka, after the construction of the White Sea–Baltic Canal, after the war. "This is a place of refuge for our family, just in case," he wrote in his journal. In Vladimir, where Great-Grandfather was the head physician, his position became untenable when officers began to return from the front—as a former prisoner, he could be denounced and rearrested at any moment, all because someone else wanted his job. He came in the summer of '46, along with his ten-year-old granddaughter. In those days, the journey from Moscow took twelve hours: first there was the train, then seven kilometers on foot, following a rickshaw loaded up with your luggage, and, finally, a steamer up the Oka.

Here, the old house on Pushkin Street received many guests—some renowned, some unknown. The town of N. was lucky to find itself located at exactly the right distance from forbidden Moscow. In the early '70s, a few years after Great-Grandfather's death, the house was looted and demolished—and so the family's relationship with the town was ruptured. The only things that remain from those early days are the fireplace tiles, which mother salvaged, and the huge linden tree in the corner of the property. The only childhood memories left are of this linden tree and of certain smells: a damp basement, dust caked by the rain.

In 1946 there was only one security officer of the NKVD in town, but by the '70s the number of secret policemen had risen to eleven—to deal with all the "enemies" that had settled here. These days, the number is hard to determine.

Europeans, in any case, feel very comfortable here. An Italian mosaicist and his wife have lived here for several years now. The vicissitudes of Russian history don't shock him:

"*Che cazzo*! We were gays before you were walking upright."

One time his wife went into an Armenian shop and he stayed outside, smoking a hand-rolled cigarette beside a crate of cucumbers.

"How much?" asks a customer.

The Italian shrugs: "*Italiano*." He doesn't speak Russian.

"I know, I know—*Italiano*. But how much for the *Italiano* cucumbers?"

The natives are used to seeing foreigners. Germans, the French, Indians, Americans—you name it. They don't consider Tajiks, Azerbaijanis, Armenians, or Moldovans foreigners, and they don't discriminate against them: What can you do? They didn't choose to be what they are.

A new worker appeared at the car wash—Surik (Suren). What happened to the other fellow?

"Gagik. They locked him up. Shot an Azerbaijani."

They gave Gagik four years, which seems very lenient.

"Not *shot*, Daddy—*shot at*," Surik's ten-year-old son cuts in. The boy goes to school during the year but helps his father in the summer.

Tourists come up on weekends, visit the Church of the Resurrection, the sculpture of the "sleeping boy" (Victor Borisov-Musatov is buried beneath it), and the Tsvetaeva Stone. The local tourist guide tells a story: in the early '60s, a student named Senya O. arrived from

Kyiv—"a boy in shabby trousers," as Tsvetaeva's daughter put it, a pure, romantic soul, the type they call "lovely" today. He had only one desire: to fulfill the dying wish of the poet whose verse had pierced his heart. "I would like to be buried," she had written, "in one of those graves with a silver dove on it." The stone Senya found at the local quarry and had placed where Tsvetaeva had wished to be laid to rest was removed after a few days. Good deeds—such as aid (mostly weaponry) for that era's "children of Dzhankoy," who were then in Africa and the Middle East—could only be performed by the government. Without the state's consent, one couldn't erect a monument even to Khrushchev, much less to Tsvetaeva. But the intelligentsia of N., and especially its female contingent, appreciated Senya's impulsive gesture. "Charming and taming them (the intelligentsia) is child's play. Go ahead, pick them up with your bare hands"—Senya had succeeded fabulously, but not everyone was impressed by his resourcefulness: he became the subject of one of father's short stories. And so the town of N. was inoculated against excessive enthusiasm and good deeds long ago. The current cenotaph stone (engraved "Marina Tsvetaeva Would Have Liked to Rest Here") was placed during perestroika. As for Senya, he now makes his home far away, in New York, and writes "pleasant poems for children, so that they don't forget Russian."

The shops, cafés, hotels, and bed and breakfasts—these are run by local entrepreneurs, who have their own distinct charm. They're accustomed to circumventing the state and despise anyone who "made a bundle" through "connections"—people like that, they say, want a bite of everything. These entrepreneurs use the language of the criminal world (*fence, shark, fall guy*), but you can come to them for help without hesitation; they might turn you down, but they'll do it with a light touch—no "unfortunately, you just don't fit our program." In fact, without the secret donations of one of these entrepreneurs, the hospital would have gone under long ago. When he first brought in his ninety-two-year-old grandmother, he was greatly surprised that neither the doctors nor the nurses had asked her what on earth she expected from them, at her age—obviously, she wanted what everyone wants: to live longer and to feel well. She received treatment, felt better. Some years later she passed away, but the grandson keeps on donating.

All institutions of practical significance (municipal services, schools, the pension fund, the treasury, the registry office) are headed, as is usual in Russia, by middle-aged women; the life of the town rests on their shoulders. They're not averse to socializing, don't shy away from a drink and a song ("How about it, girls?"), and are far more pleasant than the fellows with the leather murses. Sometimes they seem totally comprehensible, sometimes not. Here's an example. There was an internist at the clinic a few years back—tall and melancholy, very mediocre. Later he turned up in Moscow, a clerk at a drugstore. At the hospital's New Year's party, between the appetizers and the dancing, the women discussed the vegetables this internist used to sell at the market, as a sideline. His professional degradation didn't strike them as tragic, they were just sorry he'd left town: he used to sell such good vegetables.

The most important civic event for the inhabitants of N. is the Saturday market. There's no telling what you might hear between the stalls:

"God didn't grant Patriarch Alexey health."

A sigh in response:

"Or life, either."

Another pair of women shoppers:

"Why are you feeding her"—probably the interlocutor's mother or mother-in-law—"like that? Just you watch, she'll live to a hundred."

A third:

"My husband's liver is totally shot. The doctors say he's only hanging on 'cause he's got a good stomach and pancreas."

There hasn't been a high-profile murder in many years, not since the gambling industry was banned. That and the shortening of compulsory military service are, it seems, the only positive reforms that can be ascribed to the current regime. Of course, with the passage of time, things are easily forgotten: for example, after Yeltsin had bypass surgery, the number of these procedures immediately increased tenfold all across the country—but who now remembers such accomplishments?

In terms of headline-grabbing crimes, there was the armed bank robbery (the culprits shut off the town's electricity, stole a car and dumped it) and the art heist, where the thieves claimed they were conducting a surprise security check, tied up the gallery's guard and director, and made off with two canvases—one by Vasily Polenov, the other by Ivan Aivazovsky. In both cases, the wrongdoers got away with it. There was also the assault at one of the B and Bs. Thirteen of the guests showed up at the hospital after being attacked with baseball bats in the middle of the night—at the behest, it turned out, of the inn's proprietor, who took offense at a joke one of them had made. The story was reported throughout the country—a new development in the hospitality sector.

On one occasion, in 2008, the police had to get involved: someone was going door-to-door slipping leaflets into mailboxes that said all the local doctors were working for the CIA (this was before the law against "foreign agents" went into effect). The leaflets read something like this: "Alien extremists have come to feed the homeless so as to transplant organs." Echoes of the Stalinist "Doctors' Plot." No one was caught, but things eventually quieted down and returned to normal. A very Russian turn of events: no solution, but the trouble passes—so why bring it up? Forget it. In any case, the police department itself is not perceived as a danger in N. Relations between medical professionals and policemen are familiar, friendly: they too are state employees, and they have wives, children, parents—they all need doctors now and then.

Here's a story—fresh, but from Moscow. An ambulance arrives and a nurse rushes into the office of the doctor on call: "They've brought in a traffic cop!" A joyous bustle: the traffic cop has had a myocardial infarction. The cop's wife starts weeping and pleading: "He works at a desk, not on the street"—that is to say, don't take his life, have mercy. No one in N. would ever have thought of such a thing.

*

The Christian denominations represented in N. are the Pentecostals (they have a church up on a hill) and the Seventh-Day Adventists (they have a school, a university, and an institute for Bible translation across the river)—both of these groups keep a low profile—and, of course, the Orthodox, who are the majority.

A pretentious middle-aged visitor is none too impressed with the town. He sighs:

"Everything around here is so gray, so dull. And Moscow's not much better."

So what's better? "Mount Athos. The salvation of the soul...What else does one need?" In fact, he needs a lot else besides—and he needs it done well, quickly, and for free. That's precisely why he showed up here at the hospital.

The religiosity of old Olga Mikhailovna, who suffers from congestive heart failure, is far less complicated, far more cheerful:

"I'm a communist by conviction. I even pay my party dues. But I'm superstitious, you know, and I feel it isn't only your pills that help—I feel God helps me too."

Another Orthodox woman, the head clerk of an office-supply warehouse, reasons thus:

"I'll quit smoking, I promise. I consulted with the elder at the monastery about it too. A proper Orthodox person isn't supposed to smoke, isn't that so? I never smoke when I'm on a pilgrimage, but when I get back, I always start up again—my nerves get to me. I work in a warehouse, and I'm responsible for everything. By the way, doctor, you need any staplers, folders, markers? We've got tons of them lying around."

The head of the warehouse laughs. She's brought a huge bag full of office supplies. *Make to yourselves friends of the mammon of unrighteousness*—of all the Gospel's commandments, this one people keep without fail.

And then there's Nastya, a girl of thirteen with developmental delay. A nurse draws her blood and, in order to distract her, asks:

"What's your zodiac sign?"

"Don't have one," she responds. "I'm Orthodox."

The girl's answer perplexes the nurse: she's Orthodox too, after all, but she has a zodiac sign.

Anyone may enter intensive care, and priests are no exception. Sometimes they're asked to come to visit patients who are near death—to anoint them, offer the last rites.

"Is there any hope she might pull through?" asks the young priest. Extreme unction is a laborious business, so he might as well make sure. A major stroke, mechanical ventilation, several days in a deep coma. Who actually believes in miracles, aside from a patient's closest relatives?

Another priest tried to discourage several women from having abortions. He walked into the ob-gyn wing and made a powerful, impassioned speech, yet the women not only refused to listen but also gave him an earful: one was out of work, another had no husband, and a third had no place to call home. "You should have thought of that earlier," the priest responded and left.

Parish priests have precious little freedom themselves—even less than doctors do. Somehow they quickly became part of the system: school, army, hospital, prison. Not all of them, thank God, but most of them. People had expected a great deal from the church when it was still under the Soviet yoke—and even afterward, throughout the '90s—but the only thing it has actually taught them is what they can and cannot consume during Lent.

There's a lot of longing for the Soviet past around here, even among those who never really experienced it. It's best not to talk politics with patients, but if a woman has an unusual mitral valve, it's tempting to think that she herself must be interesting. Natalya is a thirty-six-year-old journalist and amateur pilot who misses the USSR:

"Now, that was strength."

So there you are: nothing interesting. She barely even lived in the USSR—but apparently Young Communists are born, not made. And the next patient is an old woman. When asked why she hasn't been taking her medications, she replies:

"Who needs us, anyway? Back in the day, things were different ..."

Her meaning is clear. Back in the day the state cared about its citizens. Both she and Natalya feel orphaned, though the latter still has her parents. The old woman is easier to understand: she's all alone. And yet it's unlikely that any of her peers in the United Kingdom would fail to take their pills because Her Majesty wasn't personally concerned about their high blood pressure.

Nostalgia for the Soviet Union is now widespread and finds expression in a series of clichés: everyone was afraid of us, and there was a lot to be thankful for—the health care was free (in what sense?), literary magazines had enormous circulations, and the state put out good animated cartoons. After the Jews came out of Egypt, they too looked back fondly on their time in captivity, remembering the "flesh pots," the fish, which they "did eat in Egypt freely," the cucumbers, the melons, and maybe even the fine Egyptian health-care and education systems.

"You who from birth / Wore orphan's garb—/ Don't mourn an Eden / You've not seen."[4] The Soviets leveled Tsvetaeva's dacha long ago. The place is now the outdoor dance floor of that very B and B where the pond is stocked with fish and guests are treated so unkindly. Across from the hospital is the Tsvetaeva Museum, where the only personal item on display is a mirror in which the poet might have examined her reflection. The young woman who works there ends her tour by reciting, in a high voice, "To My Poems" and announcing that their turn has finally come.[5]

There aren't that many real fanatics around, but here's one: his father was purged and executed in 1938, and he himself was put away for protesting against the Soviet invasion of Hungary two decades later (Khrushchev released him soon after—and he hates Khrushchev). Now he's in his early eighties, same age as Mother would have been; he knew her English teacher, Margarita Yakovlevna Rabinovich— "they sent her to the camps too"—and that's how the conversation started. He teaches philosophy, theology, and social studies at a technical institute in Moscow, and here, in the Cardiology Lab, preaches Stalinism.

What about his father?

"Sure, there were excesses… But Churchill himself praised our leader…" Even Stalinists value international success.

The professor isn't risking anything. Calm, sober K., an engineer from the Moscow region, is a different case.

K. needs anticoagulants, to prevent thrombosis. It's a high-risk matter. He has two options—one cheap, the other expensive, and neither is right for him; the cheap one requires frequent tests, which his local clinic cannot provide, while the expensive one costs nearly four thousand rubles a month, which he doesn't have.

"We used to earn good money, but things have changed since the crisis. Have to pay for Crimea."

The right attitude, it seems.

"So, are we prepared to pay?"

"Sure, we're prepared," K. replies, unexpectedly.

"And what about those who aren't?"

K. shrugs:

"They can lay down and die."

He'll be the first to do so, of course—but "*Merde!* The Guard dies but does not surrender!"[6] So be it. There's no hope for recovery in either case: both the professor and K. are grown men, established in their fields—both have read *The Gulag Archipelago*, both know about the mass executions at the Butovo Firing Range, the camp at Solovki, the Katyn massacre, yet they prefer military might, the space program, and Soviet hockey.

Not everyone, however, can maintain such ideological purity.

"Nina Ivanovna, you lived in Moscow, yes? What sort of work did you do?"

"Oh, I had the best job in the world—polisher at the First Moscow Watch Factory. You walk into the workshop…" Nina Ivanovna closes her eyes. "Oh, I still dream of that smell—there's just nothing like it."

"So why did you leave?"

"They started delaying our paychecks, so I left. What the heck do I need to swallow all that dust for?"

*

"Of all the wardens, doctors are the best," Mother's old classmate Victor Brailovsky used to say after serving a term as a "prisoner of Zion" in the early '8os.[7] A dubious compliment, but well earned. Russian health care, like its Soviet predecessor, is part of the system of oppression—release from the hospital denied, return to work prohibited, banned from giving birth, operation refused: "Condition serious, temperature normal, visiting hours from six to eight." No transfer to another hospital: "Won't survive the journey—don't ask why." Can't do this, can't do that: no coffee, no flights, no stress, no sleeping on one's left side, no driving, no heavy lifting, no setting foot in the wing without shoe covers. "What did you expect? You spend all day in front of the computer, you're over sixty (or a hundred)—it's too late for a doctor's help. You've got no one to blame but yourself. Like they used to say in the old days, if you don't commit any crimes, you won't wind up in the camps." There are all sorts of regulations, standards, plans. But medical professionals are also capable of sympathy. A senior doctor once gave some excellent advice to a young violinist who was having trouble with her back: "Just hold the violin in your other hand." They can also tie someone up in a bureaucratic nightmare and then sigh, "That's the sort of country we live in."

The idea that you should act in the interests of the patient and not in those of the institution where you work, or of the health-care system, or for "the greatness, glory, and benefit of the Fatherland," sounds as revolutionary and paradoxical as the commandment to love your enemies. Sometimes, on the very same day, one sees several patients who have been operated on completely needlessly, without any indications, at some of the country's finest medical institutions. These patients sense that they've been exposed to risk for no reason, that their conditions haven't improved, but they cannot bring themselves to believe that this is possible, just as people in the '2os, '3os, and later decades couldn't believe that they could be imprisoned and executed without cause, to meet some quota.

One patient—an internist from Moscow—has come to get a second opinion: she's been scheduled for surgery. No other complaints. She has mitral valve prolapse, moderate to severe, but there's no need for an operation yet. She herself doesn't want to understand what's wrong with her, doesn't want any information: doesn't use email. All attempts to explain the situation (the anterior valve leaflet is more difficult to repair than the posterior, etc.) are in vain:

"I'm just a precinct doctor..."

"But there's a difference between a precinct internist and a precinct policeman."

She just smiles: all she needs to know is that there's no need for an operation. Now she feels better.

She tells a story: everyone at her clinic in Moscow plans to attend a state-sanctioned protest against health-care optimization—that is, against doctors losing their jobs—but she isn't sure whether it's worth showing up.

There was a rumor that all the doctors at her clinic would be fired on Friday, at a big meeting. Well, that's reason enough for a protest. But then the bosses postponed the meeting, so no one's been fired. And maybe they won't fire anyone at all—so why protest? And what if the bosses get wind of it? What if they see it on TV?

"But isn't that the whole point of protesting—for the bosses to get wind of it?"

She sighs:

"Easy for you to talk."

A good friend, a painter who also lives in N., tells another story. Once, back in Paris, he had to paint a nude for an exhibition and needed a slender female model. So he went down to the infamous Place Pigalle and found a prostitute—a very slender woman, just the right body type. Back at his studio, he told her to undress and prepared the canvas. To his surprise, she refused to pose, and even took offense: "I'm a prostitute, not a model." There's an Italian version of the same story: "Signora, I am a thief, not a postman," a bandit replies when asked to return the documents in the purse he snatched. That's European-style professional self-respect for you—a stark contrast to our benighted physicians, who don't know how to use email, and who round out their salaries by selling vegetables at the market. "Perfectly natural," as Epikhodov says in *The Cherry Orchard*. "Abroad everything is in full complexity."

Asking acquaintances and strangers for donations, consulting textbooks, seeking the advice of colleagues in the hospital, in Moscow, in the US—here one can do what one feels is right. There are, however, illnesses that simply can't be cured in N.—both by law and because we lack the equipment and specialists; patients have to be sent to Moscow or, worst case scenario, to Region. One such illness is cancer, of any kind. The backwardness of our health-care system is nowhere more evident than in the realm of oncology: "Yes, you've got a tumor"—though sometimes they don't even come out and say that, and instead use the word "disease"—"but we have a queue of people with your condition, and besides, your EKG's bad. Go home, get your heart in order, and come back in four months." Of course, by that point the cancer's at the last stage: "treatment at the place of residence." Why should one pity the "doomed" (as the people in the Baltic states viewed the Jews during the war)? Why get all worked up? God forbid—that might lead to "professional burnout." The ill aren't pushed off cliffs or shot, they're just denied treatment. And the people are used to it: some things are important—the Olympic games, Crimea— while old biddies, and sick ones at that, don't matter a whit. Still, we aren't animals, we build "hospices": a fashionable word, and a fashionable type of institution—the authorities like it very much. (In point of fact, hospices are designed to prevent excessive care—to make sure, say, that old men with advanced dementia don't receive valve replacements; but in our case, even perfectly lucid men and women over seventy can't hope for that kind of surgery.)

An Avar man named Ahmad offered an example of true courage. His story, which ended well, circulated around the hospital.

Ahmad lives deep in the provinces, far from the town of N., and works as a locksmith. Never mind Europe or America—he's never even been to Moscow. A few years ago he began to lose weight and developed some strange pains. He went to the clinic, where they discovered a tumor. Next stop, cancer ward: complicated treatment, examination of the heart and lungs, lots of paperwork and referrals. He went to a famous clinic in Moscow, also to no avail. It wasn't yet time for a hospice (the popular term is "croaker"), but Ahmad realized he had months, not years, so he began to contact his family. It turned out he had a second cousin in Belgium, who told him about that country's excellent health-care system. Now Ahmad had a goal: to get to Belgium. He spent all his savings (two thousand euros) on a bribe for a Schengen visa; the visa didn't come through, but he got his money back. Then he bade farewell to his family and took the bus to Brest, in Belarus. From there he crossed the border into Poland (there's a well-established method) and hitchhiked through that country and Germany (where the health care is no worse than in Belgium, but his second cousin never mentioned this). Though he didn't speak a single word of any foreign language, he somehow reached Belgium, where he surrendered himself to the authorities and asked for asylum, never mentioning his illness.

Ahmad was sent to a camp for displaced persons. No armed guards in watchtowers, no dogs, no barbed wire—just a room for four in a hostel in the center of Brussels. The food was good, and they even gave him money. It takes a few months for refugee status to be granted (or denied)—time Ahmad didn't have—but he never asked to see a doctor, he just waited patiently to be summoned.

After he underwent surgery (apparently successful) in one of the primary hospitals in Brussels and finished his course of chemotherapy, Ahmad declared that he missed his family and wished to go home. At public expense, through international organizations, Ahmad was flown back from Belgium—accompanied by a doctor, who shared this story. As a parting gift, he received an enormous supply of opiates, for which, hopefully, he'll have no use.

Ahmad shows great dignity without a hint of arrogance. His valor, his desire to live bring to mind Tolstoy's "Tatar thistle" from *Hadji Murat*: "But what energy and tenacity!"

*

"Doctor, what is *apoplexy*?"

"It's when your arms and legs go numb."

"Well, my wife calls me *numbskull*—does that count?"

Understandable: A friendly pair that does everything together—shopping, drinking, giving the cardiologist a headache.

The next patient likes the hospital too. He looks around the Major Cardiology Lab:

"Marina Tsvetaeva would have liked to rest here." Also understandable: A member of the intelligentsia come from afar—took a stroll by the river, saw the Stone.

Understanding is the main condition of life in the town of N. When people hear the barking of an unfamiliar dog or the honking of a neighbor's car horn, they look through the window—there shouldn't be any mysteries.

A patient has had a major heart attack, with complications, and required attention all evening. Now, in the morning, he wants to go home.

"Must be crazy. We'd better strap him to the bed," says a nurse.

No, his mind is clear, if a bit quirky:

"Do you know today's date?"

"The day of the founding of the All-Union Pioneer Organization."

We Google it and, sure enough, he's right: May 19. How did he get here?

"Private transport."

Right. So he drove himself, somehow made it without crashing, and left the car by the entrance. Now he's afraid something might happen to it.

"We could move it for you. Just give us the keys."

"What are you talking about? Your medicine makes my liver hurt." A lie.

There's no persuading him. Oh well, one more patient released to relieve the "stress of confinement" (a marvelous formulation!): everyone has the right to go. It's early, of course—not even twenty-four hours has passed—and the risk is great, but this isn't a prison. All the electrodes and catheters are removed. But don't change the sheets quite yet: he'll be back before long. And indeed, about twenty minutes later, the phone rings:

"I'm dying...the elevator."

He had taken his car back to his garage and returned by taxi.

Another man, named Nikolay, has ABBA tattooed on his arm. He doesn't look like a disco fan, or a speaker of Aramaic. It isn't polite to ask about such things, but curiosity wins out in the end. The tattoo used to read ALLA, the name of his first girlfriend. His wife was jealous, so, in the name of love, he suffered a few more pinpricks and had the *L*'s changed to *B*'s.

Life in and around the hospital flows by as a flickering sequence of faces, characters, and situations. Over twelve thousand patients, including outpatients, have passed through these doors in the past few years—most of them more than once. If one doesn't write things down, they fade from memory: the burn victims; Volodya, the convict; the polisher from the watch factory; the devout warehouse clerk; and K., the engineer ("The Guard dies but does not surrender!"—sure enough, he had a stroke). Even the children of Dzhankoy seems like ancient history, although not even three years have passed since that day. And here's a patient who last visited in 2009 but is offended that no one recognizes him:

"You're getting old, doc. The name's Krymtsov, with a *y*." How else could one spell it?

Life in N. can be monotonous, but—"ground beneath me, and sky above me"—it's cozy, warm. Some things are touching, others annoying. The political system, as well as the mood of the citizenry, is disappointing, but one isn't given the same gift—freedom—twice. Major changes probably won't come in this lifetime; with Brezhnev, one just had to wait—there was an age gap of nearly sixty years. The soul, however, refuses to believe the worst (perhaps it lacks the imagination to do so), and then there's Mother to look after. Besides, it isn't just Young Communists who keep springing up on their own, but also members of the intelligentsia—young colleagues who overtake you before you know it. It seems everything in N. is as clear as can be. The events below, however, force one to view the town from an unexpected angle.

2.

ICD-10-CM Diagnostic Code I72.8: "Aneurysm of other specified arteries." An absurd formulation, but—one might say under other circumstances—not without its beauty.

"The death of one's mother leads to a mental illness that lasts at least a year," Father Ilya Shmain, a friend and a teacher, once said. "No matter how ready you think you were, no matter how old you might be."

The doctors did what they could: surgery, multiple blood transfusions. Four days, each filled with activity. The illusion of control fell by the wayside, as did all grudges, even those held from earliest childhood. There were miracles—of the sort only a patient's closest relatives believe in. Everything seemed to work out, except for the main thing—victory over death; disaster is often accompanied by many minor items of good news.

Instructors of creative writing in the US ask their students to write about the death of their parents: thousands of essays each year—thousands of deaths, thousands of writers. Speaking to David Remnick before an audience, Jonathan Franzen took a light tone about the death of his mother. After receiving the sad news, he finished scrambling some eggs: "I like scrambled eggs."[8] Not especially interesting—everyone remembers Camus: "Maman died today. Or yesterday maybe, I don't know."[9]

She spent the last years of her life in N., in a newly built house, aided by home-care workers—older women from various former republics of the USSR. Dependence on others is a heavy burden: she was often rude to these women, mean. This was angering to see, but now an explanation suggested itself: the ideal of equality falls apart when you're lying helpless and the other person is standing upright. It was now also clear why she had kept lapsing into German: her profound confusion about what was happening would transport her to Saxony, where she'd lived between the ages of eleven and thirteen.

Her last words: "If you give them"—in response to Father Konstantin's offer of the sacraments. He had come from Moscow just in time. An hour later, she stopped breathing. Then: notification of acquaintances, a requiem mass among loved ones, night, and—wherever you step, whatever you think about—the mystery of it.

She had never allowed herself to talk much about death—such talk was unchaste, meant to provoke pity—but there's no doubt that she wanted to be buried here. Her feelings toward the town were strong and not even entirely clear. However, no other member of the family is buried in N. (Great-Grandfather requested that his ashes be scattered in the river.) There's no plot in the cemetery.

And now it's morning, a new day, and time to ask the mayor   a cheerful, mustachioed fellow who was appointed after the scandal at the hospital—to allocate a plot. But no, he doesn't have the power: it would require a resolution of the deputies or some such nonsense, which there isn't even time to decipher.

The middle-aged ladies who actually run the town come up with a solution in fifteen minutes flat.

"Just add 'in the family plot' to the notice."

The attempt to pay them is in vain. No one asks, "You out of your mind, dear?" (as an old woman once asked Father when he tried to pay for the milk she gave him to quench his thirst on a hot day). They simply say:

"You're famous around here." They would have done the same for any actor, athlete, maybe even gangster.

At the exit, an old acquaintance of Mother's—whose Armenian

family had fled Baku in '88 and stayed at her place in Moscow for a long time, and who now heads the local branch of Housing and Communal Services—comes up and asks:

"Why didn't you come to me first?"

Make to yourselves friends of the mammon of unrighteousness; that, when ye fail, they may receive you into everlasting habitations. An oversight.

Endless activity—paperwork, arrangements for the wake, negotiations with the Fathers Superior of both churches: it would be good to have the service officiated by Father Konstantin, a close friend ("No, he's not banned"—the magic phrase that needed to be uttered). The pursuit of practical, everyday solutions in a situation that is anything but everyday.

The employees of the funeral home are not possessed of the finest human qualities, and the hospital's relations with them are complicated (one time, for instance, they mixed up two bodies)—but there's no choice, no "other club." Yet this time they behave humanely. Their pamphlet offers a huge variety of coffins, including imported models. A joke suggests itself—about "love for domestic coffins"—but perhaps it's better not to joke.[10] It's painful to know that she has spent two nights in the hands of strangers.

And then the service and burial are over. The church showed a great deal of love, both for her and for the living. And more people showed up than expected—the crowd wouldn't have been so large in Moscow. One might say that everything went well. Her old coworkers spoke of her gift for making her presence felt while keeping silent. "A captive spirit"—that's what her closest, most devoted friend called her (once again, Tsvetaeva came in handy).[11]

In terms of incidents, Father Konstantin brought a homeless fellow, whom he'd taken in to live with him at the church in Moscow. The fellow hadn't touched alcohol for a long while, but on the eve of the funeral he went into a state—got drunk and created a scene. What was the priest to do? The man stayed in the car the whole time, locked up, and people would bring him water.

*

A day passed, and then another—a big hurry to find someone to fence off the plot. There's really no reason to hurry, but something needs to be done: the illusion that one can still help, somehow. A new contact in the phone: Alexey Grave. "Grave" isn't his surname, it's shorthand for his place of work—an aid to the memory. The observation about the locals "drinking less" doesn't apply to him: he shows up to examine the plot without bringing his tape measure. Such ineptitude, but what's the use in getting mad? He'll go fetch it.

In the meantime, one can look around: the gate is open, no guards, no one selling flowers and wreaths, complete solitude. The crosses and headstones bear familiar names: her new neighbors for eternity. A little ways to the right is Konstantin Paustovsky (1968—the very first funeral, sitting on father's shoulders, the whole town in attendance), and to the left and down a bit is Eduard Steinberg, a good friend. But there are also certain faces one would rather encounter on a laser-etched headstone than in a dark alley. Many abandoned graves: an overturned stone—nineteenth-century, the inscription worn away, and very soft, from the local quarry (easy to pick up again); and there, behind a downed fence, a picturesque cluster of half-rotted painted crosses—blue, gray, and brown (they should stay exactly where they are). Here and there pitiful plastic flowers have been stuck in the ground: an attempt to maintain appearances with minimal resources. There are too many trees blocking the sun. Grass will have to be planted—later, of course, in May or June: Is there a variety that thrives in the shade? These are entirely new concerns. Well, here comes Alexey. He'll need help with the measurements.

Why do people come to cemeteries? Is the connection to the beloved dead in fact stronger here than elsewhere? Difficult to say. And why even ask? People have always come, and they'll continue to do so. The old cemetery of the town of N. is completely quiet. This isn't just the absence of sound—rather, as sometimes happens in libraries or empty concert halls, the space is actually filled with silence.

*

The following Monday, a nurse brings a pack of banknotes to the Major Cardiology Lab: here, people pitched in for you. "Thank you, but..." Feelings of gratitude, awkwardness—but chiefly surprise: Donations? What are we, the children of Dzhankoy?

The nurse looks as perplexed as she had in the case of the zodiac signs:

"The children of Dzhankoy? What's that?"

The pack is made up of hundred- and thousand-ruble notes—about sixteen thousand in total. That's no symbolic gesture: together with the state's allowance for burial expenses (just under 5,570 rubles), it's more than enough to cover a modest funeral in the town of N. As to the children of Dzhankoy—who knew one might someday wind up in their shoes?

The old cemetery soon takes its place in the large home that the town of N. has become: together with the hospital, the houses of old friends, the Italian mosaicist's studio, the forests, ravines, and expanses, "the sleeping boy," and the footpath along the riverbank, beside which a few tethered punts lie upside down. The boats awaken recollections: there was a time, over forty years ago, when one would hide under these punts, having said or done something wrong, and discuss one's actions with grown-ups—it was a sort of confessional, like the Catholics have. Beneath the punts it was dark and cool, and smelled like a damp basement. Mother and Father would sit nearby on the grass: she'd usually keep quiet, and might even doze, while he'd be talking heatedly. Much has changed since then, but the punts are the same, and N. is too: a town and a home.

Time to deal with her things. Everything unique—letters, old photographs, tape recordings, diaries—must be kept. All medical and household items, all the stuff just lying around, must be given or thrown away. Photographs from the last three or four years present the greatest difficulty. Life during these years demanded enormous effort; it was tied up in endless attempts to slow the downward slide. The photographs can't be destroyed, but it's painful to look at them. And here is a giant folder devoted to a legal case (unsuccessful) against the authorities of N. back in '73; it takes nearly all Sunday to sort through it.

There are complaints, regulations, decisions to initiate legal proceedings and then to halt them, telegrams, notifications, inventories, open letters to the newspaper *October*. The maneuvers of the old regime look perfectly contemporary: opening the house and letting the neighbors ransack it, along with the garden; allocating a new plot of land on Resurrection Hill, ordering that every piece of the house be moved there, at public expense, and then, one day, bulldozing it to the ground, having canceled their initial decree after declaring it illegal. The only difference was that they never told you to sue them—back then, you couldn't take the authorities to court.

An inventory of 1 Pushkin Street. Among the witnesses is the local music teacher, and the first item is "a beat-up grand, needs tuning." Every object is paired with a derogatory epithet: the bucket is "rusty," the cabinets are "homemade," and the quilt is "plain." The personality of the chairman of the Regional Executive Committee—whose mannerisms Great-Grandfather described as those of an old-school provincial tragedian—also seems perfectly familiar. This was his "benefit" night, and the chairman performed with the ease of a virtuoso; they say he really hated summer people. Ever since then, the lot on Pushkin Street has been occupied by something far worse, far more terrifying than emptiness: a hulking mass of gray brick—the House of Children's Creativity—which was boarded up long ago.

Great-Grandfather's diaries feature a brief reflection on having to treat one of the town's authorities: "Tonight I washed up very thoroughly in front of the burning fireplace. The radio was playing *The Magic Flute*. Earlier in the day I had to visit a critically ill patient, a member of the Regional Committee, and after encountering his disease and his unkempt home, I was all the more grateful for my own comfort and health—a blessing from God," writes a disenfranchised man in his sixty-fifth year. Meanwhile, the chairman's fate did indeed prove tragic: he got drunk, drove his Volga into a tree, smashed his chest against the steering wheel, and died at the scene.

The documents that follow are much more rousing. "The Restoration of Historical Justice," nothing less. One's own handwriting is easy to recognize. The '90s—the gift of freedom ("How mightily beat the Russian heart at the word Fatherland!")[12] The beginning of an interesting life: a meeting with the hospital's chief of staff, almost by chance. He had referred a patient to the institute in Moscow; her condition improved, and then he himself came to visit. The chief of staff shared his memories of Great-Grandfather, who had once lent him a marvelous scythe. The chief of staff had held on to this scythe all those years, waiting for the heirs to show up—bit by bit, circumstances improve. Spring of '93: the allocation of a plot of land of such-and-such a size within the town limits—here's the decree.

Construction did not move quickly. Visits were brief, in the warmer months, and only once, in early spring of '98 or '99, a sudden escape—Mother and I, together.

An awful story—best to keep it short. On a day off, an invitation to a palatial estate in the suburbs: marble, glass, ceramic tiles. Mother's classmates, who'd immigrated to the States, had asked her to send them something through their children or grandchildren. A predatory glance: "Ah, you're a doctor! Why don't you stay for lunch?" Between courses of hors d'oeuvres, the woman explains: just imagine, four babies died in her uterus, until she finally found a surrogate mother—a red-blooded Ukrainian girl, strong as an ox. The girl gave birth to their Vitalik—there he is, a big boy already, sitting at the table. But then (the women's eyes sparkle again), when she and her husband wanted to have another child, using the same surrogate (an unexpected note of joy), the fetus upped and died in the girl's belly!

Smoking isn't allowed in the house, so there's a break—shoes, coat, outside. Together, without saying a word, it's in the car and onto the ring road (it wasn't yet called the Moscow Ring Road)—music on the radio, singing, chatting. A missed turn onto Lenin Avenue—and so, might as well: off to the town of N. After all, these days, it's only a one-and-a-half-hour drive, not a twelve-hour journey. Cold air nips at the face—and it's even worse in the unheated house than out on the street. But there's the fireplace, the "beat-up piano" (both survived from the old house), vodka, smoked sausage ("You're just like your father!"). Time to warm up, both inside and out, and to recall yet another escape, which took place long, long ago.

Moscow Secondary School No. 31, fifth grade. The schoolmarm in charge of the class (neither her name nor her face have stuck—a complete fool: crossed out the word "inclement" in an essay because she'd never seen it before) doesn't let students leave early even if they bring a note from their parents. Mother pays her a visit: "You go get dressed."

It's winter: boots, a coat, slippers back in their bag, and out onto the dark street (classes only started at two p.m.). Mother: "Hurry, hurry, go!"

A classmate comes running in his slippers, catches up, grabs a hand: "Wait! Lyudmila Olegovna (or was it Larisa Valeryevna?) says you can't leave!" Can't fight at all—and yet, somehow, the classmate goes down in the snow, face-first. Now run, run, and never return to School No. 31 again.

July and August were cold and rainy, but they gave way to a nice autumn, warm and dry. Time to wrap up admissions and go down there—to rake the yellowish leaves off the grass (had to be sown several times, but grew in eventually, despite the shade), to sit a while on the bench hammered together by the same Alexey, to read.

"We must leave on one side the beliefs which fill up voids and sweeten what is bitter. The belief in immortality. The belief in the utility of sin: *etiam peccata*. The belief in the providential ordering of events—in short the 'consolations' which are ordinarily sought in religion," writes Simone Weil.[13] A step too far, isn't it? In any case, there's really no desire to contemplate such things—all interest in human wisdom has evaporated.

"The best way to see this town is from the belly of a bomber," wrote Brodsky. But that was about Moscow.[14] (The capital took its revenge on him, by means of an opulent monument: hands thrust rakishly into his trouser pockets, Italian shoes on his feet, face turned up to the sun as if he were blind.) The best way to see N., though, is from the ground—or, better yet, from beneath it. And here time doesn't flow as it should, according to classical physics—it's as if someone had raised it to the power of minus one. Viewed from this perspective, life tends not toward depletion, toward zero, but, on the contrary, toward repletion, fullness. Recent events slide onto one another, get lumped together, and what happened in fact gets mixed up with what never occurred—meanwhile, things from the distant past (an escape from school, a confessional punt on the riverbank, the linden on Pushkin Street) come to seem infinitely closer, infinitely more joyful than they had seemed all those years ago.

October 2017
Translated by Boris Dralyuk

NOTES

SVENTA: IN LIEU OF A FOREWORD

1 As TASS, a Russian government news agency, reported on April 15, 2017, "A special capsule containing the Holy Fire [was] brought to Moscow's Christ the Savior Cathedral for the Easter night service led by Patriarch Kirill of Moscow and All Russia, the head of Russian Orthodox Church. At Moscow's Vnukovo airport hundreds of worshippers met the Holy Fire to take it to parishes of Moscow and [other] Russian regions."

2 From a poem by the Russian-Ukrainian poet Ivan Elagin (1918–1987), who immigrated to the United States after World War II.

3 From the same poem by Elagin.

4 From "To the empty earth" (1937), a poem that was among the last works of Osip Mandelstam (1891–1938).

5 See "Objects in Mirror," trans. Boris Dralyuk, in *Rock, Paper, Scissors, and Other Stories* (New York: NYRB Classics, 2019).

LITTLE LORD FAUNTLEROY

1 Friedrich Joseph Haass (1780–1853) was a German-Russian doctor and philanthropist famed for his charitable work, especially in improving the treatment of jailed convicts. His grave in Moscow bears the exhortation quoted here.

PIECES ON A PLANE

1 Gavril Derzhavin, "Invitation to Dinner," 1795.

2 William H. Honan, "Roman L. Hruska Dies at 94; Leading Senate Conservative," *The New York Times*, April 27,1999.

3 "Estelle Sapir, 73, Who Fought Bank Over Holocaust Assets", William H. Honan, *The New York Times*, April 16, 1999.

4   Eric Pace, "Herbert Young, Who Fought In World War I, Dies at 112," *The New York Times*, April 28, 1999.

CAPE COD

1   The poet Mikhail Lermontov's pioneering novel *A Hero of Our Time* (1840) is known for its probing portrait of Grigoriy Alexandrovich Pechorin, a complicated yet magnetic "hero" in the Byronic tradition.

2   From Lermontov's "My Country" (1841), trans. Peter France, in *The Penguin Book of Russian Poetry*, ed. Robert Chandler, Boris Dralyuk, and Irina Mashinki (New York: Penguin Classics, 2015).

LUXEMBURG

1   "Going to the people" was a movement initiated by Russian populists in the 1860s, which sent thousands of progressive young urbanites to the countryside in order to educate the peasantry and to inspire political unrest. The peasants were largely unreceptive, many agitators were arrested, and the movement failed.

A SIN TO COMPLAIN

1   Osip Mandelstam, "Let's praise, O brothers, liberty's dim light," trans. Boris Dralyuk, in *1917: Stories and Poems from the Russian Revolution* (London: Pushkin Press, 2016).

2   The animated film is *Blue Puppy* (1976), written by Yuri Entin and directed by Yefim Gamburg.

3   Venedikt "Venichka" Yerofeyev (1938–1990) was the author of the 1969 "poem" in prose *Moscow-Petushki*—also titled in translation as *Moscow to the End of the Line*—a subversive paean to alcoholism as a way of life. It circulated in the Soviet Union in manuscript form and in editions published abroad and smuggled into the country. Yerofeyev became something of a patron saint of intellectual alcoholics.

4   From "Spring Day" (1911), a poem by Igor Severyanin (1887–1941).

THE CHILDREN OF DZHANKOY

1   The monument is to the Russian physician Efrem Osipovich Mukhin (1766–1850).

2   On October 29, 1958, at the plenum of the Central Committee of the Young Communist League, the organization's First Secretary, Vladimir Semichastny (who would later become chairman of the KGB), read a

speech denouncing Boris Pasternak, whose *Doctor Zhivago* had been published abroad. The quote comparing Pasternak to a pig is taken from that speech. The existing locales of Voronezh, Taman, Mtsensk, Abakan, Magadan, and Orenburg occur in the works, respectively, of Osip Mandelstam, Mikhail Lermontov, Nikolai Leskov, Alexander Galich, Nikolay Zabolotsky, and Alexander Pushkin; the fictional locales of Yuriatin, Skotoprigonyevsk, Kalinov, Glupov, and Goryukhino occur in the works, respectively, of Boris Pasternak, Fyodor Dostoyevsky, Alexander Ostrovsky, Mikhail Saltykov-Shchedrin, and Pushkin.

3 For a summary of the case of Yury Shevchenko (ordained as Father Georgy) and Patriarch Kirill's apartment, see "Patriarch Kirill's Apartment Buried in Sand," *The Moscow Times*, March 28, 2012, https://www.themoscowtimes.com/2012/03/28/patriarch-kirills-apartment-buried-in-sand-a13636.

4 From the second of Marina Tsvetaeva's "Verses for My Son" (1932).

5 In Vladimir Nabokov's translation, the final four lines of Tsvetaeva's "To My Poems" (1913) read: "Amidst the dust of bookshops, wide dispersed / And never purchased there by anyone, / Yet similar to precious wines, my verse / Can wait: its turn shall come."

6 Words attributed to Pierre Cambronne (1770–1842), a general who played an important role in the French Revolution and the Napoleonic Wars.

7 Victor Brailovsky (b. 1935) was a Soviet-born Jewish computer scientist and mathematician who became a "refusenik" in the early 1970s, and served as a "prisoner of Zion" for his activism between 1981 and 1984, before being allowed to emigrate to Israel in 1987.

8 Jonathan Franzen, interview with David Remnick, The New Yorker Festival, October 1, 2011, https://www.newyorker.com/video/watch/jonathan-franzen-talks-with-david-remnick.

9 Albert Camus, *The Stranger*, trans. Matthew Ward (New York: Vintage, 1988).

10 The reference is to an unfinished poem by Pushkin, from 1830, which begins: "Two feelings feed our hearts, / And these will not be softened — / Love for our native hearths, / Love for ancestral coffins."

11 "A Captive Spirit" is the title of Tsvetaeva's 1934 essay on the poet and novelist Andrei Bely (1880–1934). See Marina Tsvetaeva, *A Captive Spirit: Collected Prose*, trans. and ed. J. Marin King (New York: Abrams Press, 2009).

12 A line from Pushkin's short story "The Blizzard." See *Alexander Pushkin: Complete Prose Fiction*, trans. Paul Debreczeny (Stanford, CA: Stanford University Press, 1983).

13 Simone Weil, *Gravity and Grace*, trans. Emma Crawford and Mario von der Ruhr (London and New York: Routledge, 2004).

14 Lines from Joseph Brodsky's long poem "A Performance" (1986).

OTHER NEW YORK REVIEW CLASSICS

For a complete list of titles, visit www.nyrb.com.